Raves for *The* [barcode] S0-AVY-199

For **The Dark Ferryman:**

"The intricately plotted, character-driven saga of the Vaelinar's desperate struggles finds anchors in folklore and legend, appealing to fans of slower pacing and detailed world building." —*Publishers Weekly*

"Continuing the panoramic saga begun in *The Four Forges*, Rhodes develops her world both politically and emotionally, filling it with complex and compelling characters."
—*Library Journal*

For **The Four Forges:**

"Sevryn Dardanon is not your typical elf. In fact, the world of Kerith is not your typical elf world. In this spectacular series debut, the pseudonymous Rhodes (a prolific YA author) plays fresh variations on the standard epic fantasy tropes. Her elves, the Vaelinars, are outsiders, propelled by a magical cataclysm into an unfamiliar and somewhat hostile new environment. For Sevryn, a half-breed Vaelinar, life is especially difficult as he's neither of one world or the other. Meanwhile, human Dwellers take in the orphaned Rivergrace, an escaped slave of Vaelinar heritage, and raise her as their adopted daughter. Both Rivergrace and Sevryn struggle to survive as quietly as possible, until, by chance, their paths cross and they must help each other battle an unknown evil that's infecting Kerith. Sevryn and Rivergrace possess not only undeveloped magical powers but mysteries in their respective pasts that promise to keep the excitement level high in the next installment."
—*Publishers Weekly* (starred review)

"The first book of the Elven Ways series introduces the very detailed and well-drawn world of Kerith, in which four different peoples coexisted since the end of a devastating war, until a magestorm from another world brought a fifth people, the Vaelinars. Rhodes' use of detail will please those who like richly drawn settings and intricate plots." —*Booklist*

"Rhodes has built a fully realized world with engaging characters with a dangerous manifest destiny. The characters are complex and real in perilous times and leave you waiting anxiously to see what is resolved. A bright beginning for a new light on the fantasy horizon." —*ConNotations*

JENNA RHODES

THE ELVEN WAYS:
THE FOUR FORGES
THE DARK FERRYMAN

THE
DARK
FERRYMAN

The Elven Ways: Book Two

Jenna Rhodes

DAW BOOKS, INC.

DONALD A. WOLLHEIM, FOUNDER

375 Hudson Street, New York, NY 10014

ELIZABETH R. WOLLHEIM
SHEILA E. GILBERT
PUBLISHERS

http://www.dawbooks.com

First Paperback Printing, June 2009
1 2 3 4 5 6 7 8 9

DAW TRADEMARK REGISTERED
U.S. PAT. AND TM. OFF. AND FOREIGN COUNTRIES
—MARCA REGISTRADA
HECHO EN U.S.A.

PRINTED IN THE U.S.A.

Dedicated to:

James, Jessica, Maureen and Aaron
You are my heroes.

A Tale of Desperate Times
As told through the smoke haze of a Toback Shop

"THOSE OF YOU who aren't wanting t' hear the story of our own Rivergrace and her love Sevryn and how they came to their deaths at the hands of a Demon and a Goddess, I give my blessing for you to shove over or leave, because th' shop is nigh filled and other folks are wantin' to come in and listen."

Murmurs greeted the voice of their much-anticipated tale-teller, one of their own, a good ranch and orchard man. A willowy young woman by the door gave a fleeting smile and took the hand of the tall elven man by her side. With a nod of her head, she bid a silent good-bye to the speaker and withdrew into the bitter cold of the outside. He watched her go, the tale-spinner. A Dweller still in his prime, with his face weathered and his hair tinged with gray, a man of good stock, Tolby Farbranch studied his callused hands a moment.

Outside, the man chided his companion. "Not staying?"

Grace smiled again before kissing his cheek gently. "I know how the tale ends."

He put his hand on her wrists and drew her close to his chest, guarding her from the wind and the winter and the inevitable. "It's only the beginning. It's not done," he whispered to her temple, "but I promise to stay with you until it is."

She leaned into him, saying, "The queen calls us to her."

"And we'll go," Sevryn told her. "Together."

From the shelter of his embrace, she looked upon the Dweller town, and the shop, and the people of her beginning as if she might never see them again once they left Stonesend. After all, she had already died once.

Small clouds of fragrant pipe smoke floated out of the shop after bouncing about the rough wooden beams of the ceiling, as the audience tamped pipes themselves or squirmed to find a squidge more room for perching comfortably. Dwellers filled the room, mostly men, for the toback shop was one of their sanctuaries, but a few of other races sprawled with long legs and gangly arms, winter cloaks pulled about their bodies, as drawn in for a pouch full of savory leaf and news as the next man be he Dweller, Kernan, Galdarkan, or even Vaelinar. Women and children sat on the walkway outside and watched Rivergrace and Sevryn leave before turning their ears keenly to the speaker and spinner.

"I have in mind," Tolby said deliberately, "to be tellin' a tale of my own today, with your indulgence, a true telling, of the Demon sword Cerat, and the corrupting of the sacred river Andredia, and how they came to be undone," and the lines in his face deepened. "These are grim times, my friends and fellows, not a doubt of that. Raiders and such driving us from our holdings, taking from us our good sons and daughters, talk of war on the horizon." His eyes glanced toward the Barrels at that, his mouth turning in a grimace. "Aye, a true tale, but one I cannot say will illuminate the fates awaiting all of us, for like a weaving, there are many threads tangled in the pattern afore its true appearance can be known. So, like many things in our lives, this tale is not quite finished."

Tolby began to speak of the Warrior Queen of the Vaelinars and the shadowy weaponsmith known as Quendius, and the prophecy which knotted them together, a prophecy hidden in a child's gaming rhyme.

"Four forges dire
Earth, Wind, Water, and Fire,
You skip low
And I'll jump higher.
One for thunder
By lands torn asunder
Two for blood
By mountains over flood.
Three for soul
With no place to go.
You skip low
And I'll skip higher
Four on air
With war to bear."

A solemn tone fell over Tolby Farbranch's voice as he related the dire workings of Quendius and the smith who worked under him in forges which poisoned the river Andredia and their own swift-flowing Silverwing. He told them of how Narskap, the slave to Quendius, captured the Demon Souldrinker into a mortal-made sword and caged the River Goddess of the Silverwing in the same. He spoke to them of Queen Lariel and her brother Jeredon and the Hand of the Queen, Sevryn the half-breed. He reminded his audience of the vow of her House to protect the Andredia and its river valleys. In astonishment they listened as Vaelinars and Kernans and Dwellers, even arrogant Galdarkans and rough Bolgers were plaited together in the pattern of assassins and raiders and Demon-ridden swords. They gasped as they heard of their own Rivergrace taking up Cerat after the attempted murder of Lariel and Sevryn who put his own body in front of Cerat to save his queen and was killed, then swallowed by the Souldrinker. Then Tolby swiftly led them on Rivergrace's own journey to the font of the sacred river Andredia with her companions who fell one by one till only she faced the foul altar which made the sword and damned the river with its poisons to break one upon the other, ending the curse. There was more to the story than he told, for he did not know of all the moments within the tale and he knew better than to reveal all that he did. Still, his words were enough to send shivers down the spine of every man listening. And, as difficult as it was to speak of the deaths and hardships of friends and family, and of even more troubled times to come, he held a purpose beyond that of telling the story and its truth to those gathered there. He had a mission, as it were, to smoke out the old enemy. To warn that enemy that they knew a great deal of what had been secret, and what he planned, and that they stood together, the intruder Vaelinars, and the Kernans and Dwellers of the First Home.

He finished as the toback shop owner shuffled softly about the room, lighting candles and oil lamps, as the afternoon grew rain-cloud dark. Finally, one muttered, "Our thanks for the telling of that, Farbranch. It proves what my grand-da oft used to say."

"And what is that?" Tolby asked not unkindly of him.

"It is better to have Death knock on your door than a Vaelinar."

Chapter One

"WHO WOULD YOU DIE FOR?" A blade bit into his neck, awaiting his answer.

"My lady and my queen," Sevryn said before a rough hand stilled further words. He lay with a thin campaign blanket tangled over his knees and counted the daggers he could get into his hands quickly: four, one at each ankle and each forearm. No longer slave, no longer an unfettered street brat, he was the Queen's Hand amid a troop of her finest. What would his odds be against besting an intruder who'd crept into a military camp without warning? He sank into his Vaelinar senses. They flared out to identify the good steel made by one of their own, the edge so keen that it drew blood just brushing his neck.

Horses tied at the night lines stayed quiet. He could no longer feel warmth against his side where Rivergrace had lain curved against his body. She must have rolled away, curled into her own blankets. Sevryn, and Sevryn alone, dealt with the intruder.

"I need you to come with me. Take your gear and horse." A firm voice tickled his ear, and the knife withdrew. Then and only then, he recognized the one man he knew who could have gotten into the guarded and warded camp without attracting attention. "I am chasing matters of dire import."

He would have asked questions, but Daravan moved away with silken speed, so he got silently to his feet and followed, taking up those bits of his life the other had told him to retrieve and leaving Rivergrace, the largest part of his life and the only one that mattered, curled in sleep. He drew on his Talent of Voice, pitched in words barely audible even to himself as he walked between his friends and allies, telling them they did not feel him, hear him, or see him move among them. His Voice quieted the horse line as he took his mount out and saddled it quickly, already checking the girth when a hand tugged on his sleeve.

He turned to see Rivergrace just behind him, standing cloaked in night shadows, her body filled with that serenity and sadness that was the current of the soul that ran deep in her. Damp and chill though the air was, she hadn't brought a blanket or her cloak with her, and her breasts budded against the fabric of her blouse. He could not see her eyes or the lustrous auburn cast to her hair in the dark, but he knew them well, especially her eyes of aquamarine, of river water and sea tide, and how they would be watching him, searching his face.

"Where are you going?"

"I've gotten other orders."

Her gaze narrowed a bit and she looked beyond him. "Where is the lord of shadows taking you?"

Her nickname for the rogue Daravan, but an apt one.

"I don't know." He combed her heavy hair from her brow, burying his fingers in it for a long moment, smelling the aroma of her skin and tresses, feeling her warmth. "But I'll come back."

"Why you? Why not Osten or one of the captains

here or someone else. She used to send Jeredon when Daravan came calling." Her voice quavered over naming the queen's brother.

"Jeredon is crippled."

"Why is it always you, then? Someone else until Jeredon is ready." She shivered a bit, as if throwing off the chill. "He heals. He'll walk again someday, the healers have predicted it."

"If they're right, and that someday is not tonight, and Daravan's need is now. Osten serves the queen best at her shoulder, and I am probably better than any of the captains who are still snoring in their blankets."

"She sends you here and me there, and even when we're together, she keeps us apart. I have no work to do but follow her whims." Rivergrace took a quick breath before stilling. She closed her eyes a long moment, and he could feel her power awaken, a power that lay deeply in her as water sinks deeply into earth and stone and lies silently, pooled, waiting. He wondered if she knew she had that much strength within her. "Are you going after Quendius?"

Anger knotted in his throat at the name, but he swallowed it down and kept it there. "I don't know."

"You have to bring him back alive if you find him."

"Now you ask the impossible of me. If we do find him, he won't be taken easily, and I won't vouch for Daravan's plans. We can't tell if he's still allied with Abayan Diort or if he's splintered off with his own mercenaries, and even if we knew, it would take a great deal to get to him."

"He made slaves of my family and you."

"All the more reason I'd rather see him dead."

"I can't talk to him if he's dead. I can't find out who my mother and father were and why they sold themselves to him. What price could possibly have been worth what happened to them, what they gave up?"

She had her mother's name, but Sevryn knew she wanted more than that, she wanted to know their essence, and he couldn't help her with that. "You'd have better luck getting a Bolger to dance than having Quendius ever tell you the truth."

That brought a slight smile to her face as she must have pictured one of the bestial Bolgers capering about. He touched the upturned corner of her mouth. He would rather kiss it, but knew if he did, he would want to linger, and he could feel Daravan's impatient stare on the back of his shoulders from somewhere out of the shadows where he waited. "I promise you, I shall get answers for you someday." Sevryn leaned forward and kissed her forehead instead. "I will come back," he repeated.

She put her hand on his chest, and he could feel her strength filling him as if he'd taken a long, deep drink of her. "Tell *him* that." She turned and slipped away, and he watched her walk among the sleeping figures, her tall and slender body still a bit awkward as though she had not quite come to grips with herself after having been raised by compact and sturdy Dwellers. She turned once more to raise her hand in farewell, before kneeling onto her blankets, and then curling down to sleep, and he found himself with a bittersweet taste on his lips before he gathered the reins of his mount.

He led his horse away, hoofbeats muffled by grass heavy with dew, and found Daravan waiting for him downslope. Wrapped in his long gray cloak, the other looked as if he were made of fog, as still and unsubstantial on the evening air.

"She told me to tell you that I will return to her."

"I should have told her I was taking you. Not that she'd have forgiven me any more easily." Daravan rubbed his forehead. "How many blades do you have on you?"

"Seven." They considered one another.

"That should be enough," Daravan noted, finally. "We ride far and hard." He looped his reins about his hand. "What is the first rule of war?"

Sevryn studied him but found no answer on the man's stern face. He thought of Gilgarran. Like his dead mentor, this man moved along paths he shared with few, for reasons he seldom revealed, yet Sevryn found himself trusting Daravan. He brought forth one of Gilgarran's lessons. "No regrets," he answered.

Daravan dropped his chin in agreement. "And no prisoners. We shall be lucky to stay alive ourselves."

Sevryn nodded as a stillness settled in his chest.

She thought she heard a horse being led quietly away as she lay with her cheek to the ground, feeling the dampness of the night draped around her. She waited until the soft thud of its muted hoofbeats faded entirely away before rousing slightly, peering out from under her blanket at the sleeping camp. Raised in mining caverns for the first, near-forgotten years of her life, no night held the darkness it might for others. She could see in hues of gray and sepia, brown and muted blues, reds, greens, all the colors that would lie sparkling before her at dawn's first turning. And because she was who she was, who she had been, a vessel for a being much greater than herself, she could feel the hand of the River Goddess upon them all, in every drop of dew that touched them. Perhaps that touch even ran in her blood, in the bodily fluids of her existence; she could not be sure.

The only surety she held was that the Goddess bent very close to her this night, an oppressive weight in her thoughts and her heart. She rose, even more quietly than before, disturbing no one but the blanket which fell from her shoulders to the ground in a soundless ripple of cloth. Her steps took her to the small runnel of fresh water that bordered the field camp, no bold river or even a stream, but a brooklet, if that. By the time she reached it, dewdrops covered her like fine, gossamer clothing, tiny diamonds catching the barest illumination of the night and its stars, cloaking her from head to toe. She knelt at the edge and dipped her hand down to touch the running water. Since her earliest memories, that was how she'd found her comfort. A mother's hug she could not remember, but the play of water upon her fingers, encircling her hand, that she could remember and often sought. Icy, cold, or tepid, the temperature of the river did not matter; it brought her cleansing. It filled her with strength. It washed away disquiet and fear and left serenity pooling behind it.

Behind the touch of the river lay the soft nearly unheard sound of a woman's voice. Grace tilted her head to listen better amidst the quiet of the forest and meadow. She could not catch words, only a melody, a song of nearly unbearable loss and mourning. The dew about her fell away as if loosened, becoming moon-tinged teardrops that rained about her. They gathered into small pools that caught the moon's glitter.

They were not her tears. It was not her sorrow. Yet it flooded her, rose in her throat, surrounded her like tiny orbs of the silver-and-blue moon itself. She did not pull her hand from the water. It would do her no good to do so, and the dirge beat upon her senses.

A loss. A nearly incomprehensible loss. Not hers, though her father and mother had been torn away and an unborn sibling she had known nothing of until the Goddess granted her the barest touch of the other's soul. The loss, then, was of the Goddess. Did she mourn the sundering of their forms? That seemed unthinkable. The River Goddess had never acknowledged her openly all the years that Rivergrace had sheltered her within. She had lived most of her life unaware that her body had been a shield, a vessel, for one of the essences of Kerith summoned forth unwillingly. But with the destruction of the Souldrinker Cerat, the Goddess had been freed. Why then did she now weep as if inconsolable? Cold water ran through her fingers like the questions for which she could find no answers.

The formless element seized her. Suddenly, Grace found herself yanked down to the ground, her entire

arm and shoulder immersed, her hair soaked and trailing upon the waters. What had been a babbling of water
became a roar in her ear, a cascade of furious tide surging against her, drawing her down into it.

"Return to me what is mine."

Water filled her mouth as she tried to answer. Grace
spit it out to manage, "I have nothing."

"Thief. I am emptying!"

She could feel the silvery strands of herself drawn
thin and fought the unweaving, the unraveling of her
very being. She had been through this before, when the
loose Goddess unmade her to free herself entirely and
then remade her in gratitude. This was death and dying,
and she had already made that sacrifice. She fought it this
time, gently, protesting that she had nothing left to give
that she had not already given. "I carried you in my heart
and soul for decades. How can you not know me? How
can you not know the truth in what I say to you?" Grace
thought her heart would break as the elemental railed at
her, about her, and then the tide began to ebb.

The near inaudible song surrounding her, all but
drowned out by the frothing of the brook rising to claim
her, stilled for a moment. Then it began again, quietly,
resolutely, a new melody, of incalculable puzzlement
underlaid with strength, and the whitecapped waters
about her slowly receded until she found herself lying
across the small freshet once more, soaked, shivering,
and alone.

Grace sat up, hugging herself against the cold, and
combed her hair from her face with her fingers, hand
shaking. What happened to the world when a Goddess
began to die? What would happen to her?

She staggered to her feet. A warmth came out of the
dew still blanketing the ground, a soft current of air
which swirled about her once, twice, thrice and then
faded away, leaving her dry, except for the icy core of fear
inside her. The Goddess had given her back her life. Yet
was this a gift Rivergrace could hold onto? Was it being

reclaimed from her? She put her hand out, looking at it. Unbidden, the stalwart form of her sister Nutmeg swept through her thoughts, bringing with her the cinnamon spice of her words and nature, an upwelling of optimism and sass. Nutmeg would have had words about the Goddess, no doubt about that. The weave of life was greater than one mortal or immortal strand, and gifts given were like flowers gone to seed on the wind, out of sight, out of mind even if never out of heart. Grace closed her hand as if she could feel Nutmeg's hand within her grasp, keeping her always anchored to the practical nature of life.

She made her way back into the sleeping camp and fell into an exhausted, dreamless sleep.

Lariel watched her silently from her tent canopy, the night framing Rivergrace's slender form as she gave way. She could only wish the evening would embrace her again, but she doubted it would. She had too many thoughts running through her mind for sleep to calm her again. She'd seen Daravan go to Sevryn and take him away, and then Grace follow, and none of it had been a surprise to her because he'd pierced the wards she'd set up, alarming her. Like a knife parting shadows, he'd slipped into the camp, and none had sensed it except for her. He did not even know he'd awakened her. She wondered if she should have challenged his boldness at taking her Hand from her, and had decided against it. Daravan kept his own counsel and it was unlikely he would tell her his plans lest she block him. He would report to her later. His presence had been a surprise, awakening her from a dream which she still saw vividly in her mind: Abayan Diort standing on a bed of flames and wearing a fiery crown. A woman watched him from a distance, a slender graceful woman but the dream had bled all color from her, casting her in shades of dusk. Was it Rivergrace who watched him . . . or herself? Omen or a shred of restless sleep? Lara had no way of judging, and even if she should fall asleep again, she knew that the moment had been lost to her.

Nor could she let herself dwell upon it. That way would take her down a path Lariel could not afford. She must keep her eyes upon the horizon which stayed boundless, and if a singular, undeniable path presented itself, then and only then would she let herself travel it. As her grandfather had told her shortly before he died, when she began to dream, to truly dream, it would be the death of all that she knew to be Vaelinar.

She could not let that happen.

A slight pain arced through her left hand, and she looked down to see her fingers crabbed into a tight fist, the scar of the missing finger pulsing in soreness. Lara opened her hands slowly. A hundred twisted paths and one true one might lead into the future, and a hundred true paths and one twisted one might lead away from it. Of all the Talents Vaelinars could summon, the one they could not was certainty. No one could sift through destiny and its myriad of choices and say, this is the one you must take, this is the best and only road. She was as blind as anyone.

As for Rivergrace, Lara knew that she had come to a fork in their friendship when she must assert herself as a queen. That Rivergrace had Vaelinar blood in her veins seemed certain, although her maternal lineage had been untraceable and her father's line altogether unknown. Lara saw that which Grace did not: why would two Vaelinars allow themselves to become enslaved to one such as Quendius, giving up not only their lives but that of their child? They had made a pact with a Demon, surely knowing that they did so, but to what advantage? They had to have been outlawed or in hiding, and if they had been, there would have been good reason to cast them out. Lara did not want to lay the burden of her parents' past upon Rivergrace's shoulders but the truth needed to be known. Grace held unknown qualities within her, and as Warrior Queen, Lariel had to be able to assess them.

She would not have another traitorous line such as the ild Fallyns facing her, if she could help it.

Lara dropped the tent flap back into place and retreated to her own blankets, kneeling upon them, rather than lying down. She bowed her head in meditation and stayed until dawn.

A merciless sun beat down on the queen's finest.

"I want to understand how you could lose an entire army."

Rivergrace looked across the landscape to Lariel Anderieon who sat on her hot-blooded Vaelinar-bred horse, her wrists crossed casually at his withers, her easy posture belying the irritated tone of her voice. The *tashya* mare pawed the ground, telegraphing her rider's annoyance. The bulky general being addressed merely held himself quiet, waiting for the queen to finish. "We were hot on Diort's tail." Lara stared down at a valley baked by an unseasonably fierce late autumn sun, floodwaters having left a slick of clay over the basin, now crackled and dried like tile over what had once been fertile fields. The river which had cut through, bringing its life with it, was gone, the bed nothing more than a cut in the soil, pebbles and sandy bottom gleaming. Its source had been broken within the stone foundation of a narrow pass which had once protected the valley. "First Sevryn, now this. Was it easy to lose an army?" The sun glittered off her mail, and she shook her head, her hair falling loose from the jeweled net which had bound it, silver-and-golden tresses tumbling down to her shoulders. She put a hand up to retrieve the net and yank it aside, frowning at Osten whose horse flanked hers. The general's face wore his perpetual weathered grimace, his expression pulled by the great scar which cleaved his face in two, a death blow meant to do more than scar him but which, miraculously, had not. His voice rumbled in reply.

"Not as easily as it might appear, Lara. We know Bistel harried them down from the north, and sign pointed them here." Osten stood in his stirrups, easing his body a moment, before settling back onto the saddle. "And we know the Galdarkan's been here." He surveyed the damage done by the war hammer Rakka where it had split the valley and the small pass which had once guarded it wide open, sending the brook which fed its fertile valley into a flood before rock slides had shut it down altogether. They could see the fractured lines running through the valley floor up into the meager hills where the village perched on hummocks and hills. The stone spine of the mountains ringing the area, barely tall enough to be called such, lay bare with chasms chiseled open in a web of flaws. It was not the first time Diort had struck his hammer and the Demon within had thundered open the very bones of the world. But why here? What would he gain by loosing the Demon here? A few heavily laden carts trudged from the devastation, a handful of family members to each cart, the pitful survivors of Abayan Diort's attack. Others had either already fled or joined Diort's army in fear for their lives. Lariel's hand twitched on the reins in distress, and her horse tossed her head in a nervous response.

"I know he's been here. It's where he's vanished to that concerns me." Her gloved hand cut the air. "I want someone down there to talk to the villagers." She looked to Rivergrace. "You have Dweller upbringing, you know the farming life, but you can promise them nothing. I know this will go against your grain, but hold your tongue. They think we Vaelinars can heal all that is wrong with their world with our magic, and curse us whether we do so or not. If we helped everyone who pleaded for our magic, we would create a world full of beggars who refuse to do anything for themselves. I won't have you contribute to that."

Her brusque request shook Rivergrace and scattered

her thoughts about Sevryn's disappearance in the night. "But—" protested Grace softly.

"Rivergrace," Lara answered softly. "No one can heal the earth here. All we can do is find Diort and put a stop to him." She put a heel to her horse's flank. "Stand down the men. More than a handful of us will panic them. Grace, come with me."

Pursing her lips in quiet obstinacy yet obeying Lara's order, she reined her mare after the queen, and they descended down into the valley. The beautiful red-and-gold leaves of autumn had fallen, but the flood had drowned their glory in mud, and the horses soon trotted over baked silt, puffs of dirt greeting the strike of each hoof. Rivergrace looked down, feeling the water below which had sunk into the earth—deep, still water. Spring would bring the life back to this land again, but the people who had lived here couldn't wait through a harsh winter in that hope and with the fear that the demolished pass which they could easily have guarded against raiders and Bolgers was now laid wide open, a shattered gateway into their midst. All but a few had already fled.

Lara signaled a dismount as the carts and their Kernan drivers halted, looking at them with expressions both frightened and curious. Rivergrace slid to the ground, one hand on her mount's neck. She wondered if any of these farmers and tradesmen had ever seen a Vaelinar before, thinking from the widening of their eyes that likely they had not, although they'd undoubtedly heard many things about them. She knew what they would see: a tall, handsome folk with tipped ears and eyes as bright as gems with streaks and specks and whorls of color within color, eyes unlike any ever seen before on Kerith. Those eyes were not native to Kerith, belonging to a people some God or forbidden magic had flung into their world centuries ago for reasons the Vaelinar could not remember and the races born to Kerith had no way to discern. She knew what they thought if they thought the worst of them: invaders, slavers. She took a deep breath, feeling the old manacle scars prickle high on her wrists. All but faded, the pain could still chafe at her now and again. Vaelinars were often no kinder to their own than to others. Hammered onto Kerith, they had suffered no less damage to themselves and their culture than this valley had from the Demon Rakka. She dropped the reins of her horse into a ground-tie and stepped away, letting a soft smile curve across her lips, hoping it would ease the looks she faced.

Lariel had been ill at ease, and no wonder. The Vaelinars were strangers in the lands of Kerith, their existence here at the forbearance of the native peoples. Or perhaps not forbearance, perhaps they'd supplanted those originally in control here. Yet they weren't exactly conquerors, although they were treading a fine line there. The Vaelinars had brought with them intelligence, experience, and magic, and used all they had to establish new domains among those who had been born here.

Rivergrace had been isolated from her people for most of her young life and had only recently started to know them intimately, her previous view of them that of her adopted family of Dwellers who had long protected her from her strange beginnings. Vaelinars guarded each other's backs from the native peoples of Kerith, yet within their own society they could be vicious and deadly as the assassins sent after Lara proved. The queen faced not only murderers from within but civil war from without. Her own seneschal, Tiiva, head of her household staff for many, many years, had sent death after her before disappearing. Did Lara think that Tiiva had conspired with Abayan Diort? If she did, the Warrior Queen hadn't confided that to Rivergrace, but there was a doggedness about this pursuit that suggested it.

Grace didn't understand the politics of the Vaelinars and took what solace she could in the countryside, looking at it with the eyes of a Dweller as Lariel and Osten approached the head of the raggedy caravan. Her feet took her wandering off to the side, to the bed of the river that had been, and she knelt there, reaching out. She sifted the pebbles and soft dirt and sand, thinking of the fish that had swum in the river once, their fins fanning the sediment, of the water cold and harsh in the winter and soft and languid in the summer. There were prints on the far side bank, from animals which had come to drink as if not believing the water had gone. A wilted weed tangled across her palm, drying out, dying, as the whole valley would, slowly. Rain and runoff might fill this riverbed again, but ... she looked up. The hammer strike had shifted the rocks in the hills to block the water from the river, and she doubted it would ever run true again. Like high desert land, rain would fall here and sweep away, disappearing into porous, infertile sand that would not, could not, hold it. The river's source spoke to her from the depths of stone, a wounded presence that struggled to be free, to be whole. She sighed.

A tiny sigh echoed hers, and she looked up into a small, oval face. A hand reached past hers to finger the dirt. "Grampa says we hafta leave because of the river. Without the river, we can't live." The Kernan lad looked askance at her, brown eyes crinkling a little at the corners, as if she were too bright to watch directly.

"He says that, does he? He's probably right, don't you think?"

"Probably. He's awful old, and you don't get that way bein' stupid."

She smothered her reaction. "Indeed. I'm going to walk up. Would you like to come with me?" She stood, dusted off her hand, and held it out to him.

He studied it, then her. He wove his fingers into hers carefully. "You're not like the others."

Rivergrace nodded. The bane of her life. She was, and she wasn't, like the other Vaelinars. She wasn't sure if he meant that she did not wear mail and carry weapons like the others, although she did have a short sword slung on her left hip. With the eyes of the young, he might be able to see that imperceptible aura that she wasn't quite

Vaelinar, and was most definitely not anything else of Kerith either. Not a tall and arrogant Galdarkan, the nomadic guardians bred by the long-ago Mageborn race, nor a humble Kernan who populated these lands in the greatest numbers, and certainly not a short and sturdy and boisterous Dweller. They began to walk up the riverbed toward the broken landscape, leaving behind the elder Kernans telling what they knew of events to Lara and Osten.

"I'm Barton," the lad said.

"I am called Rivergrace," she answered, half-listening to him and half-listening to something dancing on the wind, the voice of the water if it had such a thing.

"They came a few days ago," he offered. "Lots of Galdarkan lived here, they came out to listen to him. Grampa said only a fool doesn't listen to a man with a sword if he wants to talk before using it."

They skirted a fall of granite and slate. "Then what happened?"

"He said . . . Diort . . . that we had to leave. Come with him or leave by ourselves, that it wouldn't be safe."

"Not safe?" But it was Diort who'd splintered open the pass which held the village close, as if a wall had been built by nature to cozen them. "Did he say why?" She paused to help him up a boulder as they began to climb cautiously over the edge of the rockfall. Pebbles skittered after them as they moved upward.

"Grampa muttered something about Mageborn and badlands. Stuff I don't understand."

Nor did she, yet. She did know that when the elder civilization, the Mageborn, warred and the Gods of Kerith stripped the magic from them in angry retribution, backlash currents of chaos anchored into the lands where the Mages had established their kingdoms. The badlands to the east, the wastelands of those wars, expanded and contracted erratically except where the Vaelinar lord Bistel's holding of Hith-aryn seemed to keep the tide at bay. The great aryn trees the Vaelinar had brought with them in seed and staff sprang up in groves like windbreaks and bent their limbs against the chaos like a shield. Here, though ... she was uncertain how close or far they might be to an errant spear of wasteland. The wasteland was rumored to move, to devour. But did it? Would Diort have lied to them to force them into his alliance? What good had it done him to destroy their farms and village here? Or did he intend to destroy something else along with it?

She said to Barton, "But your grampa didn't go with them."

"Nope. We're Kernan. A lot of Kernan went with 'em, too, but he said, soldiering brings trouble, and no matter what a soldier said about glory, he still needed a farmer to fill his gut."

"I see." The corner of Rivergrace's mouth tugged. The Kernan sounded much like her Dweller foster father Tolby. They reached a high point, where she could look up at the smallish peaks the river had once tumbled from before running down into the valley. She still could find no sense in Diort's destruction, although the aryn trees bordering the rim to the north stood withered as though winter had already swept through savagely and they but hanging on until the spring. Too early for that, she thought, they had only just dropped the few leaves they would let go at the season's turning. Aryns were mainly evergreens, although they did shed a few golden leaves from their deep green boughs at autumn's touch. Did the aryns falter here? And if so, why? They were far enough from the edges of the badlands. She frowned at that as she considered what had been river and had become flood. She pushed the aryns out of her mind as her senses attuned to the pitch of the roots of the water. Fire answered instead to her shock, heated tongues licking the inside of her mind. It leaped at her awareness of it. It wanted her to release it, and she shivered at its intensity. She took a deep breath to clear her thoughts before seeking for the water which was her Talent, her affinity, and part of her soul. It came, quietly, wet and silken as she called it, and she listened to see where water ran deep in the ground about her, also ready to answer.

Barton waited long moments before saying, "You're listening, aren't you?"

She gave him a look of surprise before answering, "Yes."

"I'll be quiet, then." He squatted down, balancing one elbow on a knee so he could cradle his chin in his palm, and he stayed there, with the patience of those who are used to farming, where seed doesn't sprout overnight nor great things happen in a single day.

Grace perched on a ledge. Tilting her face, she could feel moisture on the slight breeze that stirred. She was not that high, or far away from Lara and her guard, but she could look down and see that they were still deep in talk, with a little bit of hand waving and gesturing, as they gleaned details and dropped persuasions of their own. She wasn't sure if they even knew she had wandered off, but undoubtedly they did. Little escaped Lara's notice.

She stretched out her hand, her palm over the rockfall. She could feel the river, blocked, down below. She could feel its ache, like that of a caged creature, knowing yet unknowing of imprisonment or how to obtain freedom. It might spring forth with heavy winter rains, or it might burrow deeper below. Sweet water, good water, despite the health of the forest edging it. No sense to that, she could not catch the pattern. She tried to see as Vaelinar did, or as she'd been told they did, although few had ever tried to instruct her in their ways or Talents. The world consisted of elemental threads of fire, wind, water, and earth, to be plucked, braided, and coaxed into a weave if one had the ability, but she could not see Kerith in that way. To her, the world was an already completed fabric, a tapestry of beauty, and she only knew that fresh water, river water, called to her. It bathed her soul, no matter how fierce or how serene. She knew sweet water from

bitter, tame water from wild, and it knew her. For a moment, a fear swept over her of the Goddess who might
reach through it to her, and then that fear bled away.
Water was hers, whether by virtue of her Vaelinar nature
or the shield she'd been for the River Goddess, and she
could not deny it. She put aside whatever protest Lara
might give her against working her magic, to do whatever she could. Had Lariel's heated protest brought the
flames to her mind? She had no answers, but they had
gone, and water remained in its rightful place.

Her hand tingled. She looked to Barton who watched
her unblinkingly. Water needed to burst through the
stone. "Think you could help me move a few rocks?"

He stood, puffing his chest out. "I'm strong as a mule!"
he declared.

Rivergrace rose. "This one, and that one there, and
maybe that one down below," she pointed, and they
stepped to.

If she had had an affinity for earth, she thought long
moments later as she paused to rub the sweat from her
forehead, she might have known that rock did not move
as easily as it might look like it would, and that this slide
was bound and determined to stay anchored in one way
or another, for as soon as they rolled one small boulder
out of the way, two more tumbled into its place from
above. They barked knuckles and ankles and toes more
than once, yelping with pain as they skinned their hands
and twanged their elbows. Barton wrestled with great
enthusiasm as his face grew apple red and sweat dappled his thin tunic darkly. They finally stopped, panting,
and looked at one another.

Barton said, "It's like wrestling goats, m'lady." He
rubbed hands that must have stung on his trousers.

"You know, you're right. That's exactly what it's
like!"

"You know goats?"

"Oh, yes. I grew up on a farm and orchard. I spent
my days gathering eggs, milking goats, and picking ap-

ples for cider," she told him. If her family were with her now, they'd make short work of moving this rockfall, she thought fondly.

"But you're a lady!"

She looked down at her dust-coated riding skirt and boots, standing in gravel up to her ankles. The cuffs of her shirt she'd rolled back, but red clay and silt had stained them anyway, needlework embroidery likely never to come clean again. "Hardly," she laughed at herself. "At any rate, this looks like one billy goat I can't wrestle into the pen."

"Maybe." Barton chewed his lower lip in thought, or perhaps he was merely sucking the salty sweat from it. He jabbed a finger at the boulders. "That one," he said. "It looks like that one is the one you need to move, if you're trying to shift the slide in that other direction."

She craned her neck. "I think you're right!" She picked her way carefully over the loose ground to the recalcitrant boulder bigger than both of them put together. A push and a shove hardly made it do more than rock a little in its place. She pulled out her sword, shoved it into a crack beneath it, and began to lever it out. The metal made a deep, throbbing sound as she pried at the boulder, and Barton scrambled over to put his scrawny shoulder to the thing. It fought them both, giving a little and then sliding back into position stubborn as if it had an ornery, billy goat mind of its own. She stopped to breathe deep and finally caught Lara's voice calling up to them.

"What are you doing up there besides ruining a good sword?" Lariel stood, hands on her hips, head tilted up to them, the glory of her gold-and-silver hair catching the sunlight, her face creased in query. Her blue, gold, and silver eyes flashed in the slanting sun.

"I'm ... I have to free this." She thumped her palm on the rock.

A very long moment passed. She could see the disapproval flash over her features, quickly followed by a neutral expression. She swallowed, knowing that she had provoked a rare anger. Lara snapped a wave at a guard standing to the rear. "Marten, get up there if you can and help m'lady Rivergrace before she snaps good steel in two and impales herself as well." She turned about abruptly as if to shut out the sight of Grace and the boy.

Marten flashed a grin up at Rivergrace, before springing up the rockfall as gracefully as a stag, even with the gravel and sand that loosened under his boots and cascaded down the hillside every which way. He eased her sword from its leveraging position and handed it back to her with a tsk at the notched blade. "Which way?"

"Thatta way." Barton jabbed a thumb as he warily gave ground to the guard.

"All shoulders to it, then." Marten dug in his heels and true to his order, put his shoulder and hands to it, waited till Grace bent down and then Barton, and they took a deep breath in concert.

Three heaves and the boulder finally gave, squirreling out of its cradle with a quickness that almost pitched all of them face first, but Marten caught his own balance, then the two of them by the scruff of the neck to save them from going over, as the boulder fell. The rockslide behind it gave way, moving slowly at first and then cascading down furiously. A gurgle sounded behind Rivergrace as water began to trickle up. The guardsman took her by the elbow.

"As welcome as that looks and sounds, I fear that if we don't move, we're in danger of being inundated." He steered her off the hillside back to the track that she and Barton had originally taken up, even as the font grew in size and intensity, becoming a waterfall springing from the side of the escarpment and tumbling down into the forsaken riverbed. Barton leaned over to dash his head in the water's spray with a whoop of joy.

"Do you think," Lara said softly, as they sat by the

evening fire, "that you will mind the boy getting all the credit for freeing the river and saving the village?"

"Not a bit." Rivergrace leaned forward as the Warrior Queen tweaked her ear gently. "They'll probably remember my name when it floods."

"Not a doubt of that."

"I heeded what you said to me, but I couldn't help it. The water called. It had to be freed, for its own nature as well as for their sakes."

"What's done is done. You would do well to remember my words in the future, though. We have been through a lot of heartache over this, Grace, and you'd be a fool to toss away our experience." Lara rubbed her hands together, bringing Grace's gaze to them, to the missing finger on her left hand, wondering if it ached in the cold the late fall night brought to them. Lariel did not often go ungloved in public, but this was not public, this was the queen leading a war troop on a scouting sortie, and when she did not have gauntlets on, she went bare-handed like any other trooper.

Rivergrace looked back to the ground, remembering the finger Lara had taken off to work deep earth magic, for the blood and flesh sacrifice to lead them on another quest, much different from this one. They had won through that. She didn't know if what they did now in pursuit of Abayan Diort would bring victory or defeat, or even if it could be ended in their lifetime. He came from a line of Galdarkan who'd been created to guard Mage Kings and fallen, and what ruled his mind generations later, none of them knew. Lariel had set a destiny in motion. It would be like trying to wade across the great sea, knowing that it stretched much farther than the eye could see or even imagine, and that you might fail before you accomplished reaching the other side.

And for the hundredth time since he'd left, she wondered how Sevryn fared.

Chapter
Two

DARAVAN DROVE HARD into the night, taking the horses as fast as they could go over even ground, leading them over treacherous stony impasses where they could not safely ride. Following him was like racing after a storm cloud, wrapped in ash gray as he was, as elusive as Daravan appeared to be in the threads of darkness around them. His horse moved under him as though not needing bridle or stirrup to guide him, spurred only by the will of the man he bore. He reminded Sevryn of Gilgarran, the only man on Kerith who'd taken notice of him as a half-breed living by his wits on backwater streets and decided he was of merit, not only because of his Vaelinar blood but because of who he'd become. Sevryn carried the Vaelinar magic in his veins although he did not have their remarkable eyes. Impossible to have the Talent without the multi-colored eyes, the eyes that could see into the elements of the world around them . . . but he had it. Everyone until Gilgarran had overlooked him and Daravan, often called the lord of storms, was very like his old mentor. Daravan would weigh you with his eyes, gray and silver as he was himself, the gaze not piercing, so you'd never guess that he'd taken your measure within a pinch of your soul. Then, like Gilgarran, he'd keep the secret of what he'd learned buried deep within himself until he needed to draw it out.

For all of that, Sevryn wondered how and why it was that Daravan had plucked him out of Lariel's troop. When they dismounted to lead the horses through a thinning copse of trees, he asked, "What luck drew you to me?"

He got no answer until they'd reached the other side, and he'd almost forgotten the question. "You were snoring loudest when I came through. I said to myself, 'that's the one I need, he'll be well-rested.'" Daravan stopped his horse, twisted the stirrup to put boot to it, and swung up to settle lightly.

"My luck, indeed," Sevryn said dryly. "To what do we ride?"

Daravan grinned. "Cutthroats, assassins, and Vaelinar honor. I have hopes that you'll stand at my back, and prove of some use there."

"I'll do my best."

"That goes without saying."

They reached a wide, rolling river much later in the evening, and Daravan reined to a halt. He sat his horse calmly on the riverbank as if waiting for some divine sign before crossing, and perhaps he did.

Sevryn dismounted to let his horse get a breather and eyed the sky. No lightening yet on the horizon, no sign that dawn might be near, although the night predators seemed quiet and those who rested and hid in the darkness stayed silent naturally. After very long moments, when he feared the calm would put him to sleep on his feet, he asked, "Are we waiting for a third?"

"No, the Ferryman."

Sevryn's eyes widened. He knew he had not slept in

the saddle nor could they have traveled far enough in half an evening to bring them to the banks of the swift and angry Nylara River where the phantom Ferryman docked his Way, his Vaelinar-created ability to negotiate a ferry across a treacherous river no ordinary being could tame. No one could safely cross the Nylara without him, and all paid the Ferryman's toll although the traders had always chafed under the paying. From one side of the deep and wide-cut river to the other, the Ferryman went back and forth as though chained to those waters, but Sevryn knew better. He'd discovered quite by accident that, if he'd a mind to, the Ferryman could bring you from the bank of the Nylara across to the bank of an altogether different river if one had the strength of will to ask. He'd paid a toll in coins and wondered then if the Ferryman would ever request or collect another sort of payment altogether.

Although the Ferryman had come to the Nylara River when the Vaelinar created the Way for the boat, no House claimed the creation of him, and no House or Hold or Fortress knew where the tolls he collected went. Had the Vaelinar-created Way chained a God, one of the Gods of Kerith who had abandoned their peoples in anger, to mortal waters? They did not know. They only knew when they'd needed a boatman, one came, and they dared not turn him away, or so whispered Vaelinar tales said. The making of Ways was an art forbidden centuries ago, yet there were those bloodlines who still attempted it although the knowledge of how to do so had been secreted away by those jealous of their power. The thought of the phantom being traveling from his anchor on the Nylara stopped words in his throat.

"I promised a price," Daravan said flatly, "a long time ago. The Ferryman answers to me."

The tone of his voice said that he would not be explaining further. Sevryn swung back into his saddle and waited for the impossible. They had ridden into the depth of the night, into its darkest tide, when souls floated out in their sleep never to be drawn back to the flesh again, when unspeakable Gods demanded even more unspeakable deeds of those who sought them out, and when mortal men plotted to gain immortality. He stared across the wide river and thought again of Rivergrace whose mere touch changed the water she approached, who could not tame the tides or currents but rode them. The river ahead, little more than a steep-sided brook, looked still enough he thought they might be able to ford it easily, but Daravan had other needs than just to cross this one span. He needed to cross country and quickly. It could be their escort might not show till dawn or later. The Ferryman had been known to keep certain personages waiting, as if out of spite. If a being without material needs in this world could hold a grudge, this one did. The Oxfort caravans were often kept waiting half a day or more, but then the young heir to the trading dynasty, Bregan Oxfort, had once cut the Ferryman down. The fury and magic unleashed had cost him most of the movement in one leg and arm for a decade of his young life until he recovered slowly, and as for the Ferryman, he'd disappeared entirely for a few breaths and then reappeared out of nothingness again, as intractable and unknowable as before, as if those who watched had merely closed their eyes for a long blink. Many learned from Bregan's foolhardiness. The Ferryman was not untouchable, only nearly so. Out of Sevryn's reverie and a darkness gathering on the farthest bank, a specter emerged.

A deep black hood and long cloak hid whatever shape, body, and face he might have. He strode across the river without breaking the surface of it, an eerie apparition that seemed solid but whose passage did not affect the water. A shiver ran down Sevryn's spine. This being strode through the nightmares of all the children of Kerith whose parents had ever met the Ferryman, and although he knew it well, Sevryn took a step backward himself. Daravan did not seem to notice as he dismounted.

The Ferryman halted. To Daravan he said, "Half a silver." To Sevryn, he added, "You cannot cross."

"He travels with me."

"He cannot cross."

Daravan's jaw tightened, and he slapped the end of his reins across the palm of his hand, but Sevryn stepped between the two. "He's only a tool," Daravan told the Ferryman, "but one I deem necessary for this journey."

"Let me accompany him." Sevryn pitched his tone carefully, bordering on the Voice of persuasion that was part of his Vaelinar Talent, but he didn't dare coerce the phantom as he would an ordinary being. The darkness within the hood turned to face him. Sevryn knew from past encounters that he would see nothing within, but he looked in reflex anyway. An abyss faced him for a fleeting moment and then a wisp drifted across the vision. He looked into a flat surface, like a pool of deep water, still and reflective, a bottomless pool facing a night without stars or midnight sun. Slowly, an image floated into view upon the surface. Indistinct, it wavered before his examination. Sevryn fought to envision it, and a blur of a face stilled in front of him, a blur that gained focus, until it grew distinct. He stared for a moment, expecting himself and not recognizing the features that sharpened in front of him. Then he caught it. The face he looked into, hidden in the depth of the Ferryman's hood, was not his own but that of Daravan. He looked sharply, and the likeness remained, the wrongness of it striking Sevryn to his core. Then the moment passed by, and he stared back into the abyss. Whatever else he might have said to persuade the Ferryman, he lost.

"The closing of our agreement grows near."

Daravan shifted weight. "It shall, one day." Did Sevryn hear more than uneasiness in his tone? He stepped back, as if to free Daravan from whatever the Ferryman might ask of him, but the phantom faced Daravan once more.

"Done, then," he said. "But the consequence lies upon you both."

Daravan hesitated, then dropped his chin in agreement and fetched out the coin piece from an inner pocket in his shirt, dropping it upon the hand the Ferryman held out.

"Stay close," the being instructed them. "Do not let me out of your sight." The Ferryman turned to ford the river, his movement through the water undetectable. Daravan tossed him a glance, but he gestured that he knew the drill and Daravan hurried after with Sevryn on his heels.

The river swallowed him up to his chest, cold as ice. His horse snorted at his back, throwing up his head and tugging on the reins in protest as they began to ford against the current. Sevryn kept his eyes on the back of the Ferryman's unfurled cloak, not knowing their destination but knowing if he lost either the specter or Daravan, he could be more than merely left behind. What magic the Ferryman worked he could not tell, but he did not wish to be in its wake if it went awry. They strode across a river that spanned more than its bed, more than its shore, more than this night. He felt it in the very marrow of his bones and in the hairs prickling at the back of his neck and in the tightened sinews of his neck as his body tensed.

The river fought his passage. It pulled and surged at him, trying to drag him away like two great arms wrapped about his legs pulling him down. Sevryn slogged after, trying to keep close and falling behind by a hand's length with every step. Fear shrouded him. He grasped his horse's stirrup with both hands, driving the horse after the others with his Voice as one might use a whip to keep the animal moving, dragging him along with its passage.

Sevryn spit river spray from his mouth as he gulped down a breath to shout for Daravan to stop or slow for him, and then he felt it. Idiot. Gilgarran would have boxed his ears for it. He wasn't just crossing a river, and he'd known it, knew it when Daravan had said he waited for the Ferryman. He just hadn't *realized* it down to his marrow despite his knowledge. He traversed a Way, one the Ferryman built with each stride ... and one that ended not far from his wake. He could see it now, rippling like a haze over the still water that surrounded the phantom form, and he cast his thoughts into it, anchoring himself on the Ferryman as he had to his horse's saddle. The pull and drag on him eased slowly. Sevryn thrust closer to the two men ahead and the Way opened fully to him.

From impeding him, the river now seemed to carry him, as though he journeyed along a bridge just over its waters. Its icy touch still inundated him, but the level dropped to his knees, and even his horse found the going much easier. Now, though, now he could see things reflected in the still water mirroring the Ferryman, things he wished he could not see. A black crimson flowered on the current, pooled and growing. He could smell the coppery smell of fresh blood, and he could see bodies, gashed and writhing, carried downstream past them, white-skinned and copper-skinned and even light gray ash, rare among the Vaelinar. Soldiers. He saw a Vaelinar warlord carried past on the river's crest, his eyes sightless in his despair. Sevryn thought of the battle of Ashenbrook which had brought the great Kanako to death. But this was not the river Ashenbrook. Or perhaps it was, and the Way took them across it, opening up the past like a fresh wound. The blood and the bodies moved downstream, below them. He saw other things, timber on the waters with log runners poling their harvest, trappers washing their snares in the waters, a hunt or two of wild animals bounding through the shallows. A wildfire that paused only to lick at the dampness and then gutter down to nothing but glowing embers as the night passed. They drew along the Way closer to the end of their journey.

In the shadows of the shore ahead, he could see a figure coming to the water, wrapped in blues and coppers, her russet hair unbound and shining to her shoulders, her hand in supplication to the river's edge as she knelt to it. His anger rose in him. Not Rivergrace. The Ferryman would not show Rivergrace to him! She did not belong entrapped in the Ferryman's doings. He let out a bellow. "Let her go!"

"It is as it is," the Ferryman answered.

Rivergrace looked up, unseeing, as they staggered onto the shore. She pulled her hand back with a slight smile, tucking a stray bit of hair behind one ear, and turned away, unharmed, untouched, unknowing. She did not fear fresh water, never had and, he prayed, never would.

He did not relax until her ghost faded into the evening air.

On dry shore, the Ferryman turned to Daravan and said in a low voice Sevryn was not meant to hear, but did, "One day you shall serve me as I serve you."

They stood like stone, the two of them, then Daravan nodded to their escort. Behind him, the first rays of dawn began to lighten the sky. They were no longer in verdant forest, but at the edge of a salt marsh, and the river behind them could barely be called a freshet. Sevryn could hear the cries of the kites off the bay as they rose into the air and hung over the inlets, waiting for fish to break the waves. They had come the length of the west coast of Kerith in one night. He mounted his horse without waiting for Daravan's signal. Whatever awaited them, Daravan and the Ferryman had turned the earth in its tracks to get to it.

Daravan waited until the Ferryman had gone before he pulled a vial from his saddlebags and passed it to Sevryn. "Two swallows," he counseled. "No more."

"What is it?" Sevryn took the vial and sniffed at it when he uncorked it. It held a musty, smoky smell under the medicinal odor.

"An antidote for *kedant*."

He'd been hit with the viper's poison before and

nearly died of it. Assassins favored coating their weapons with it. Those of Vaelinar blood had a particular weakness for kedant. Sevryn swallowed. It latched onto the back of his throat with a burning heat that made him swallow convulsively again and again, as he thrust the vial back to Daravan, his hand shaking, tears in the corners of his eyes. Finally the awful potion went down and smoldered in the pit of his stomach. "*Velk!* I am not so sure that isn't worse."

"I hear that." Daravan corked the vial and returned it to storage.

"We're meeting the Kobrir?"

"Perhaps."

He'd said assassins earlier, and they were famed for their skill and elusiveness. Sevryn respected them as much as he hated the Kobrir. No one knew how many there were, or even if they were of the race of man, so supple and quick were they. But they weren't invincible, any more than he was. His only concern was that Daravan seemed uncertain of what they rode to meet. What Daravan did not know might only inconvenience him but could mean the difference between living and dying to an ordinary man. Next to the full-blooded Vaelinar, Sevryn knew he was ordinary.

Daravan pointed across the salt marshes. "To the bay. We'll have a little cover from the abandoned village there. Take to the shadows, use them as well as you can. And, Sevryn," he paused. "Your Voice will be of little use. Keep to your other skills."

"All right." In a pitched battle, Daravan had just saved him time and effort, although it would have been nice to have advantages.

They rode toward the bay and its sky curtain of floating kites, their calls sounding thinly. They found their enemy waiting for them beneath the scavengers.

"Go to melee and keep them there," Daravan said, kicking free of his stirrups and leaping from his mount, pulling his sword and hand shield as he did.

Sevryn followed suit and found himself in pitched battle before he could inhale twice.

The sun beat hotly on them. Sweat ran off him in sheets. Feint, a thrust to the exposed flank from his left, and his opponent went down.

Screeching filled his ears, as did the hard breathing of Daravan at his back, and his own rasp. His katana ran with blood as did the wicked dagger in his off hand, and puddles of it pooled at his feet. His own body howled with the fierce joy of the fight, and he wanted more. Heated blood, tortured sounds of death and dying. He stoppered a growl in his throat, instead kicking sand over the pooled blood to keep from slipping. The enemy ringed them, their fallen lying where they had dropped them, but more stood than decorated the bloodied marsh. He'd expected Kobrir or perhaps even Ravers, but what faced them now, he held no name for.

He did not want to put a name to the ferocity that raged within him, and he tried to ignore it like the old ghost of an ancient demon. Blood hunger echoing inside him should not be heard.

But he did hear it.

"Still with me?"

He pulled himself back from his thoughts. "I am." He weighed his weapons in his hands, keeping an eye on the warriors who did the same.

"Marked?"

"A scratch or two. You?"

"Well enough. Tough buggers. Try for their knees, or what passes for them. Bring them down. Then . . . I think their eyes are at their throat level."

Daravan had a better assessment than he'd been able to make about the eyes. The knees he'd discovered for-tuitously, or they'd have cut him down long ago. They wrapped themselves in rags, disguising their look, skin, build, but they did not move as a race of Kerith did or as the Kobrir did. The cries of the kites above had grown faint when the fighting started. Screeching instead came from the ones they faced, fighting and wounded. It tore at his ears and his thoughts, making it near impossible to think. Perhaps they knew it, these devil fighters. A group had come in at pole length, swinging weapons similar to a harvest scythe, but they'd dispatched that half a dozen quickly with thrown daggers. Now they stood at melee and had for a bit, furious sorties balanced with breathers such as this one while they assessed one another.

Sweat ran through Sevryn's hair and soaked his shirt. His cloak wrapped one arm. He could feel dampness running down his trousers into his boots, not an inch of his skin that did not sweat profusely. Or he hoped it was mainly sweat.

To Sevryn's far right, one moved. The faintest of twitches, but he could guess that it was the start of a lunge that the others would copy in a wave, and he could ill afford that. He stepped away from Daravan's back in a sweep of his own, aiming across the throat, which seemed to be mid-torso, and the thing went down in a spurt of blackish red and a squeal cut short. He moved back into line an instant before they charged. Blades flashed. He took aim low, then high, his hands moving in a blur, his mind thinking only of staying alive. His thoughts hummed, his hunger fed. Warmth splashed his hands.

The breather he'd gotten was forgotten, and his muscles began to knot into numbing weariness. He'd been marked four times, one deep, when Daravan stumbled against his back, then swung around. He heard a thud behind him, and one of the fighters fell at his right foot, twitching into death.

"A thought."

"Aye?"

"Run a wedge through them. It should break this last wave, unless they've fighters in reserve I cannot spot."

"With you, but it'll leave our backs open."

"Dispatch the fore and spin about."

"Done."

In a fluid, synchronized movement, they left each other's back and joined side to side. As the enemy bunched, ten of them, momentarily confused, Sevryn let out a loud, hoarse cry and charged ahead, Daravan at his elbow. He dove and rolled, legs kicking out and sweeping four down by brute force, getting back on his feet before they did. His katana swept through them, and wetness sprayed upward. He spun about. His cloak-wrapped forearm took the brunt of a chop. He rocked back on his heel to counter with a thrust and dropped the being where it stood.

Three bore down on Daravan who grunted as he punched with his knife-filled hands, and Sevryn put his attention to the last three standing. He had to bet that Daravan would stay standing long enough for Sevryn to put his away and turn back to help.

One froze as he swung his katana, and his body crumpled over his sword. Sevryn pulled it free with a spray of blood. The last two let out harsh screeches, turned as one, and ran.

He dropped his sword and reached for a last throwing dagger. Daravan shook the dead off him and put his hand out. "Don't."

Sevryn didn't. Air rattling in his lungs, he bent to pick up his knives and went to one knee in dizziness. He lifted his head to watch the two pelt through the shambles of the ruins and disappear toward the waters of the bay. "Letting them carry word back?"

"Most definitely."

He'd get to his feet if he could, but it seemed beyond him for the moment. His blood thundered through his body. His mind sang, not with melody but with the cacophony of metal meeting metal and flesh meeting death. It was not a song he wished to remember, but it took him now at full flood.

Daravan gulped a mouthful of air himself. He took a hand and dagger off the closest attacker. "Take a breath," he managed. Shading his forehead, he peered at the sun, now at noon height over them. "We came to spare someone this welcome." He kicked bodies out of his way before kneeling himself and taking deep gulps of salted air.

"Antidote worked well."

"Good, that. I wasn't sure."

Sevryn raised an eyebrow, turned his face toward Daravan.

"Messed about with it a bit, had some failures, seemed it should work this time."

"Glad I could help clear that up."

"Don't mention it." Daravan sucked down another deep breath, and then grinned hugely. Sevryn put his boot to his hip and knocked the man over into the sand.

Over the noise of his breathing, Sevryn could hear the sound of a carriage bouncing its way through the broken street lanes of weathered seaport ruins. Still laughing, Daravan rolled to a stand and gave Sevryn a hand up. He got to his feet then and cleaned his sword quickly before sheathing it. Then he gathered up his daggers and throwing stars as he moved through the bodies. He opened up the hoods and cloaks to look at a thing he'd never seen before. Its mottled skin, eyes far out of place for eyes, its six-fingered hands with supple claws, high-ridged head pate brought a belligerent desert lizard to mind. The sight brought sourness up the back of his throat, and he spat to one side. "What are they?"

"I think, my lad, that you are looking at Raymy." Daravan took a second hand for a trophy. "Not that any of us have ever faced them since our First Days, but their fighting prowess is legendary."

The Vaelinar had appeared on Kerith, thrown onto the western coast by a catastrophe none could explain, from their world to this, and as they grew more settled, they'd come to realize that if the Mageborn had survived, if the Raymy had not annihilated much of the fighters before, they would not have gone unchallenged in their supremacy. But the Mageborn had incurred the wrath of Kerith's Gods and lost their magic as they battled one another after the Raymy defeat, when it seemed that holding small domains was no longer enough and the Mageborn decided one or another had to reign supreme. In disgust, the Gods had turned their faces from the races of Kerith. The backlash of their punishment and the self-destruction of the Mageborn generated a maelstrom that swirled about the continent's southern interior and created badlands no man would ever rule. Still, the Raymy were legend, one he'd never thought to meet. He toed a body at his feet.

"Then Lariel's fears are true."

"Perhaps. Or perhaps it only seems reasonable that they send a scouting party across the seas now and then to see what might face them if they return. If they had, and met with less resistance than ours, who would know today?" He tucked one of the hands into his belt and carried the other with him. "Let's see who approaches."

Despite the heat pouring off his soaked body, Sevryn pulled the hood of his cloak up to shade his face. His body stiffening, he forced himself into a trot after Daravan, and they rounded a fallen heap of building to accost the carriage driver.

Bregan Oxfort stood up in surprise, as he reined his horses down and he set the brake. His trader finery had been exchanged for field leathers, his gold filigree leg brace glinting in the sunlight over them, his hair tied back, his Kernan handsomeness settling into a mask of neutrality. "Lord Daravan! A surprise to see you here."

Sevryn found no less a surprise in seeing Bregan. Son and partner to one of the foremost trading dynasties, and not known to be doing his own dirty work, his appearance in the hinterlands, in the salt marshes of a tsunami-destroyed bay, could only raise far more questions than he could answer.

Daravan cut the air with a bloodied hand. "A

fortunate one for you, Trader Oxfort. We chanced upon an ambush."

Bregan paled. He sat down on the carriage seat, the vehicle squeaking slightly under his weight. A robe hid whatever the small vehicle bed behind him might carry, nor did he give the slightest sign of body language that he worried about a cargo. But he most certainly knew it was there, even though his light blue eyes rested firmly on the two of them. Bregan Oxfort was not the type of man who did not know. Kernan eyes, holding only one distinct color, plain eyes signaling no power such as rested in a Vaelinar, gazed solidly on them. "A friend sent me down this route, asking me to assess the site, see if it might be suitable to invest in. The tides along this bay have been harsh, but it was once a good fishing port. We hoped time had healed it. We'd like to rebuild here."

"Your friend has some questions to answer, then." Daravan tossed the clawed hand next to Bregan's leg. "Take that to your guild library and see if you and your associates can identify it, and what was waiting for you. I'll be contacting you to see what you can discover from it."

The Kernan stared down at the grisly remain. "The two of you are bloodied." He kicked the severed hand down into the wagon well.

"We had some opposition. They set a goodly number against you."

He nodded. Rings upon his fingers shot colored gleams into the air as he let the brake off and regathered the reins to turn his carriage about. "Consider me in your debt, Lord Daravan."

Daravan gave a half bow. "It cannot be ill fortune to have a family such as the Oxforts indebted to me," he returned. Bregan gave a wave in answer and clucked to his horses, and they set off in a high-stepping trot.

Daravan waited until the sight and sound of the carriage had disappeared from their senses, hidden by the leaning ruins until the lane took him into dunes etched by wind and where scrub brush had all but swallowed the old road. "I'd heard he was still a good horseman, for all the stiffness of that leg. When did he give up riding?"

"He hasn't. And he's a decent off-handed swordsman now, although not as good as he was before. He had it beat into him that he could train the other hand." Sevryn dropped his hood, relieved that Bregan had neither recognized him nor even tried to, a faceless shadow at Daravan's elbow.

"Then he should have been riding here. Faster and easier than a carriage." Daravan rubbed his chin. "Saved him, did we?" he said softly, as if mulling it over. "Or had he come to a meeting, with trade goods in the wagon behind him?"

Chapter Three

ON THE BARE-BONED side of a hill, overlooking golden-brown fields where autumn harvest had reduced the crop to row after row of broken stalks which cows and goats now grazed slowly, a fortress sat watch. As weather-beaten and dun as the land about it, it hardly rated more than a glance or two, first for its sheer size and second for the broken tower at its corner, a tower not for defense or offense but for imprisonment. If not for those, it might be dismissed altogether. The sharp peaks and cuts of a hard-spined mountain range leaned heavily upon it, imposing and dangerous, an implacable wall of stone. Winter would bring snow and ice and carry the shards of it on every breeze to the tower. A wind from the twilight-colored skies caught on it now, howling and whistling as though tearing loose or perhaps tearing down the impediment to its path. An answering howl came from within before fading to a thin hoarseness and then bleeding away altogether. Hoarse, rasping words followed, piercing the veil. "I am done.

Now the bright and beautiful shall fall, one by one, into ruin." Then, nothingness.

In the silence that fell briefly over the barracks and outbuildings, no one looked up, although a few shrugged their shoulders in relief before putting their muscles back to the chores awaiting them. Of little imagination, they did not hold superstitions about what they heard. They knew whose tortured throat had uttered the ululations. Their master's hound, as they called him, had been locked up for many days now. Or perhaps, as it was rumored about the rough fortress, he had locked the others out. Their ears had not the wit to hear more, nor their eyes the sagacity to see more, though many of them held a trace of Vaelinar in their bloodline. They were the chaff of the fields, and they knew it. They would work till the last ray of sun glinted across the landscape, or their master would exact a terrible discipline from them. Soldiers made into farmhands and blacksmiths, they toiled at what they must to survive. When the wars came, then would come their glory and their prosperity. They had been told that, and they believed it. That was a soldier's lot and they had been chosen for it. The wind picked up again after a moment, unsubstantial and wavering. The tower remained silent.

Inside the tower, in a room locked from the inside, a spare, ragged man sat, his hollowed gaze upon a row of water jugs, most full and untouched. No crust or rind of bread could be found, nor any sign of meat or fruit. As lithe as any Vaelinar could be, he bordered more on skeletal, his strength wiry at best, whatever handsomeness his features had held long ago given way to gauntness and madness. Hair that might have been a lustrous brown in his youth was now lank and gray and corded back at the nape of his neck, his eyes flat and barely showing the jeweled multicolors of his people. Yet, as emaciated as he was, the very bones of his body shouted out his breeding. No one would mistake him as any other than Vaelinar.

He put a hand up and stroked his throat. His voice, if he had one left, would be raw and ragged, but his throat felt empty, as though there were no screams left to issue forth. Narskap nodded to himself and dragged one of the water vessels to him before drinking deeply, water cascading down his chin and over his chest. He dropped the jug wearily when he'd finished with it and it rolled about on its clay side, droplets running into a meager puddle. He looked into the wetness thinking to see himself there, scarcely more than skin and bones, hair pulled back into a severe queue at the back of his neck, his forehead peaked and high, the tips of his ears elegantly pointed, the only mark upon him that could be called one of Vaelinar quality. The rest of him could hardly be said to be so. He dressed in rags, he sat in sweat and dust, the tower confining him little more than wood and a bit of mortar here and there in the more severe cracks where the elements drove themselves in. Boards in the roof overhead rattled without cause. It was shelter but only just.

He gave a shrug. Dust drifted off him, a shroud of madness and delusion, and softly swirled to the floor around him, lesser motes floating on the air to be caught and studded by rays of sunlight managing to find their way inside. With a heave he found his feet, his body wavering back and forth with effort as though incapable of staying erect. He lifted trembling hands until he curved them into a position, holding an imaginary sword, a great sword, before him. In that pose, his body steadied. He found a gravity as he molded himself into a sword warrior's stance. His hands tightened about that which he dreamed.

It had been his burden. He knew the heft and swing of it, the runes which had engraved it, the channels carved in it for the blood to run off, the elaborate hilt, the shining length of it. Narskap knew it as well as the smithy who'd fashioned and imbued it. He knew the Demon which had sung in it. Shoulders tense and sinews straining, he went through a series of movements with it. Guard, parry, thrust, balance, slice, he glided through them all. Cerat the Souldrinker, the Demon-ridden sword which only he could wield, filled his hands. He had become one with it then and moved with it now as if it were a part of him, imaginary blade stroking the air. His exertion increased, movements quickening, until he had stepped from exercise into battle, meeting a foe. Parry, gather, lunge, block. A spray of crimson washed the air in front of him, blinding him from the last of the sun filtering in through the cracks of the weather-beaten tower. He did it all, the sword in his mind forged to thrust as well as slice, doing all while the Demon cried in a thin, high, eerie song for blood and the mortality of the flesh it carved.

At some point, he became not the man imagining the sword but the sword imagining the man. He knew the bite of each hit, the wetness of the blood splashing down it, the thrill of the death and the taking of the soul inside himself, the eating of the mortality and the fear of the opponent. He was cold metal which became warmed by the fluids of the dying and by the hands gripping it firmly, giving it freedom to attack and the strength to move. He felt the nock of each slice to the bone once armor gave way. He felt the jolt of meeting a shield or parry and finessing beyond to drink again. He bathed in the blood of his enemies, and everything which lived was his enemy. He sliced the air until his wielder began to shake with effort and then ... then ... he faced that which he had never encountered before. Entities which imbued the sword along with Cerat, powerful entities and souls, and a girl who bore the blade as a charge threatened his being. She carried him heedless of his bloodsong and power, she carried him to do a thing which only she could do, and he unable to resist her. She a stripling yet ... a cord, a wire ... he could not break. She lifted him a last time and struck him across a bond of magic and stone. He let out a demonic yowl.

And shattered. His existence ended in broken shards and splinters of steel. His voice fled shrieking to the nether realms, freed and yet exiled. Dream collapsed, and the man fell in exhaustion.

His legs gave way, folding under him, and Narskap collapsed into a heap on the floor, chest heaving, his clothes sodden, his hair lank and sweat-slicked to his head. He reached for another jug of water, hand shaking wildly.

He stayed his hand as a cloud coalesced from the jugs in front of him. His arm shook wildly. A mist of fine drops ranged upward, becoming a spray, then a dense fog and then ... a being. She hovered in front of him, silver and blue and gray, with wings of dark marine blue spread about her form, or perhaps it was a massive cloak unfurled. Power radiated from her, and the room chilled with her presence. The lumber bones of the tower creaked heavily as if they fought to contain her, dry wood hit with a burst of sudden moisture. She brought with her the smell of summer rain on heat-baked stone and the burning odor of fresh struck lightning. Dampness surrounded her, made the air heavy to breathe almost as if he were underwater. Her eyes held the deep blue of a bottomless mountain tarn and they were fixed on him. Her hair cascaded about her, colored like many waters. She did not smile as she beheld him.

Nor did he express awe or fear as he looked upon her. He merely reached for a clay jug that her presence did not affect, drawing it close and draining it. He cradled the empty jug with one hand. "Goddess," he acknowledged. "Although not of me and mine."

"Man who dreams of being a sword and sword who dreams of being a man," she answered. Her presence spread until it flooded the room save where it reached him, and then it was as though his body dammed her from reaching farther. The cloak curled like whitecaps cresting on a windblown lake but stayed a finger's breadth from touching him. Dewdrops as bright as jewels dappled over his sweat-stained skin and clothes. Behind him, the wood stayed as dry and dusty as it had been although he had the sense it would have gulped her down if it could have, wood that had once lived and ached to do so again. She beckoned. The mists about her rippled. Her face stayed smooth and her godly beauty did not change its mask, but Narskap thought a mortal disappointment might have lanced through her eyes for a moment. "Which are you?"

"One might as well be the other. Both are tools."

"Does a tool live? Does it feel, inhale, stretch its soul toward the unknown? Does it talk with a God? Does it know worry and fear?"

"I exist. As for the rest determining what a man is, even the smallest animal in the field goes to sleep at night, worrying that it will hunger when it awakens in the morning."

She looked down on him. "You hunger."

"In a way that no Goddess can fulfill." His fingers tightened momentarily on the empty jug he held.

"There is nothing I can offer you." Neither a statement nor a question, bordering on both.

"Nothing that I would want from you, no. You do not exist to me."

"It is not wise to disbelieve in the Gods. Or to argue with them."

He cut the air between them with the side of his hand. "You can always leave."

"I came to look at the being which caused me distress."

"Both your observance and revenge could have come from on high if you are as you believe yourself. The omnipotent do not need to visit their targets." He seemed unperturbed.

"But not as satisfying."

Narskap grunted softly. "Nothing gets satisfaction from me."

"I will."

"To do that, you would have to exist."

"Do you think existence depends upon you and your recognition?" The Goddess made a scoffing sound. "You don't have to will it, for it to be so." Her image gathered a bit, becoming more solid, her eyes growing icy and her face sharper. She almost looked as if she were a Vaelinar herself with her expression so planed. "You wait for your partner, but I tell you the Souldrinker is blocked from leaving the nether planes again. You wait fruitlessly for Cerat. Even your years will not extend long enough for such a thing to happen."

He blinked. "A concerted effort. The world must be ending if the Gods align."

"We often agree on the important things," she said in a cold fury. The winged cloak about her unfurled and rippled as if in a distressed wind, a wind that howled both inside and outside the tower. The clapboards rattled around him, although the floor he sat upon seemed solid enough. Dewdrops and condensation ran off him in chilled rivulets.

"You will wander the earth as lifeless and soulless as you profess to be. That of you and yours will not be satisfied until quenched by the blood of destiny." The voice of the River Goddess rose strongly as she spoke, and when she ceased, the room fell into an absolute quiet broken only by the sound of droplets hitting the floor.

The wind began to howl again. "You have cursed me," Narskap observed mildly. "Even worse, with nonsense."

"Or blessed you. As for the nonsense, time will give you proof." A ripple like that which moved across water ran through her. The wind growled louder, a storm moving across the land. The apparition spoke again. "I know that which can destroy you." She shrank yet again, growing more solid, more mortal-sized, and ever more threatening. She loomed in front of his face, her cloak-wings wrapping about him, and she leaned down to whisper a word or two in his ear. His pale skin grayed further. Then she drew back and flung her arms out, her presence once again billowing forth and claiming all of the tower that she could. "You will never touch one of us again," she told him.

"I should never have been able to touch one of you before," he said dryly, reminding her of his ability.

Lightning struck once, very close, followed on the heels of the blinding flash by thunder which shook the entire fortress with an ear-shattering rumble.

And then she was gone.

Narskap sat very still for a moment or two, counting his heartbeats. It might have been raining outside, he was not certain, for his ears still rang with the boom of the thunder, and the heated smell of lightning filled his nostrils. When he recovered, he reached forward, sweeping over four of the clay jugs, revealing four very sharp arrowheads chiseled and struck from a jewel of red-gold.

"Interesting. She did not sense me." Quendius stepped forth from the tower shadows at Narskap's back.

"Indeed, Master." He picked up an arrowhead, cradling it carefully. "An important bit of knowledge. As for the omnipotence of godliness, she is wrong on several counts."

Quendius reached his side. He wore his long ivory fleece vest over dark leather pants, as supple as the well-muscled legs they covered, his ash-gray skin looking as though he had been dusted lightly by the fires of the forge he commanded. His dark eyes narrowed as his gaze examined the object Narskap held up for him. "Well shaped."

"Cerat cannot leave the planes whole. But his essence, quartered, can. We have achieved what he wished, even under the nose of the River Goddess. She came to advise us of triumph, already too late to know she had been defeated." Narskap tapped each of the four arrowheads. "He has already imbued that which I have shaped for him." A loud hum began from the arrowheads as if awakened to his thump. Quendius knew that hum, knew the impatient song of a Demon whining for obedience.

"And what now to finish them?"

"Aryn wood for the shaft." Narskap looked into his master's face. "If you would procure that for me, you will have an arrow that armor cannot turn aside. Even flesh and bone will not stop it, until it has taken the blood and soul it wishes, and then it will return to the archer's hand. Your quiver will never be empty as long as Cerat is thirsty, and he is never sated."

Quendius smiled briefly. He shifted his weight to bow over the arrowheads. "Aryn wood."

"Bistel Vantane guards his aryns as a Kernan guards his daughters. But I have faith that you can secure wood for the shafts and a matching longbow. Once I've strung the longbow, all you need is to be bonded to it."

"And yet you call me master." Quendius put a fingertip to the arrowhead held by Narskap. He could feel the heat within it, hear the buzz like that of an angry hornet. He trusted that all was as Narskap told him, and that Cerat had divided himself to enter the plane of mortals which fed him so well before. "It will return to the archer," he repeated.

"Once the bow is made and strung and initiated, yes. It will drill through flesh like a hot dagger through freshly churned butter."

He grunted in satisfaction before remarking. "I will presume the ritual involves blood."

"With Cerat, there can be no other way."

Quendius removed his finger from the arrowhead. "I'll see to it." He withdrew to the door, unlocking the four locks which secured it, each a thick and heavy dead bolt. As ramshackle as the tower looked, it was not. The timber shaping it was thick and solid. Its cracks might let the elements in, but it would never allow its occupants out.

Narskap heard him leave. He did not for a moment wonder how his master had gotten into a tower locked from the inside nor why the Goddess had not sensed him. Had Quendius even been there? Perhaps not; his master had left days ago on another mission. He knew, better than Quendius even, that the weaponsmith could step through dark spots in the otherwise bright firmament of Kerith. He'd been at Quendius' side when it happened. A day or more might have been lost or gained, but shadow swallowed Quendius even as madness swallowed Narskap. Or perhaps it was only his madness that made him think Quendius could travel through shadow. It was not a Talent or a magic that the Vaelinar held. It was more like a blight on the world and Quendius a worm who could wiggle through the corruption. Narskap shivered. His thoughts turned to the problem at hand: getting past Bistel to harvest the wood from the famed Vaelinar trees known as aryns. Nothing less would suit his purpose.

Inwardly, the words of the Goddess echoed in his head, particularly those which she had whispered to him. Like an arrow of Cerat, he mused. Straight to the heart and through it. She had intended to hurt him, and she had indeed pierced him. If he'd had a heart.

Chapter
Four

He watched Daravan ride off, north and to the east around the looping bay after a last admonishment to tell Lariel their suspicions but to couch them with uncertainty. And to make sure his audience had no listeners but the queen, not even Osten. As for the trader they'd saved, Daravan wanted nothing said. He would handle that, he'd told Sevryn, and Sevryn had little doubt he would. The Oxfort dynasty held more power on the First Home continent than any bloodline or warlord, and it would be crossed, if at all, with great diplomacy. Sevryn took a hand off a carcass for himself after kicking and shooing away the kites who'd come down to claim the spoils.

Blood soaked his clothes, drying stiffly in the slanting sunlight. Some of it belonged to him and some to Daravan, but the vast majority was the red-black blood of the foe and it stank. The whites of his horse's eyes showed as he watched Sevryn as warily as he would a stranger while Sevryn wrapped and tucked away his grisly souvenir. Sevryn pulled firmly on the bridle with a word or two, testing the tie-up to a driftwood stump and sat down to pull his boots off so he could bathe. He would not ruin his boots in the sea, not even for a recalcitrant mount. He waded into the surf, the salt water stinging the cuts and scratches peppering his body, even as the chill made him clench his teeth. The foam drew back with the tide stained red by his bathing, and he stepped out of the water as soon as he could, wind off the bay cutting through him.

Sevryn pulled a saddlebag open and ate while the cold breeze dried him, cutting jerky into strips and chewing it down as best he could. He had a cheese in there, too, but decided to save it and warm it by a fire in the evening. After he finished, he drew out all his weapons, the ones he had recovered, and began to oil and clean them. He honed the ones with the harshest usage, but there were nicks and notches that a smithy would have to finish off for him. Shivers came and went over him as his clothes dried in the chill wind, and he finally put his blades away. He cleaned his boots in the same way, but they would have to be redyed and treated. The bloodsong in him bled away with the sea wind.

The kites came back with their shrill cries, a dark cloud of them, swooping low to the marsh, and he knew they had come to feast on the carrion left for them. With that thought, he pulled his boots back on, mounted with an encouraging word to his horse, and put his heels to the animal's flanks. The blood on the water, the cry of birds squabbling over the dead, the winter chill of the wind, all filled him with the sense that he had a need to get back to Rivergrace as soon as he could. It spurred him harder than the urgency to take his grisly trophy to the Warrior Queen with word of a possible new foe. He rode back the way they'd come, the wind off the sea already whipping the sand and dirt over their tracks, obscuring them. When he came to the freshwater river cutting across the marshes, he paused at its bank holding little hope that he could call on the Ferryman to aid his return. He kicked the horse into the water with a jump and a leap and they were through, heading south and to the east, to the line of forested hills where the horse could graze when they halted for the day and he could catch fresh game.

Aching a bit and tired, he let the horse carry him toward the verdant line while he scanned the area, trying to pick up threads of the trail that Daravan had forged bringing them here. As much a sign of their journey as broken branches and hoofprints, an aura lay over it. Sevryn stared across the landscape, sensing an aura he could pick up and gather, a gossamer-fine thread that he could braid into a stronger thread to guide him back. He caught a shimmering of gray mist and fine sable. Daravan had brought them to the Ferryman, a trail which carried them farther, faster, than physical abilities could otherwise. He should have sensed it. He could now. With a snap of will, he anchored his senses to it, separating it from the natural elements of the world, a passage of unnatural speed and effort, a Way that faded with every breathing moment as it had been meant to do, a thing created to be transient and unobtrusive on the structure of the world. He wondered that he could find it at all, knowing that Daravan must have expended more strength creating it than needed, rather than use too little and fail as his need to arrive in time had pressed him. He wondered that Daravan had been on his feet when they'd come to the bay. What effort had he expended, and of what stuff was he made? As far as Sevryn knew no one had created a Way in his lifetime. The methods for doing so were guarded by each House, if any even remembered. There were many who'd died trying to forge a Way, far more unsuccessful than succeeding, but even that had claimed its toll. Only the Ferryman could cut distance as he had. It was rather like two halves of the whole, this journey of theirs and the Ferryman and the Vaelinar had made the Ways.

So it was that Sevryn urged his horse onward into the fading day by another riverside just before the setting of the sun.

He spurred his tired mount across the river, feeling the water rise about them till it touched the bottom of his boot soles and breasted the horse. Weariness sucked at him as did the current, slowing their progress to a slogging walk and he chirped to encourage the horse, mist soaking them both. But the river grew no deeper, nor did it go higher than his boot shank. He pushed worry from his mind and fixed it on the Andredia, the sweet and sacred river that flowed into and through the valley kingdom of Larandaril, the river which would take him to Rivergrace.

Sevryn's horse gave a startled whuff as it staggered out of the water. He didn't need to urge the animal away from the river, as it gratefully clambered onto dry land. He stared back at the water, the hair at the back of his neck prickling uncomfortably. He rubbed his hand across his nape as he took stock of where they stood, but didn't know where he was. Hopefully, that condition would be temporary when he had a chance to scout in the early daylight on the morrow.

In the thick of the forest cover, night pressed down as the sun lowered, leaving him shivering. Dry kindling and branches soon made a fire, and the two of them stood close to it while they warmed, and soon the horse dropped his head to crop at the grasses as Sevryn squatted by the flames. He listened to the calming noise of the animal searching out tender shoots left behind yet untouched by frost, and the crackle of the wood as it burned.

He had grown up in towns—towns, villages, backwater slums of cities, with his hair long and shaggy over the pointed ears that would give him away as a by-blow of the Vaelinar, his clothes nondescript rags that would not give away his age or height or build, for he aged slower than the other wretched children of the streets.

Another useless castoff of a feared and sometimes hated bloodline. He didn't even have the Vaelinar eyes, the eyes that signaled the ability to manipulate magics of the world. No one had a use for him, no race of Kerith and certainly not the Vaelinars. His mother had brought him to a village and then left him to search for his father when his prolonged childhood had so burdened her that she had no choice but to abandon him. She said she'd return, but she never did, nor did anyone who might have deemed himself a father come to claim him in her stead. He was not wanted, except by himself. Every road had been a choice for him, a conscious decision to survive or fall by the wayside. He took care to move from village to city to town, leaving when the years made it obvious that others matured while he did not. He had a talent for making things listen to him and bend to his will. He used that to calm the recalcitrant beasts of trader stables and caravans as a stableboy, a menial job that gave him coin to get through from time to time. Other seasons, he made a living through salvaging and stealing that which was not held dear or close by others. He learned to fight to protect himself and he taught himself to throw daggers ... to amuse himself and to hunt. He hadn't had much of a life until that day that Gilgarran fell on him from a second-story window and looked into his face and knew exactly what he looked at despite how Sevryn tried to dissemble and to persuade him otherwise with his Voice.

Gilgarran had taken him in, groomed him, taught him intrigue and spying and weapons and diplomacy, and the two of them had never looked back until the day Quendius sliced Gilgarran's head from his shoulders when Gilgarran breached his outlaw fortress and forge. Of his own almost twenty-year captivity by the weaponsmith, he thought and remembered little except that which sometimes rode his dreams. The memories had been scarred over and hidden for a good many years till made raw again by circumstances, but he would not dwell on them. They were as if they had happened to someone else, and so he treated them that way. To think otherwise would invite insanity or self-pity, and he'd already moved beyond that. Far beyond. His escape had brought him to yet another Vaelinar who'd recognized the potential in him: Queen Lariel and her brother Jeredon, and he had not left their service since.

Not even for Rivergrace. He thanked the lost Gods of the Vaelinars and the stubbornly absent ones of Kerith that he'd never had to make the choice.

Lara's title had not come by way of a dynasty, although her grandfather had been the Warrior King. She had, through a series of trials that Sevryn and most Vaelinar were not privy to, earned her designation. He could not say what she'd sacrificed, but he could say that he found her fair and tough-minded and formidable. No word had ever been breathed of what Talent she held. There were those disgruntled Vaelinar who claimed she had no Talent, that her remarkable eyes of blue highlighted by gold and silver were empty of the magics of her people, but he would deny that. Secretive she could be, but without Talent? No. She possessed whatever she needed to be Warrior Queen of the contentious Vaelinar, and more.

As for her brother Jeredon, he was like a brother to Sevryn as well. Tall and graceful, diffident about politics and more at home in the forest than in the halls, Jeredon strode across the lands as a hunter and caretaker, not a warrior. Since his wounding in a rockfall, he'd been paralyzed from the waist down, though healers proclaimed he retained some feeling and movement and that he would likely heal completely, given time, that nerves and tendons and cartilage had not been severed, only severely bruised and traumatized. The one trait he shared with his sister, impatience, made his recovery all the more difficult. Lariel did not need the burden of his infirmity. No one but Jeredon complained of it. Indeed, Rivergrace's foster sister Nutmeg waited on him hand

and foot and said not a word in complaint. The sturdy Dweller lass had pulled a starveling Vaelinar child from the River Silverwing and made a sister of her, and she'd accept no less a miracle with Jeredon's recuperation.

Sevryn poked a branch into the fire, stirring up those already burning a bit, and watched as an ember flew up with a hissing spit, then burned out. Actually, that was not quite true. Nutmeg could box the prince's ears with the best of them, and give him an earful of Dweller parables, always pragmatic and often humorous, and she never let Jeredon wallow in regret or slack in his rehabilitation, for all that she was little more than torso high to a Vaelinar. The Dwellers of this world were the salt of the earth, no less, and the Gods blessed them even as they had turned deaf ears and blind eyes to the other races of Kerith. Sevryn had not been raised as a Vaelinar, so he wasn't brought up with the knowledge that they'd lost all they'd known, even their memories of their true roots and heritage. He missed nothing but what he had been given from the day he was born, and never thought back on the generations before him.

Not true for other Vaelinars; not for those original lost who still lived. Not for those who fought to claim an intangible something they felt they had lost, whether it be rulership or superiority or dominion over the earth they trod. Not for those who would do anything to regain that which they had been banned from forever.

Sevryn wondered if that was what drove Quendius.

He stabbed his poker branch into the flames and left it there to burn as well, knowing he wouldn't gain an answer that evening, and perhaps never. He would not, however, give up trying to find one. He wondered if he had already made the choice the Ferryman had demanded of him.

He dozed a moment, eyes half open, his hands going slack, his mind drifting off to things he hadn't felt in the battle, hadn't noticed until now ... the smell of the blood exciting him, the sight of it streaming down his blade and pooling onto the sands. His heart leaped in momentary excitement and he tasted a yearning at the back of his throat.

He dreamed of something he was not, but had been . . . once. The feel of cold iron bound him by ankle and wrist, shame as white hot as forge-heated iron filled him. Old scars of body and soul ran achingly through him.

The shock of it flung his eyes wide open, his body in a still wakefulness. The afternoon had grown late, the sun's half-hidden rays slanting low across the vista.

"City lad. You ought to know better than to sleep in the wild."

He knew the voice before he saw the shadow separate itself from the dusky images thrown by tree and bush, and the being squatted down in front of him, the burned-out fire separating them. Even among the varied Vaelinars, his soot-colored skin was a rarity, and he dressed to accent it, wearing leather breeches of charcoal hue, and a rich ivory long vest which fell open as he settled himself. Quendius spread his hands out to the cooling ashes in futility, but Sevryn doubted he wanted embers to warm his hands. The man he knew preferred the heat of blood.

"You followed Gilgarran to his death. Would you follow Daravan there as well? It is better, lad, to lead. Always better to lead."

"Kill me and be done with it."

Quendius grinned. "To the point."

Sevryn levered himself to one elbow, eyes locked on the other. He did not move beyond that, nor did the expression in the other's eyes give away any intention.

"When Gilgarran brought you to my forge above the Silverwing, I thought you nothing more than a servant dogging his boot steps. Him, I knew. I knew his reputation and his canniness. Knowing that, I should have paid more attention. You were the weapon he had hidden up his sleeve although it didn't save his life. You did what he intended. You brought my forge down, and you brought back word of what I had been doing." Quendius clenched one fist and released it. "I kept you alive because I thought you had only been a by-blow tagging along behind him. If I had known, you'd be dead already.' "

"We've something in common, then. We both regret the other is living."

"And what of my hound? Do you have him marked for death as well?"

Sevryn flicked his gaze around quickly but found no one else. "Where is Narskap? I thought you held that leash close."

"He is hunting other quarry. One you should worry more about than yourself."

Sevryn froze his expression before the other could see the emotion that ran through him. Before Quendius could see that his words marked him like a brand. Before Quendius could verify that he cared far more about Rivergrace than he did for himself. Before he could hand Quendius another weapon to be used in this private war. "One lives for oneself or not at all," he remarked, with just a shadow of his Voice upon it, pushing conviction and trust. *Do not think upon Rivergrace, Quendius, do not think of her at all.*

After watching him closely for a moment or two, Quendius moved smoothly to his feet. A massive though lean man, he towered over the prone Sevryn. The years had not aged him much, if at all, although his hands showed more calluses and scarring, the signature of his trade as a weaponsmith and a warrior. He crooked a finger at Sevryn. "We are both alone, it seems, except for our regrets. Yours should be short-lived." He cast a look about the area. "The day grew cold early. It is a shame you neglected your fire, though that neglect suits my purposes." He gestured, and Sevryn followed it to see an empty sack lying nearby on the ground. "It will seek your heat. And, when it does, sooner or later, it will strike you. I won't bore you with the tale of why I even had it on me, but I did. If, for some reason, this doesn't kill you, I'll find another way." Quendius took a calculated step backward. Behind Sevryn, his horse let out a nervous whinny.

Sevryn moved his chin a bit to see the thing lying close to his pants leg—green-and-yellow scales, a long, flattish, diamond-shaped head with a beautiful red whorl mark—the kedant viper. Quendius gave a dry chuckle as he took another step backward, into the shadows. "May you have the unquiet Return you deserve," he said as he left.

Sevryn did not move, except to measure his breathing in long, slow, shallow drafts while he watched the serpent. It would strike, inevitably, for that was its nature, to hunt warm-blooded things, even as it took shelter with him. Far from the rocks and sands which the sun heated like a hearth for its existence, it would be unsettled and even more aggressive than usual. Time crawled, even as the kedant viper did, edging up along his leg and thigh toward his torso and the hand he held very still. He stretched his senses out, the senses Gilgarran had tuned for him, Vaelinar senses for which he had the Talents if not the eyes, even as Quendius had the eyes, eyes of obsidian black with silvery shards in them, without the Talents.

He found no sign of the other, although the edge of the forest had begun to stir with those seeking shelter for the night and those seeking to hunt by cover of the night.

Now or never.

He reached down and grabbed the viper by the back of its neck. Fast but not fast enough, for it struck him on the hand as he did so, and fire stung him. Sevryn bit off a harsh word as he sprang to his feet, drew his dagger, and sliced the vicious thing into shreds. Then he stood and felt the kedant venom raking him.

He waited. Sweat broke out and poured down his face, his neck, his torso, as though he stood in a downpour.

His skin danced with the fiery ache of the poison, and his heart sped up to the rhythm of an unheard but frantic drumbeat. His hand shook. It swelled slightly, crimson around the puncture marks. His vision blurred as he stared at himself, wondering if he had miscalculated.

Then his eyesight cleared. His pulse calmed. The feeling of a thousand crawling snakes under his skin began to retreat. The fire was the last to bleed out of him, leeched away by the approaching dusk, and he did not know how long he'd stood, waiting to see if Daravan's antidote had been strong enough, still remained potent enough in his body, to keep him alive.

His horse threw his head up with a snort. He cleared his mind and then his throat before speaking a Word or two to calm his animal. Then, to calm himself, he walked to the river's bank and knelt, dashing the chilled water over his face. He had outlived the intentions of Quendius once again. As the water dribbled off his cheekbones and chin, he trailed his hand back into the tide to cup a drink.

That's when he felt her. Saw her, with every fiber of his soul. She touched a river somewhere, thinking of him. This was no mirage the Ferryman taunted him with, no threat Quendius had laid upon him. He saw her by another river, a northern stream, blue-white with cold water. Rivergrace lifted her head as if sensing him as well, her eyes searching across the current, looking for him. But she was not there for him, nor was he for her, except by the fleeting touch of the passing river. He would warn her, but the moment passed, leaving him only with the knowing of that instant. Nothing more did it give him. No warning and no comfort.

Chapter Five

"WHERE IS MY father?" Bregan stepped down from his carriage, sunburn aching on his skin, the taste of salt from the southern sea still on his lips. He'd driven all day and night to return to the guild, and the horses blew and foamed where they stood exhausted in their harnesses while the guild lads hurriedly attempted to unbuckle and lead them off.

"In his offices, Master Oxfort."

"Turn them out. They won't be good for much, I think I lamed the right wheel horse." Bregan leaned back into the carriage and grasped a small bundle he'd wrapped in his coat. "I want the boxes returned to the guild vaults. I have an inventory on them and if anything, *anything*, goes missing, it'll be your head or your hands. Understood?"

The head lad bowed stiffly.

Bregan turned abruptly and made his way through the guild to the elaborate rooms that comprised his father's offices, not caring who had to scramble out of his way. The Oxforts had built this branch of the guild and although he was only the son, this was his kingdom as much as it was his father's. Or so he had thought until Daravan had tossed a gory souvenir into his lap and told him of an ambush.

He did not knock. He burst through the great double doors, striding past the sputtering secretary who manned the outer lobby and into the vast room which housed Willard Oxfort.

His father looked up from a stack of papers and his face immediately creased into a heavy frown. "I may be old, and I may be contemplating retiring, and you may be my heir, but I do demand respect."

Bregan ignored him. He tossed his pungent bundle onto the desk, scattering papers and scrolls in every direction. His coat lay damp and sticky with ichor from the thing it encased. "As do I. Smugglers, you said. Opportunists who think they might have found a mote in the eye of the Jewel of Tomarq and who might sail our coasts with profitability to both of us. So you sent me to strike a few deals. Inconsequential but intriguing, you said." He fisted his hands and leaned them on the desktop. "You sent me into an ambush, dear father, and if the Gray Man had not been there, you would have lost your goods and me into the bargain. *Or perhaps that was the bargain.*"

Willard Oxfort lifted his hand, pen still gripped in his fingers, his cuff ink-stained, and stopped just short of using the stylus to open the crude bundle in front of him. His dark gaze flicked to Bregan's face. "The Vaelinar knew of the meet?"

"He was there before me."

The frown creased even deeper. "We have a leak from within our walls, then. It is well for you, this time, but it must be stopped. Our business," and the senior Oxfort tightened his jaw on that, emphasizing his last words, "must remain within our boundaries. As for the other, it was to be a discreet meeting with no more than privateers. What is this, then?" He poked at the bundle with his pen.

"Daravan asked that you see if you can identify it."

"I should know the remains of a petty seaman?"

Bregan unfisted a hand, lifted it, and shrugged aside his stained coat to reveal the remains within. Truncated arms lay curled on the leather, paws bloody and clawed. Willard choked a breath inward. All color fled his face.

"What is this?"

"He asks that of you."

Willard dropped his pen and held his now empty palm over the things. His hand shook slightly. He let out a shallow breath before answering, "Raymy."

"You're certain?"

"Aye. A scout hits our coast every now and then, as if testing our resolve and our Shield. I've seen this perhaps twice in my lifetime, once trailing at your grandfather's heels and again just after I had married your mother. You can't mistake it once you've seen one." He flipped the stiffening coat back over the arms. "We can't know that it was an ambush. The Gray Man was there, interrupting whatever might have occurred." He scrubbed his hand over his sweating face. "Quendius meddles and has dragged us into it." He shoved himself away from his desk. "I shall be retiring to my estates for a bit while I handle this matter."

"And I?"

"You shall send word to Daravan that it is Raymy. Use one of the Vaelinar birds. It will find him, no doubt." Willard gave a disapproving grunt of the magics involved. "Tell no one else. We have strategies to consider."

Bregan straightened. His father's words had not mollified him. He would have his own options to put into place. He left for the guild nests, uncaring of what his father might do with the gory bundle he'd dropped in the middle of guild business.

"Get on with you, now. Ye'd think touching the water would kill you. Slide in, or it'll be me you have to fear." Nutmeg tossed her head, thick wavy amber hair falling over her shoulders and down her back, her hands on her hips, her mouth in a twist of disdain. The object of her scorn sat in his carriage chair, one brow quirked, knowing that if he got to his feet, her nose would be about navel level on him, but that did not diminish her scolding one bit. With her standing and him seated, they were nearly of a height. She buried the end of the torch she carried into the rocky bank of the underground cavern as if to emphasize her determined words. Her voice filled the hollow with its rich, Dweller accent and no-nonsense tone. Yellow light flickered from the torch, which flared wildly before settling down to cast a golden glow over the pool's black waters. Sunlight rarely found its way here under the rocky roof and it could have been midday or midnight for all they could tell. A faint aroma lay over the cavern and its pool. It smelled of herbs and a touch of sulfur, neither pleasant nor unpleasant. He wouldn't want to drink it, he thought, as he stared into its inkiness.

"It's late," Jeredon answered apologetically. "Tomorrow would be a better time for this."

"There's never a time for this. Right hand for the queen, all matter of problems, all the councils you hold. It wouldn't be late *this* eve, but you dallied all the day long." She crossed her arms across her white peasant blouse and laced vest, her full bosom bouncing just a touch. "Th' water's hot, they tell me, day or night, so there's no reason for you to be malingering."

"It's always better when you're in here with me."

Nutmeg's cheeks flushed. "As sweet as that exercise is, it's not putting you back on your feet."

"I wouldn't be so sure of that." Jeredon leaned out of his chair and dipped a hand into the water lapping the stony bank at his feet. The water indeed held a heat from the heart of the earth which had birthed it. The pool circled his hand with invitation. "Being her brother means obligations, Nutmeg."

"A-course it does. And you being on your feet, hale and hearty, would make it all that much easier on everyone, wouldn't it? Don't think I haven't seen the scuff marks from dragging your boots across the council floors, walking on the crutches when you shouldn't be. I know you've been up when the doctors told you no and what would be best for you. This—" And she jabbed her pragmatic Dweller hand at the grotto. "This is what the healers ordered. Now strip down, or I'll do it for you." A glint in her eyes and the dimple in her chin told him she would do exactly as threatened, and enjoy it.

Truth to tell, if she'd been a Vaelinar woman, he'd enjoy it, too. But she was scarcely more than a girl even amoung her own people, Rivergrace's adopted sister, and had lived a mere fraction of his years. She had none of the willowy sharpness of the Vaelinar about her, and her thick hair waved down over rounded ears, and as she gave an impatient huff at his silence, her curvaceous bounty seemed to breathe an invitation to him that he had no intention of answering. Yet she filled his arms as no other, and shared her sweetness with him as if he'd been her only lover, and he supposed that he had. He cared too much for his time with her. He was a prince, and his life was as much for Lara to barter as her own.

Jeredon stripped off his tunic and shirt, slinging his weapons harness over the arm of the wheeled carriage chair that had become his second home. As good as a hot soak sounded, the stubborn streak in him reared its ugly head. What was it some men found irresistible in bossy women? Give him a quietly determined lass like Sevryn's Rivergrace in place of his sister Lariel or this Dweller force of nature who glared him down now. Although, Jeredon reflected, Rivergrace might well just crook a finger at Sevryn who would then use his Voice, sweeping him into the watery basin whether he willed it nor not.

He'd evidently been moving too slowly because the moment he slipped his boots off, Nutmeg dropped her shoulder to the chair and gave a shove, tipping it over and dumping him into the pool with a sputter and surprised wave of his arms. The hot water claimed him. His near-numb lower body failed him as he knew it would, but he stayed upright as he flailed his arms about, churning up the pool. The sight of Nutmeg shedding her own clothes down to her simple white chemise stopped him, and when he stopped struggling, the water bore him and he could sense a rocky ledge under his feet which deigned to feel as little as possible.

Nutmeg hopped in. "Don't be looking at me like that. I've been swimming with my brothers since I was knee-high to a shadow."

"I'm not looking at you in any way at all, but if I was, it was only to see if I were bobbing right side up or upside down." He managed to sound rather contrite, he thought.

"Don't be pouting, it isn't fit for a Warrior Prince." She reached over and took his hands.

He managed a snort.

"Now," she told him. "Practice your striding, with the water holding your weight." Her small firm hands bore calluses as did his, something he scarcely found on the hands of a Kernan woman although the Vaelinar women fought and trained at trades and crafts just as any man might. Only the lower classes of the women of Kerith worked as hard as Nutmeg had in her young life. Dwellers were the salt of the land, and they all worked, a sturdy practical people with a riotous sense of fun. She gave him no respect as the Warrior Queen's heir and second-in-command; whatever he got from her, he'd earned as himself. She drew Jeredon toward her as he tried to take halting steps and strained to command legs, feet, and buttocks that no longer seemed to belong to him.

He had feeling. Not much, but some. And there were days when he experienced a violent stinging up and down his afflicted limbs, so sharp and angry that he thought he'd fallen into a hornet's nest, and it almost drove him crazy because there was nothing he could do about it. Better that than no feeling, no hope at all, the healers told him. The roadways from his legs to his mind had not been severed but harshly bruised and battered. They healed excruciatingly slowly, and no one could tell him if he would heal completely. He mourned the loss of himself. Nutmeg hounded him about it. Better to feel something than be dead flesh. He knew that. He *knew* it, but liked it not. He could barely remember the days when he'd first begun walking, a hundred years and more ago by Kerith reckoning, and he hadn't had as much trouble then. Was he relearning now or just reminding his body that it knew what to do when it healed, that it knew how to heal?

Nutmeg towed him after her. "Now, just drift. Let me do the swimming. You be a lazy log in the water." She swam on her back, the chemise slicked to her lush body, as unconscious of herself as his legs seemed to be of their mortal state.

Jeredon closed his eyes, letting the hot waters soothe him. He had to admit it felt good. It felt bracing. He could nearly stand on his own without braces or crutches and his backbone did not scream in pain where he could feel it, or ache dully where he nearly could. No. In these waters, he could just float and *be*. They swam in circles for a long while.

The warmth of her hands around his left him. He opened his eyes to find himself a good ways away from the rim of the pool. The torch had burned halfway down. Nutmeg clambered out and perched on a flat rock.

"You can't leave me out here."

"I'm not leaving you anywhere. If you get left, it's 'cause you gave up." She cupped her hand to rest her chin in it, gaze considering him.

"I couldn't walk in if I wanted to. There's no bottom here."

"You're certain of that?"

"I can feel enough to know when something is solid under these dead feet and when something isn't."

"Swim in, then."

"Swim? I can't kick."

"Neither can a four-legged animal, in the way you mean, and I've seen quite a few lakes swum by them."

Jeredon grunted. She wanted him to paddle in, half crippled, dragging his dead weight after him. Well, why not? He'd drown out here eventually if he didn't. With powerful thrusts of his arms and shoulders, he brought himself closer to the rim where she observed. He scraped his shin on an underwater rocky ledge then, a burning pain that flared and numbed almost as quickly, and tried to get his feet under him.

His body wouldn't, couldn't respond. He let out a sharp yell of frustration and then clamped his jaw tight on his anger. He raised his eyes to Nutmeg's. Her mouth opened, but he beat her to it. "I know. Let the water hold me."

She nodded.

With a deep breath, he forced the tension out of himself. The pool gathered around him as if it were a being, holding him, cradling him, and when he sculled again, he propelled himself to the water's edge, and heaved himself out with the last flagging energy of his arms. He sat panting for a moment.

A feeling shot down his left leg. Not a pain, but a feeling. He rubbed his thigh. The touch of his hand made an impression, though faint. A tear in his breeches showed him where he'd barked his shin underwater. It would bruise but whatever bleeding it had done, it had finished, and the minerals of the pool had washed it clean.

"Finished?"

"More like done in, but, aye, I'm finished." Jeredon took a deep breath. He reached for his crutch and the carriage chair, and Nutmeg came to help him as well, and between them, they got him seated. He felt tired but good. The twisted throbbing in his back had gone, without his even realizing it had been there all day, for days, bothering him.

"We'll come back tomorrow."

He inhaled. "Might be a bit soon for that, but the day after, I'll make time."

"Your promise on that, then. I won't spit as we're all clean." She held her hand out for a shake, an impish gleam in her eyes.

He shook it solemnly.

He could have done worse for a nursemaid, he thought, as she dressed him, then herself, and got behind the chair, helping to push it with a determined grunt even as he propelled it with the force of his arms upon the wheels.

Something dribbled upon his face, two or three drops, and he put his head back to see if the cavern roof overhead seeped with moisture, as grottoes often did, but it seemed dry. He put his finger to his cheek and tasted the drops.

Salty, as if someone crying had splashed upon him.

He said nothing but bent his will upon the carriage chair to get it moving quickly.

Chapter
Six

THE MOON CUT a thin line through overhanging clouds, the edge of its image limned in faint pink and gold. Quendius tilted his head back to observe it. The sky held winter in its grasp but had not yet chosen to release it. The weather and the illumination served his purposes. He saw well in the dark, perhaps from the years he'd spent mining in tunnels and caves, perhaps because of his otherwise useless Vaelinar eyes. It was not a Talent, no, but it was a thing he could depend upon and use to his advantage.

He reined his horse to a halt and tied it to a shrub, fragrant leaves crackling and filling the air with their aroma as he twisted the leathers into a knot. His horse immediately dropped his head to crop wearily at a few browning spears of grass as Quendius pulled his sword and moved into the stand of fine, vibrant aryns lining the valley. The blade, a precursor to and much less than Cerat, sent a weak hum along his fingers and into his wrist, the vibration wrought by the lesser Demon which inhabited it. A violent being, as all Demons were wont to be, it made sure the sword would strike with uncanny accuracy into the flesh, and strike deeply, but it was no Souldrinker. That one you dared not draw without blooding and blooding well. That one Quendius had only wielded once, and it had nearly torn the soul out of him before Narskap had picked it up and managed it, at a terrible cost to himself. Narskap, being what he was, referred to himself only as the arm of Quendius, for he had no will but that which Quendius gave him. The howling fits which came upon Narskap could last days or weeks, and Quendius had no doubt it was part of the price he paid for having conquered the Souldrinker.

A bit of errant moonlight struck his blade, and it flashed a cold blue. Quendius moved downslope to the massive aryn trees, small saplings pushing up from between the great, gripping roots of the mature trees, saplings which would be dug up and replanted elsewhere, or the canopy of the parent trees would suffocate and choke all sunlight and rain from them. He chose the branches he wanted with care, for he wanted both strong and pliable wood, well-grained, and the aryn had the trait of drying well and quickly, so he hewed off green branches, ignoring the deadwood which had fallen sporadically about the grove.

Bistel Vantane would try to kill him if he were caught. The aryns lived unhurt and well-nurtured, for it was they who held back the edges of burned-out, chaotic Mageborn magics that ravaged the countryside. How they took it in and cleansed it or absorbed it, no one could quite be sure, only that it was done and had been so for centuries. Quendius had no qualms about taking down the sacred wood. If Bistel wanted so badly to salvage Kerith, why did he not extend the groves deep into the Scars, the blasted lands, to see if they would continue to thrive and cleanse? Or did Bistel have a keen sense of the limitations of his power through the aryns and their Way that had flourished upon his borders? Either way held little concern for Quendius. He would rather see all in ruins if he could not someday hold it under the heel of his boot.

When he held a sizable bundle under his arm, of lengths nearly as tall as he was and as big around as his wrist, he decided he'd hewed enough. He moved back through the trees as the wind of the night murmured through them, and they protested his butchery of them. Twigs snatched and pulled at his hair and vest, tangling as he brushed through them. Roots seemed to buckle upward from the ground to trip him up or rap sharply against his shin when he stepped around them. He knew that none of it was true, only fanciful tales such as the Dwellers might pass among themselves, and the depth of the night only served to give the fancy credence. He did not believe that the woods lived as a man, as a Vaelinar lived. He did not believe that it was a miracle which had caused the trees to spring to life on Kerith, far from the lands in which the aryn had originally been grown and harvested. He believed only that it was an uncommonly fine hardwood, good for working, excellent for crafting. The deadwood was used for jewelry and mosaic tiles, to be inlaid into other woods, but never for weapons, bows, arrows, hafts, or staves, an unwritten decree of the Van-tane family. Much of the deadwood was burned on the turning day, when winter melted into summer. Quendius doubted the bonfires made a difference one way or the other. The seasons would come and go as they always had, before the arrival of the Vaelinars and after their final leave-taking.

He slowed as he wandered the groves, enjoying his trespass of Bistel's grounds without chance of discovery, for Quendius knew Bistel was not at his stronghold though he did not know why. He might be out tracking his eastern borders, looking for sign of the Galdarkan warlord Abayan Diort, once under Quendius' thumb and now little more than an uneasy ally, but Quendius did not bother about that. He would use Diort, willingly or not, when the time came. And, if now, Bistel tracked him instead of watching his own backyard, so much the better.

A bit of dried wood cracked under his step. The sound popped loudly in the nighttime, and Quendius paused. He heard a rasping shout in response.

"Who goes there? Step out and name y'rself, laddie."

Quendius stayed a moment longer, weighing his options. Then he decided it might be fun to answer the summons, and so he did, moving in the direction of the breathy voice. A beam of moonlight illuminated the spot where the old gardener stood, leaning on a scythe that was more of a staff or cane than a sharp-honed tool for reaping. He was Vaelinar, his hawklike features sharp and lined, his mahogany skin tanned to a deep, rich cherrywood color like well polished wood, his silvery hair with a pinkish hue that reflected the deepness of his coloring. Quendius knew him to be Bistel's man, bent and gnarled in his service and that of the aryn groves since he was knee-high and although Bistel was a few centuries older, Magdan looked ancient while the warlord appeared still in his prime. Gardening must take a worse toll than making war, Quendius thought as he moved into the patch of moonlight, forbidden aryn cuttings under one arm and ill-used sword in the other. He dropped the bundle to free himself.

"What have you done?" the old gardener cried hoarsely. He put the end of his scythe out and jabbed the pile of cuttings. "Bistel will have your hide."

The shadows and the twilight must have hidden him still. Quendius stepped forward closer, making certain that the shaft of light shining down on the small clearing revealed him fully, and Magdan stepped back in answer, with a rough hiss.

"Your lord is not about to flay anyone."

"He'll come at my whistle."

"Even if he does, it'll not be soon enough to save you."

Magdan's jaw flapped a moment as he seemed to draw into himself. Then he put his shoulders back. "The aryns are not to be touched."

"They've not only been touched, I've chopped off what I will." Quendius scanned the trees about them. "It's been a dry fall so far. I might even torch them before I leave."

Magdan hissed again. His tough and gnarled hands gripped the haft of his tool tightly. "What do you want from me?"

"Nothing that I can't have whether you give it to me or not." With a dry laugh, Quendius lashed out, his sword cutting through the old man's tunic. Fabric caught and fell in limp shreds. Magdan shook, not with fear but with anger, and his eyes shone fiercely in the dim light, which was anything but dim to Quendius. He pulled his scythe into a defensive position across his body, set his bowed legs, and gritted his teeth.

"I've stopped brighter lads than you," the old gardener forced out.

"Perhaps." Quendius cut through the air again, this time across the elder's breeches, leaving his legs bare against the evening air. His legs, like his hands and face, were weathered and etched with the working of the soil and recalcitrant thorns and branches, weeds and rocks, tendrils and lashings. Hard work, gardening and farming. "I'll give you this, old goat of a man, you've backbone. For that, I'll let you return to your lord. I don't care if you carry word of me or not. Better perhaps, if you do." He withdrew his blade slightly. "I am Quendius."

Whether the old man considered his name to remember it or not, he could not tell, for Magdan's answer was to lunge at him, business end of the scythe sweeping across the air, catching on his vest of curried wool, brushing across his bare skin with a burning slice, but not deep enough to slow his reaction. He jabbed, and jabbed deeply, the other crumpling in front of him with a bubbling gulp and hiss.

Magdan did not die. Nor would he for a bit. Quendius pulled back. He cleaned his sword in the dry dirt about them before sheathing it. His sharp eyes caught sight of the winter-woolly mountain pony the gardener had staked not too far away, as well as three young saplings dug up and bagged, resting next to a small cart to carry them, gardening by light of the moon like a superstitious old Dweller. Luck for this harvesting, it seemed, had escaped Magdan this time.

Quendius heaved him up, over his shoulder, like a sack of meal and dumped him onto the cart bed. He threw the saplings in as well, and untied the mountain pony from its staking. "You'll be home by morning," Quendius told the ashen-faced gardener. "You should live that long." He tugged the ragged wrappings of the shirt tightly about Magdan's chest. Then he slapped the cart pony on its rump, hard, and the startled animal jumped in its harness, bolting away and dragging the cart thumping behind it. It would, once the scare left it, find its way back to the stables.

Quendius took up the heavy bundle of cuttings and returned to his own mount. The beast's nostrils flared at the smell of fresh blood on him, but did nothing more than that, used to the smell although not liking it.

Quendius rubbed his knuckles under the creature's chin. "You know who the master is," he told it, before lashing the aryn wood behind the saddle pad. The horse grunted and shifted its weight unhappily at the burden, but it would bear that, and him, and more if he asked that of it. It had been trained to do so. He turned its head toward his fortress. He wondered if the gardener would live to repeat his name.

Bistel rode in, midmorning winter sun on his shoulders, to find his courtyard in commotion. The gardener's cart stood in the center of it, ringed by stable and farm lads, and a healer, bloodied rags tossed to the ground, and aryn saplings half falling from the cart. He dismounted. "What is going on?"

"It's Magdan, m'lord," the head lad said, swinging about, face pale. "He's been done for, m'lord, and he won't tell anyone what happened or let us move him. He says he's dying, and we're to clear the courtyard because he's Returning."

Bistel felt a coldness in his core that the winter sun would not be able to warm. "Do he says, boys. Take your leavings of him while you can, and keep the yard clear. I'm the only one who stays." He thrust the reins of his horse into the hands of Verdayne, a tall lad of Dweller blood mixed with something more, who stood quietly at the tailgate of the cart. Verdayne looked up at him, worried lines knotting his brow and the corners of his eyes, but said nothing except to wrap his fist tightly upon the leathers.

"We don't want to go." The boys jumbled around, giving him room to approach the cart but hanging about with stubborn looks on their faces.

"This goes beyond death. You don't know what you ask to witness."

Their mouths all tightened. The healer, Ninuon, stepped back. Bruises of effort and fatigue cast shadows under her eyes. "I'm sorry, Lord Bistel. I've done all I could, but I cannot heal that wound, and I cannot . . . I cannot give him the peace he deserves."

Bistel looked over the rough-sided cart. Blood seeped into the old wood where Magdan looked as if he'd been thrown in carelessly, and Ninuon had straightened him out as best she could without harming him further. His clothing lay in shreds about him and great pain etched the grooves of his weathered face. Bistel's hands tightened on the cart.

"Magdan."

"Lord," the gardener rasped. "I made it back to you."

He did not know if waiting for him had begun the change in Magdan's dying. He hoped not, for what had begun would be excruciating, and he could not change or alter it. None of the powers he had in this world would save Magdan from the Return of his soul before his life had gone. A rare occurrence, a frightening one, and one he would give anything to keep another from experiencing. He could not explain why it happened so, but it would be as if the Gods of their home world and the Gods of Kerith fought for the soul, a physical tug-of-war for something so ephemeral, so precious, so elemental. And it sometimes happened before the flesh died and had become insensitive. Bistel fought on battlefields and he knew a war when he saw one, and he could see one beginning now. One of Gods and spiritual planes and possession.

He could see the edges of the gardener's dying body blurring, the flesh growing translucent. He put a hand on the back of Verdayne's neck, the gardener's apprentice, and the young man looked up at him, eyes brimming with unshed tears. "Look away," he said.

"I can't." Verdayne swallowed tightly. Despite his Dweller heritage, he came nearly to Bistel's shoulder, his thick, curling black hair hiding ears that, just barely, tipped slightly. His eyes of dark, nearly purple blue sparkled with his grief. Vaelinar blood ran in him. Bistel did not guess that. He knew it well. He nodded to Verdayne before reaching down to grasp Magdan's rough hand tightly. "I cannot save you."

"I know." Magdan coughed. Blood bubbled from his cracked lips. "Home calls for me."

Bistel tightened his grip. "It should be a blessing."

"Perhaps it is, on the other side." Magdan ceased to speak, fighting for a moment. His flesh grew more transparent, the blood running through his veins showing visibly.

"You go where we all yearn to go. You will chase the memories taken from us, greet the loved ones left behind by us, know the mystery of our lives." Bistel leaned into the cart. He kissed the rough forehead of his old friend.

"I must tell you." Magdan shuddered heavily. "I was digging up saplings."

"By the fullness of the moon, no doubt."

"Aye, Lord. I caught an intruder."

Or, rather, the intruder caught him, Bistel thought. And did his best to murder him. "Do you know him?"

"No, Lord, but he gave me his name." His voice was as wispy thin as the snow white hair tousled about his head, barely audible to Bistel's hearing. "Quendius," he said.

Bistel's hands clenched about Magdan's, causing pain where he did not intend. "Are you sure?"

"He could have lied. But I know a smithy's hands when I see them, and he held a forge-hot hatred." The gardener fought for a deep breath, and Bistel could feel the sudden tension in the hand he cradled. Magdan hissed sharply, his back arching, his whole body going stiff.

"Don't talk."

"One last." Magdan's mouth gaped like a fish brought out of the water. "Take care of Verdayne."

"You know I will." He rubbed his hands over Magdan's rough ones. War had toughened his hands, but centuries of farming and gardening had knobbed this old man's hands like a cobbled pathway. Magdan clung to Bistel.

He drummed one heel in protest as his form began to disintegrate, skin from flesh, flesh from bone, his soul burning like a fire from the inside out, escaping.

Returning.

The stable and farm boys around him cried out, and Ninuon fell limply to the ground, caught by the wash of agony emanating from Magdan. The healer curled in empathic agony. Bistel braced himself. Magdan's face contorted. His skull yawned in horror and his throat uttered one last word. "M'lord," he gasped.

Then his form shredded to nothingness as his soul flared through it, a starburst of colors Bistel would never be able to describe or forget. The gardener's substance in his hand flared, and then, with a sudden whoosh, the apparition disappeared, leaving him holding nothing. Bistel staggered against the side of the cart. The bloodstains splashed about the boards began to smoke and then burn, and Verdayne dragged him away just before the entire cart exploded into flames taller than all of them, bright red orange against the day, and burned until nothing was left but ash.

Bistel coughed and rubbed his eyes against the smarting of the smoke. He had never before seen a pyre like this although it seemed a blessing. Usually the flesh remained, rended savagely by the struggle. He placed a hand on Verdayne's shoulder and gripped him tightly. Magdan had fostered Verdayne for decades and the lad would miss him almost as sorely as Bistel and Bistane would. "An uncommon death," Bistel said quietly. "Magdan did not wish to be uprooted and fought it, just like one of the grand old aryn."

Verdayne breathed then. "Aye," he answered as though he understood, a little. He brushed his face with the back of his hand.

Some Vaelinar did not just die. Some Returned, their souls grabbed back by the place where all Vaelinar had once originated, and the phenomenon was not kind or beautiful to watch. Bistel had seen it before, rarely, and he hoped to never see it again. He rubbed his hands against his riding leathers, an uneasiness settling deep within him that his own death would be just as difficult.

He turned his head as two of the lads helped reed-thin Ninuon to her feet.

"Quendius," he said flatly. "No one here forget that Magdan named his murderer. If I should die before he does, tell it to Bistane."

Chapter
Seven

SUNLIGHT DAPPLED THE treetops fitfully and the morning breeze had stilled when Sevryn caught sight of a landmark which he knew, a broken spike of a granite peak behind the trees. The structure of black and gravelly gray poked out of tree branches as though someone thrust out a hand. Raptors liked to sit upon it, and so it had garnered the simple name of The Perch. There was no mistaking it. He turned his horse's head toward it, for it stood sentinel at the edge of a small Way known as Hunter's Cut, a pass through an otherwise impassable and implacable ridge of stone. Hunter's Cut stayed open through wind, rain, sleet, snow, and ice, although it was only the width of a horse and man walking abreast. Traders couldn't use it unless they led beasts of burden on foot through it, and some traders were canny enough to make that sacrifice. Mostly, it guided hunters and trappers home through the harshest of winters, and that alone was enough to ask of it. It would provide a Way home that cut days off the journey through the worst of weather. It would get him where he needed to be.

A hawk sat on the farthest tip of the Perch as they approached, head cocked to take note of his passage through the forest. Keen eyes fixed on Sevryn as they traded looks, then the hawk ruffled his wings slightly to turn his attention elsewhere. Sevryn closed his knees tight, hurrying his mount to the edge of Hunter's Cut. The forest parted reluctantly as the rocky spire pushed out of the soft dirt of the forest floor, the foot of the mountains which backed it, all sharp, sheer flints of stones that even the surefooted would hesitate to cross. Now and then an evergreen sapling determinedly broke through crevices, growing wherever sun and rain and stone would give enough for one to root. The sheer determination of growth had always been something Sevryn admired. He'd seen it in the cities where he'd run in the shadows. Give the land a week or a season without human hand on it, and growth would spurt. It might be weedy and useless to the eye, but it would then give shelter to other creatures, all banned and unwanted by humans but still a part of their world. There was life that refused to be denied.

The Perch itself only pointed the way to the cut. He rode back and forth a bit before finding it, the overlapping rock front fiendishly hard to spot. He'd been through it once or twice in the dead of winter riding at Gilgarran's back. He could not describe the eerie feeling of riding on the Way with impassable snow and icy peaks surrounding them, yet the floor of the cut itself had held green shoots of tender spring grass and soft shrub branches catching at the horses' hooves. No wind had piped through the rocks, but snow droplets would melt and cascade wetly down the stone walls, leaving ice-cold puddles for the horses to splash through. Winter might be held at bay in Hunter's Cut, but nothing could keep it from sending small reminders that it existed and held sway over the outside world. Gilgarran had once warned him of that, saying nature could only be held at arm's length at great cost.

He found the crevasse and urged his mount forward. The beast trotted a few steps into the cut and then came to a stiff-legged halt, head down, and snorted. He shook his head, reins rattling when Sevryn urged him onward. Sevryn stretched in the stirrups, casting a look along the stony ground to see if prints or broken greenery might tell the tale of another taking the Way and saw little fresh sign of any consequence. Clouds in the skies above drew closer and grayer, the weather growing heavy with threatening rain. He put a heel to the recalcitrant beast's flank. The horse flicked his ears back and stayed his ground.

"Now then," Sevryn told him. "We're on the queen's business. You were bred for that. Serve her well and you'll have green pastures to retire to, with sun on your body and warm oat mash in the dead of winter. Do any less than the best you were bred for, my tashya, and you'll be working the land for a Dweller or Kernan family, putting your shoulder to the harness and knowing the lash even when you're tired. Not that it isn't a noble occupation for a horse to work the land, but not for one of your hot blood, eh?" He pulled his water skin up and took a short swig, giving the horse a breather and a chance to relax against the bit. When he'd done so, Sevryn nudged the horse forward again.

The horse took a few steps with an uneasy swing of his head. The snap of the rein ends against his neck did nothing but make him halt in his tracks again, four legs braced, and his ears down.

With a sigh, Sevryn swung off and pulled the reins forward to lead his mount after him. It would do him good to stretch his legs a bit and perhaps his horse was more leg-weary than he'd gauged. Riding in Daravan's wake had perhaps taken more of a toll on the horses than on the riders. He could feel the dampness in the sky. Did Hunter's Cut hold off rain as well as snow and ice? He rather doubted it, and hunched his shoulders against the inevitable. The horse let the reins grow taut before giving a chuff and reluctantly trailing after. Sevryn broke into a slow jog.

The horse threw his head back in a violent start, whipping the leather reins through his hand in a red-hot motion that left his palm and fingers stinging. His mount reared up, twisting his body about, and bolted back the way he had come.

"Halt!" Sevryn's Voice lashed the air.

He could hear the grunt as his horse plowed to a stop, somewhere beyond the Way's opening. He slogged after it, his hand afire, and found the mount, head down, shuddering, panting, lather foaming his neck.

The horse rolled a white-ringed eye at him. Sevryn grunted back at the beast. He knelt by the side of a small stream running along the gravelly crevice and dipped his hand into the water to cool the fiery welt.

His thoughts whirled into an icy river washing up to his knees. He could see Rivergrace afoot coaxing her mare across, one hand wrapped in the coarse black mane and the other in bridle reins. It was not the scene the Ferryman had showed him, but it sent a tremor of need through him. Shouts rang through the forest and across the river, and from upstream, riders bore down on her, her and the queen's troops with her. Bolgers leaned over their small, scruffy mountain ponies, their faces stretched in war yelps, bows and swords in their hands. He could feel the fear lance through her body as she urged her mare across the river, the water dragging at them both as the raiders bore down on them. He could hear orders shouted from Lariel and Osten and see arrows slicing the air. This was far, far worse than anything the Dark Ferryman had given him in vision. This was what Quendius had goaded him about.

He tore his hand from the freshet. With a muffled curse, he grabbed up his mount's reins. No time to waste, no time to coax a stubborn beast. Rage surged

through him, rage and the need to be in the battle. He
put a hand to the creature's ear, twisting it as he mounted
and righted before letting go. Then he slammed his heels
into the horse's sides. "Now *move*," he Voiced, and sent
them plunging headlong into the Hunter's Cut.

Her skirts dragging wetly at the hems, Rivergrace paused
in the riverbed, her hands full of horse and leather, but
her senses filled with Sevryn. She could smell his odor,
tinged with seawater and salt and horse and woodsmoke.
She could feel his heat and hear his frustration in his
breathing, so close to her, so close that she turned in
the water, but no one stood behind her. She had just
turned back to her mare, pushing against her, hurrying her against the current when a horse screamed. It
thrashed and died, an arrow piercing its neck as it fell
into the river, throwing its rider free. Whoops split the
air as Bolgers yelped and growled, raiders riding down
on Rivergrace and her companions through the river,
spray flying from the pounding hooves of their rugged
little ponies.

"Stand back and hold!" Lara yelled as did Osten, and
the trooper whose horse had gone down managed to
drag himself aside, choking and sputtering as he did so.
The archers spurred their mounts onto the far bank and
unslung their bows, nocking arrows as fast as they could
pull them from their quivers.

Rivergrace froze for a thumping heartbeat or two.
Then she slapped her mare on the rump, sending her
bolting out of the river and splashing after the horse.
An arrow hissed past her, slapping into the river ineffec-
tively. The Bolgers pulled up, circling their tough little
ponies in the churning waters. She looked for the age-
toughened face of her old friend Rufus but did not see it
among the others. She hoped for a moment they might
be clan Bolgers of the area, just defending their lands,

but they looked nothing like farmers and hunters and craftsmen. They wore boiled leather, with the insignia of a red hand on it, nothing she'd ever seen before. And they screamed for Vaelinar blood.

Lara wheeled her horse about as an arrow whistled past her and thunked into Osten who bellowed in pain and anger. His horse reared up and crumpled on his hindquarters, legs giving way in the deep and fast-moving stream. The mount rolled and came up with Osten unhorsed and still cursing, holding onto the stirrup as he pulled the arrow from his breastplate. He tossed it away in disdain, pulling his one-handed sword and slapping the flat of it across his horse's rump. The animal threw its head up with a squeal, bucking out of the river, dragging Osten's bulk alongside. He heaved into position on the muddied bank as two of the Bolgers lunged at him in a spray of water. He braced his hefty legs and swung backhanded across the assault.

One Bolger head went rolling in mid-yell, and the other rider caught the blade deep in his shoulder, unseating him and sending him into a sodden heap in the mud. Limp, he slid into and under the river's waters. The two shaggy ponies whinnied sharply and pounded into the forest, their slack reins flying about their necks. They disappeared into the crackling shrubbery. Osten kicked the first body aside and set his boots in the mud, yelling out orders, his deep voice underscoring Lara's higher authority.

Of little use as the troopers and the archers fell into lines, Rivergrace took up the reins of the loosened mounts wherever she could, dragging them off to the shrubs and tying them there, fighting with horses twice as big but not half as stubborn as the sturdy ponies she'd grown up with, Acorn and his tough little stallion son Bumblebee. She shouldered her way between the tashya horses the Vaelinars favored, those hot-blooded animals with sculpted faces and long flowing manes and the need to run in their veins. They stamped their hooves and shook themselves dry like puppies and chomped at their bits but did as she bid them.

She viewed a rout as she took up a position in the clearing, drawing her short sword. Jeredon would be gnashing his teeth at the line of the archers, broken apart and sent running by Bolgers who hung off the flanks of their ponies, using them as shields. She set herself as the attackers thrashed relentlessly downstream toward them. The initial group of raiders had been joined by two dozen or more. Whoops rang through the trees. Osten waded through bodies to join Lara shoulder to shoulder at the forefront. He bellowed his defiance. Grace slipped behind a bending sapling, and her movement caught an attacker's attention.

A raider followed her. Baring his curved tusks in a ferocious grin, he charged with the reins looped about one forearm and hoisted his sword in the other. She waited as the pony erupted from the river in a spray of mud and foam before taking a step outward. She swung, one hand over the other on the hilt, cutting into his thigh deeply as her movement made the pony swerve into her blow. He hauled on the reins in yelping pain, bringing his mount about sharply. It lost its balance on the slippery bank, going down on top of the rider. When it regained its feet, the rider stayed facedown in a spreading pool of crimson. Rivergrace took a shaky breath, stepping back into tender green branches of the sapling. Red droplets ran off the edge of the sword onto trampled mud and grass.

Lara and Osten shouted at each other over the cries of battle. She could barely hear them, words torn out of their mouths and swallowed by the riot of sound. A body surged past, borne by the river's current. Its Vaelinar silvery-and-black hair in a long twirl about a bloodless face, the form threatened to disappear forever in the waters. Rivergrace plunged after him and dragged the corpse back to shore, looking across at their men who'd taken to high ground at the far side. She left him with his arms folded across his body.

Upstream, a whistle split the air, sharp and keen as a sword blade. Grace's attention jerked to it.

A tall, proud Galdarkan sat atop a tall, proud horse. Both of them shone in tones of gold and bronze, but the man wore a diadem which caught the sun. He watched from a knoll at the river's bend, and at the whistle, the Bolgers wheeled. They reacted to the sight of him by regrouping into a ragged unit and charging down on Lara and her troops again while the Galdarkan watched. Had the whistle come from him? Had he given the order to punish them all for trespassing? Did he hope his raiders were up to taking down the Warrior Queen? He turned and rode into the forest upriver, melting from sight as if he had never been.

Rivergrace shouldered aside a riderless Bolger pony as it staggered into her through the scrub brush. The creature ambled off, covered with blood that might be its own or its missing rider's. The sword hilt turned in her slippery hands as the raiders crashed into the wall of defenders poised to protect Lara. Blood slicked the river. The hot, coppery smell of it sickened her. The low moaning and fresh screams filled her ears. None of them cared if those which came after to drink with the dusk or the following dawn would find the river fouled. None of the warriors noted, as she did, the sounds of scavengers already flying in. Carrion eaters would wing in flocks and scurry on paws to tear the flesh of the dead. Their only care was for the matters of men and rulers, not for waters which were meant to carry life and had filled with death.

A sour and bitter taste filled her throat. A hunkered raider lumbered at her, short ax in his hand and a feathered arrow in the back of his shoulder. Grace put her hand to her protective sapling and retreated a step as the Bolger squared away to face her. With a grunt, he moved closer and she released the sapling. It snapped into his face and she plunged her sword in after, shoving it deep into his flank and pulling it free. With a surprised look and a gnashing of his teeth the raider dropped to his knees and died.

Rivergrace took a deep breath. She dropped her sword as anger filled her. Sweet water cried out to her as gore filled it. A silver-blue mist rose across her vision, heated tears filling her eyes at the desecration. She flung her arm out, curving her hand and pointing her fingers to the river, a vision of a wall of Bolger raiders bearing inexorably down on them, riding through the water as if it were a road built for their carnage. Their battle poisoned the earth and water about her. The fury came to her, hot and heavy, burning away the bile in her throat, searing away the shock of the cold river and the fear.

She let out a cry. It came from her throat, melodic and high-pitched, winging across the air and through the noise of battle in a lance of sound, pure and beautiful in its anger. She ordered the river to do her bidding, and hers alone. She ordered it to forbid trespass.

The waters rose with a noise that filled her ears. With a sound like a wind in high tempest, an inferno answered her call, turning against all nature. The sun seemed to fall into the river, its brilliance setting the very waves alight. Fire danced across it in a torrent of flame. A tongue of flame crested in orange-red and blue magnificence, and licked down upon the riders.

Ponies screamed in terror, and voices shouted in disbelief. In moments, mere beats of her heart, the flames swept through the war party, sending the ponies bolting in fear. Their frenzied flight from the fire pounded the riders into the banks and trees, stunning all those within reach of the river of fire. Not a rider stayed on horseback. Not a weapon stayed in hand. Not a sheath or quiver could be recovered. The battle had been swept away from them on raging wildfire. The Bolgers fled.

Silence fell. The fire crackled and slowly dissolved into a smoky black residue along the waters, hissing into nothingness.

Her curved hand wavered as her arm dropped to her

side. Grace took a step back, and only the green sapling with its springy strength kept her from falling. Its branches embraced her.

Lara sheathed her sword and crossed the distance between them in four great, running strides, her lithe body coated with blood. She threw an arm around Grace's waist, holding her up. "What, in the name of all the Gods of the Vaelinar, was that?"

Grace looked at her, seeing her only dimly for a moment, then her vision sharpened, and she could hear her own heartbeat again instead of the thrumming, the roar, of the river. And she looked out as the sunlight abandoned the river, leaving the water to resume its swift flow downstream. The ragged troopers still standing did as instructed, pulling all of the dead onto dry land. She had no words for what might have happened, for what she might have felt tearing through her flesh and into the river. With each new heartbeat, she lost the sense of what she might have seen.

"The river burned."

"Sun, in our eyes . . . I don't know." Grace shook her head.

The Warrior Queen's gaze went very still before Lara put her gauntleted hand over Grace's bare one, and squeezed. "We'll come to an understanding of this." She released Rivergrace. "Osten! Get bonfires built for the dead and gather the troops together."

Rivergrace watched her leave. She put her hand to her throat, raw and chilled. She could still feel the authority of the unknown words which had been torn from her, the outrage and the power. She did not know where they had come from or where the sound fled, once uttered. The ache in her throat bore witness to an event her mind already shuttered away from her. She sank to her knees.

Rivergrace shivered, suddenly aware of the cold and the death around her.

Chapter Eight

SEVRYN SPURRED HIS MOUNT down the narrow rock passageway, stones clattering under his hooves as Rivergrace's need spurred his own. He would lame the horse and be on foot if he didn't slow, but he couldn't. He would force Hunter's Cut to bring him to her side if he could but held no hope of turning that Way into another road. He bent low over his horse's neck, urging caution out of him and speed into every stride. Shale brushed his elbow as they took the crooks and corners of the Cut at a breakneck pace. He slowed only when he had to, until the horse's breathing grew ragged. Then, with great reluctance, he slowed his mount and swung off, leading him through the narrow tunnel of stone and rock with only a clouded sky overhead telling him that they were not buried in granite.

He pulled his waterskin down and tipped it to the horse's muzzle, wetting his mouth and waiting till the breathing grew steady, then coaxed the rest of the liquid down his throat. It wouldn't be enough to satisfy the horse by any means, but they would have grass and water once out of Hunter's Cut, even if only for a few moments while he caught his bearings and headed for Grace again. The pause cleared his mind of the rage which had been pulsing through his veins. She would be no safer with him than she would be with Lariel and Osten. He knew that, in the marrow of his bones, a fact which had escaped him until now. Something desperate had ridden him, spurred him, even as he had done so to his horse.

He smoothed his horse's forelock and straightened the bridle before strapping the emptied waterskin back onto the pack. When he started off again, his horse followed him quietly, head hanging low and easy. Sevryn wondered at the creature's behavior before settling into a stride he'd learned from years of trekking behind Gilgarran with his love of the open road.

He'd jogged long and far enough that his shins ached and his heels felt the jar of every step when the sky overhead rumbled in more than a threatening manner. He might have seen the flash of lightning from the corner of his eye, but the thunder left no doubt. They were in for rain. His cloak in shreds, he had little left for shelter. No matter. Once through Hunter's Cut, he would have a clear path.

Thunder rumbled again. Sevryn ground to a halt, his horse's nose bumping onto his shoulder as he did, the beast giving a low, worried whicker. He glanced upward, at the slivers of sky seen through the rocky pass overhead. A brilliant blue shone back at him, streaked with streamers of blackening clouds. He had the eerie sense that he saw not the sky, but that the sky saw him . . . noticed him, as if for the first time, and was taking its measure of him as a being. An icy reaction shivered down the back of his neck as something or somethings sifted through him.

Time slowed. The wind halted in mid-gust. The boiling clouds froze in the sky and beyond it, a deeper blue opened, like the slit of an eye. He stood, head thrown back, while his very being peeled off him layer by layer. He'd been dissected before by foreign hands with far greater power than anything he could conceive. This time was no different except that, as each layer fell away from him, touched by a cold assessment, he felt a weight of judgment. Sevryn could explain it no other way. It felt as though the Gods of Kerith peered down at him, examined the threads of the Vaelinar-made Hunter's Cut, and plucked at the elemental strings braided by the Way, distorted from the nature of their world. It could not be what he imagined. It could not. But as he stared upward, he felt an icy anger as they sifted his very being and something within him answered. A white-hot defiance rose burning in his chest. He took a swelling breath to shout at the sky, and then choked it back as the earth moved below him while a muted thunder sounded again. He could feel the vibration under his boots. It gave way to a rolling motion, as though some great creature shivered and slithered its way under the ground. The reins grew taut as his horse threw his head back with a grunt. The ground swelled. He staggered and his elbow struck the side of the mountain sharply. He hadn't moved. It had.

He took another step. A shower of gravel rained down the side of the passage in front of them, a cloud of grit and dirt hanging in the air. They pushed through it, both of them coughing and blinking. He looked down the narrow passage of stone and saw a dark, spidery crack beginning to open up on the flooring. Not wide, but growing, heading toward them.

A pressure beat on his eardrums. His hearing grew muffled and faint. Sevryn moved forward hesitantly, and his horse hurried to stay with him now, as though afraid of being separated.

He'd been in places where the earth danced and the rocks heaved upward. Terrifying long moments when the world reshaped itself and even city walls could topple. This was not one of them. He realized that when the sky began to bleed colors and fell in on them.

His only clue of warning came with that ominous rumble of thunder that beat on his ears like a great, bass drum, and then colors swirled out of the leaden sky and melted into Hunter's Cut where they puddled onto the ground and the dirt and gravel greedily sucked them up. He'd never seen anything like it.

Sevryn turned on his heel to go back.

Behind him lay a great, dark, yawning void. It stretched wider and wider like the maw of a beast hoping to devour him.

He had two thoughts. The first was to run like hell and the second, to hope that his horse hadn't noticed it. He tugged on the reins and followed his first impulse. Auras hung before him, curtaining the passage.

He pushed himself through them as though he ran headlong into a silvered mirror. Colors shattered, wailing as they did so, like a fragile, dying animal. Shards fell about him and melted as they touched, snowflakes too wet to hold their shape or substance. Rainbows hung from him and then gave way, their prismatic colors dazzling his eyes before they winked from existence. Behind him, at their heels, the void made a noise like a low, rolling thunder, a basso profundo growl.

He held no concept of how far they'd come, or how far he'd yet to go. All he knew was that Hunter's Cut was coming to a violent, terrible end, and he would be trapped in it. Whatever forces had created the Way and held it together now seemed to be unraveling.

He stumbled, and his horse nearly plowed over him. He halted over Sevryn, trembling, nervous sweat dappling his neck, chest, and flanks. The beast rolled an eye at him. Sevryn put his hand up and cupped his muzzle to comfort him. He got back to his feet.

"Come on. I'll get you out of this."

His voice sounded dull and faint, barely audible to himself, but the horse flicked his ears and nudged him.

Sevryn let him lick the salt off his palms before urging him forward. The cut had widened. Or rather, it had fallen up, a cracked eggshell stone and gravel, sloughing away as they moved through it. The void which had swallowed their back trail now entrenched either side of the remaining trail, and each sheet of granite that sloughed away disappeared into its maw of nothingness.

He'd seen the chaos of the badlands. This was nothing like it. He'd looked into death itself, and not found it like this, although the River Goddess and the sword Cerat had held his soul then.

No, he'd never seen anything like *this*.

Beyond, a brilliant ray sliced across the melting colors of the sky. It looked as if the sun lanced through. He followed its point.

He and the horse burst free of Hunter's Cut as the ground beneath them gave way, and the abyss sucked them back in. Sevryn leaped from the saddle, grabbing for purchase. With screams of fear, his horse fought to scramble after him, his hindquarters sinking into nothingness. Sevryn set his heels and pulled on the bridle, grabbing a handful of mane and anchoring the beast. With a mighty heave, the horse found something to kick hind legs against and scrambled onto solid land, where he fell to his side, panting and trembling with fear. Sevryn looked back into the casade of black as it wavered across the firmament. In the river of nothingness, he saw Rivergrace. She stood in water to her knees, icy blue-and-gray water, one hand flung out in command. The river moved as she bade it, turning in its bed, against itself, rising in a curl of tide. Her face paled and her eyes of aquamarine, eyes of serene and gentle expression, went coldly silver as she faced raiders bearing down on her through the river. Sevryn would have gone back to her, through the Way, even as it twisted and died within itself, but Lariel rose between them. Sword in hand, her other hand knocking her helm from her head to free her sight, hair of platinum and gold cascading about her, the Warrior Queen swung, a great roundhouse of a slice. The blade whistled thinly through the air close enough to take his head, except that he ducked in sheer instinct and the blade continued in its orbit, straight at Rivergrace.

The Way collapsed, all darkness swallowing both women in a riot that spun about until he could see nothing of them but smears of riotous color, and then they were gone. The earth shook. With a great groan of stone on stone and wood creaking against wood, the mountain itself gave way in an avalanche of gravel and dust and dirt. On his knees, Sevryn watched the landslide.

If anyone were to ask him how the world could end, he could tell them. It would end with the slicing of his heart in two with fear for his love. And then the world would collapse.

In his wake, a crescent of darkness pulsed across the mountains, and Hunter's Cut existed no more, something dread and terrible in its stead. He did not think anyone could survive a passage through that.

A Way had ceased to exist. A twist in the laws of nature, had nature gone insane trying to unknot itself?

Or had something even worse come to bear?

What of Rivergrace? What had he seen? Omen or deed or his own deepest fear? He got to his feet and dusted himself off. He tugged on the bridle and his horse came to his hooves, shaking himself off with a tired whicker. Sevryn closed his eyes a moment, reaching within himself, taking himself back to the river where she dwelled, always drawn to water and where he'd felt her earlier. He had to know if she breathed. If she lived. If her soul still kindled a flame in this world. His body shook with effort as he reached for her. Search for the Way, Gilgarran had taught him, that is woven through all things existing. She was a Way unto herself, and he fought with every fiber of his being to find her. His own soul spun out, far and wide and away until he thought it would be the death of him, then he felt a flicker, a knowledge of Rivergrace. She lived, then. He knotted his fist and brought it to his chest as if he could hold her secure there, a whirl of water and fire, a sigil that represented her and no other. His soul came back wearily and he fell back, eyes snapping open.

A rest for the horse and himself, and then he'd find his trail. They would move south and west, so he would ride north and west. The Vaelinars would return to Larandaril. When he got to his feet, he'd ride there with the paw of an enemy which should no longer exist, and tell Lariel of the destruction of a Way without cause, and he would claim his lover and then, and only then, could he put his world to rights.

That battles had been engaged, he knew.

Who or what set the rules of those engagements, he could not determine. Yet. But they would not take from him the one he loved, the one he would die, again and again, to protect.

He would witness that to his final dying breath.

Sevryn got to his feet, weak in every limb, but alive. He took the reins of his mount, chucked him under the chin, and led the horse off to a patch of grass yet green, and then Sevryn gazed at the autumn sky to get his bearings.

Chapter Nine

SHE LIES IN AN EDDYING CURRENT under the
surface of the water, gazing up. Frosty edges melt
away at the banks framing her view, but the day is coming when the entire river will be iced over, even if only
at dawn. Her blood cools even as the water does or perhaps, since she is a Goddess, the river only reflects the
winter of her form. She ponders that for the most fleeting of moments. Once she would have known which it
was. Now, she no longer does. Does she exist because of
the river or does the river exist because of her?

The current sluices upon the bank as she frets in her
thoughts. The last vestiges of ice shred away freely, melting into oblivion as they go. She knows anger. It tastes
like coppery iron on her lips. It sings through her body
in miniature, fiery rivers of its own. It is foreign to her
in that she does not call up the anger but it exists on its
own. She no longer has control of her own existence.
She has told the others of her predicament, or believes
she has, and they have no care for her. They have their

own concerns in the immortality of their world. Their creation is not as they willed it, and that weighs upon them all. They have pushed her aside as if she no longer matters in their pantheon. How can they betray her in such a way?

She will storm. She will let the winds rise with her and push her along in a heady, out-of-control fury for ignoring her and her needs and fears and strengths and torrents of her element. But no. No, she will not storm in water. She has decided to withhold that, she remembers. Instead, she will rain punishment upon their heads, those who ignore her. She forsakes them as they forsake her. That is a godly vengeance. Yes.

She feels one of the people approaching the cove where she lies in her river. She feels the heat of the woman's body, the echo of the coppery smoke lying upon her lips, the tumble of her thoughts as she stumbles toward the river's edge for water. The Goddess floats upward toward the sky and the brightness of the sun upon the surface. It stokes the fire within her. She feels the lick of yawning need in her essence. It swallows her. They have done this to her. The one who used her has done this to her. She will not accept it one moment longer. She will take back what she is missing, bit by bit, flesh by flesh. This is one of the living who defies her, if not the one she seeks, still a breather of air and sunlight as the woman she hates is. It might even be the woman she seeks. The one who has stolen from her.

She rises in the water. Need and anger cloud her vision. Is it the one or is it not? The smell of flesh and blood overwhelms her. She cannot tell! To hesitate is to lose her quarry, so she takes the Kernan who kneels at her side with buckets, seeking to fill them at the river. The woman screams and struggles within her hold. The Goddess thrills at the fight. It fills her emptiness. A rage erupts in her. She is not to be ignored or stolen from! Not by any flesh. Her fingers tighten like river-grown ironweed about her prey as the Kernan shrieks. She builds fangs and sinks them into the struggling, frightened woman. She drinks deeply of the iron-tinged blood. The flesh struggles. It cries out in abandonment as she rends it. She shakes it savagely with the teeth she has built for herself as the flesh begs her for mercy.

The River Goddess has none. She has never had a need for mercy toward flesh. Her concern is the earth and the growing things which come from within it when she graces herself upon and through it. The struggle and fear of the being fills her as nothing else ever has. She revels in it. The knowledge that she has taken its life fills her even as she also knows that this is not the one she hates and needs. No matter. It fulfills her for this moment. She rends the being into shreds of lifeless matter and leaves it strewn upon the riverbank.

The Goddess sinks slowly back into her waters. Confusion and a crimson tide swirl about her. She has lost the rhythm of her world and its cycle and her part in its concert, stolen by the very one who kept her safe for so many years, who kept her by the river and who took her intimately to its waters whenever the two of them felt the need. That was past although it is still in the now for this river goddess because it is like a dark pool, a quagmire in the bed of a gentle stream, that sucks down water and mud and stick and life into the nothingness of dead earth deep, deep below. When she considers this now, as she drifts back and forth, feeling the call of her lands for water, for rain, for stream and flood, she angers still. There is no calm for her. None.

She drifts through the world, always in the now, uncaring of the concepts of yesterday and tomorrow in the river called Silverwing, and in all its tributaries large and small, and in the droplets of rain that run into those branches, and in the mists and fog off the river which carry her, scattered, back to the sky. She lives in the icy banks and the frosted rivulets, and in the downpours and floods. The only thing that can diminish her naturally is her own state of being.

She had remade herself. Spun herself free of the cage
of steel which held her and of the vessel of flesh which
she found for herself to protect her essence sundered by
the steel, and she had braided herself anew. Her fingers
tremble and dance through the air as she remembers
the moment of reweaving the strands of her existence.
Yet a splinter of the Demon lies within her and because
it does, she knows that a crucial element of herself lies
within the vessel of flesh that must be reclaimed.

The River Goddess dances on the bank of the Silverwing, like a will-o'-the-wisp, in angry confusion. She
shakes at the chaos tumbling inside her ephemeral form.
She has been stolen from. Betrayed. In despair and
anger, she withholds herself from the cycle of rain, of
tendering her care upon the lands which so desperately
need her. She cannot spend herself; there is so little left.
She will not evaporate into oblivion gently! She will rain
fire upon the earth if she must to redeem herself. She
will take back what the flesh owes her, if she must rend
to bits every scrap of mortal walking within her realm.
This she knows. She will lay them low to regain what she
is owed.

Homecoming was never what he imagined it would be.
He had seen, in his youth, joyous welcoming at the door,
or at the edge of the field or pasture, young ones running to see their father, to be hugged and swung about.
Mothers with toddlers hanging on their apron, standing in the doorway, waiting to be favored with a flashing grin. Demonstrations of returning and the resultant
happiness to be found in that action. Dwellers were the
most conspicuous, but he'd seen the Kernans celebrate;
even the arrogant Galdarkans had been known to show
a sentimental streak now and then. Not one of those re-
turnings had involved him, but he had watched, envied,
hated, on the sidelines.

Quendius pulled up at the stable yard, his horse grunting in relief to be shed of the burden of his weight and the aryn wood, and a Bolger hobbled over to take the reins. His leathern face grimaced as he gave a bob. "M'lord." He did not look happy. No one enjoyed having the taskmaster come home.

Quendius tapped the bundle of aryn cuttings. "Get these to the bowyer. I've taken an accounting, and it had better not be short. Master Narskap has a use for them." Narskap was no less feared than he was in this camp, and with good reason.

The Bolger made a chuffing noise and dipped his chin. He shouldered the bundle as if it were dry tinder wood instead of heavy and dense branches, and dragged the tired horse off behind him.

Quendius shouted after him. "When did the howling stop?" He gave a glance to the tower.

"Yes'erday."

Quendius nodded, and the Bolger resumed his trek. Quendius tilted his head a bit, looking at the fortress and tower. Perhaps it had only been in his imagination he'd been with Narskap when the River Goddess appeared, perhaps he'd already been on the trail and Narskap had communicated the need for aryn wood while he was about. He flexed his fingers as if he could grasp the elusive ability within himself that was almost a Talent and almost a curse. He could bridge distances. Sometimes. Not often enough to depend upon it or well enough to be entirely sure of where he would travel when he did. Close to his destination, yes, but not always there. There could be an advantage to it if he knew how to shape the fugues, but he did not. He imagined his ability as a sword, sometimes solid and sharp when he wished to swing it, but more times than not, insubstantial and limp. Had Kanako or Anderieon forged their Vaelinar destiny with a wet noodle? No. Nor could he. So the Vaelinar blood ran thin in him, good only to hate. He would not call it magic from his bloodline, he had none. More likely it was a result of the places he traveled across, the Scarred lands, the Mageborn blasted lands, and forces that stirred unpredictably there. He had seen nothing that he could reliably harness to his advantage. He slapped dust off his thighs.

Bistel Vantane would see, when he rode the borders of his land and the lands adjoining that his precious aryns had begun to lose the war against the plague of the Scars. A Vaelinar who harvested both men and grain, who reaped the blooded and bloodless, Bistel would have to make a choice. Would he go to Lariel's side or would he make the borders his own private war, against an enemy unnamed and not understood but equally deadly? Quendius would be curious which the old man would choose. Bistel did not look old, but he was, enduringly, one of the last Vaelinar left from the first days, and that edge of prime existence he clung to would fall away as suddenly as if he'd plunged over a cliff. Quendius had seen it happen before. He enjoyed waiting to see it happen to Bistel.

He sent word to Narskap's tower that he had returned, and then went to his own retreat, and stood at the edge of a great table, mapped from edge to edge with what was known of these great lands and tapped his dagger speculatively at the map's perimeter. Who would move where, and how soon? And would any of them look to the west?

"SHE'S IN HIGH TEMPER. They've called for healers, stabled the horses, and done little else," Jeredon said to Sevryn. His arms wheeled his chair across the grounds, moving to keep pace with Sevryn's booted strides. A night in Larandaril, in what served as his own bedroom, had eased the pains of the past few days, if not the worry. He'd said little to Jeredon upon his return, and his friend had accepted that, with a hurt look in his eyes, but no admonishment in his words. They had an unspoken agreement that Sevryn's findings would await Lariel's arrival. This morning had brought word of spotting the queen's patrol at the borders.

He responded only, "The news I bring won't do anything to ease that."

"Thank you for the warning. Perhaps I should hitch a goat to my wagon to increase my speed of retreat."

"From what I've seen of you and goats, I doubt that will help much. You'd both insist on going separate ways."

Jeredon chuckled, although a bit breathlessly. He added, "If you see a Dweller chugging after us, run for it. I left Nutmeg behind and forgot to tell her Lara and Rivergrace were riding in."

"You'll pay for that."

"No doubt of it."

Sevryn lifted his chin, and his strides stretched, taking him ahead of Jeredon, as he saw the group by the stables, Rivergrace surrounded by dusty and bloodstained troopers. He recognized her movement, her presence a moment before he could actually see her features because he knew the way she made her way through the world. She worked among the healers who'd come out first, bringing out litters for the wounded and tending those they could on the spot, but his attention stayed on her alone. Her auburn hair caught the low-slanting gleam of the late autumn sun, burnishing it in red-gold highlights as she wove among the litters, bending here and touching briefly there. She couldn't replace the high healers of the Vaelinars but she had a soothing ability of her own which aided any she touched. She wore blues and golds and grays, and he would have known her anywhere, just by the way she moved her hand to her brow, lifting back a strand of hair that had fallen across her face, or took a step across the yard. If he had been blind, he would have known her by her voice, her step, and her aroma; if deaf, by the silk of her skin and the gentleness of her touch; and if dead, he still would have known her, as he had once before, by the brilliance of her soul.

She turned as if hearing his thoughts, let out a soft cry, and began to run toward him. Troopers laughed as she jostled through them before they could step aside for her.

Sevryn caught her by the waist and swung her once. Her face lit ever so briefly with a smile before the quiet worry curtained her expression again. The blood on her was not hers, he could tell that immediately as he ran his hands lightly over her shoulders and arms before catching her hands. "I thought I might miss you, that Lara wouldn't be bringing you back here, but this seemed the only place to go. The tides may be determined to carry us apart."

"It doesn't matter as long as we're equally determined to return to each other," Grace finished for him. She considered him thoroughly, her gaze searching him from head to toe before relief lightened the color of her eyes and she smiled.

"Confirmed," he said, pulling her close and kissing her forehead. "We're both all right."

"I felt you," she answered. "At the river's crossing."

"When you were in battle?"

She turned her face aside. "I don't remember much of anything but the horses panicking and the yells, the fighting."

"And that was before you ran into raiders," Jeredon added dryly as he rolled his wheelchair into the group. "I know how my sister drives a war party. No time to think, just well-honed instincts."

"You may not think, but I do, and aplenty." Lariel heard him, striding out of the stable's wide doorway. She stripped off her riding gloves, and leaned over to pull her brother's hair affectionately. "We could have used you out there. We'll be needing archers trained."

"They did not acquit themselves well?"

"They did well enough, but there are fallen."

"What happened? How bad was it?"

"This is best discussed elsewhere. We are in Larandaril, the center of my power and my holdings, my dreams and my desires ... and there are those who listen to every heartbeat, every sigh. After Tiiva, we know this now."

"What do you intend to do about it?"

"This." She waved a glove overhead in signal. A moment passed, a sighing of breath, and then from the mews beyond the stables, hawks took to the air two by two, loosed like flights of arrows, with shrieks of joy at being free to ride the wind. War hawks, not the usual messenger birds, but birds which would not be stopped in their errands easily and which would, because of what they were and how they had been trained, reach their destination.

Human banter paused a moment as they all considered the birds climbing fiercely into the skies, circling once and disappearing, each pair winging in a slightly different direction.

"Where do you send them?"

"Wherever I must. All the signs tell us this will be a long, dry, and unseasonably warm winter, so I gather a war council. No longer will we speculate on the wisdom of fighting a war and how. Now we plan the assaults. No sense in waiting until Spring. The enemy won't."

She gave Jeredon's hair a second tug, before slapping her gloves into her belt and beckoning at Osten's burly bulk. "Join us when ready? I'll be at my gate."

The general raised an eyebrow before nodding and returning his attention to the healers aiding his fallen troopers. He would be along when this duty was discharged.

Sevryn traded a look with Rivergrace even as she laced her fingers tightly with his. No one trespassed through Lariel's gate to the inner pavilion of Larandaril. Few even knew of the pavilion, although one could note her absences and assume she had gone to her quiet place, the meditative hideaway to which she sometimes disappeared. No one had a key to this innermost heart of the Anderieon kingdom but the ruler of the moment and, in memory's time which stretched long enough for the Vaelinar, no one outside had ever been invited in. Larandaril held still the vibrant greens and golds as though untouched by black frost of coming winter, but the green had deepened and the golden leaves shivered as if the next strong wind might bring them down. Even this valley could not resist winter entirely. What magic it held, its heart lay in the queen's pavilion. Disbelieving of the invitation, they watched for a moment as the Warrior Queen strode by, and followed only when she gave them an inquiring look over her shoulder. The light-heartedness of her actions toward Jeredon immediately became shadowed by her destination. Jeredon shrugged to no one and began to wheel his chair after her, the cartwheels lurching uncertainly in the raked and wood-chip-strewn grounds of the stables.

Out of breath and apple-cheeked with exertion, Nutmeg caught up to them, her skirts flying, no more than elbow high to the shortest of the Vaelinars. She grabbed Rivergrace with a cry of happiness and hugged her tightly before rounding on Jeredon to block his wheeled chair, hands on her hips and eyes sparkling with indignation. "You can cart yourself from here to the end of Kerith," she told him, "but you'll not escape a scolding from me."

"I wouldn't dream of it. Such scoldings, I am certain, keep men such as myself in line. All of Kerith would suffer if your mouth should suddenly go silent and there were a dearth of them." Jeredon pulled a contrite face to reinforce the solemnity of his words.

"Does this run in your family, m'lady Queen, words that fall from the mouth without end and without sense?"

"If it did, I wouldn't admit to it. And good day to you, Mistress Farbranch," Lara said mildly, although her eyes of silver and gold shone a little as if the sun illuminated a hidden gleam in them.

Nutmeg dropped a hasty curtsy, neither low nor graceful, but sufficient. "Mark my words, I'm glad to see all of you, Your Highness, and most especially my sister. I hear that others aren't so fortunate and there will be mourning this evening."

"Your gossips are well-informed, as usual." Lara glanced down at her brother Jeredon and then back to Nutmeg.

"I told her nothing!" Jeredon protested before shutting his mouth as if deciding silence might be the wiser course.

"It was not from him. There were women at the ovens and in the laundry and the sewing rooms. They felt their husbands fall. They shrieked and clasped their bodies and toppled themselves, as if struck by the same blow. I've never seen such a thing. Is it Vaelinar, to know when your mate has been harmed?"

"It has happened, but most do not share such a close bonding," Lara assured her.

"More than likely histrionics," muttered Jeredon, "which seem to be at a high this time of the season. One female falters and the rest topple."

Rivergrace, however, murmured so quietly that likely only Nutmeg and Sevryn heard her as they stood the closest, "I have felt such a thing."

Sevryn squeezed her fingers a little, finding them cold in his hand. Osten caught up with them, slapping the dust off his riding mail, and lifting a waterskin to take a deep draught from it, before taking a stand next to Lara.

Nutmeg did not seem to notice the tension in the War-rior Queen. "He never tells me anything," she declared, her glance flicking disdainfully off Jeredon and back to Lara, "but excuses to avoid work the healers and I've set out for him. Despite long hours at the maps and with the stores' keepers, he's gotten some exercise, to good ad-vantage, I think, even though I nagged him into it. He'll be able to stand and toast Sevryn and Rivergrace at the engagement party. No dance, but definitely a toast."

"Meg," Grace said softly, putting her hand on the oth-er's forearm. "There won't be a party. Not for a while, at least."

"No party? What nonsense is this!" And she swung about on Sevryn as if he'd made the rash decision.

Despite himself, Sevryn took a step back. Jeredon made a choking sound, and when Sevryn looked to him, he'd ducked his chin down and had one hand over his face scratching at the bridge of his nose. Osten crossed his thick arms over his chest and managed to have little expression on his bisected face.

"That was my decision," Lariel interrupted. "Mistress Nutmeg, we've had a long ride these past days, and have much to discuss of war and mourning. Although I seldom stand on decorum, I think you'll agree with me that celebrations are not the focus of any discussions we have planned this day."

Nutmeg tilted her head, looking up at Lara's fair beauty, and pursed her lips as if in thought or argument with herself before answering. "On the contrary. I'll not be knowing, Highness, what your family schooled in you, but mine taught me that love is one of the only things that makes war bearable or worth the cost. If you toss that away, then it doesn't matter whether you win or lose at what you're doing."

Osten made a gruff humming sound at the back of his throat. Other than that, the burly and scarred general made no movement or expression in the midst of the stillness that had fallen.

The corner of Lara's mouth twitched ever so slightly. "We were headed to a brief council on affairs that I was . . . schooled . . . in. Shall I presume you will join us, Nutmeg?"

"Only as Jeredon's nurse and cart pusher. I don't know anything about planning for wars. When you're ready to talk about th' bonding party, then I've an idea or two."

"I daresay you do." Lara turned on her heel. "Keep up, all of you."

She led them across the stable grounds and toward the gardens which bordered the manor houses which had become, over centuries, the heart of the Anderieon holdings in Larandaril. Beyond that lay a grove which few ever entered except for Lariel, and at its heart, a gated pavilion. With a twitch of her hand, she produced a key seemingly out of nowhere which made Nutmeg's amber eyes grow big, and Rivergrace's face go thoughtful.

Grace entered last, hanging back, and taking one final look over her shoulder as she passed through the gate, she saw that the pathway which had brought them to its latticed arches disappeared as if it had never existed. Would the pathway exist again when they left or would it remake itself, in the tradition of the Vaelinar, a maze of possibilities which only Queen Lariel could traverse safely?

Her worry bled away the moment she stepped through the gates. Inside, the heart of the land lay in springtime. Flowers bloomed, their perfume on the air. The spears of grass held that new tinge of green, of tender young shoots just pushed from the soil. She could hear the gentle burble of the Andredia River which came to shore, somewhere near the carved benches and font, she guessed, under the bend of trees heavy with new growth. The only thing unenchanting about the place was the lack of living things. She could hear no rustling in the undergrowth of tiny rodents or insects scurrying about their business, nor could she hear the chirp or song of birds in the branches. They might be the only things alive in the pavilion besides the flora. How could such a thing be? How could the flowers and trees fruit and seed without the insects, the birds? It could not, not and be natural. She felt a frisson of fear at the magic which created such a place.

Grace looked down as her boots whispered through a branch, and she saw the unmistakable bitten ends of a leaf trail around her ankle before it whipped away on the stem. She smiled then, to herself. It was not that nothing living trod here besides them, it was that the queen hid their presence away, so that nothing living might be used to spy against her, later. The smile faded with the realization that even a sanctuary was not truly a sanctuary for Queen Lara.

Jeredon pointed a finger at the bench and raised an eyebrow at Nutmeg who pursed her lips but sat down in a bunch of skirts and petticoats, folding her hands, and becoming primly quiet for a Dweller. Sevryn drew Grace close to him, hip to hip, as if unwilling to be away from even the slightest touch of her.

Lara did not settle on the bench, but leaned her back against the slender trunk of one of the trees ringing it. "We were attacked by Bolger raiders who had been as finely drilled and outfitted as any troopers we could bring to field. They scattered our defenses and would have brought us down nearly to the last man standing but for two things: 1) the river we were fording working as much against them as for them, and 2) Abayan Diort did not order them to slaughter us so much as test us. Having done what he instructed them to do, the raiders pulled back but not before leaving us with an impression. If Diort can hone an edge like that to his Bolger troops, we must consider gravely what he can do with his Galdarkans and Kernans. We cannot afford to be in a civil war with this commander. We must, therefore, bring him down as quickly and uncivilly as we can, before he consolidates himself and his troops. We may be too late even in that. Street gossip from the cities tell us that the Kernans and others have begun a resurgence in the religious belief that their Gods will begin speaking to them soon, instructing them against a great calamity which will befall civilization. As we know, religious fervor goes in cycles but this seems inevitable and due, as well." She tugged on her dusty tunic, her loosened chain-mail corset chiming faintly as she did so. "I would like to say that this had all been a strategy to inspire him with overconfidence and lure him into a trap, but unfortunately, I cannot. We have not fought a true war in centuries, even among ourselves, and it catches us—if not unaware, then unprepared."

"I won't ask this lightly, Lara, but are you certain it was Diort who sent the Bolgers after you?"

She lifted her chin before answering Osten. "He appeared near the end of the rout, looking over the skirmish, and then whistling them off. Why would you doubt anything other than that he'd ordered it?"

"Because I haven't seen or heard word that the Galdarkan welcomes Bolgers among his troops as raiders. Laborers and craftsmen, yes, but not raiders. Quendius used them in my experience, and still does."

Her eyes narrowed a bit. "Diort and Quendius work in concert."

"They did. Diort's movements this last season indicate that he has left his alliance with Quendius and consolidates his people on his own. I think that any involvement he may have had was coerced and Diort no longer sees fit to bow his head to the other."

"He called them off."

"Or they noticed him and decided not to be caught between two armies? I play the contrarian here, my queen. It seems unlikely that Diort would have moved upon you and then drawn back when he could have taken you. Remember that I was up to my knees in Bolgers, so my observations may be a bit . . . inaccurate," added Osten wryly.

"So noted. But, it remains that we were routed by raiders when we shouldn't have been, and he was a witness. Yes, I am humiliated, but more than that, I don't like to give a man hope that taking us will be easy. Whatever his reason for being there, it remains that Bistel engaged him, and we went out looking for him after to ascertain the strength of his troops. He saw us in weakness and that can only encourage him to trespass again. Are we in agreement on that?"

Osten gave a half bow, graceful in contrast to his massive build. Jeredon and Sevryn murmured agreement as well.

"Will we have time to prepare?"

"If the winter holds as predicted." Nutmeg agreed with an affirmative chuff, which Lara ignored, adding, "It will be a long, relatively dry winter according to weather folklore and our own observations. Osten will be taking muster." Her brilliant gaze turned to Sevryn. "You had other news for us?"

"Nothing which would lessen or soothe anything you've told us thus far. Daravan gathered me in the night to take me on a sortie with him. We encountered a small war party by the southwestern bay shore. I took a souvenir. Before I show it, however," and he paused a long moment, "I have a second, unexpected tale. I traveled as quickly as I knew how to return to your side. The Way known as Hunter's Cut exists no longer. It came apart as I traversed it, and I swear to you, I don't know how or why." He paused. "It was as if Kerith noticed me, and saw the bondage the Way put upon it, and threw it off. I can't support that. Only that Hunter's Cut is ripped apart, and in its stead lies a whirl-pool of chaos that has ripped the mountain apart."

"A Way disintegrated?"

He nodded. "I've never seen power like that, and there is no reason that I survived it except that I had an extremely swift and frightened horse under me."

"Could it have been an illusion?" This from Jeredon, his jawline firm except for a tic of muscle.

"I've never known one of us who could cast illusions, let alone one like that. I can send a scout back to take a look at it to confirm that it is destroyed."

"That will be done." Lara's voice was low, yet disturbed. "You may have been there by coincidence." Her lips thinned as thoughts filled her eyes.

"It remains," Jeredon said tightly, "that no Way once established has ever vanished."

"Perhaps," murmured Lara. She raised her hand. "As awful as this is, it's not the news you raced to bring me."

"No, Highness, it is not. I cut this from an enemy." Solemnly, he took his grisly souvenir from inside his vest, where he had the limb in an oilskin pouch. He opened it and passed it to Osten who took it and began to examine it with a great sniff of curiosity. The appendage looked even more bizarre than he remembered.

Lara did not touch it, but her gaze fastened on it and did not stray. Jeredon poked a finger at it, examining a length of retractable talon.

"Intelligent?"

"Very and the most wicked fighter I've ever come

across. Daravan says to tell you that he believes it to be one of the Raymy, although he is getting confirmation."

Nutmeg drew her breath in with a hiss. Lariel merely paled a little, her eyes darkening in contrast to her fair skin.

"This is true?"

"He says it may well be."

"He isn't a man who would stir us up in vain," her voice drifted off. "I cannot let us be sandwiched between two enemies. Abayan Diort will be destroyed before those things make land. Destroyed or bowed to us, entirely. You are dismissed, all, and not a word outside these gates. Jeredon, I want you to recruit and train archers as ably as you can before we go to council. Osten will give you whatever men you think suitable. Sevryn, send that scout out you recommended. Thank you for your attendance." She opened the gate with a wave of her hand, and their leave to go seemed obvious.

Not another word did she utter until she was alone, and the gates had swung shut behind her guests. The silence seemed complete when she whispered, "And there you are."

A shadow stirred. She did not turn but said wearily, "Have you brought confirmation, Daravan?"

A tall, broad-shouldered shadow separated itself from other shadows on the other side of the river Andredia. He crossed its narrow bed in a single leap to gain her side. "My pardon, Lara, for seeming to eavesdrop on you. I did not wish to interrupt."

"You didn't surprise me, although I'm surprised that Sevryn didn't sense you. He's keen that way."

"Preoccupied, I think, with the news he had for you."

"They were Raymy?"

"According to sources, yes."

"Have you reason to doubt them?"

"Not at this time." He pushed his cloak and hood off his shoulders. "I hate bringing you news like this."

"Think how much worse it would be if you hadn't

caught them, to bring it to me." She let herself sit on one of the curved benches. If it had been the one where Nutmeg perched, no vestige of her warmth had been left behind. The stone held a chill that the garden itself tried to deny. She watched the Andredia flow by.

"You need to rethink your position with Diort."

"Never."

"That sounded intractable."

"It is."

"You can't afford not to consider options, Lara. Osten had a point, if you'd been of a mind to listen."

"Giving in to a tyrant who impresses his people into following him isn't an option."

Daravan took a moment of silence before asking mildly, "You're certain that's what he is doing?"

"I've seen evidence of it myself."

"But not in all villages, cities, and towns. Many take up the sword and follow willingly."

"Many aren't willing to wait to see what destruction he intends to bring them before he extends his rule over them. With that war hammer in hand, who could refuse him? I won't let him follow the path that Quendius has set down for him."

"I'm not so sure Quendius has a hand in this."

She looked at him sharply. "By what reasoning?"

"Quendius is, by all observation, someone who revels in destruction and subjugation. Diort has done little more than unify, although as much by power as by seduction, I'm willing to admit. He had destroyed, twice, but the dam he took down last year held contaminated water, water that the wasteland had been seeping into, and the city it bordered was no less contaminated. The area you visited held sign of dying aryns, did it not? He is not wanton with his actions, no more than you are, unlike Quendius. I believe Abayan Diort is at odds with Quendius. He was never more than a reluctant ally, and now he knows his strength. He is of Kerith, to the bone. Quendius is of nothing and cares for nothing."

"And he will stop at nothing."

Daravan dropped his chin in a nod.

"I can't meet Diort as an equal if we haven't beaten him."

"You think not?"

Lariel blushed faintly. "I presume that to be the case. Even if I wish alliance, it would have to be out of strength, or he'd absorb us the way he has the common folk. We will not be absorbed, Daravan. Whether we go down as one, or Stronghold and Holding by Stronghold and Holding, we will not be absorbed meekly. You know that."

"I'm not suggesting that. There is more than one way to forge an alliance."

"And who would you suggest I hold up for him to marry? Which one of us would suit him? Myself? Someone else? He may already have the woman he wants in the traitor Tiiva."

"If she went to him. Perhaps only the best would do. If you married an ild Fallyn off to him, we'd never have a truce." Daravan chuckled dryly at the thought. Contentious to the core, there was not an ild Fallyn alive who did not think that they could and should replace Lariel and her brother.

"I'd rather not think on it." Lara folded her hands in her lap, slightly bruised and swollen by her sword handling, and chafed the stiffness out of her fingers lightly.

"Then what it is you're not telling me?"

She glanced up. "Do I tell you everything?"

"Decidedly not. But I thought you might share this time." He sat down on the bench, not too far from her, but not quite close enough to touch. She could smell his horse's sweat on him, as well as the perfume of her pavilion, and his own unique, masculine scent.

"Abayan didn't call his raiders off. I deem that he would have, but one of us rose against his maneuver in such a way, we were all surprised. And she has little or no recollection of it, nor does anyone else in the troop.

Only I saw, and remember. Even Osten seemed foggy about it, so that I question myself. But I saw it. I know I did."

"What happened?"

"She built a fire on the water against the raiders, Daravan. I have never seen its like or even guessed it could be done. She raised a tide of fire on the river and brought it down on them."

"It can't be done." He didn't ask, she noted, who Lariel referred to.

"Rivergrace did it."

"Her Talent is water. We all know that. And you're telling me she has no memory of it?"

"Dazzled at first, and then seemingly unaware of what she'd done altogether. Or afraid to admit to me that she had. Osten doesn't remember seeing it, only that the raiders fording the river turned back in disarray. None of the others remember even that much. The waters were running red with blood."

"I've never heard of an ability like that. Perhaps to set fire to oil on water . . ." Daravan's words trailed off.

"No." Lara eyed her hands briefly. "Not like that. None that I know of."

"Perhaps it wasn't her but something other. Hunter's Cut didn't collapse without provocation. We've often wondered how long it would take the Gods of Kerith to acknowledge us, to work against us. Perhaps those days are here?"

"Did you come to encourage me with that news? First tell me the Raymy are returning, and now hostile Gods?" She laughed, in spite of herself. "Is there never any good news about you?"

He took one of her hands and brushed his lips across her knuckles with more of a breath than a kiss. "The good news is that you were born to be a Warrior Queen, and now it appears we have need of one."

Chapter Eleven

BISTEL VANTANE REINED in his horse, and eased back in his seat, stretching his long legs in the stirrups for a moment. Intermittent sunshine bore down on him, through long thin clouds that scattered across the sky, forming a blanket only to wisp away before blanketing again, rain or snow from the chill of it, that might or might not fall that evening. The rider at his flank reined in, quiet and solemn. Bistel looked down across the Dweller and Kernan homesteads, five of them laced together in a massive farming operation, one that might equal one of his own winter grain fields. They had worked hard here for generations; he knew the heads of the families back to their great great grandfathers and perhaps even beyond that, if he cared to remember. He had not, from those early days. He would be one of the first to admit that the disdain the Vaelinars carried toward the first races of Kerith had been one of their greatest faults. It was a fault still resting in many Vaelinar. Not him, or so he hoped. He had finally learned.

"You know them all," Verdayne noted.

"I do. And so did Magdan." His gloved hand twitched slightly, and Norda tossed his tashya head in response, dancing sideways under him. His hand moved down to stroke the red-gold hide. They'd come three days' ride from home and it would be three days' ride back or longer if the weather did not hold. A tashya did not have the stamina of the sturdy Dweller mountain ponies, but there was no discounting a tashya's speed or intelligence or willingness or smoothness of ride. Norda blew his nostrils. He would call for the Ferryman, but the capricious phantom might or might not show. It seemed others were learning of that being's abilities if one's strength of will were strong enough to compel him. He had his suspicions the ild Fallyns had learned the secret long ago, but now Daravan and even Sevryn were moving great distances in an untimely manner. He wondered about the unnamed and unknowable creator of the Ferryman and what he had harnessed by Voice, voice ruling over the air which resided in water, for air was undoubtedly a component of water or else how could fish and all other creatures which lived in it breathe? As for the distance, the Talent ruled earth. He had known, in his youngest days, Vaelinar who could leap from place to place in the blink of an eye. Not far, mind you, but far enough that a sword stroke or arrow's flight might miss them. That Talent had faded long ago, except for the ild Fallyn ability to levitate.

An exhalation disturbed his thoughts, and he glanced over his shoulder at Verdayne where an impatient look faded abruptly. "I shouldn't have brought you. This isn't an easy task before us."

Bistel sat for another long moment before reaching up and removing his half helm, freeing his short-cropped snow-white hair to the afternoon wind. The chill in the air intensified, and the sky took on that sharp blue hue that matched his eyes somewhat, both of them signifying a tempest to come. He took his farglass from the quiver sheath by his knee, put it up, and examined the farmlands, particularly the barrier of aryn trees to the southeast borders. The fields had been shorn of their summer crops and winter crops that could stand, no, make that thrived on the cold, barely pushed up through the soil. It looked barren from here, but his glass showed the shoots growing upward. He sat immobile for long moments as the farglass sharpened in focus, bringing the trees into detailed clarity.

"How do they look?"

"Not as they should." Their strength tempered only by their beauty never failed to move him. A man of war, he found peace among the massive trees which had grown from a single staff from the old country, a staff which should never have sprouted but apparently had been green wood, like its carrier, a green young boy sent off to war and flung from one world to another. Once planted, that single aryn had sent off saplings and seeds, determined to replicate itself, and he had carried them, transplanting and planting accordingly, to watch them thrive. Magdan had eventually grown to help him in his quest, and then Verdayne to help Magdan. The aryns had a quiet, deep magic of their own, a steadiness which held against fire, flood and drought . . . and chaos. He'd carved an empire with the aryns to fence it off and keep it safe. Now he could see the black threads of disease winding and coiling in their emerald beauty and it felt as if those same dire threads squeezed his own heart. After long moments, he lowered the farglass and slipped it back into its sheath.

Verdayne commented on their mission. "Magdan would say you've no choice."

"Would you disagree with him?" Bistel found and held the young man's gaze, blue upon blue, so dark the eyes looked like indigo.

"He raised me like a father. I won't ever live to gather the experience he held, but I might naysay this. Those are farmers down there, Lord Bistel. Can't they cull and burn the stands clean?"

"They will ask me the same thing. I will give the same answer: no."

Verdayne made a noise in his throat. "It's true, then. You've sap in your veins instead of blood."

"Sometimes I think it must be so." Bistel looked away from the boy who was both Vaelinar and Dweller. "If that were true, though, my blood wouldn't be running through your body."

Verdayne flinched. He pushed a hand back through his dark, curling hair, hair that would one day be as snow-white as Bistel's, although it would not be the color of winter wheat first. "I cannot speak like that."

"No, you cannot. Not yet. I won't put you in that position. One day, though, you'll be known. It can't be helped. You have my love of the aryns even as Bistane has my ability for war." Bistel gestured downslope. "Usually welcome in this valley, today we will blow in like an ill-wind, and leave in bad graces." He closed his knees in signal, and Norda moved down the gentle slope toward the farmlands in a long-swinging gait that showed no trace of the gelding's tiredness. Taking the trail down to the main dirt road with ice from last night's frost still melting in the deep ruts, he crossed to the Dweller great house of the farmer who held the bulk of the land. A reedy line of blue-gray smoke trailed from the chimney. They would find a warm welcome even if it were only for a moment.

Bistel did not slow his horse as he reached the valley floor, nor did he turn in his saddle, but he did look over his shoulder as the feeling of being watched washed over him. A hot, hostile gaze tickled at the back of his neck and shoulders. He freed his bow to nock an arrow, letting his feet guide the horse. "Verdayne, ride on in and do not stop."

The lad did as told. Bistel toed Norda about to see nothing in the heavy forest edging the farms, nor did he expect to with a glancing survey. All he could do was telegraph his awareness so that whatever watched him would know that an attack would not be unexpected and, indeed, ill-advised. He did not relax the bow string until he reached the great house's swinging front gate, and even then the back of his neck burned. Reluctantly, he swung his bow back over his shoulder after replacing the arrow in its quiver.

A Dweller boy clattered out of the stable yard, his vine-woven hat flying off his brunet hair as he skittered to a stop in front of them. "Lord Vantane! Derro, m'lord! Master Verdayne! May I take your horses?" Words spewed from him like a river flooding in a spring thaw, his cheeks apple red from the cold and his excitement, his hands waving in the air under Norda's muzzle. The tashya stepped sideways with a snort and threw his head up. The Dweller paid no attention to his deficit in height, springing up to put a hand to the bridle and lowering the proud horse's head to a manageable position. He then stroked Norda soothingly. Bistel swung down, saying only, "Remember this is a tashya horse. Quarter him in a corner by himself till he settles and we're ready to leave. No feed and just a sip or two of water."

Verdayne's horse was more biddable and went quietly beside the prouder Norda who always held himself as if he knew it was a warlord he carried.

"Aye, m'lord, it'll be done as you ask." With a nimble hand, he caught the coin tossed him. The lad led Norda away, singing a merry song that Bistel barely caught the words to, a popular song in the taverns that season.

"What song is that?"

"That one? A ditty about the Ferryman taking a wife. Bistane can sing it by heart already." The first shadow of a smile in a day or two crossed Verdayne's face.

Bistel turned, stripping his gloves off as he approached the house. Faces must have been pressed to the window shutters, for the door was thrown open before he had one bootheel on the step. The farmer himself came out, Pepper Straightplow, tugging on a coat over his work clothes, his sons in a wing behind him.

His hand brushed his sword hilt, and then paused as Verdayne put a hand on his elbow. The warlord in him flexed a bit. He shrugged away a momentary guilt. Old habits, distasteful as they might be among the civilized, make for old men. He relaxed his hand on his sword hilt. Master Straightplow never stopped beaming, having not caught Bistel's movement or, if he had, not comprehending. His sons, gamboling along in their father's wake like so many fuzzy puppies, certainly hadn't. Bistane would have slit someone's throat by now in reflex to so much boisterousness he thought wryly, as Straightplow put forth a square callused hand. Verdayne released his hold on his arm.

"M'lord Vantane, so good to see you! And the young master. You bring dry weather with you, for a bit anyway."

"So it seems, Master Straightplow. The moon was feathering the clouds like fine lace last night, so I doubt the weather will hold for more than a day or two longer. It would be nice to have rain, if it's been as dry here as it has been up north. Forgive my imposing on your hospitality without notice. I won't be here long."

The smile bled from Straightplow's round face, and his side chop whiskers slanted downward as his expression fell. "Trouble, then?"

"So it is."

The farmer shooed his boys away, four or five of them, Bistel couldn't count them as they jostled and tumbled around one another, and then held the door himself. "Come in, then, sit, have a drink of something to take th' bite out of the wind and tell me what it is."

Bistel kept his news until they had done just that, Farmer Straightplow uncorking a bottle of the finest apple brandy Bistel had ever come across; the Dweller lectured as he poured three stiff drinks and seated himself. He fought with straightening his coat sleeves a bit before looking into Bistel's face and saluting him with the brandy. "This," he declared, "should put a spark in your kindling."

Bistel sipped at the rich amber liquid, feeling its smoky glow with its heavy accents of apple and fermentation slide down his throat. He told himself that it was a good thing Magdan had not lived to come with him to do the deed he intended. He would have balked at the inevitable even as Verdayne sat silent, not drinking, but cradling his cup. He waited a moment while the brandy warmed him through his bones before agreeing. "A fine brandy."

"Made by Tolby Farbranch of Calcort. Used to be of Stonesend before the raiders burned him out but the man knows his apples, be they juice, cider, or brandy." Pepper Straightplow took another long sip before setting his cup aside on the small pedestal table near his elbow. He settled back in his chair, folded his hands over his slight paunch, and waited.

Bistel looked upon him, remembering the generations of Straightplows before Pepper he'd dealt with. Pepper looked like them, the Straightplow features passed down man to son without seemingly any interference or contribution from female looks in the line. He wasn't sure if it was remarkable or not. He rarely treated with those of Kerith himself, leaving it to retainers, but the Straightplow family had been an exception. Until now, an exception founded in good judgment.

"Master Straightplow, there isn't a moment in my life that I have regretted bypassing the petitions and granting your family and associates these lands. You've done well by them and for them, and been generous with your tithe to me. These times, I fear, have passed."

Pepper sat up straight. "M'lord, if there's been an offense, I wasn't aware of it. Tell me what I can do."

"Nothing. There's no easy way for me to say this, and there is nothing you did or can do. The aryns on the boundaries are dying. Black thread infects them, and all I can do is burn them to the ground and salt the land they stood in."

"Harsh," said Pepper quietly. "Are you certain?

Surely we can cut and burn where needed, but not all the groves."

"Neither you nor I can take the chance. Black thread thrives on the aryns, but it will spread, and we can't let it. The waste is encroaching on your lands, Master Straightplow. I've come to reclaim the deeds you hold."

Straightplow sucked in his breath as the color left his face. Verdayne took a big gulp of his brandy.

"Lord," the Dweller said, but Bistel interrupted him gently. "All of you and yours and the others living here must leave, immediately. Take whatever you need to pack, but you must be gone as soon as possible."

A gray sheen lay over the farmer's face. "What could we have done?"

"Nothing. You have done nothing but that which is right and good."

"Then why are you doing this to us? This is my home. Has been our home for centuries, as you well know, m'lord Vantane. I can't just pull up like that, not like a peddler with a wagon. Where would we go? It's almost winter. What would you have us do?"

"I've no choice, Master. Trust me. Black thread is virulent. It won't only infect the trees, but the soil itself, and the water, and the people who live near it. It's like a plague, Straightplow, and I'm asking you to flee from it. I would have you go here." Bistel pulled an oilcloth bundle from inside his leather vest. He laid it on the table between them, took a knife to the lacings and let it fall open. "Deeded land. Yours. As good as the land here, for groves and orchards, pastures and fields. South and west of here, some days' ride, a little warmer, wetter climate but flat surrounded by hills much as your lands here. They are and will be yours. No Vaelinar or anyone of Kerith can take them from you except by act of war."

Straightplow's glance flickered down and then up. His brows etched heavy lines across his face. His thick hands clenched and unclenched. "I already have lands."

"I can't let you stay."

Verdayne coughed as another strong draught of brandy seemed to catch in his throat. Both men waited till he settled.

Straightplow put his hand on the deeds. He said sadly, "But this is my home."

"I have known the time when it was not. I saw the beginnings of your family settle here, by my leave. Now I must take it back and tell you to move on." Bistel looked at him, keeping his tone mild. It would not be easy. He had known that.

"You've said it was no fault of mine."

"Straightplow, try to think of this as a rescue and not a punishment." He stood, towering over the sturdy Dweller. His knife still out, he tapped the point on the deeds as he spoke. "These papers will not compensate for your buildings and the history you've invested here. Besides the deeds, you will find letters of credit. You'll need them to rebuild. But this land is virgin, and a good farmer such as yourself and your family will find much benefit in working it. It's your choice whether to go there. It is not, however, your choice on whether to leave. You have a handful of days, regardless of the weather. I will be back in force to ensure that you've moved on, if necessary. Harsh, I understand, but I know how to deal with black thread."

Straightplow cocked his head slightly, looking up at him. Thoughts rumbled through his eyes as loud as wagon wheels but he did not express them out loud. Finally, he said, grudgingly, "I was always told you were a good man, for a Vaelinar. We'll be gone in the five days, if not sooner. We'll take your deeds, Lord Vantane." He paused. "We may be short-lived, but we will remember these lands and what happens to them."

The corner of Bistel's mouth crooked slightly. "Then I pray you shall not be able to remember when black thread ran rampant here, and took the lands, and corrupted them beyond redemption."

Verdayne got to his feet, a little unsteadily, and

Straightplow looked long and hard into his face. The Dweller said quietly, "Give my regards to Master Magdan."

"The good Magdan passed from us several days ago."

The farmer's attention snapped back to Bistel. "My sorrow to you, then. Would he have sent us away?"

"He would have done," Bistel answered evenly, "what I told him to have done. But, he might have advised me to take a milder course. When there are families such as yours, Pepper Straightplow, I prefer to be safe rather than sorry."

"T–there are aryns," Verdayne stammered, "and in the spring, I'll bring more saplings and . . . and seed."

"Then you will know where t' find us, young gardener," Straightplow said quietly. He folded the papers up and tucked them inside his vest. He took their hands in his and shook them.

Bistel and Verdayne left the farmer's great house. They rode out without a look back, knowing that the family gathered on the porch to stare after them. He could give them words and papers, but not an explanation. He could not explain that for which they had no understanding.

The aryn trees which had stood as long as he had planted them, a barrier and border against the Mageborn chaos to the south and east, had begun to wither and die. A black fungus had begun to splotch their brilliant leaves and crack open their greening branches, rendering them vulnerable to more disease and devouring insects. Magdan had left him a legacy of notes and samples, and his moonlit night to harvest saplings had been to replace the stricken trees that he could. But the old gardener had not understood that this was not a battle he could win. Perhaps it was a mercy he'd died without realizing that. The chaos would not be held back much longer. What would happen to these lands, so close on that border, he could not predict but he'd seen the chaos move before and it was not pretty. No, not pretty at all, even to Vaelinar eyes which could see the threads of all the elements in the world as they were born and twisted and woven into life, broken into death, and reborn again. He rode into the grove, pointing out the destruction to Verdayne. The trees murmured to him and from the look in Verdayne's eyes, he could see that his son was enough like him that he could hear them as well. Both of them wept quietly as they destroyed the trees of their Vaelinar legacy with fire and salt, both the affected and the clean, until smoke and ashes swirled into the sky as if night had fallen.

Chapter Twelve

"**D**WELLERS ARE A BLOODY FORCE of nature," Jeredon muttered. He managed the ramp and got to the door before Sevryn and Grace, waving to get it opened for them. Nutmeg had flown past all of them to get dinner ordered and Rivergrace's room freshened up. Sevryn chucked Jeredon on the shoulder as they went past him.

"And aren't you happy she is? She means to get you on your feet."

"I can get on my feet. It's staying there I can't manage, but the healers say it'll happen in time. She makes too much of me. She should be where she's happiest."

Rivergrace paused by Jeredon, her hand brushing the back of his quickly. "She is where she's happiest."

He ducked his chin. "You need to explain it to her. She can't be looking at me with those eyes of hers."

"Why not?"

"Because, Grace, I cannot look back."

She hesitated in confusion a moment, and Sevryn

took up her arm. "I'll explain it to both of them," he told Jeredon, before sweeping her inside with him.

"Good." The door shut, leaving Jeredon outside as he'd intended.

Rivergrace waited until they were on the stairs and past the bustling staff which manned the heart of Larandaril for Lara and Jeredon. "Whatever was that about?"

"Stay with me tonight."

"You're changing the subject, and I can't." But she leaned into the warmth and strength of his arm. "What is it Jeredon was trying to tell me?"

"That Nutmeg adores him, and he can't return her feelings."

"Can't or won't?"

"That scarcely matters among the Vaelinars. There is no way for her to be happy here."

Rivergrace frowned slightly, and he wanted to smooth away the faint line in her brow as she did. "And the two of you think she doesn't know this?"

"I think Jeredon hasn't the heart to send her away and hopes someone else will do it for him."

"She'll leave when he tells her he doesn't need her anymore. I know my sister. She can be stubborn, but she's never been a fool."

"That stubborn trait must run in the Farbranch family."

She laughed softly at him, the frown lines fading away as she did.

"Aderro." His mouth brushed her temple. "This isn't about Lara or dear Nutmeg; this is about the two of us. Stay with me tonight."

She knew a little of what he could do with his Voice, although he'd never used it on her nor did he now. He could whisper to the trees and convince them to let him meld into their being. He could coax the recalcitrant into agreeability. He could calm panic, turn loyalty in its tracks, bring forgetfulness to the aware.

All with a soft sentence or even just a word or two. He would not convince her to love him if she did not wish to. She curved her slender arm about his waist. A delicate heat spread from her touch. Her long hair brushed his shoulder as they walked. She said not another word, but when the time came at the top of the curving stairs for them to part, he to his apartments in the west wing and she to her rooms in the north, she matched his footsteps.

Rivergrace watched him bar the door behind them.

Someone had anticipated her visit, for in the cupola at one end of his apartment a bathtub stood, filled with water that still steamed and flower petals strewn across its surface. A drying sheet lay demurely upon a nearby footstool near a folding panel that could be drawn at the entrance to the cupola for privacy. Rivergrace let out a soft sigh of anticipation upon seeing the tub.

He took her elbow. "Hurry now, while it's still hot."

She chucked her clothes with all the glee of a child readying to jump into a welcome pond in midsummer's heat and left them in a pile with no more thought than that, letting out a sigh as she sank her willowy form into the tub. He thanked the Gods that she was still without artifice, that her pleasures came honestly and sensually without calculation and that he could enjoy her in each moment as it came to her. He crossed his arms and put a shoulder to one of the great carven armoires nearby and watched her splash about, first lying at the bottom of the tub without so much as a toe or a nose showing, then surfacing with her dark auburn hair streaming about her bare shoulders and upon the fragrant water.

"This," she said, "is glorious."

"I agree."

"Come join me!"

"In a while. You, my lady, are dirty with far more need of the tub than I have. I bathed at the racks this morning. Take all the water . . . and soap . . . you wish."

She tossed a handful of water and petals at him,

laughing as he tried to dodge and could not in time.
"You've grown slow for a warrior!"

He had. The corner of his mouth quirked. "My wounds
are a bit unyielding. Perhaps I could use a good soak."
He moved toward the tub, the fragrance of the herbs and
flowers in the water rising toward him, along with her own
aroma of innocence and sensuality with the barest hint
of musk. He stripped his leathers off and kicked them to
one side, then his shirt and under breeches, but she did
not shrink as he leaned over. Instead, she reached out and
with wiry strength pulled him into the tub with her. Water
surged around them, and he coughed out a mouthful of
soapy water, laughing.

Rivergrace ran her hands over his newly stitched cuts
and the many dark bruises mottling his skin as he settled into the tub next to her. Her touch both soothed and
aroused him, her slim fingers tracing each cut, her
mouth making noises of distress. "I shall kill Daravan
for this."

"Harsh words. And he would be as hard to kill as I am."

"There was kedant on the blades that carved you."
She gently smoothed a puckered cut, bringing fresh pain
to the purple-and-pink sutured flesh, then the pain and
more eased away as her touch soothed him.

"How can you tell?"

She looked up at his face. "I know you and kedant
well. Once you've been quickened to that venom, it will
always mark you more harshly than one who hasn't
been. Remember that, or it'll be the death of you when
you least expect it."

"Daravan had a potion for it."

"He knew they'd have poisoned blades?"

"I rather imagine he suspects the worst of any
encounter."

"He'd better not ever encounter me when I'm this
angry with him. He used you."

He tried to sound stern. "Rivergrace, I am the Hand
of Lariel, and it's my service to be used."

Her mouth curved truculently. "Not in this manner." Her hands dropped to his skin again, finding and stroking each bruise, each wound, and as each fire of kedant burned away, an ember of desire kindled in its place. They curved so closely to each other in the overflowing tub there could be no way she didn't know the effect she had on him. He dropped his face to nuzzle her neck.

She moved slightly in the tub, twining her legs with his, and meeting his mouth with hers, and both of them were silent for a very long moment as he tasted her, as lush and sweet as he remembered. She drew away after that kiss and put her hand on his chest as if to stop him for a moment, and he waited.

Her throat swelled a bit as if the words didn't come easily to her before she spoke, her eyes of aquamarine and other river blues and grays watching him. "I saw you in the river."

"And I, you."

"No one told me this could happen."

"It doesn't happen."

She toyed with the small triangle of fine, burnished gold hairs on his chest. "It's nothing we can depend upon, then. It may never happen again."

"There are other bonds."

She turned her face so that she could lean against him, cheek to cheek. "I thought perhaps it was part of being Vaelinar."

"Perhaps it is part of being us." He slid his arms around her, drawing her close, molding her body to his. Where their skin touched, his body warmed. He kissed her again, thoroughly, until she moaned softly against his mouth. He ran his hands over her, feeling the slender strength of her body and then the fullness of her breasts, and she moved onto him, taking him into her before she was fully ready, and the tightness of her made him hiss in pleasure, but he held back. She was not ready yet, she only wanted that joining, not the joy of it, not the heat of it, not yet. He would stroke her and kiss her and bite her neck until she arched her back and pleaded with him to move. And then he would.

She braided her fingers into his hair. As she did, she murmured, "I feared I would feel it if you died."

He had feared the same but protested against her lips as he returned that he would never, never die. She sank her teeth ungently into his lower lip to still his words. "You've already died for me, and I for you."

"And was it so bad?"

"It was . . ." and her words faded away, and she touched him, and he sank into a sensation he had never known before, the water from the bath rippling about them, still hot though cooling, a brand upon his skin as he realized the chill of death, her dying.

The chill lanced through him and she gasped as she felt it also, both of them cold as ice within the embrace of each other.

Flesh to flesh, yet he moved through her and she throughout him, both of them as insubstantial as wisps of river mist, yet he could feel the swirl of fire at the center of her being, even as she touched the whirlwind that comprised his being, his Talent of Vaelinar. So began their knowing of each other from within.

She pressed again his flesh to live his lunge with a word of Voice, to turn the sword Cerat from its intended target to lodge deeply into him instead. She knew the moment, the slicing away the cord of his soul from his body, death so swift that pain only followed after briefly like an echoing cry, and the true pain of being taken by the Souldrinker. In raw and sheer pain tempered only by fear, she felt his death and more terrible than that, the moment Cerat drank his soul.

The moment replayed itself in him and he shuddered from its echo. He took her wrists in his hands to brace himself and felt the weight of the blade when she took it up, the sword twisting violently in her hands in an attempt to break away from its new master. He brought her hands to his mouth and kissed her palms, a balm against the ache of it. Her eyes widened, seeing him and not seeing him, even as he beheld her and yet found himself held blindly inside the sword. Her torment cut into him as deeply as the wound which had killed him as he held both her trembling hands to his lips. *Anguish welled up in her from Cerat's very touch, from its vileness and the death it had wrought and the souls it held entrapped within it, and she unable to bear any of it but that she must. It was all she had left of him.* He realized then she would have put it down again, dropped it like a firebrand searing her flesh, but she could not bear to leave him behind. Sevryn released her hands to put his forehead to hers, and fresh tears on her face bathed his cheeks and tasted faintly salty on his lips.

And then it was like this, he told her without words, in the river of thoughts that flowed between them. *A biting iron cage about his being to be endured only because it was her hands which carried it and her presence which steadied him, that and a silvery essence which eased his own torture, a being as light in its divinity as the Souldrinker was dark in his. Sevryn rode on her shoulder when she carried Cerat high, and trailed in the dust when her will faltered and she dragged it behind her, and he knew when she raised it with the last of her strength to strike at the abomination which poisoned the sacred river Andredia, shattering both the sword and the curse.*

They both knew the moment when the sword Unmade them. He, released from his bitter metal confinement to feel his soul drawn across the aether to whatever true home the Vaelinar had lost behind them, and she Unmade as a weaving is unwoven by its weaver when a flaw is found and the fabric rejected. He nothing more than a zephyr in the world, and she a cobalt thread, uncoiled and spun out to nothingness, when the River Goddess gathered her up and rewove her, Making her once again into a mortal. Even as she had done to him, braiding his soul back into his body, Making him whole once more.

The water cooled about them, as Rivergrace sank

onto his chest, gasping for breath. He held her tightly
to him. His strong hands went to her hips, pulling her
onto him firmly and then caressing her supple flesh to
the small of her back, kneading, rocking her on him, his
mouth seeking hers before she could gasp again, this
time a small moan of remembered passion. And then
they were making love, heedless of the confines of the
tub and its tepid waters, the crush of petals still floating
upon it, their bodies hungry for each other until Sevryn
felt he would explode yet held himself back, his hands
stroking her, his mouth tasting, loving, and teasing her
until she gave a soft cry, shuddering, and a blush raced
across her features. He did not hold back then, coming
with a muffled shout as he buried his face in the curve of
her throat, his hips thrusting himself into her with one
last, powerful stroke.

They lay together quietly for a long time, so long
that he thought she might have drifted to sleep and he
feared to wake her though the tub had become cold and
stayed warm only where their bodies pressed together.
Her hand stirred on his shoulder, then moved to her ear
where she tucked a long, wet strand of hair behind it.

"I cannot stay," she whispered to his jaw.

He half smiled. "As it must be, then." He rinsed her
slowly, using the heat of his hands to take the chill from
the water before he did so, each handful as intimate as the
lovemaking they'd just shared. She let him tend to her,
kissing each bruise and scrape she'd suffered. He dipped
his head over her inner thigh to enjoy the fragrance of
her satisfaction before she tugged on his hair in protest
and began to climb out of the tub. Laughing, he caught
her wrist to help her up and out. His fingers closed about
the faded scar of her long-ago slavery and a heat in it
drew his surprised gaze. A new scar traced over the old,
a wavering line that brought to mind a meandering river,
the welt angry purple-red as if newly healed. She took his
hand from her wrist quickly as she gathered up a drying
sheet to wrap about herself.

"What happened?"

"I cannot say, because I don't know." She shivered slightly and moved to the banked fire across the room, gathering her clothes to prepare to dress as she did. First, she dried her hair as best she could as he watched.

A knowing had arced through him, a recognition of the sigil even if she did not. "Grace . . ."

She pulled her boots on last, then crossed to him, wrapping her damp drying sheet about his waist. "It's only one more scar among others," she told him. "It's nothing. I'll see you in the morning," and she slipped through the doors before he could say another word.

He would hold his peace for the night, then, while he pondered what he thought he knew because the soul in him had shared captivity with the River Goddess and he had felt Her anger through the flesh, Rivergrace's body, that She'd branded. Only a fool would refuse to listen when a God tried to speak.

Though she'd wanted nothing more than to tumble into his bed and sleep what was left of the night curved against the strength of his body, she knew she couldn't stay. It would not do to flaunt her disobedience in front of Lariel.

Rivergrace moved cautiously along the wing and landing, listening for servants or those who moved through the late night shadows. She heard heavy footsteps coming her way and the low thrum of voices growing louder. She could see blurred forms illuminated by sconces lending a low glow on the polished wood walls. She moved quickly into the shadows.

"Field strategy I understand, but this maneuvering between the courts, no. Never mind that she's sworn her loyalty to you—the lass purified the Andredia when you could not. For that alone, you should grant whatever boon you can to her. What drives you to be contrary, Lara?"

From the huge silhouette overshadowing Lara's slim

form, and from the rumbling bass tones, she knew it could be none other than Osten Lariel spoke with. She bit her lip as she withdrew under the staircase, into an alcove where the banisters joined and turned from one landing to the next, and she prayed the shadows hid her.

"There are as many facets to this as to the great gem of Tomarq. Mostly, however, it comes down to protecting Sevryn in spite of what we may or may not owe Rivergrace. To do so, Grace must be introduced as a Vaelinar, but I can't in all conscience. She is not Vaelinar as you and I are. There is something in her I don't recognize, and to embrace her bloodline as one of ours is incautious. I'm caught here, Osten, as friend and leader. Yet, what choice do I have with Sevryn? He's a half-breed with eyes that reflect that far more than his ears or his bearing even though he draws consideration from the Strongholds and Houses because he serves me, and I value him. They are not quite sure why or what strength he has that I value, but they warily respect that. When he marries, if he marries anyone less than a full-blooded Vaelinar, his children will be regarded as even less than half-breed. But, as you and I have seen time and again, love goes its own way. Denied Rivergrace, if he loves again, it could be anyone. If I lose or pass from power, he and his children will have only their own merits to be weighed upon, and those merits will be judged foremost through their bloodlines."

"So you would take Rivergrace from him?"

"Or present her as a daughter of impeccable parentage. Yet, we both know she was held as a slave under Quendius, negating her background by that very implication. Quendius is not a fool. He had reasons behind his enslavement that may entangle all of us. She may well be a half-breed herself, though I don't recognize Kernan in her."

Steps on the staircase near her slowed. Rivergrace sank farther back into the shadows, pressing her palms against the wall to stop the shaking that had begun throughout her entire body. She stilled her breathing as her heart drummed in her ears.

"We're not the most prolific of races," Osten rumbled mildly. "The Dwellers and Bolgers populate these lands easily. We are the shyest of breeders. Only the Galdarkans have as few issue as we do." He paused. "You're not hinting she could be a cross with Galdarkan lines? I've never heard of children from such a pairing. Impossible, I thought."

"Perhaps all but impossible until now. I don't know, I don't want to speculate, but I must. I have to consider Rivergrace's well-being. We owe her, yes. But at what price? If there is Galdarkan in her, then I have to account for the Mageborn and their twist of bloodlines and what magic they might have wrought upon them. The Galdarkans sprang from matings between the Mageborn and the very Gods of Kerith themselves, tales tell. Do I discount that? In my own experience, yes." Lara gave a soft snort. "But this is not our mother world or our own Gods, so perhaps . . . yes, perhaps stranger things have happened."

"Bah. You talk like an archer aiming at a charge. Where to fire, so many targets . . . and while you hesitate, you're overrun."

Osten gave a soft grunt as if Lara had elbowed him for that remark.

"What I do, for now, is keep them apart, and delay her introduction. Once I introduce her and acknowledge their betrothal, I've given my validation and that, I cannot give. Not now, not yet."

Rivergrace listened to the floorboards creak as they moved away from her, with Osten's muted thunder of a voice rumbling still, though she couldn't decipher his words. She stayed there until they were gone, quite gone from her, and then stood longer till the trembling had left her body. When she moved out of the shadows, her feet carried her down one path while her thoughts raced down another.

Chapter
Thirteen

*D*EAR MOM AND DA,
I hope this finds you and my brothers well.
Seasons are different in Larandaril. Milder, I guess.
I can't see how apple trees can fare well here, without the snap of winter to them. So I am missing the
seasons like they were at home. Meaning our old
place along the Silverwing and not in the city. Is
Hosmer a captain of the Town Guard yet? I can't
wait to see him in one of those silly hats. Tell Garner I used one of his card tricks to bet Jeredon into
doing more exercises for me! And tell Keldan that
the pastures here are full of the fine Vaelinar horses
he loves so much. They are proud and sassy, like
their riders. Grace will be writing you soon, too,
but the queen has her busy on scouting rides. They
look for poisoned water along the borders where
the blasted lands lie and where the Galdarkan Diort
rides. I think the queen looks for more backing for
her war, too, but those affairs are too vast for me to

worry about. I have my hands full with Jeredon and Rivergrace and Sevryn!

Before the night draped so deeply about the manor of Larandaril that it would curtain it away from the rest of the world, Nutmeg came from the rooms she shared with Rivergrace, drying her hands on her skirts and tucking her hair behind her shoulders. She placed her letter in the downstairs box for the postal rider and listened to the soft murmur of the servants as they retreated to their own rooms behind the main staircases. They spoke candidly of the queen and her brother, of the archers who'd fallen and the injured troopers and their families, as well as gossip among themselves. Because they were used to her bustling behind the scenes—had she not just been drawing baths in both Rivergrace's quarters and Sevryn's?—they thought of her as one of themselves, rather than a guest. They did not seem to notice or care that she overheard. It was one of the few advantages of being a Dweller amid so many Vaelinar and Kernan. She was seldom mistaken for a royal guest. Thus it was she heard that Jeredon had refused to come in for the night.

Trying not to frown, she made her way downstairs and to the main doors. She paused, hand on the latch, then changed her mind altogether. Retracing her steps, she went roundabout through the kitchen and out the back toward the gardens and the laundries. Chill came in as she opened the door, making her wish she'd brought her cloak out with her. She chided herself in place of her mother Lily. It was winter or nearly so, with the first snowfall not far away. Up north, the trader caravans already struggled through ice and sleet and passes closing with sudden storms. She ought to know that.

Nutmeg crossed the stepping stones placed for longer strides. She could smell the stringent scent of the soaping racks and laundry tubs around the corner of the building, but she did not head that way. She turned, instead, toward the gardens, where stepping stones became a graveled pathway. Against a line of tall shrubs, she saw the profile she expected.

She quashed the chastisements which rose in her. He was a grown man, and indeed, as Vaelinars lived, Jeredon probably had seen more seasons than Tolby, Lily, and she all put together. He was not heedless of taking care of himself, only that he put the needs of Lariel and others first, disliking the fuss that his injury caused. He heard her approach, no matter how cautiously she walked, darn those tipped Vaelinar ears. He turned his head ever so slightly.

"Come out to chide me?"

"No." She folded her hands in her apron, seeking a little warmth. "Only to make sure that you're all right."

"We have dead."

"We die every day, all over Kerith. It is only you Vaelinars who do not die so often."

A dry chuckle. "A valid point. Still, I trained men who did not survive their encounter with the enemy. I failed them." He knotted the hand he had resting on his thigh.

"And there will be more who'll die if Lara takes us to war, and it won't be your fault. My da always said that if you shake the apple tree, you'd better be prepared to have fruit, good and rotten, fall on your head."

"My sister does things for reasons she doesn't always explain. She sees things, I hope, that we can't."

"Her magic?"

"Maybe. Maybe it's just her training and instincts. My grandfather trained her to be a warrior. I trained to be a forester and a hunter. I can teach archers, but I can't instill battle into them. She wants me to teach more, as if being able to use a bow and arrow will be enough."

"Remember my mother's tailoring shop? There are those who spin thread. Those who weave it into patterned cloth. And, then there are those who take that cloth and cut and tailor it into dresses, curtains, cloaks, sashes. Are you asking me to measure their worth? Each depends on the other, don't you think?"

"Are Dwellers always so down to earth?"

"Whenever we're not in a tree." Nutmeg hugged herself against a touch of wind that reached her despite the grove that sheltered the gardens. "I came to tell you to come in."

"Thank you. I will, soon." Jeredon turned his head to face her for the first time since they'd begun exchanging words. "There will be many of us together again, soon."

Nutmeg thought of the convening of Vaelinars she'd observed in Calcort, to discuss their treaties and differences, and to hear petitions from those of Kerith who had been wronged or displaced, or thought they had been, by the arrival of the invaders. Those days, and the blazing hot summer, and her family's new beginning in a city rather than the far-flung orchards of her youth, seemed far behind. There were many of the Vaelinars she did not particularly care for. She'd seen many of the noblewomen who'd come to her mother's small tailoring shop. They'd been grateful for the trade, and while the Vaelinars did not have the inbred arrogance of the Galdarkans, sometimes they had been shrewish or sly. There was something about them a practical Dweller did not wish to trust.

"We will be convening at Hawthorne," Jeredon continued.

She sucked in a breath sharply. The grand city of the western lands? Far bigger than even Calcort, she'd heard, a city built on an island, connected by many bridges of architectural wonder to the mainland.

"There will be much to see, Nutmeg."

"I'm going?"

"I doubt any of us could leave you behind. However . . ." and his eyes of green and gray and gold took a measure of her. "There will be no more scolding. You've nursed me and I am grateful, but you have to mind now that I'm the queen's brother, and her heir in this, and one of her commanders."

It took a moment for her to think upon it, that she would go with Rivergrace, and that she would see things many a Dweller had never thought to look upon . . . the great sea, where the Shield of Tomarq ruled over the never-ending waves . . . that his words did not sink in at first. Then she realized he was taking her to task for her care of him, and her face flushed warmly. "You want me to act like the servant I am."

"No." He put his hand out and caught hers, untucking it from her apron. He had held his warmth in the chill of the night and his touch felt comforting. "You're a lady at Lara's court, never forget that. Nor what we had. But you cannot treat me like . . . as if you were a laundry maid and I a bundle of old clothes."

"I don't treat you like that!"

"Oh, aye, but you do! Slap me about in hot water and bump me up against a washboard, all the while telling me it's good for me, and it's what I need." He took a deep breath. "I walk, and soon I'll have the strength to stay on my feet."

"Yes, but I've heard the healers as well as you have. I don't mean to be understanding all they've said, but you've been bruised badly and deeply and it will take time for the healing. Rush it, and you may lose what you long for. Like the merest babe, you cannot just get to your feet and run! You've got to creep about first and then stand slowly and—"

"Hold that damned Dweller tongue! I do what I can, and what I must. I can't spend a season or two swimming about. I haven't the time!" His hand closed tightly about hers. "And you can't be arguing with me about it. I will do what I will, and you've got to abide by that."

Nutmeg bit her lip. She knew she must have taken on the look that her recalcitrant cart pony Bumblebee often did, for Jeredon's own eyes narrowed.

"Have we an agreement?" he said.

As if she could stand by and watch him undo himself. "Have we, Nutmeg?"

With her free hand still under her apron, she made a sign of warding which any of her brothers could have told him meant that she was going to lie and was sending the bad luck out of it, and she nodded. Her hair tumbled about her face, and she tossed it back.

"Good, then. And now for the hard part. You can't be looking at me like that."

"Like what?"

He sighed. A sadness crept into his expression. "I'm Vaelinar, lass, and you're Dweller. You can't be hoping what you hope. It's not possible for there to be anything stronger between us—"

She snatched her hand away and said hotly, "It's a wonder you can sit up, let alone stand wi' a head filled with stone as yours! Good evening to you, m'lord Jeredon. I'd wish you sweet dreams, but it's clear your thick head is already filled with them!" And she turned abruptly and left him before he could say another word.

At the kitchen door, she put her sleeve to her face to catch any hot tears that might have spilled free, before bolting into the house and up the shaded part of the stairs, her heart thumping wildly which told her that that, at least, hadn't broken.

She found no need to creep quietly into Rivergrace's rooms, as they were empty, and the hot bath she'd drawn cooling down unused. She turned down the quilts, made herself ready for bed, and crawled into the center, where she usually slept. Grace, when she came in, would take one side or the other. If she came in. Nutmeg let out a long, quivery sigh and gave herself to sleep.

Beyond the reach of the great manor house and the stables and mews and outbuildings, beyond the touch of anything Vaelinar built in the heart of Larandaril, her feet came to a halt on the bank of the Andredia River. She sank to her knees and then lay on her stomach as if she were that small child again who used to sneak out of the loft of the Farbranch homestead and go down to the Silverwing and trail her fingers through the waters. Little enough light to see herself in the Andredia as it rushed by, little enough light to see that it was a river and not a stream of ever-deepening shadows, little enough light to reveal anything to her that she might ask of it. River-grace put her hands in, feeling the push and pull of the cold water, the silken flow of it about her skin. She could feel the ice in it from the mountains, the silt carried in it from the lands it passed through, the promise of life and the promise of unknowing strength when it should begin to flood. The Silverwing had always held an awareness of her, on some deep and primitive level. This river did not seem to know her although she had freed it from foul corruption at its font. She did not expect that it would. Water was not a creature that roamed the world, it was a force within and without the world that shaped, often careless of its effect.

Hands numbing from the cold, she decided to pull free. The river rose about her fingers and tugged back, holding her as tightly as if she'd been fastened into ice. Grace crept back on her stomach, arms stretching, and hands unmoving.

A moment of panic flashed through her. She could feel the river as if it had hands of its own, holding onto her tightly, dragging her down to its shore, determined to pull her in. She got to her knees to brace herself. The mossy bank gave her little purchase. Too much of a struggle and she would tumble in headfirst. The Andredia swallowed her arms to her elbows and greedily sucked up her bare skin for more. Head down, being drawn in, she saw then that a silvery luminescence filled the river and hands did indeed grip hers, hands of flesh that never warmed, hands the temperature of the water itself, hands that would refuse to let her go.

Give it up.

The voice without a throat of the River Goddess flooded her mind. *Give it up. Return to me what is mine. Come to me, if you would, be one with me.*

Heedless, Rivergrace fought back. She had nothing belonging to the Goddess, and nothing she wanted lay at the bottom of that riverbed. She twisted and turned her arms in the manacle hold of the being which pulled her, bit by bit, fighting into the depths. Her thoughts, invaded, spun in a maelstrom about her. The solace, the cleansing of the water became a murderous sinkhole sucking her into it. That which had cocooned and protected her for unknown years now actively sought to drown her, to destroy her. What could she give the River Goddess? She had nothing, nothing but mortality, and that she knew the other did not want. She'd kept nothing from the immortal being who'd shredded her down to the last fiber of her flesh and soul before reweaving her. Yet, it was not enough. The other wanted more. Of what, she did not know and could not offer. Choking and clawing at the water, Rivergrace fought back. Anger and frustration battered her mind and soul as the Goddess drew her down into the water.

When the chill splashed her face and water seeped into her nose, Rivergrace reared backward with a strength born out of sheer terror, gasping for breath. Her arms wrenched free, aching with bitter cold, the pull gone so suddenly she sat back on her rump. Lurid marks ringed her wrists and fingers. Chafing her hands, she staggered to her feet and away from the Andredia. The howls of dismay, of comfort and threat, of longing and want, followed her as she retreated. The river splashed up against the crumbling bank in a curtain of white foam and drops, splattering her. With each drop that hit, a stinging word beat at her mind. *Return. Come back. Mine. Give it up. Stay with me.*

Rivergrace turned away from the river and ran, wobbling with numbing cold and drenched from her nose to her toes, as the river ... or perhaps now it was the wind ... howled after her. What was she that her very life offended and threatened the divinity of Kerith? She had had her bloodline and heritage torn away from her. What more did the Goddess intend to take from her?

Trembling from the violent cold encasing her, River-grace stumbled up to her rooms and stood by the banked fire, hoping to thaw herself out. The flames seemed to sense her need and licked upward from the coals, re-newing themselves without being stirred or her needing to add more kindling. She shed her clothes into a sodden heap on the floor, dried her hair, and then slid into bed, hoping that she would not awaken Nutmeg.

Futile. When her still cold feet grazed the warmth of her sister, Nutmeg's eyes flew open. "Grace!"

"Ssssh. Go back to sleep."

Her soft admonishment, which used to work when they were very young, didn't. Nutmeg put her arm out and drew her close, her warmth blanketing both of them, her crisp chemise crinkling as she did.

"Your hair is still damp. How can you stand it? The river is so cold in winter."

"It clears my mind." Then the fear, the disappoint-ment, stirred in her. Rivergrace began to cry, softly, un-bidden. Nutmeg stroked her hair, braiding it gently so that it would not greet the morning in untamed curls.

"What happened?"

"The river tried to take me," she managed, putting her forehead to Nutmeg's nightgown. "The bank gave way and it swallowed me up, wouldn't let me go. It was as though it had hands and was determined to drag me under! I've never been afraid of drowning before. I've always gone to the river, always."

"I know, Sister, I know."

She swallowed tightly. "I never thought I would find water that did not lift me up or cleanse me."

Nutmeg's hands slowed as she cajoled Grace's hair into obedience. She could hear the sadness, the forlorn note, in her sister's voice, and echoed it. "I never thought I wouldn't be able to climb a tree tall enough to get me close to my dreams."

"What is going to happen to us?"

Her sister's voice, muffled and thinned, in answer.

"I don't know. But I do know that fearing it won't make it any easier or cause it to go away. The river gave you to me, and by all the water drops on Kerith, it's not taking you back. You have my word as a daughter of Tolby and Lily Farbranch on that. We Dwellers have strong roots."

WINTER SUN, BRILLIANT BUT PALE and brittle as if it might shatter in the cold, streamed in across the hearths of Larandaril. Song greeted the early risers as Bistane straddled one of the kitchen chairs dragged into the dining room, all doors flung open to allow his melody passage. Nutmeg heard it as she scampered down the stairs in hunger. His voice rolled in a merry tune that belied its words.

> "... *Proud Nylara River holds her dead most dear*
> *Only the Ferryman can cross her tempest bed*
> *Wrapped in shadow but casting none,*
> *Boatman who alone can tame her shores.*
> *But oh, no one passes without a toll, a toll*
> *No one fails to pay the price.*"

She stopped at the bottom stair, looking back over her shoulder, wondering if she should warn Rivergrace or if the other would even pay heed to Bistane. With a shrug, she decided that a hot breakfast was more important, her stomach growling in agreement, and Nutmeg scurried into the kitchens to grab a trencher of whatever she could find. Almiva, one of the younger cooks, her hair held back in wispy brunette strands, her face dewy with the heat from the ovens, ladled a coddled egg out for Nutmeg. "Listen to that man," she said. "Rode in late last night after days on the road, and up this morning warbling like a songbird. Ought to be a poet that one, not a warlord." She paused, head cocked, to catch another word or two before waving Nutmeg on. Bistane held a steaming mug and saluted her as she passed to grab a seat at a nearby table. The aromas of her meal wafted up to make her mouth water as she gathered up her spoon and fell to eating.

She'd heard Bistane sing at Spring fairs and Midsummer balls, his magnificent voice filling grand halls, and he did it because he loved it. He had no audience now but herself and one or two other early eaters, and the kitchen staff which hung back near their ovens and pots and pantries, listening when they could around the bustle of their morning chores. Even for all the Vaelinars in this manor, he was handsome. His eyes blazed dark and light blue, and his hair was charcoal black, with a soft glistening to its tied-back waves and a deep blue cast to the darkness. His father's hair held that same blueness, deep in its white. They were both, like the war hawks from which they took their lineage and name, the Vantane, fierce and yet direct. The music, the poetry in Bistane, could be heard in his singing as well as seen in the way he walked and the way he wielded his weapons. A little shiver danced across the back of Nutmeg's neck as she realized this.

"In Hawthorne they tell this tale in whispers
Of a pretty lass with skin snow pale and berry-stained
*   lips*
The healers foretold a strange destiny

Of short-lived years unless she found true love
And so her family looked to make her a wife

Her family could not bear to hear it said,
But no one wanted to gain a love just to lose her,
Until a Kernan from the north answered their plea,
He'd love her till her last breath and not just for
*   money*
Yet she looked into eyes that promised only lies."

She thought of great and grand Hawthorne where
Grand Mayor Randall lived and ruled these western
provinces. A magnificent city, built on an island, with
bridges that connected it to the shore, and she wondered
what it might be like there. Rumor said that Lariel intended the war council to convene there, and if it did,
she might be going there in a week or so. She would
have to keep a sharp eye out for what the citizens wore,
and if the fabrics held bold patterns and colors, and then
send word to her mother of what she'd seen. Rivergrace
would be aghast at seeing the great sea. She'd seen it
once herself, and it had made her knees weak even as
her ears filled with the sound of its roaring waves. She
fell to daydreaming as Bistane sang on.

"She begged not to leave them, that his vows weren't
*   true*
But they hugged good-bye, telling her he meant best
She kissed them farewell as her life was sold.
With dowry purse sealed, the husband steered her
*   down the road*
Impatient for home across the wide and furious
*   Nylara."*

Someone with a voice that bordered on coarse yet me-
lodious sang loud enough that his guild office filled with

the noise, and Bregan Oxfort gritted his teeth against the interruption and sat with his hand covering his left ear, but he could not mute it enough. The slanting winter sun came streaking into the room, setting his leg brace on metallic fire even as it did little to actually warm the limb. The song put him in a foul mood, but it was everywhere on the city streets this season and now some trader had brought a troubadour into the guildhall salon and he could not even escape it here.

"Oh, you stay at the banks till he's good and ready,
For the Ferryman knows he rules that shore
The wild Nylara answers only to his barge and him.
Only the worthy can board his boats, and
He'll take the measure of your cargo and soul
The weight of your very soul, your soul,
Oh, the weight of your soul."

The grinding of his teeth did little to drown out the cursed song either, nor did the scratching of his pen on the papers he glared down at. Bregan lifted his gaze, looking out the glazed windows at the nearby span, one of the Seven Sisters which bound Hawthorne to the mainland. Built by common hands, the Kernans and the Dwellers and the Galdarkans, wonders of engineering that the Vaelinars could not lay claim to. One of the few, but all the same, his people could claim it, and any time one wanted to dispute who ruled these provinces, he could point out the city of Hawthorne even on a wintry day like this, when forbidding clouds swept in from the sea, heavy with threatening rain. For half a crown, he'd forgo the bridge and swim to shore if it meant he could get away from the tune.

A knock came at the door. He pulled his attention away from the bridge long enough to bark out permission to enter. An apprentice pulled the door open wide enough for his long thin face and long hooked nose to peer in at him, letting the room flood with sound from the nearby tavern singer. His anger must have showed, for the apprentice broke into a series of nervous, almost petrified coughs rather than spit out what he had come for.

Bregan waited as long as his short temper allowed before growling, "Either tell me or leave."

"Your father, Master. He sent this." The apprentice held up his shaking hand.

"Toss it here, then and get out." He didn't intend to hear another lyric about the abusive suitor and his poor downtrodden bride who was all but dead from his care of her by the time they reached the Nylara. The apprentice managed to drop the bundle of letters in his lap amid another fit of coughing before bowing and backing out as the singer revealed the husband's deciding to cross the Nylara without the Ferryman and his goods-laden barge being tossed on waves as it swamped and the Ferryman watching as he and his bride began to sink.

The door shut. It could not totally muffle the relentless singer as the heartless husband offered the life of his bride for passage across the river, and the Ferryman accepted. The irony of it was that his acceptance saved her soul even as it doomed that of her husband, but the girl hardly cared by then as she passed into the shadowy immortality of the phantom Ferryman. Shouts accompanied the gods be praised, last verse.

> *"The banks of the Nylara are in stormy tide,*
> *Passing o'er the river looks grim*
> *There's no one crossing from side to side*
> *We're all a-waiting on him*
> *He'll come when he's ready and not a whit sooner,*
> *For the Ferryman's taken a wife, a wife,*
> *Oh, the Ferryman's taken a wife!"*

Bregan popped open the waxed sealing string on the packet. Several notes from his father fell open, as if the man could not confine all his thoughts to just one letter.

Actually, as was his wont, each missive probably concerned a single topic. It made for ease of concentration among his underlings and for record keeping, and even though it was his son whom he addressed, Willard Oxfort was not likely to change decades of dictating habit. Also, it was likely at least one of these letters had not been copied for the files and archives and had been meant for his eyes alone. The smell of the wax was still new, meaning his father had probably written these no later than last night and possibly even this morning.

Bregan tapped the letters open with an unhappy grunt. The old man could sit in his gentleman's estates, retired from everything but meddling while he still rode the caravan trails as well as handling the politicking his father set out for him to do. Meanwhile, actual leadership of the various traders' guilds was kept dangling just out of his reach like so much bait by the elder Oxfort. When he had proved himself, the mantle would be settled on his shoulders. Proved himself! Did the brace he wore mean nothing? He would have had the old man assassinated years ago except that, unfortunately, it seemed he still had a thing or two to learn from Willard Oxfort. His gaze fell on the letters in his lap.

One of those things seemed necessary to be learned at the lunching hour. He glanced at the small timepiece on his desk, a thing of extraordinary gears and water flow that needed to be turned but once a day, at the darkest hour. He had apprentices who would come in and do the chore, although he was often working that late himself, if not on the roads. If he took a carriage, he could make the lane of the Gods by the time indicated. He shoved that paper to the side and read the other notations sent him. One involved the marketing of forged items by various Bolger clans and if one might benefit by getting them to elect or assign a three-man council to unify the bargaining process or not. The last detailed a possible new trade route east which would undercut one of the Elven Ways, thereby

saving on tolls and permits, although the road would
be exceedingly rough going at first, having not been established or trekked. Willard thought armored caravan
beasts might make their way through the undergrowth
to help establish the route, and did Bregan have any
input on the matter?

He dropped that last with a sigh and rubbed his eyes.
He had worked the last two decades of his life trying to
find a way to skirt the spiderweb of Vaelinar influence
that cobbled the lands together. Much easier hoped for
than done. The scarring of the southern and eastern
lands by the Mageborn Wars left gaping holes in the firmament, not only of the land itself but of the atmosphere
about it. The very wind could not be counted upon, nor
the waters, for the elements themselves had been turned
and corrupted. Ofttimes, only the Ways could skirt those
lands safely, or if not a true Way, only a road laid down
by the Vaelinars. He hated that, hated it far more than
that despicable Dweller song about the Ferryman of the
Nylara. And the Ferryman, who'd taken the youth from
his body and the strength of his limbs, he hated with
every fiber of his being.

He kicked his leg aside and stood, the brace moving
with an oiled smoothness to cage his weakness. Kerith
belonged to those born of Kerith, placed by the creating hands of the Gods to inhabit these lands, but the
Vaelinars were like an insidious parasitic plant that
managed to seed itself into every crack and entwine itself upon every living thing it could possibly feed upon.
If it were up to him, he'd kill them off one by one, quietly but surely, but it was not. And, indeed, that would be
an insanity even he could not carry out. Quendius was
another matter. Bregan was not certain what Quendius
had in mind ultimately, but for the moment, he wanted
to see an ending to the Ways as much as Bregan did.
That made him a useful ally. He wondered if his father
held his own alliances with Quendius, cutting Bregan
out of his own future.

He glanced at the clever clockworks again. Opening the door to his offices, he gave a shout for a horse as he grabbed his cape, and he could hear the apprentices scattering on the landing below him to do his bidding. He could hear threats echoing in the stable yard as underlings scurried. He would not throttle the lad who did not have his horse ready by the time he strode into the guild yards, although he had the temper to do so. No. The lads were not responsible for his unhappiness, and they would not, for the moment, bear the brunt of it. Quendius had spoken to Willard only of smugglers, and as of this moment, he was still uncertain of what ultimate outcome had been planned for him. Was he to have been assassinated by those who waited and were driven off by Daravan and his lackey? Or was there to have been a historic meeting, corrupted and befouled by Daravan as only a Vaelinar can twist happenings? Did he trust Quendius or not? And that, he supposed, was the ultimate crux of the matter. That Quendius had come to him, a sly whisper on the night wind, was undeniable, and yet Bregan supposed it would be too much to assume the man held as much contempt for the Vaelinars as Oxfort did. Far too much.

A horse waited for him, one of the hot-blooded elven breed, and Bregan curled his lip as he mounted it. The nervous beast danced a side step or two as he bent down to make sure his right boot fit the stirrup properly. The feeling in the leg came and went, and he'd learned the hard way that he could not ride well if the leg had gone into one of its numb spells. Today he could feel pins and needles, but that did not reassure him. The arm did not need to be braced, although he could no longer use it with the strength and accuracy he had before. No matter. His sword fit his other hand equally and lethally well. He turned the mare out of the guild yard, flipped a coin to the stable lad who looked the most hot and mussed and had probably done most of the work (or the yelling), and headed onto the public streets.

The mare stretched her legs in a long-striding walk, her head up and ears flipping back and forth to catch the sounds on the city streets. He could smell hot wax, cooking fish, and the salt of the sea. As they moved closer through the trade and market streets toward the small row of temples, the aroma of incense grew stronger. The horse flared her nostrils at the unfamiliar odors. Some smelled sweet and others pungent and still others downright unpleasant, the last meant to keep away the spirits of the deceased Mageborn who had brought a downfall to all the Gods and temples and believers. He had little faith in anything that held sway on Temple Row; he'd seen much in his years on the road that influenced his judgment of mortal flesh. He slowed his mount down as the streets grew crowded, and even the riding lane filled with the jostle of bodies, all it seemed, intent on going the same way he was. The thought passed through his mind that he ought to turn back; he disliked crowds, and he could see nothing here of any use to him, despite his father's instructions. There would be an interrogation later, as always, if he had done as bidden by his father, yet that did not influence his decision one way or the other. He simply took a shorter hold on the reins to calm the mare as they pressed onward. It was his own curiosity, the interest in what his father might be thinking about, and what profit might be had by this visit that kept him going.

From the growing press of flesh about him, Bregan thought he might have forgotten an observance day. He searched his mind for a religious rite that might explain the growing numbers descending upon Temple Row and could not find one. Yet here they were, flooding toward the Row, their lunches carried in sacks or gripped in their hands, meats still steaming, juices dribbling onto the paving stones where dogs darted in and out among the crowds to lick up the goodness. He caught words and breathless phrases over the jumble of noise and clatter of horse hooves. One of the priests was going to speak, one who had a reputation for fiery rhetoric and insight-fulness and just plain entertainment, one who promised to cast enlightenment on recent Events and Omens. Bregan stifled his disgust at the thought of being forced to stand in one of the squares and listen to inflammatory talk, but the assignment might have its possibilities. There was always trade in fear: goods for protection and retribution against that which might attack you. Even if reason should prevail, the short market should be profitable.

Letting his senses guide him to the square teeming with activity and anticipation, he forced the mare into the crowd, making his way to a corner where he would have good access to the oratory and be able to cut through a nearby narrow lane to leave quickly if he so desired. That lane now held little traffic, being out of the way and not nearly wide enough to accommodate more than a person or two at a time, and the flow of listeners into the Row coming from much easier directions. He held his riding whip in his right hand. There was no need for tremendous speed or accuracy to protect himself with that; it was mostly to keep the opportunists away from himself and his mount. He could feel people sizing him up and, wisely, turning away. He noted the Town Guard lining up around the edges of the square, their red-and-gold tabards quite visible among the more drab colors of the crowd.

It was then, too, he realized that he saw no Vaelinars, veiled or otherwise, among the onlookers. Likewise, no Bolgers—who commonly skulked around the edges of the city—could be seen anywhere. Not being seen did not mean there were no elven about, but the Bolgers lacked that sort of discretion and freedom of movement in the towns. In the countryside, that was another matter altogether. A flurry of activity rippled by one of the temples and he saw tall, thin Kernan emerge, flanked by young apprentices. They wore light blue and light green, with a silvery border, and he could not for the life

of him remember what God or Gods that symbolized.
This man, not a youth but showing no true lines of age
on his face, thin to the point of being spindly, with hair
of nondescript brown bound back with leather thongs so
tightly that it left his hooked nose to be his only promi-
nent and interesting feature, stood between two youths
wearing green and silver. Did he look as if he waited to
be noticed? Bregan watched him closely. No. He looked
more as if he were steeling himself. A reluctant prophet?
Or one as yet unused to and unsure of his effect on his
people?

His mare snorted as someone brushed her hindquarters and he flicked his riding whip that way, cracking the
air, a warning to give them distance. A muttered curse
and a stumble followed. The horse flicked her ears before quieting. As she settled, so did the crowd, but only
because the Kernan priest raised his hands, palms out to
them. A hush settled over the square, packed shoulder
to shoulder with listeners, with only a pocket or two of
exception. Bregan sat his mount in one such area.

The two youths in green and silver set down vases
filled with incense sticks and knelt, lighting them quickly.
They stayed on their knees. The priest waited until thin
blue-gray smoke curled from every one of the herbal
sticks before clearing his throat.

Not a good voice, Bregan thought, when the other
began. He wouldn't be heard by most of his audience.
The next few moments proved him wrong as the man
began to talk, his words growing more powerful and
distinct with every breath. Bregan scanned the people
about him, listening. Acoustics of the square. Of course.
The great speaking rooms at the guild were built for
such, and he should have recognized it when he saw it.
As cobbled together as Temple Row seemed, it was anything but. Every architectural feature here from shrine
to temple to shrine down the Row had been placed deliberately. Coincidence, then, that this priest emerged
from a temple facing the square most propitious for such

talks? He did not think so. If he did, he'd be an even greater fool than the enthralled common folks about him. They paused, sack lunches in their hands, fistfuls of food halfway to their mouths, caught up by his words.

As for what the priest said, it held no deep meaning for him. The spindly man merely recounted recent events that any tale-spinner at a toback shop might tell. Bregan quickly lost interest in his words and surveyed the listeners instead, wondering what it was his father had wished him to observe.

Then he heard it. Words caught his attention like heavy rocks dropped into a still pond. "The Gods are bending close to us again. They will speak as they have spoken to us in centuries past, voices to guide us and to punish us. This I know for a certainty, because I have heard their whispers. Surely they will get louder! Surely they will return to thunder in our ears! We must prepare to listen. We must brace ourselves to be chastised before we will be led by them again. Are you ready?"

A blending of voices called back, echoing among the buildings and columns, shouts of joy and fear and derision. Did they believe him? They must. They pushed and shoved against one another now, lifted small children among them to their shoulders to hear better, pointed and shouted. Lunches forgotten, hooded cloaks against the promised rain pushed back to see better, bodies crushing closer to hear better as if this priest knew for a certainty what they had only dared hope.

How, after all these centuries, could they believe?

A better question, Bregan thought, as he reined his now nervous mare close. How could they not? How could any people stand forever as forgotten, shunned? How could they persevere against that without hope that they would one day be forgiven?

What day would the Gods speak? The tall priest did not know, but it would be soon. The judgment was upon all of them, even as the Warrior Queen built her troops for a war that would envelop them all. She would be

called to the Court of Gods as all of them would be, accountable for her deeds against Kerith. The Gods had
been watching the Strangers and come to a decision
about them, and their trial would be at hand along with
all the other peoples of Kerith.

The moment of clarity faded for Bregan, as his
thoughts raced ahead, tumbling over one another with
an eagerness he had not felt in years. He could use this
building tide. Oh, yes. This fervor could be used.

He put a heel to his mare, reining her out of the crowd,
moving slowly for the listeners still stood in rapt attention, their faces uplifted to the speaking priest, and he
ducked her out of the way along that narrow, ill-used
lane. He looked back once.

And saw, in the shadowy threshold of the temple behind the priest, a visage. He should not have seen it. He
knew he was not expected to. What man would expect to
be noticed in shadows the color of his sooty skin?

Quendius stood listening, as well.

The clouds opened up. A spattering of fat, heavy, and
cold raindrops began to fall. It would be a deluge in
a handful of moments, dispersing the crowd far more
quickly than the Town Guard could. Bregan put his whip
to his mare, then, to urge her down the lane and away
as quickly as possible before his attention had been noticed. He did not want those flint-dark eyes to look his
way.

LARIEL SAT IN A QUIET ALCOVE of her rooms, a small retreat built to overlook the gardens from a corner of her apartments. From its windows, she could see the Andredia below, a bright blue-and-silver ribbon among the greenery of Larandaril. Even winter frost hardly touched here, although it did, and would, despite the evergreens which flourished everywhere, and the winter grasses which the wind sowed prodigiously and which even the rodents and grazers could never quite keep cropped down. Here was a land which the harshest of seasons might never touch more than briefly. The only seasons which affected it were those of man, and the deadliest one of war loomed now on the country's borders. It had already survived a season of plague, and she wondered how resilient her country could be.

Those boundaries threatening to be breached lived and breathed with the magic that was Larandaril as well as the land itself. No one crossed them unless one of the Anderieon blood gave them free passage. She was safe here as she could be nowhere else, and yet she knew it could be an illusion. Had not her friend and confidante, Tiiva, the last heir of House Pantoreth held the keys to this manor for decades, and still planned her death? Had attempted it once in Calcort through the assassin Kobrir and attempted it a second time through Quendius, Narskap, and the great sword Cerat? What safety remained for Lara, then, if not here?

Despite seeking, Lariel had not yet found the fled Tiiva Pantoreth. Death and betrayal still awaited her from that source. Lara gave a dry chuckle. *Join the crowd*, she thought wryly. *May you all have a very long wait.*

Still, although the thought of her death weighed on her, it didn't weigh as heavily as concern for her lands and the people she tried to protect. That, she supposed, was as it should be.

She had other business to attend. Lara put her hands palm down on her knees, and took in a deep breath, preparing herself. A momentary distraction caught her attention as she took in the missing digit on her left hand, the purpled scar at the point of amputation, and then she dismissed it. A scar only in the sense that it disrupted that which others called beauty, but a trifle to be considered in the overall scheme of things. She had been trained to be a warrior, and the toll of such a life came in scars and maiming, more to be feared than the loss of life. To be maimed meant she might live but without the ability to act as she chose. This was a warrior's legacy, and the only one she shrank from. If she could find a Way, she would have it be the one which led to victory without the fight, before the battle, a subjugation or compromise of wills before the massacre of bodies. Such a Way would be worth universes.

She took in a second deep breath, willing away the sight before her eyes, and looking inward, centering on that which rested inside of her, waiting to be called forth. This, one of the least of her abilities, and yet at times one of the most valuable, was to extend herself into the senses of another, giving her vision where most could not see, knowledge which might otherwise take days or even weeks to gain. She worked at plucking the threads of the living things she sought, bridging them to hers. She had not the ability to twine them together for more than a few moments, but that would be all she needed. Whether now, when she sought to look through the eyes of flesh, or later when she sought to anticipate the actions of another, moments were all she had to touch and learn and plan her own decisions. It worked the same with lesser or greater beings.

Hawks loosed against the dimming sky, like arrows shot into the horizon. She'd ordered them sent out and seen them taking wing, and she linked her memory of that moment with their passage now. Hawks winged their way to the northeast, across Hith-aryn where the aryn trees blotted out the hillsides and fenced off the wide-ranging fields of grain against the wilderness of the blighted and scarred areas left by the Magi. She could hear the beat of wings against her ears, feel the pulse of strain rush in her bloodstream, see the land below as they banked in tandem, drawing near their destination. She could feel the crisp early winter wind like a tide carrying their flights, bearing them, coasting when wings had grown weary but the destination was in view. The lord of the aryns would have them in a moment, unrolling the message she had sent, the ripple of destiny come his way. Bistel had already sent Bistane to them in anticipation, but this would be her formal declaration and call for mustering.

Lariel's breath fluttered in her throat. She closed her eyes, wiping away the brilliantly colored view of Hith-aryn, and pulled to herself the senses of other hawks, wings outspread, as they spanned the forests of the north over the libraries and lands of D'Ferstanthe. She could see through the eyes of the bird the vibrant colors of the northern forests, the streams flowing with ice-cold waters and lumber being sent downstream, chimney smoke rising from the many scattered cottages and, as they neared their destination, even the image of a great, lumbering giant of a Vaelinar came out into the courtyard to look upward at them. Azel d'Stanthe in his usual robes of indigo, broad shouldered with a bit of a girth at his belt, glasses glinting in a beam of sunlight escaping the clouds which had been rumbling in from the north all day. Lara could see his eyes on the birds, see his lips purse, and hear a sharp whistle pierce the air which caught the hawks' attention and brought them swooping in lower.

Another message delivered.

She shook herself lightly. She forced herself northwest, to the harsh coastline and countryside where Stronghold ild Fallyn reigned. Only one hawk flew here, meaning that the other had been lost somewhere along the way, faltered, or perhaps even died in the effort. When the sharp fortress walls came into view, Lara made a noise of disdain and broke her contact. Lara did not stay with this hawk long enough to see the wild beauty of Tressandre ild Fallyn as she moved off the parapet to call down the hawk to her wrist, where sharp eyes would meet an even sharper and more predatory gaze of verdant green flecked with smoky gray and leaf green.

Southward to the cliffs surrounding the bay where the Shield of Tomarq reigned, she found herself already hooded and in jesses in the tower of the Istlanthirs and Drebukar, message scroll already taken and delivered. Blinking against the enforced darkness, she found one last hawk body to will herself into, wings wearied by a long flight eastward . . . and found herself falling in pain and confusion from the sky. Wings beating, she flailed against the ground until firm hands enfolded her, stilling the wings and drawing them close to her body, drawing the arrow from one wing and straightening it gently. Hawk eye sharp, she looked into the tattooed face of Abayan Diort.

With a hiss, Lara burst away, drawing her soul back,

heart beating as wildly as that of the injured bird, the feel of the man's wide and strong yet gentle hands still upon her. She heard his firm voice coax the bird into heeding his attentions as he freed the arrow and cupped the wings to its sides, letting it know that no further harm would come to it, should it settle in his hands. The hawk would struggle but another moment before succumbing to the commanding nature of the Galdarkan who held it. Lariel wrenched free of the bridge she'd built. She spat to one side. With another hiss and shake, Lara got to her feet, leaning on the window's frame. She had not revealed much in the letters she'd had sent, but Diort would undoubtedly know and understand. He had taken the bait.

Without having a Way into peace, she would settle for a trap.

She took a deep breath and rose to her feet, putting her chin up, preparing to go downstairs and talk with the others to begin a war.

She never got in a second breath before the vision took her and swept her up.

Abayan Diort faced her. They crossed blades and he threw her back on her heels, keeping his block across his chest, the sword glinting silver in her eyes. And behind him . . . oh, behind him lay an opening to a land that called out to her, a land of such indescribable beauty that her throat stilled even though her heart thumped wildly in her chest and *he held her away from it*. Home. She knew it had to be home and that a Way had wondrously opened onto it and this man, this arrogant Galdarkan denied her.

Lara shuddered as the vision fled as suddenly as it had come upon her. She lifted her hands to her face to stop their shaking and to clear her eyes. The incident filled her with resolve. The clearest vision that had come to her yet, and it stiffened her spine. Bistane had refused the position which Osten now filled, but if he could have seen this through her eyes, he would know why she must

stop Diort in his tracks. He stood between them and all
that they hoped for most dearly. She could not allow
that, any more than she could allow him to distract her
from the enemy which would come from the western
sea.

She stood up slowly as her breathing steadied. She
saw her path clearly.

"It's the middle of the day. I thought this sort of thing demanded blood in the dark of night." Quendius squinted
at the tower's shutters which had been thrown open for
the sunlight even as he mused that once again the servant had sent for the master.

Narskap canted him a look part annoyance and part
fear, rather like a skittish wild pony about to bolt away
before sizing him up as a threat. "You are safer with the
sun at its brightest."

Quendius waved away Narskap's concern. "We do
it whenever the time is best for the most fortunate
outcome."

"That time is now. All preparations are ready." Narskap put a hand to the table where he had a longbow
shaped and waiting to be strung and four arrow shafts
waiting to be fletched and finished.

"The wood is seasoned already?"

"I swallowed a God of fire long ago," Narskap said
wearily. "Kilns are not a problem. The wood is dried to
my satisfaction." He picked up a very sharp knife, the
blade long, thin, and slightly curved, a flensing knife. He
could draw far more than blood from Quendius, and
quickly, if he wished.

Quendius flexed his arm thoughtfully before present-
ing it to Narskap. They both knew that if Narskap and
his knife slipped but a notch, he would be dead before
Quendius bled out, a left-handed dagger through his
eye. He did not hold it, but he didn't have to, it rested

in his wrist sheath and it would spring into his hand the moment he needed it. They had a mutual respect for one another's abilities, but also Quendius believed in not trusting anyone. Narskap washed his instrument in some tolerably good liquor that he poured from the jug, and he poured a shot over Quendius' proffered arm as well. Then, quickly, he sliced into the blue-veined surface to bring blood gushing to the fore and twisted the arm in his hold to let the crimson splash over the bow, shaft and arrowheads lying in wait upon the table. Then he took a clean rag and knotted it quickly about Quendius' wound.

Without another word, he squatted by the low table and began to make the arrows. Quendius waited a long moment before saying, "That was it?"

Frowning, Narskap looked up. "Did you expect more? Shall I bring a Bolger shaman in here to grunt and shake things about and burn odious herbs?"

"I only wondered if your Gods needed a bit more ceremony."

"Ceremony." Narskap rolled the word about his mouth as he said it. "No. The only thing they require of you is a taste." He returned his attention to the shaft in his hand, fletching the flights to it with quick and sure movements.

"Basic creatures, the Gods are."

"They know what you are, and what you are not," Narskap said, his tone now absent, his attention upon the arrow he crafted. "And through them, I know." His gaze flickered up, eyes intent again. "I know that you are not wholly Vaelinar."

Quendius shifted his weight. He had killed men for thinking far less than that, and he sifted through the options in his mind as they fell like sand through a primitive timepiece. Narskap had looked away again, immersed in his work by the time he'd reached a decision. He did not trust Narskap more than he trusted any other man, for Quendius trusted no one at all, but he knew his tools,

and Narskap was the best he'd ever used. One did not
break or allow a tool to rust needlessly. The wind picked
up outside and whistled inside in a thin, faint piping. The
work would be done shortly, the glue dried and the string
wound tightly, and then the bow itself must be strung.
He wondered if Narskap would do it or summon him
again. He wasn't sure if Narskap still had the strength
needed to bend the longbow into accepting the string-
ing. It would be in tune with the irony he felt: that the
Gods had given Narskap the ability to make a weapon
he could not use, just as they had given him knowledge
that he did not wish. Quendius balled his hand into a
fist. He had known for years what he was not, but never
what he *was*. Good tools were difficult to replace. The
thought stayed his action.

Quendius turned abruptly and left the tower. He had
other tools in place that were far less worthy, and he decided to consult one now, knowing that this tool would
be broken, and soon.

She barely turned her head as he entered her quarters. She would have heard him, of course, for the lock
was not a subtle one and rattled quite a bit whenever he
opened it. She sat at a window, at a writing desk which
he had wrought himself in his younger days as a wood-
worker, her elaborate dress in folds about her, the weak
sun illuminating her coppery skin. Her pause in giving
him her elegant attention was long, and deliberate, her
slender fingers poised on a pen as she made notes or perhaps she was sketching something from the elongated
window. Bold, to sketch in ink, but then Tiiva Pantoreth
made few mistakes and was disinclined to eradicate the
ones she did make, for to do so would be to admit them.
She had been Abayan Diort's, but when her fortunes in
Larandaril fell, she came to Quendius. He had few delusions about why. She had not explained herself, but
he took it as an action he would have committed. Find
the strongest and ally yourself there. He let her stay but
warily. She had, after all, betrayed both Lariel and Diort.

He had no illusions about her either. He did, however, have uses for her.

"You were seneschal for Lariel for many years, and I have a need to know how to move in and out of the manor house with as little detection as possible."

Her hand put the pen aside, and as she swung more of her body about to face him, he saw three quarters of her profile with one shapely brow arched. "If one can penetrate the living borders of Larandaril, I could perhaps show you the shadows of the manor. However . . ."

"You doubt I can breach the border."

She shrugged.

"If I'm not worried, you shouldn't be. I want you to sketch entrances and exits of the building itself for me, the likelihood they will be guarded or warded, and how. I want to be ready when I get there."

"Lariel."

"Who else?"

Another lift and dip of her shoulder, the materials of her dress rustling as she did so. "It would be a mistake to think that killing her would stop the war."

"Oh, I don't want to stop it. I want to ensure it."

Her mouth quirked. "That may well do it, then. All right. It will take me a mark or so to finish it." She turned back around, pushing the paper that she had been working upon out of the way and drawing clean sheets out of a small pile at the desk's corner. Here in the outlands, paper was a valuable commodity, but Tiiva had always had all she wanted. She, in herself, had been a valuable commodity.

Quendius thought of waiting, then thought better of it and left.

Chapter Sixteen

EDGES OF A NIGHT still purple hung about the fortress walls of the ild Fallyn, but they did not blanket the sleeping. Tressandre stood, then paced, her wild honey-colored hair tangled about her shoulders and down her back, the illumination of smoldering torches bringing alive the highlights of her eyes. The verdant green of her eye coloring increased in the shadows, rendering the lighter streaks of spring green almost unseeable. She twirled a short spear in her hands, the sinews of her wrists tight and strong as she did so, the lines of her body slender and yet taut, expressing her impatience as well as her energy. About to step into the courtyard, her brother halted, the look in her eyes stopping him. She pivoted, her back to him as she passed. Beyond her, straw targets had been all but destroyed and other stains lay pooled on the ground, dried and yet still pungent. He did not like to face his sister in one of these moods, but he had little choice. Alton knew she undoubtedly waited for him, and it would be better to greet her when they were alone rather than have her catch him in front of the troops. Unless she had changed her mind and was going with him after all. . . .

He stepped into the courtyard. "Early," he said. "Even for you."

"The world doesn't stop changing just because I have slept in." She halted, planting the butt of the spear between her booted feet, her fingers wrapped just underneath its sharp point.

"Nor does it because you haven't."

She stamped her spear, and her lips thinned.

"Joining me, then?" He pulled his riding gloves from his belt and pulled them on.

"No. I'm taking a small contingent to the heart of Larandaril. She'll have to open the borders for me."

His brow went up, the one with the small scar, nicked by a dagger held by Tressandre when they were much younger but just as deadly. "To what purpose?"

"An innocent one, I assure you. Healers for Jeredon's sake. A hope of meeting this new Vaelinar who serves our queen, the half-breed or whatever she is who created such a fuss last fall. And I will take two hands of archers, as a show of our good faith as well as the forces you take to the muster."

Alton leaned a shoulder against the courtyard arena wall. "Very politic of you. I thought Lariel had refused services of our healers, saying they weren't necessary."

"She has, and they may well not be. Jeredon is still struggling with paralysis and weakness although word has it he improves steadily." Tressandre lifted her spear and began to rotate it again.

"You think they hide something?"

"No. I do think, however," and she looked at him from under a fall of blonde and silvery hair, "that there is more than one way to gain the title of Warrior Queen."

Alton said flatly, "Jeredon."

"He is her heir."

"And if you cannot best her, I have no doubt you can defeat him."

"In so many words, yes." The spear stopped in her hands, and she gestured to the walls.

"I thought you had your hooks into Sevryn."

She turned away for a moment, giving him a view of her flawless profile. "He is a half-breed. I would never be satisfied with such, although he had his purposes."

"He serves the queen well."

"As he served me, but there is more than service, Alton. There is fulfillment. Are you satisfied with our austere northern domain, Brother? We have timber, yes, and furs, yes, and our fine horses run the open pastures when the seasons allow, but we are fenced in by our relative poverty, and that is no accident that we live where and how we must, and—"

"Larandaril is the summer kingdom," he finished for her.

"Indeed, it is. Then there is Drebukar, which bordered her mountains on the west, the mines of which produced, among other gems, the great stone which became the Shield of Tomarq. Although its like may never be seen again, we know that gemstones and fine metals built the treasuries of both the Drebukars and those of Larandaril."

"And they won't share."

Tressandre smiled slowly. "Those mountains now lie fallow, but we both know that mines can play out or become too dangerous to work, or that treaties may be made, which say too much of a good thing can flood a market and make it worthless."

"Tsk. A conspiracy to control the gemstone trade? Who would dare such a thing?"

Tressandre's hands whipped about, and Alton found himself with the spearhead digging into his sternum.

"Do. Not. Mock. Me."

He moved the point away. "Never, Sister. I know the whip that drives us both." He inhaled deeply. "Old tales say a new Way being laid down that ridge of mountains exploded out of control and destroyed part of the House of Drebukar, which is why it now aligns with Istlanthir, and that to set foot on those ridges or into those mines means a death which is neither painless nor instant. Thoughts of those mines were put away decades ago. Building a Way has never been easy . . . nor the methods for doing so shared. If you were to go a-hunting in those mountains, we might lose the true treasure of the ild Fallyns." He watched as his sister shifted her weight and tilted her head slightly to eye him.

"Now you attempt to dissuade me by flattery."

"I only tell the ruthless truth of ild Fallyn Stronghold. You were meant to rule. It would be sweet to gain power, but we both know it won't come by riches alone."

"No, which is why a war is so . . . desirable . . . right now." Her smoky voice lingered over that word in a way that sent a shiver down the back of his neck. "Many things can be accomplished under its cover."

"What do you want me to do?"

"Nothing. Take our forces as planned and head to the muster. We are under suspicion and likely to remain that way, so it's best that you stay in her eye as much as you can. While I do what I can." And the corner of Tressandre's mouth quirked slightly.

"You will think to keep me advised from time to time?"

"Brother. Do you think I would not share with you?" She stepped close to him, very close, her warm breath grazing his cheek as she spoke. "As I share all things with you?"

"As painful as that sharing can be," he returned, and turned his mouth to meet hers for a long, full moment, savoring the touch of her lips and taste of her mouth.

She broke away first. "Pain is what gives us joy later."

Alton watched as she turned her attention to what remained of the straw targets, her body barely concealed beneath the minimum of body armor she wore, and the gauzy scrap of a blouse that hid nothing and promised more. He put the tip of his tongue to his lips to remember

the taste of her before crossing the courtyard to the gate,
and into the dawn where their forces waited with horse
and wagon for him to lead them. He had no doubts
whatsoever in his mind about who led him.

Sevryn woke as he usually did, instantly alert and aware
with all touches of whatever he had been dreaming
shredding away from him immediately. He sat on the
side of the bed, feeling the early chill of the morning
dance along his bare skin as the warmth of the covers
bled away. He ran the flat of his palm over his stomach
and trailed his fingertips over his rib cage. Grace was not
a healer in any traditional sense, whether a Vaelinar one
or an alchemist of Kerith. Her touch was a soothing balm
that cleansed and washed away the wounds it found. Her
presence could work its way deeper and deeper, layering
through the hurt until all was cleansed and mended, the
way water worked its way through stone, slowly and inexorably. She seemed almost unaware of her touch and
its effect, for her calling was not that of a healer but that
of water, and whatever way it might enrich and soothe,
it did. Their togetherness in the night had bled the last
of the kedant and its antidote from him, and worried out
the knots of bruises and wounds, and even the scarring
had faded to near nothingness in the bare light of dawn
that filtered in through his shuttered window. Sevryn
touched his flank again, where he'd been scored deeply,
and found it only slightly tender, the flesh pinkish but
seamless as though he had barely been wounded at all.

He had fallen asleep, determined to seek out Daravan this morning before that one slipped away into the
shadows he favored. He had told no one yet of the meeting with Quendius, and now his resolve faltered. He had
been filled with kedant after the melee, and antidote
or not, he knew its fever had racked him. Had he seen
Quendius, or had it been only a venom-riddled dream

as his body fought off the effects of what he'd been through? His body no longer held the mark of fangs if it had ever held them ... he had been healed too well. The most he could relate would be a vision of anxiety and threat, a paranoia that Daravan could not take for anything more. Had he seen and spoken with the villain, or had he not? He no longer knew.

Sevryn scrubbed his hands over his face. He knew that Daravan would think him addled and rightly so. Better to hold his tongue than to appear the fool, especially in these days. There was no doubt the enemy would be afoot, and when he spoke of such things, he needed to have proof. He had nothing tangible he could show but the uneasiness on his spirit, toward both Quendius and the intentions of his queen. Armies could, and would, move on his word in the near future. He had to be circumspect, and he had to be infallible. Kedant-laced visions were neither.

He got to his feet and stretched, deciding that what his mind and body needed was a good stint in the arena, where he did not have to think overmuch. That, too, would keep him alive.

Morning hung fitfully over the arena, a leaden sky promising a day of gloom if not rain, and its chill dappled the soldiers and bowmen who sat at the edges of the training grounds, cleaning or repairing their weapons and armor. Sevryn found a willing sparring partner in the person of one Taitrus, a tall, amber-eyed Vaelinar who had some Kernan blood in his lineage somewhere, befitting the bulk of his body, but that Kernan heritage was a generation or so ago. He stood taller as well as wider than Sevryn, a good sword and shield man, and the corner of his mouth quirked as they sized each other up. He'd seen Taitrus going out on detail but had never fought by his side, so they were both unknown quantities to each other. Sevryn knew that the soldier saw him for a half-breed without the multi-hued eyes of power that marked the Vaelinar blood that ran true, just as his

own amber eyes showed only the golden-brown color
of his Kernan blood. Taitrus flexed his sword arm, his
head tilted a little, gauging Sevryn's balance as they
squared away. The soldier also knew that Sevryn was
the Queen's Hand, and that accounted for much, both
said and unsaid.

They traded a few blows, solid but unremarkable, taking each other's measure in reach and balance. Sevryn
could feel the pulse quicken in him slightly. He parried
a hard hit, felt it vibrate throughout his forearm into his
elbow, and grinned. Taitrus was not going to toy with
him just because he rode at the Warrior Queen's side.
They sparred deliberately, warming up even as the hidden sun added no warmth to the day. There was no rain,
no frost, no snow, but the day was indisputably winter. It
held its cold decisively, and only their movement heated
them as their blows began to quicken. The arena filled
with the sound of their weapons striking and slicing air,
and the murmur of a small audience watching and perhaps placing a few side bets. Sevryn backed off a step,
took a moment to swipe the back of his hand across his
forehead, and threw Taitrus a grin. "Street rules, to first
blood?" he suggested.

The soldier grinned back. "First blood," he agreed.

And street rules meant no rules at all. They balanced
on the balls of their feet, knees flexed, and started to
fight in earnest. Sevryn took note of a slight stiffness in
the other's left leg, and played on that, even as the other's longer reach kept him moving and weaving. They
worked on each other, swords clashing but also feet kicking and a roll through the dirt now and then to dodge or
unbalance the other. Taitrus fought well, both clean and
dirty, and they grunted at each other in mutual appreciation of their skill. Heat ran through his limbs and sweat
dripped from his chin as they hit, parried, dropped back,
lunged into striking distance, free hands and feet working as often as the sword hand, blows thudding off their
forms. He could feel the heat pooling and then rolling

off his body and thought for a moment that the kedant still held him, but there was no scent of it in his sweat. An inferno built in his veins, as though the sword and fist play built a fire in a forge, stoking it with every stroke. Taitrus matched him well. He slapped the other across the hip soundly with the flat of the blade, sending him staggering. Taitrus righted himself and winked. "You're more than a pretty boy for the queen, eh?"

Sevryn chuckled at that before dodging a well-aimed kick, spinning away from it, the momentum sliding off his movement. For a space of time, they forgot their swords for fists and boots, dodging and jabbing and tripping when they could close on the other. Taitrus was swifter than he looked, but Sevryn had years of growing up in city backstreets to guide his survival instincts.

Then the soldier struck him in the jaw, fist jolting him.

Sevryn rocked back on one heel and shook his head to clear it. His ears roared a second, and the burn of the hit filled his face. He parried quickly, not letting Taitrus drive in closer on the heel of his reaction. Something stirred in Sevryn. His vision went red for a moment, as though a curtain of blood poured down from his brow. He blinked as Taitrus fended off his parry, blocked, and turned slightly away from him, exposing his own flank. In the street, that would have brought a kidney shot. His hand fisted. The veil across his sight cleared, but slowly, like a red-shot sunrise fading. He could feel a thrum in his ears, his pulse thickening, a catch in his throat.

The sparring became more than an exercise, much more. He wanted to take the arrogance out of this soldier, the quickness, the expertise. He wanted to pound him into the ground until the blood ran, and then he wanted the blood. . . .

A soft rumble came out of the back of his throat. The growl rattled through him, cutting off his breath for a moment, and Taitrus shivered a bit before he spun about on his heel to meet Sevryn. They had exchanged few words up until then, except for a "Nice one" or "Well hit." The less breath wasted on talking, the more stamina the fighter held. But the atmosphere changed with Sevryn's growl. Taitrus dropped his shoulders in defense and waited for Sevryn's next move. No apology. None needed with street rules.

Sevryn whipped around, sending his heel slamming into the other's shoulder. Taitrus staggered back on his stiffening leg, as Sevryn tumbled back into balance and lunged while the other fought to turn away. He went for the weakness, and Taitrus sensed it instinctively, both pivoting a little awkwardly even as he swept his blade down. Both of them grunted as they hit, Taitrus taking only a swipe as the flat of his sword knocked Sevryn aside with a blow to his shoulder. Sevryn rolled as he went down and came up, anger roiling through him.

Taitrus settled himself, moving his sword from one hand to the other, his gaze leveled on Sevryn. A glint lay at the back of his eyes, a sudden knowledge of Sevryn's intent. The heat coiled and rippling through his body lessened and Sevryn shook it off. An angry fighter only had honed instincts going for him, strategy thrown to the wind, and often even his instincts were not enough to save his life. And this was not a fight, this was a spar, this was training. His thoughts cooled.

They circled one another, looking for an opening, catching their breath, shaking off the stings of their last blows. And, at the back of his mind, Sevryn felt a whisper. A stirring. It made his scalp crawl from the inside out.

Taitrus took advantage of his reach and slapped at Sevryn, his blade sizzling through the air and catching him on the side of the head before he could weave away, and the burn of the hit brought a snarl from him as he fell away from it. His blood boiled in anger, his lips curled with a feral sound.

Sevryn choked back the growl that threatened to bubble up from the depths of his throat. He knew that sound, knew it from the core of himself, from the time he had existed only as a soul and Cerat had swallowed him whole. He did not know where the Demon manifested, only that it was very close and leaning on him as only the Souldrinker could. It wanted him, but more than that, it wanted the death of Taitrus. If it had hands of its own, it would take Taitrus by the neck and shake him as though he were some vermin to be slaughtered. Barring that, it wanted Sevryn to dance in the man's blood and to bathe Cerat in the man's essence and soul. It knew how to reach Sevryn.

It came from within.

Sevryn showed his teeth. Cerat whispered along his bones. *A training accident, a blow twisted awry into a fatal stab, it would be so easy* ... It would be so g*ood.*

He pushed the thought away, but it bubbled back up, a fountain that would drown him. Taitrus jabbed at him, and he blocked it, shrugging it off. He could feel the bloodlust rolling off him.

Sevryn dropped his sword to the arena floor and kicked it away in the dust. Eyes widening in disbelief, Taitrus shrugged and then tossed his sword away also, knotting one hand into a fist and curling the other one. He danced a step toward Sevryn. He beckoned, a slow grin returning to his face.

Sevryn clamped his jaws tight and moved in deliberately. He would not take long, he did not dare. Not if Taitrus wanted to be able to walk out of the arena that day. Taitrus was his sparring partner, but the real battle would be against Cerat and the need to kill.

Chapter
Seventeen

SLEEP CAME FOR ALL BUT TWO in the spacious apartment rooms of the queen where candles guttered low and Jeredon sat, his long legs sprawled out in front of him, one hand absently rubbing his right knee as if a deep, unconscious ache pained him. Lara stopped and squeezed his shoulder before moving past him and dropping into the cushioned chair opposite. "I'm sorry to keep you so late."

"Osten, when he decides to talk, will rumble for days."

"I had more to say than he did. Our archers are trained for the field, not for sniping from trees and rivers. They did poorly."

"Our general is minded in that way."

"He is. You're not, nor is Bistel."

The corner of Jeredon's shadowed face pulled. "Bistel declined to head your troops."

"I know." Lara looked into the banked fire which barely held enough heat to chase the cold from her rooms. "We have his backing, and yet we don't. The talking, for now, is done. We've training to finish. But that's not why I asked you to wait up for me."

"It isn't?"

"No." Lara wearily tugged off the black sash of mourning from her upper arm and let it drift to the floor. "I know you'll be handling the replacements capably. What we need to talk about is Nutmeg."

He dropped his gaze a moment before meeting hers steadily, as if gathering himself.

She added quietly, "I hear you've refused yet another request from the Stronghold of the ild Fallyn to send healers."

"I may not be the man our grandfather wanted me to be, but I have some grasp of the situation. Tressandre will seize the opportunity and come here if she thinks she can get away with it. Alton will go to the muster. She couldn't replace you directly, so she will come at you through me."

"And?"

"I'll let her. Let me do this for you."

"You can't let Nutmeg come into harm's way between you."

"I wouldn't." He shifted his legs restlessly. "Even Meg doesn't know how well I can stand and walk, and I don't intend to let her. This is one advantage we have, my disability. I'll draw the attention you can't afford to have. And I won't let Nutmeg come to harm. Not from Tress anyway." He looked away then, into the glowing embers of the banked fire.

"If it weren't for Nutmeg, you wouldn't be walking now."

"Don't think, don't ever think, that I don't know that."

"And that she adores you."

"I know," Jeredon said tiredly. "I've tried, but she warms me like that fire does. Can I not share her spark a little longer?"

"All I ask is that when you put her aside, do it soon and gently. She deserves happiness among her own, and contentment, and nothing more than a few brief but treasured memories. Not a life of longing and regret."

"That cuts."

"All the more reason," Lara replied softly.

"I will. Soon. When I can find a way to tell her."

"You have to find the means. This is something that can't be, for either of you."

"Don't you think I don't tell myself that? I have hounds of our bloodlines that will live longer than a Dweller, yet it makes her burn all the brighter in my eyes."

"You can't let her grow old and bitter while you do not. You can't lose her that way, Jeredon, it will tear the heart out of both of you."

He did not answer, but his breath sighed out of him slowly.

Lara got up and rested her hand on the top of her brother's head. "None of this will be easy for any of us." She withdrew to the bedroom of her apartment, leaving him staring at the fire as it guttered lower and lower, yet refused to burn out.

Lara hadn't realized she had been hearing Bistane's voice until she slowed in her descent and it filled the stairwell. Another song she hadn't heard before, and with the simple cadence and rhyming scheme of a bar song, it detailed the efforts of a Bolger to get a God to notice him, despite all the obvious omens that he would really be much better off if a God didn't notice him. The misguided attempts of the Bolger caused ever more trouble until a smile tipped her lips as the clever ditty wound around upon itself to end. The listeners below broke into scattered applause and shouts of appreciation. She paused on the final step, wondering if Bistane had deliberately brought levity with him.

He appeared in the hall as if her thoughts made him materialize, one hand held out. "A fair morning it is," he observed, "but fairer still for the smile you bring." As handsome as his father, there could be no doubt Bistel Vantane had sired him, but he looked younger than he was, even younger than Lariel, and she hated for a moment that he made her feel weary. Perhaps he held his youth because he stood in his father's shadow, Bistel so dominant and still in his prime, but the reason didn't matter. He made her feel *old*. She pushed the feeling away and forced the mirth of the song back into her thoughts.

"The smile is yours," she said and took his hand.

"It might fade. My father has sent me a reply to your call."

She raised an eyebrow.

"He will not attend."

Did her fingers grow colder in his hand? She hoped not. She kept her voice level as she answered, "Does he give reason? Lord Vantane knows that we will miss him sorely."

"He sends word that he will retain a pittance of troops for his own use, and he sends assurances that he will not stint in his support of your decisions." Bistane's voice stayed as light and unconcerned as if he still sang a whimsical melody, but his eyes were shadowed.

Her mouth twisted a little. The warlord of the north was showing both his approval and disapproval of her actions, and keeping an important part of his support at his own disposal. She supposed that the adage that half an apple was better than none would have to do. She squeezed his hand so that he would not take offense at her slowness in response to the news. "Then you will have to appreciate the fetish I am having made for my helm," she told him.

"Indeed? Do I get a guess at its appearance?"

"You'd never guess it in a thousand tries." Lariel let him tuck her hand under his arm as he escorted her to the breakfast hall, where the last remnants of the morning meal were being stored away, but the head cook peeked in and beamed when she saw Lara. Her booming voice notified the kitchen that they were not quite done yet providing and she wanted a platter of coddled eggs, fresh fruits, and a meat salad.

"You will join me?"

Bistane released her arm reluctantly and seated her. "A bite or two only. I ate earlier. I worked late, but rested well and was up early enough to have a brief word or two with General Osten. I saw Jeredon readying to leave for his therapeutics."

"Did he? He usually does that at the end of day."

"Not to sound like a laundry maid with gossip," Bistane noted as he seated himself beside her, but his eyes were twinkling as he said it, "but the young Dweller lass who seems to have appointed herself as his nursemaid was in a fury when she found out he'd gone on without her. Reminded me of the days when my father learned I had forgotten to pen the hounds for the night or hood the hawks. I would not want to be Jeredon when she catches up with him."

"A sound judgment, I'd say." Lara paused as maids hurried out to bring her the fruit and meat salad and assure her that the coddled eggs, on fresh toast, would be following shortly. She put a plate aside for Bistane and let him have his pick of the fruits as she began to devour the greenery, spiced with bits of freshly roasted meats.

He peeled himself a fruit and then selected one for her, his slim dagger held in strong, capable hands. She watched him out of the corner of her eye, catching thoughts at the edge of her mind wondering what those efficient, knowing hands might do to her. . . .

She shoved the errant notion away. Bistane was eager, as always, to put out the hope that he could share her bed, but she had never, never, been tempted to consider it as well. A warmth rose in the pit of her stomach, and she fought to keep it there. She could feel the flush rise

in spite of her efforts, between the swell of her bosom
and up her throat before she managed to sit back and
let a cool breeze from a nearby opened shutter bathe
her. Bistane quartered her fruit and arranged it for her
convenience without seeming to notice her sudden quietude. After a moment or two of the breeze playing over
her, she found her voice again.

"I'll miss your father's abilities."

"You will have them. He knows of the situation within
your house and has deemed his independence a better
option." Bistane paused as if judging what to say next, and
then added, "Some of the stands of aryns are failing."

She relaxed a bit then. Bistel had not abandoned
her. He would fight his own battle, partnering hers. She
might not agree with what Lord Vantane had in mind,
now or in the future, but she couldn't overlook his skill
as a warlord. "I understand," she murmured.

"He thought you might. It might be wise, however,"
and Bistane spoke to her ear, whispering, his warm
breath stirring her hair and along the curve of her neck,
"to mislead the others, particularly ild Fallyn, about his
intentions."

She nodded and leaned forward, away from his mouth
and breath and voice, to pick up the fruit he'd rendered
for her. A sigh followed her movement. She managed to
swing away from him slightly as she straightened. "Until
your forces arrive, Lord Bistane, I hope you'll find time
to work with Jeredon and the contingent of archers we
need trained."

"As you will." His eyes smiled upon her.

She thought she saw a calculation reflected at the
back of them, but she could not be sure. He would not
be Vaelinar, however, if there were not.

For the rest of their meal, she chose topics of light
interest, drawing him out about his new repertoire of
songs and the northern weather. They agreed that it was
a dry winter, exceedingly so, and because of that, they
might be wise to deal with Abayan Diort before the

end of spring when it would normally be best to march
an army. It seemed that it did not matter how trivial a
conversation might be, it would inevitably turn to what
loomed in front of them. She ate sparingly and neatly,
wanting to be away from Bistane and his eyes that kept
an admiring and interested gaze upon her whenever she
looked up. She did not understand the sudden current of
interest that thrilled through her, nor did she wish him
to sense it. Perhaps she needed a tonic. She'd have to
find the herbalist and have a quick word with her.

Lara put aside her plates. She touched the back of Bistane's hand lightly. "I've a chore or two before I will be
taking the field in practice. Perhaps I will see you about
later."

"That, milady queen, would be my greatest pleasure."
Bistane stood and drew her to her feet. She escaped
without a look back but felt his gaze upon her.

"Vaelinar," declared Nutmeg. She spelled it quietly. "V
a e l i n a r. I think it means a people who are scared
of their own shadow." The cavern echoed faintly with
her voice, and the slap of water, but she heard nothing
else, not even a breath. She crossed her arms defiantly
over her bosom, knowing that Jeredon had to be there,
that the staff had seen him go out with his cart and his
chair, and that he'd gone out without her. Sunlight skittered fitfully over the mouth of the cave as clouds blew
by quickly in a winter wind that seemed to be growing
stronger with every gust. She should not have come
after him. She knew that. He would laugh at her again,
but she couldn't not have come after him either. Raised
with three older brothers, she wasn't about to let one get
an upper hand, even if that male had a Warrior Queen
for a sister.

"Perhaps it *means* shadow. Would you then be afraid?"
His voice shivered mockingly through the hollows.

She narrowed eyes with vision not yet accustomed to the flickering dark of the cavern. "I have fought Bolgers, raiders and Ravers. I've stood toe to toe with three brothers. I've Tolby Farbranch for a father and Lily Farbranch for a mother. Why would a shadow scare me?"

A sigh followed her words, or perhaps it was just the waters of the pool lapping along the rim of stone. She tapped her foot impatiently.

Jeredon emerged an arm's length away to fold them on the stone's edge and look up at her, his expression aggrieved. "Woman, you disrespect me."

"Perhaps. Even worse, you disrespect yourself."

He stammered a word in reply, and then shut his mouth firmly. It was a fine Vaelinar mouth, she thought, well shaped and full, not like a thin-lipped Kernan who always looked as though the harvest had been poor and lean. She sat down so that he would not have to crane his neck to look up at her. The heat of the earth below her that warmed the waters also took away the cold of the morning. A faint fog rose from the pool, wispy and insubstantial, yet hiding the true nature of the cavern.

Finally, Jeredon said, "I do, do I?"

"You do. You're the heir to a Warrior Queen, not because of your blood but because she chose you for that position."

He slicked his hair back from his face. "You seem to overlook that heritage."

"Me? A Farbranch? Where, as the Dwellers love t' say, the apple doesn't fall far from the tree?" She reached out and pinched his nose. "Lariel is no one's fool. If she needed Osten or that Bistane or anyone else for an heir at her back, she'd put them there. She's not stuck with you, near as I can tell. I admit I'm no Vaelinar, thank the Gods, to know how you all do things, but my ears have been filled with talk since I got here."

Jeredon moved out of reach. "My sister is loyal to a fault."

"You being the fault?" She rocked back. "I suppose she wears her armor because she's loyal to it?"

"No, because it may well save her life."

"Oh, and her judgment in that case is sound enough, is it?"

"There's a difference between me and her mail."

"Aye, and that difference is, you're thicker. She ought to be wearing you about instead!"

Jeredon gave a long blink, then his face twisted to one side, and then he began to laugh despite his efforts to hold it back. Finally, he covered his face with his hands and muttered, "I should know better. Isn't there a proverb or something about arguing with a Dweller?"

"You'd be meaning the one about the farmer and the great stone in his pasture. He tried a brace of ponies to pull it out, but it wouldn't budge. So he went to the village and borrowed a team of those great long-horned steers the traders use on their caravans, and they pulled and pulled, but the stone wouldn't budge. So the farmer thought about it a bit and decided the stone needed convincing. He was a young lad, the farmer, and the land was new to the plow and to his family, being part of a bride price. That huge bit of rock ruined all his plans for plowing and planting and harvesting. So, he went out to have a talk with it about moving to one side or maybe becoming part of the new house's great room wall or such, but the stone wouldn't answer him. He sat and argued with it for the better part of the day, then went home when it was dark, determined not to give up. Sure enough, come the dawn, he was back in the pasture arguing with that stubborn bit of granite."

Jeredon made a smothered sound that she couldn't quite decipher. Nutmeg raised her eyebrow but continued on. "Well, that newly married farmer was even more obstinate. He went out every day to argue with the rock. Soon the weather began to turn a bit and it became clear to all those who knew farmin' that the time to get the crops in was nearly past. They urged him to simply plow around the rock and get on with it. Even his wife's father looked a bit gruffly at him, but he would not give up. And then, one morning after three long, hard weeks of arguing, he rose and trudged down to his pasture. 'See here,' he says to the rock. 'You may be made of stone, but I am made of Dweller stock and I'll be here arguing with you until the sun turns blue.' At that, the stone gave out a great, rending groan and split in two, and then again and again and again, till there was nothing left of it but a heap of gravel. So, the farmer kept his word by taking the gravel and putting it into the foundation and wall of his home's great room once the spring planting was finished." Nutmeg took a deep breath. "You'll be meaning that story?"

Jeredon made a strangled sound before managing, "Yes, that's the one. If not that one, another just like it."

"You're sure? Because it might have been the tale about why the Bolgers grew tusks—"

"No. No, no, I'm sure that's it."

"You thick-headed dunce. There is no tale about why the Bolgers grew tusks, they were born like that from the beginning!" Nutmeg leaned over, hand outstretched to give Jeredon a thorough dunking, but he ducked away quickly and she overbalanced to find herself falling into the water with a loud splash. She bobbed up quickly like an apple in a barrel, spluttering a bit for breath.

"Now that's what comes around for trying to man-handle a poor, defenseless cripple."

Her dress floated about her like a colorful cloud as she began to tread water. Her hands nimble, she unfastened it and pulled it off, tossing it onto the bank she had so recently occupied. It took a bit more doing to pull her boots off and toss them over as well, and by the time she had, her hair had come out of the twist she'd so carefully put it into that morning and cascaded down onto her shoulders.

"I will," Jeredon offered, "get you a new pair of boots. Those are likely to be ruined."

"A new pair would be welcome. Those were getting to be a bit thin at the sole, due no doubt to traipsing around after you and your sort on your adventures."

"My sort? What happened to all the praise you were beginning to heap on me?"

"Changed my mind. You're a lout, and a great one at that."

Jeredon pulled back. "Now I'm thickheaded?"

"And you're not? So tell me this, Jeredon Eladar. You rolled down here in your chair all nice and independent, tipped it over, and slipped into the water—but of the two of us bobbing around all cozy in here now, which one of us is going to be getting back out without help?"

"Well, I. That is. Hmmmm."

"Is that an answer?"

"I'm thinking."

"Do that." And Nutmeg rolled over in the water, her ivory chemise molding to her body as she did so, kicked her legs free, and headed for the shallow part of the pool where she could climb easiest onto the bank. "I do hope you find an answer before you wither completely up."

"Or turn into gravel." He grabbed her by the ankle.

He hadn't lost any of his strength, really, she thought as he pulled her to his side, or the handsome looks of his face except for the white pinched marks around his mouth when the pain bothered him overmuch. And now, with his hair slicked back, she could see the fine points of his ears, and the carved delicacy of his cheekbones in a face that was nonetheless very masculine.

"Now you're looking at me like that," Jeredon said quietly.

She stared at him, at eyes that carried no color in the cavern but of the darkness of the water, pooled deep and dark and true. "I cannot help it," she answered.

"But you have to. There is no place for you at my side."

"Only if you wish it that way."

"Nutmeg . . ." and Jeredon suddenly buried his hand

in her hair and drew her to him, and then covered her mouth with his, in a long soft kiss that brought her to a moan as she answered it. She wrapped her arms about his neck and curved her body to his, feeling his strength and his need. He broke away long enough to protest, "I cannot feel this way."

"But you do, and it proves you are healing, and you are still a man." And she kissed him then, as hot and desperately as he had kissed her, and he stopped arguing with her.

Chapter
Eighteen

BREGAN FOUND HIS father still at his estates though it was well after the breakfasting hour. He was neither surprised nor delighted to do so, but had accepted the likelihood. In the same trend, he did not seem overly interested in haste about turning over his empire to Bregan. It had not failed to occur to Bregan that he might have to succeed in the way that Willard did from his sire, Ruman Oxfort, in a hostile takeover.

He was five days late in arriving for their appointment and knew that their meeting would be even more difficult than usual. He swung down from his horse, feeling the leg brace take the weight of his leg easily as he did so, pondering whether takeovers were a family tradition or simply a way of proving that one was, indeed, old enough and strong enough to be the successor. It didn't seem the sort of thing he could discuss with his father. Not if he wished to have any legs at all left to stand upon.

A stable lad ran out to take care of his horse as soon

as he stood free. Her freckled face beamed as she stroked the creature's neck and led him off. She wore trousers like the other lads, and he was not sure how his father had managed to be so equitable in his hiring. Perhaps he hadn't even noticed the new lad was a female. He stripped his gloves off, slapping them against his trousers before tucking them away. He did not relish this meeting.

Willard heard his steps upon the tiled flooring as soon as he entered, and recognized the cadence from the normal stride and the braced one, movement that he couldn't disguise even if he tried. His voice boomed through the wing of the estate. "Bregan! Is that you?"

"And no one else, Father."

"High time! High time indeed. It's been five days since I sent you to Temple Row. Come here and explain."

He followed the thunderous voice into his father's study. Books and scrolls were thrown everywhere, the window shutters stood wide open to the gray fog of the day, and a smell of toback lingered in the air. His father sat, feet up, vest unbuttoned and his dark eyes sparkling sharp, like those of a rapacious bird looking for scraps. His boots lay next to the ottoman, and his stockings looked as though he'd been walking around in them all morning, a damp leaf pressed to the bottom of his right foot.

Bregan looked about for a place to sit, found a chair under a small mountain of scrolls, and then decided to sit on the edge of his father's desk, the cleanest spot available. "Temple Row," he began, but Willard Oxfort launched into a speech of his own.

"A revelatory mess that is. Gods listening, readying to talk to us! Bah. Too late now to head that off at the pass, so we'll simply have to deal with it. Make arrangements to meet with the leading clergy in the towns and villages, bribe them off. I'll have a small surtax placed on the goods to offset the costs, but it's going to hit us in our purses. Better now than later, though. This kind of thing can be quite difficult to deal with, especially with the Galdarkans and Vaelinars rattling their sabers. The people will be looking for fear and miracles, don't you think? Well-placed bribes all around should take the wind out of their sails, although there will be a dirt preacher or two who won't listen. The Kobrir will have to deal with them." Willard took a deep breath and Bregan took the plunge.

"Not necessary, I've dealt with it."

"You'll have to—what? What do you mean?"

"I've been busy these past few days."

"Too busy to come speak with me, that I know. Busy at what?"

Bregan tapped his hand to his ear. "It's a godsend, a bloody gold mine, Father. I've got contracts with potters along our routes, the wheels spinning and the ovens fired up. We're going to be the leading suppliers of relics. Listening niches, small idols, offering bowls and basins, you name it, whatever might please the Gods in whatever small way, we're going to sell it to them. Don't head this off, embrace it!"

"Embrace it? What in tree's blood are you talking about?"

"This trend comes up every few decades. The people hunger to be heard, to be spoken to, as they were centuries ago. Having had it once, they want it back again."

Willard chopped at the air with his hand. "The Gods cut us off. You can't gamble good capital on their capricious whims."

"I'm not gambling on them, Father, I'm gambling on the people. We've made money off their whims since time began."

Willard narrowed his gaze. "And when the Gods fail to speak?"

"Put the blame where the blame lies, then. The Gods alone are responsible for their conduct. We will have done everything possible to court their attention. We will have been sanctimonious and flattering and eager and respectful." Bregan spread his hands. "What more can they ask of us? We will have given it our all, and you must never forget, Father, that the Gods act in their own time. What passes as a year or even a decade to us might only be a breath in their world. We shall also sell *patience*."

Willard sat back in his chair, dropping his feet from his settee to the floor, and his sharp gaze mellowed a bit as he thought. Bregan leaned forward from his perch. Willard's fingers moved, and he knew his father was counting subconsciously.

Their eyes met again. Willard said quietly, "There could be money in this."

"Fountains of it. And, for a time at least, unnoticed by the Vaelinars and anyone else of note. I can funnel it away as I please."

"To what end?"

"I'll be hiring more caravan guards. Vastly more."

"And ..."

"We'll have our own army, Father. An army that will stand when the Vaelinars and Galdarkans have cut each other to bloody ribbons. An army that will stand forth to protect our trade routes and Ways as well as our people as needed."

Willard grunted. "You may have to. We can't trust Quendius."

"I was meant to be a dead man."

"Perhaps. Or perhaps he had indeed arranged a treaty of sorts with them, and you were sent in good faith by him. Either way, you would have suited his purpose. You alive, with trade goods to seal the bargain, or you dead, to whet their appetite for conquering these lands."

Bregan looked at his father. The man had an exterior that showed nothing, ever, unless he willed it, and the look on his father's face now held no more awareness of anything other than the simple act of having finished putting his boots on. "If it is the Raymy ..."

"All the more reason for the Gods to lean close once again. It will be seen as one of the signs of their returning to us, if we play it right."

"If not . . ."

"There will be panic in the streets, and the coast will be stripped. I suggest we secure warehouses inland, well fortified and stocked. Food as well as religious relics will become our mainstay. Do it quietly, though, no sense tipping our hand."

"Buying grain stores will alert attention."

"I trust you can handle it." Willard surged to his feet. "Can't you?"

Bregan slid off the desk. "Of course."

"Good, then. I've meetings to attend, and I'll keep my ear out for stirrings, as well. You've enough coin for these investments?"

"I do."

"All right, then. Spend your seed money, and I'll reimburse you off the books."

"So, if anyone notices, they will think your trader son has taken the bit in his teeth and gone bolting his own way."

"Unsanctioned trading and investing, yes. If they think I back you, they will either give us competition we do not want, or they will trip the panic before we're ready. Either way will cost us money."

And all the risk would be his. But not quite. He would only be risking coin. Those who stayed unaware of the fact the Raymy might be massing again would have their lives at stake.

Willard waved him out the office door. "Distasteful as you find it, I want to be kept apprised of everything and it will be best to do it in person."

"Done, then."

"Good. Have the staff fix you a breakfast before you leave." And with that, his father dismissed him as he picked up his coat and cane and prepared to leave his estate for a day or week in the city proper at the guildhall offices. Bregan watched him go, turned, and eyed the interior of his father's study. Would it be worth going through the books and scrolls to see what mission of knowledge had prompted the chaos?

Time, it seemed, might be of the essence. He had places to be and deals to put in place.

Bregan headed for the doors, only a breath or two behind his father.

Chapter Nineteen

TIIVA ROSE FROM HER WRITING DESK in a swirl of color and fabric, her gown one that Quendius might have seen before but could not remember if he had, nor even cared particularly, except that he wondered where her seemingly inexhaustible supply came from. A bemused expression played over her face as she put aside her pen and capped her inkwell before turning to face him fully. Sconces on the wall burned fitfully to augment scant light from an overcast day, giving her copper skin a glow. She was, he supposed, a beautiful woman although he did not particularly find her so even though Abayan Diort had, which was why Quendius kept her. Experience had shown him it paid to know what others valued. She moved with a surety and confidence that amused him as she tilted her chin to meet his gaze.

"Been hunting?"

He held the bow in his off-hand, the quiver with four arrows in it across his back. "Not yet," he answered. "Perhaps in a short while."

"Are the maps I sent you pleasing?"

"They are most complete, as far as I know."

She pushed one hand into a pocket in her skirt which rustled as she did so. "I have hidden nothing from you."

"What do you know of the borders?"

Tiiva pursed her curved mouth in thought a moment. "Only that mountain passes are a natural gate. There are two, one to the west and one to the southwesterly side. Larandaril can also be approached over the mountains from the east, but the passage is difficult and not easily accomplished. Nor would it be secret. The border is well-watched, and the slightest breach of it is sensed almost immediately."

He had a small parchment in his quiver, and pulled it to spread out over her writing desk, a compact and well-done map of Queen Lariel's domain. "Here, then, and here?" He traced the mountains passes with familiarity.

"Yes. Do you have doubts now about getting as far as the estates?"

Quendius gave a sharp shake of his head. "No doubts. I simply wanted to know whatever it is you know."

She watched him trace his hand over the map. "It would be presumptuous," she told him, "with my span of years akin to yours, for me to relate everything I know to you so easily. But what I know of the entrances and exits to the manor now rests at your disposal." Tiiva paused. "Has there been any word from my cousin Galraya on a ransom?"

"Your cousin sent word that you are sorely missed from the family but that your duties have been taken up by another."

"I see." She watched him reroll the map with a few snaps of his wrists.

"There appears to be no love lost between your kin."

"There are casualties in any endeavor." She took a slight step backward.

He replaced the map in his quiver and drew out an arrow. He wondered if she could hear the faint, Demon thrum in it that he heard when he touched it. The polished wood shone in his grasp, the grain of the aryn tree plainly visible in its striated beauty. The jewel shard glittered, its cruel edge sparkling. It gave him pleasure to hold the weapon. "We are at war."

"You and I?"

"Do you think I might ascertain that?"

"I think, Quendius, that your intelligence far supersedes mine and you know far more of the world than I."

"Now you seek to flatter me." He turned the arrow in his fingers, admiring the fletching. "I ask myself why you seek refuge here, rather than at Diort's side."

"A question you did not ask at the time you took me in." Her hands sought, and found, the back of her chair as if she might lean upon it. Or grasp it to use. A shield? A weapon? Her face maintained a slight smile on an otherwise neutral expression. She had Vaelinar eyes, however, and he'd learned long ago he could never trust Vaelinar eyes. He carried them himself, with not a hint whatsoever of the power they promised. Whatever power he had, he'd gotten through work and planning and the sweat of his brow and the blood of his enemies, not by some insubstantial current of magic running through the fabric of the world. What ran through the world was life and death, and he knew both of them intimately. He did not trust anything handed to him, as Tiiva had done with herself.

"Power attracts power," Tiiva offered.

"Abayan Diort looks to become a Galdarkan emperor."

"Perhaps. But what does he rule? Tribes who live in mud villages and goat tents, and pitch their homes at the edge of Mageborn chaos where nothing thrives. Anyone can become king of nothing."

He noticed her hands grasping the back of the chair had gone white around the knuckles. "Why join forces with him at all, then?"

"I thought he had potential." Tiiva's mouth twisted wryly about the words.

"And now he does not, but I do."

She shook her head, hair of spun red-gold shimmering around her shoulders. "You are like playing with fire, to a child who has no concept of the vastness of the element. It consumes, it preserves. It has dimensions for use that a child cannot possibly grasp nor hope to tame. You are beyond my knowing."

He was meant to admire her candor, but it meant nothing to him. "Did you hope to know me?"

"In some small way, yes. I would hesitate to ally with someone I had absolutely no understanding of, and I cannot provide value for you without knowing what you wish."

Did she think she argued for her fate? He had already decided it. His silence fell upon her.

"I have my uses," she said defensively.

"I'm certain you do." He swapped the bow and arrow in his hand and nocked it, hearing the string stretch as he did so.

Her face went pale under its natural coppery sheen. She moved when he did, but even her unnatural speed and grace was no match for the flight of the arrow. It struck home, *thunk*ing deeply into her arm as she let out a cry of anger and surprise. She fell with a second gasp to lie writhing upon the floor in a spreading pool of crimson as the arrow shaft sank deeper and deeper into her, working its way through her flesh and bone as Narskap had promised him it would. He stood over her to watch its progress.

He had not missed. He had wanted a wounding, to incapacitate her, to bend her completely to his will. She writhed upon the floor. Pain tore words from her mouth, and Tiiva thrashed soundlessly, her limbs flailing in her agony. He could almost hear Cerat's hum of satisfaction as it devoured her from the inside out. The blood which had seeped out began to disappear as rapidly as it left her, absorbed by the Souldrinker. It appeared excruciating. Kill shots, when he made them, would be most interesting.

The arrow ate through her arm and then leaped into the air, to his hand. He held it for a long moment, smelling the stink of fresh blood and mortality upon it, but it was clean. Not a smear of crimson nor a gobbet of flesh decorated it. It might never have been loosened upon a target. He returned it to his quiver.

Tiiva lay with her eyes open and back arched, her hands knotted with her arms thrown akimbo with an immense red flower through the sleeve of her gown, expensive fabric tattered about the ruin of her flesh. Her copper color had gone gray. The bleeding had stopped, absorbed by the arrow. He wouldn't even have to cauterize it, he thought. A last look of consciousness sobbed out of her into stillness.

"Yes, I'm certain you will be of great use," he told her slack body.

Chapter
Twenty

D ARAVAN RODE INTO ABAYAN DIORT'S
encampment, taking note of the many tents and
wagons and cooking bays without seeming to. The
tang of the horse lines and middens and the smell of
woodsmoke lingered on the air. Still, as his casual gaze
took in the sights, he made note that this was not nec-
essarily an offensive army hidden among arid hillocks.
The wagons and larger tents held community groups of
women with babes on their hips and backs and children
playing with sticks and stones, as well as moving along
the horse lines grooming or sitting with elders repairing tack. This could well be a recruitment movement,
headed back to the east to one of Diort's burgeoning
cities, bringing nomad Galdarkans home. If not, Diort
had no heart to be taking babes to war.

He recognized the golden tents that pantomimed the
Pavilion of the Sun on a rise which overlooked the encampment. His escorts took him to the foot of the knoll
and motioned for him to dismount. Before he could

reach it, Diort came out and stood, framed by the canopies, his flaring eyes of jade set off by the golden tent and that of his own bronze-hued skin. He wore a woven headpiece that both swept his hair back from his forehead and protected his temples, setting off the tattoos on his cheekbones which marked his rank and bearing. He closed the ground between them, wearing an expression of mild curiosity, a man among the few who could look Daravan in the eyes. The Galdarkans alone matched the height of the Vaelinars, although their frames were more muscular and coarser, and their skins almost universally of bronze tones, from light to dark, and their eyes of green or blue tones. They had been made, it was said, of a union between the Gods and the Mageborn, bred to guard the Mageborn from the rigors of a physical world while they tamed a spiritual one. More likely, they had been specially bred to guard the magic users from each other and the jealous spats which had eventually led to the full-blown wars. However that had come to be, Daravan knew that here was a Galdarkan devoted to his own heritage of guardianship now for his people. But did he also wait for the return of the Mageborn after a thousand years and more?

Daravan doubted the Gods would stir a finger to see them brought back. They had destroyed those the Mageborn had not killed already and disowned all the peoples of their world. But he would be a fool not to fear the return of native magic wielders of Kerith. The pools of chaos they had left behind were disturbing maelstroms of destruction, and if but one person could utilize or awaken them, he feared for the world itself. In all his years roaming these lands, he had never met anyone with even an inkling of this worry, nor did he dare repeat it in case it might find a way to echo into the sleepy minds of Kerith's Gods. Not even within the Vaelinars who worried overmuch about many things had he found a murmur of his concern. They worried, yes, about the attention of the Gods, and the Kerith-born wondered when they might be in the Gods' favor again, but Abayan Diort had never given any sign of waiting for his kings to return. When he spoke of his destiny at all, it was as a unifier of wanderers who needed protection. If his attitude was a weather vane, Daravan prayed it would be a true one.

A slight breeze ruffled the mantle upon his shoulders. Daravan inhaled deeply for a moment, found no hint of rain upon it, and closed within reach of the Galdarkan.

"Do I greet an envoy, a friend, or a spy?" Diort asked of him, a smile on his face.

"I would lie if I did not say all three, depending upon the candlemark of my life."

"And a long life it has been. Therefore, such circumspection must serve you well, even in the camp of a potential enemy. If you're spying today, you are a poor one. May I offer you a cooled beverage?"

"If you will let me sit and drink, that would be most appreciated."

Daravan waited as Diort signaled two men who had flanked him in the canopied shadows of his tent, and they slipped away to do his bidding. More, he could be sure, waited in the shadows. He sat on a hide chair when Diort did. Diort wore a war kilt, of a sort, and a half cloak folded upon his body, giving warmth and yet lending good access to the war harness he wore strapped across his chest and shoulder. The great hammer rested at his back, much like a great sword, its grip aiming at the sky, its head in the curve of Diort's lower back. When Diort sat, he did so at ease, seemingly unaware of the massive weapon and weight he carried. Daravan thought he heard a buzzing in his ears, like that of hornets for sweet nectar, but he couldn't be certain. Did the thing hold a kind of life to it, that it sang to the Galdarkan? And if it sang, what tune would such a thing carry? He had not heard of Demons who communed, but this one did, it seemed.

Daravan flicked his attention away from the weapon

as he settled in the chair, and the leather creaked as it shifted to hold his weight. Abayan waited until cups arrived and his men faded to a discreet distance from them, their hands near but not on their weapons. Daravan did not wait for his host to drink, but drank deeply, signaling a trust he did not quite feel. Diort followed without hesitation. The watered juice was indeed cool, with a slight hint of sweetness and another flavor he could not identify except that it refreshed with a tang. The warlord watched his eyes and noted that he had taken a quick sweep across the gathered army on the grounds below them.

"Do you count my numbers? I would be a fool to have them all on display for you."

"And we both know you're not a fool. Actually, I was looking at the mix. Mostly Galdarkan, with a scattering of Kernan and Dweller. No Bolgers."

"I have Bolgers. You haven't looked far enough south. Not the raiders who slapped your queen a bit; they were rogue, but my clan chieftain is a good man with a forging background. He does metalsmith work and repairs for me. His name is Rufus."

"Who keeps the raiders?"

"Again, no proof, but I'd say it is Quendius."

"Not a stretch of imagination there."

"No. Quendius runs a small army of very hard and ruthless men. He never intends to stay and rule, just drill through and destroy what he can, get what he wants, and get out."

"Not your tactics."

"No. Any alliance we had was based on the need to comply at the time."

"And you've no need now?"

"No, thank the Gods. I won't move openly against him yet, and so he leaves me alone." Diort shifted a little uneasily in his chair, despite his words.

"But the day will come."

"Perhaps. It seems I have other concerns for now."

He took a slow sip of his juice while judging the posture of the man opposite him, and Abayan mirrored his actions. Diort lowered his cup to add, "For today, then, may I ask what compels you to visit me?"

"I'm here, unofficially, on behalf of the Warrior Queen." Daravan leaned forward, his voice pitched so that the only one who could actually discern his words sat close to him and the others would know only that he spoke in a mild, unthreatening tone.

"Unofficially. You carry no papers and no seal, then."

"Not at this time."

"Interesting. And do you allow me an unofficial response, or do you intend to hold me at my word even when I cannot hold you at yours?"

Daravan lifted a shoulder and let it fall. "I haven't heard it said that you are dishonest. It costs you nothing to listen."

"That's where you are wrong if you're here to distract and delay me. These people need solidarity and a home. Our days of wandering have to be over." Abayan leaned forward on the table, resting some of his weight on his well-toned forearms. The scars of a fighter decorated his arms. "I'm glad to have good proof of my word, and I expect no less of the queen . . . but you're another sort altogether."

Daravan said dryly, "Again, I suppose it would depend on the hour of my life. However, my deeds today are not for myself but for Lariel Anderieon, and so you may count upon what you expect."

"But I have no expectations. You've not given me any."

Daravan cradled his unfinished cup of juice. "Is this a good time, then, Warlord Diort? I take it you're listening?"

"Only a fool would forget to listen."

"I know it seems, on the surface, that Lariel determines to go to war with you, but only because there seemed no alternative if you were entangled with Quendius. That bond seems sundered, and so gives rise to the notion that there are options that can be explored. She's concerned that you're pressuring people into a nation who don't wish to be under your rule. If you can dissuade her of that, there are alliances which might be more advantageous."

"True."

"There are alliances of fealty. Of blood and marriage. Of commerce. And of partnership."

"Among others." Abayan Diort leaned on one elbow, his chair creaking companionably as he did so. He showed no sign of his feelings other than that he listened. His jade eyes, like his face, remained implacable.

"The question, of course, is which would be the most appealing to you and do your following the most good, a question which has a complex answer. You would wish ties that aid, not constrain, and lessen, not greaten, your strife. An alliance and truce that go beyond a mere marriage."

"A marriage is not mere, depending on the woman, Lord Daravan."

Daravan allowed himself a flash of a smile. "Corrected. While the Warrior Queen hesitates to offer herself, she has asked me to convey that it could be a consideration."

"And what if I want children? It's said that a Galdarkan/Vaelinar match is sterile."

"It is not uncommon, is it, to have a second wife for heirs if the first is infertile? All parties accepting, of course, and there would certainly be no slight felt if such were the case. Only if she were to be humiliated and put aside without honor or estate, which I know you would not do. In fact, you look to me like a man who could handle two wives."

Diort's mouth twitched. "There isn't a man alive who is able to, but thousands who think they can." He put a hand palm down on the table, fingers spread. "I've heard no terms that make me think this would be a bargain. If we meet in combat, and I dominate, these lands fall to me, ripe for the plucking, along with Lariel."

"If you meet in combat, excepting the rout you witnessed at the river a few days' past, I cannot predict who might win, but I can predict that there will not be enough survivors of either army to stand alone. You both may well waver on the threshold of annihilation, and what sort of victory is that? Quendius will wipe out the remnants, his work having already been done for him."

"Does she know that?"

"She," answered Daravan slowly, "is a very wise woman."

"I would hate to settle for second best." Diort stood slowly. His jade eyes crinkled at the corners from the sunlight flooding the encampment.

"If not her, there is another ..."

Abayan glanced to him.

Daravan cleared his throat. "She has asked me, independent of the queen's offer, to put herself before you." He shifted in his chair purposely. "Lara has kept her hidden, and she's not been publicly embraced by the court, but I imagine you've heard some tales of her. She holds the Talent of water, and no one's been able to measure how strong it is. Your lands to the east are often in frequent need of good wells."

Diort's nostrils flared slightly as he gave a mild snort and said, "I can hire a dowser."

"This woman cleared the Andredia of corruption and poison. Think of it, Abayan, sweet water when and where you need it. With water, even stone can bloom."

He blinked.

Daravan pushed his lies a little. "Rivergrace asks only for peace. If you agree, she's naïve enough to politicking that she would leave the details to such as you and I. Consider her suit as well." Daravan left his cup sitting on the table.

"A queen or a foundling with rare magic. I would be a fool not to consider either, if either considers me."

Daravan thought of mentioning the Raymy and then decided against it. If the Galdarkan's intelligence was good enough, he would know. If not, Daravan didn't wish to let him know the coast seemed vulnerable without the Jewel of Tomarq and that Diort might not have to move a finger to have Lariel beg him for an alliance when the ancient enemy came after them. She had strength in her current position, and he would barter with that, whether she liked it or not. He stood, matching Abayan's gaze. He'd lit a fire in the man, and felt pleased to note it. "You have much to offer each other. My thanks for listening."

Diort dropped his chin in acknowledgment. He beckoned to his pavilion. "I'll have my men show you out. There are areas which, despite your sharp eyes, you've not seen and I would rather keep to myself for the moment. I'm certain you understand."

Daravan reflected on the way out of the hills that he understood war all too well.

Chapter
Twenty-One

GRACE SAT ON THE CUSHIONED LEDGE of her window and watched the mists of evening curl outside. The hour had grown late, but she hadn't found sleep yet and had finally given up on her bed. What was she that Sevryn avoided her, and Lariel no longer felt she could trust her, and the Goddess who had cradled her had turned against her? She had come so far, only to falter. She tucked her hair behind her ear and then traced the tipped outline of it gently with one finger. Vaelinar and yet not. Whole and yet not. The fog billowed up against her window, and she put her palm to it. She could feel the dampness in the air, the crying out to be fulfilled with rain and yet to be denied it. She reached out and plucked the thread of water as it spun through the air toward her before realizing, too late, that the River Goddess might be trying to trap her.

With that thought, she lost herself.

Water of the deepest blue dragged Rivergrace plummeting downward. These were not the waters which gave her peace and hope. These were bitter cold and sharp and biting against her skin, swallowing her whole and flooding her with fear. Gray shards of ice lanced through the liquid, numbing her as they swirled around her, biting and tracking her plunge into the depths. She struggled against the fall, but another held her arms, clasped her from behind within an iron embrace, murmuring harsh words in her ear.

This is my kingdom and you live here by my will, not yours. Give up to me that which you have stolen, and I will let you rise from here unharmed. Keep it, and you will remain here, chained until your flesh dissolves and your bones decay and all that stays will be your fettered soul. Keep that which you have taken from me, and all whom you have loved will become as nothing more than ash on the face of this earth while you cry after them and your tears feed my demesne. You will witness every agonizing moment of their mortality while they search uselessly for you and mourn your loss and struggle with lives which I shall knot and tangle in hopelessness until their return to dust. Neither they nor you will ever know peace. But you and I have sheltered together, and I am not heartless to you. Let go that which you hold that belongs to me and I shall reward you for its release, keep you close in all your long days to me, and you will prosper in your freedom.

Grace fought for breath against the grip upon her body, her ribs and arms bound tightly, the cords on her throat straining, but she could not breathe and every sense of her body screamed silently against the death pressing in on her. Her hair and the other's hair tangled about her, long streamers of ribbon flailing about her face and shoulders, a net through which she could barely see the endless blue of the water as the River Goddess bore her down and she sank like a stone. She prayed for that moment when her toes would touch a sandy bottom and she could kick upward, she could be centered, she would know where the surface lay above even if she could not hope to reach it in time . . . but nothing met her feet. The fall seemed endless and her lungs about to burst.

Pray for drowning if you will, the Goddess hissed in her ear, *but that mercy will never come. Not until I allow it.*

They fell deeper where sunlight could barely touch the water, and its blue became the color of a storm-filled night, dark and turbulent and unknowable. Her hair veiled her face in a gossamer curtain as she fought to keep her eyes open, feeling that if she closed them, the weight of the water would keep her from ever opening her eyes again and she would be truly blind in this kingdom. And if she could see again, what would she see? A troubled Sevryn who had gone to the arena day after day since their one night together, and who would barely speak to her after, battered and bruised and quiet, turning his face and eyes from her when they met. A love who would not, could not, share his mind with her though she could see a deep troubling which he could not hide from her, no matter how marked from training he might be. Would she seek then her sister, an absent Nutmeg who devoted herself to Jeredon's well-being, her cheer and glow undeniable but meant for another now and not for Rivergrace's comfort? Perhaps her gaze would fall upon an unbending Lariel who would neither avow nor disavow Grace's own existence as a Vaelinar, though as Warrior Queen, she held all of their fates in her hand to crush or set free with a blessing. Did she truly wish to hold these in her thoughts any longer, as painful as they had become?

A tremor ran through her. That she thought such things chilled through her, and she knew they were true thoughts, but they were not the ones by which she loved and lived. They were only clouds that might drift by, darkening her momentarily, but they were not what commanded the way she lived.

She would not be turned as a weapon against herself! Rivergrace dragged a hand free and sliced it through the water in dismay, silencing the intruder in her thoughts where the River Goddess' voice had invaded so slyly she almost could not tell her mind from the other's. A quiet coldness bled from inside her head, a feeling so real she could not believe that crimson did not stain the waters capturing her. A frustrated hiss followed her small triumph.

Give me back what is mine, and I will be gone from you, and you from my kingdom, with my blessings. Hold onto it, and this cursing will be but the beginning of many. . . .

Grace found her voice. "You unraveled me into a single thread of life and soul, and then rewove me after I had given you shelter for twenty years. You held me as a child and only gave me up to live a true life when you couldn't hold me any longer! You tore me from my father and mother in floodwaters and let them die because you had no strength, and I became your vessel to shelter you. When I found the strength to grow, so did you, and we survived. You took everything from me, not once, but twice. I have nothing of yours, nothing!"

Midnight-blue water churned about her in swirls of ice-white anger and silent rebuttal. Tiny bubbles danced through the froth and burst against her skin in staccato and painful stings.

One arm freed, she reached across to free her other arm, her hand splayed across the pale-as-marble hand of the Goddess, a hand without warmth to it, with strength that seemed to melt as she touched it as though it were nothing more than ice. She pried the fingers off her forearm and then shrugged the cloaking weight of the Goddess off her.

"I won't let you take my freedom from me again! I am alive, and I am someone, not a shell holding your crippled essence. Give me that due, as I give you yours!"

The water screamed.

Her senses flooded back. Rivergrace came to herself, thrown across the room into a tangle of blankets. Her pillows tumbled to the floor and the hollow at the far side of the bed where Nutmeg usually slept, was yet still cold and empty. She brushed her hair from her face and stared toward the window for a long moment, feeling her throat pulse with the agony she had just experienced. She put a hand there, to feel it, to assure her that her heart still beat, that her body did not struggle for life and breath as it had. Dew sparkled upon her skin, and she felt her hair lying wetly upon her head as she pushed herself from an otherwise dry bed as dawn broke fitfully through the windows. She combed her hair through, smelling rain and lake water upon it. She put her hand out to a mound of blankets, feeling for Nutmeg just in case, but found no sign of her except for pillows that had been pounded into a hollow to match the small one in the mattress.

She might as well be up and about as, no doubt, all the others were. She held little hope that she could find someone she could speak to about her vision. She'd asked before, vaguely, of one of the Vaelinars who healed soul as well as body, only to be told that dreams of suffocating water were dreams from beyond birth, and of the mother, and influences that weighed upon the mind. That much, she knew without arcane knowledge or study. As for it being only a dream, the manifestation had lain about her like a mantle. The River Goddess haunted her. She would until she had what she wished from Rivergrace or saw her dead and beyond surrender.

She washed her hair quickly, not waiting for warm water or help, unable to bear the smell of the Goddess upon her. She dressed for a day where winter had finally crept in, solidly and in gray tones, rain drizzling quietly against the manor through a fog. She found no sign of Sevryn at the dining tables, and made her way outside to the showering racks where she could hear Bistane's clear and handsome voice singing, a ballad that seemed to fit the somber tones of the morning.

*"At summer's last bloom, at winter's fall, at sword
    blade ever turning,
The war came to an end on the banks of Ashenbrook.
Through fields of death the river ran, its waters laced
    with blood,
Bearing a fallen king upon its tide, carried onto his
    Returning.
Spring has come and gone in time, with grasses ever
    greening
Still the Ashenbrook flows through killing fields,
Its dark and bitter waters running through banks of
    clay and bone.
Only men can sing of memory, of war and its darkest
    gleaning."*

He sang of Kanako's death, the Vaelinar warrior who
had quelled the uprising of the Bolger clans once and
for all, a bloody conflict that had cost both the Vaelinars
and the beastlike Bolgers dearly. It was their greatest
and dearest triumph. She could not think of them united
in an army that could sweep across the lands and slaughter all of Kerith they faced, but they had once. She could
not think of Bolgers at all without thinking of the one
she'd befriended in the mines where she had spent her
earliest years. Rufus, with whom she'd shared bits of
meager food and who had brought her flowers from the
outside. His nature was fierce and gruff but honorable,
and she could only think that the war his people had carried had risen out of desperation and misunderstanding.
She ducked her head against a spattering of raindrops
from the eaves of the outbuilding as she approached the
showering racks.

Barrels rested on overhead catwalks, and loosed
water on those standing in the stalls below, a primitive
but quick way of showering off sweat and dirt. Her father Tolby had built a similar arrangement, stalls that
ran under barrels with spigots, in order to spray herb
dips over his livestock. She could see Bistane, his bare

torso rippled with muscle, as he turned under a spray of cold water, his song giving way to the process of getting cleaned. Beyond him, she could see Sevryn toweling off his head and shoulders and called out to him. Both men pulled on their leggings as she drew near. He frowned as he looked back at her, but he came out of the racks, his hair wet and glistening, bruises purpled against his skin, scars she knew intimately a faded white line against his arms and flanks, a rough towel in one hand and his tunic in the other.

"Aderro," he said, and his eyes warmed even though his face looked solemn. "What are you doing here?"

"It's plain to see," Bistane said, jostling him slightly as he joined them, "that only one thing can tumble a maid out of a warm bed so early on a bitter morning. She's come to hear me sing and catch a glimpse of me." He winked as he pulled on his shirt and began lacing it over his well-muscled chest. "We all know it wasn't to come hear you sing."

"I sing."

"Of course you do! Like the croaking of a drunken Bolger. Now, Rivergrace, lass . . . I'll bet you sing. Raised by Dwellers, surely you do." He appraised her, a teasing smile on his finely etched features, his eyes of sharpest, cleanest blues that seemed to look not at her, but through her. She caught a sense of what it would be like to meet him on the battlefield. A frisson of fear ran through her.

"What would you know of Dweller songs except those you hear in taverns?" Sevryn nudged him back, as he pulled on his tunic and tugged it into place with the slightest of winces.

"Ah, lad. I know the Dwellers sing their orchards into blossom, and chant their beers into brewing, and even move their looms to the beat of a drum. There isn't a moment in their lives go by that a song doesn't run through it. Isn't that right, fair Grace?"

She had not thought upon it before, but now that

Bistane spoke of it, she knew that he was right. Her family and the others she knew did weave a song throughout their daily lives, from the humming of her mother Lily as she tailored a fine new gown, to her brothers who whistled and jeered at one another as they did their chores, to Nutmeg who knew all the new dances and tried teaching them now and then to Grace who held few of the virtues of her nickname. "It seems you know my family well, Lord Bistane."

He finished lacing his shirt, and tilted his head, looking both at her and beyond her, and his tone saddened a bit. "Lass. Not only your family but many before it. Although my seeming to you is young, my life is filled with generations of families."

"Lived long and learned little," Sevryn gibed. "Lyrics from the taverns and bathhouses about sum up your wisdom."

"Hey, now! Perhaps it's time you and I have a go at it in the arena. I feel my virtue and honor need protecting."

"You can't defend what you haven't got. You lost your virtue long ago." Sevryn put his hand on Rivergrace's shoulder even as he answered lightly, "I won't be held accountable for your actions from beyond my birthing."

"I am wounded!" Bistane placed his hand upon his chest. "Fair lady, you must witness for me. I should demand a duel. Although . . ." and his tone trailed off. "I will be defending myself enough, shortly. I should not alienate the very man who is likely to stand at my back protecting me from the Demon who crosses the borders of Larandaril even as we speak."

"Demon?" If a Demon had pierced the borders of Larandaril, her disturbing dreams perhaps had reason beyond her own fears. It could not be Cerat. She knew his touch almost as well as she knew that of the River Goddess, yet if there existed one such a thing, there would be more. Like raiders, like Ravers.

Bistane tossed his toweling aside onto the shower

racks and dried his hands on the thighs of his pants as he answered her. "A She-Demon, Mistress Farbranch, one of biting meanness."

"Surely Lariel or Osten is putting together a detail to go deal with it? And how can such a thing get past the borders?"

"Just such answers as I'll be sent to get. I had hoped Sevryn might join me."

"I wouldn't count on any alliance with me, Bistane. You're on your own against that she-force and the grievances she brings with her.

"Wounded again! Perhaps mortally now. Is there no honor among soldiers?"

"Not this time."

Grace made a perturbed noise, and Sevryn's hand rubbed her shoulder gently. "How can you joke about such a thing?"

"Is not laughter a weapon? One I think such Demons would flee all the quicker. They have no sense of humor, for that would imply the warmth of life, and that they are bereft of as well."

"How can you stand to sense them?"

"That's not all there is to the world." The levity left his face for a moment as he looked keenly at her. "Can you not see it? Feel Kerith? Is it true, then, that you freed the sacred Andredia River with little sense or knowledge of your skills? You were raised as a slave?"

Sevryn's fingers tightened on Rivergrace's shoulder, so firm that she nearly cried out both from the surprise and pain of the grip, but instead she inhaled deeply, reminding herself that although she was in Larandaril and this was a gathering for war, not all who came here were true allies or friends. "I was enslaved, yes, and as for my skills, I'm learning to look upon the land as you do."

He gestured. "Lara's kingdom is fair. What do you see, even on this gray day as the sky teases us with a hope of rain?"

She knew from the days Lariel and Jeredon had spent

with her what she should see, the elements that ran like
fine threads throughout all the firmaments that existed,
that her Vaelinar eyes were remarkable orbs that could
recognize the very *being* of what they looked upon, and
there were days when she did see just that ... for a fleeting
moment or two. It was not something the Vaelinars saw
constantly, but they did recognize it when they focused
upon it, and depending upon the talents and skills of their
bloodline, they could manipulate the threads of those elements. Sevryn was the only one of Vaelinar blood who
did not have the multihued eyes and yet held the magic
within him. For that reason, he was invaluable to Lariel
who was one of a handful or less who knew he had skills.
Others, such as Bistane, dismissed the possibility of certain potentials within him, and in his position, it helped to
be overlooked and underestimated. Yet, after the night,
she feared to touch those threads of the elements.

"I don't see as you do, Lord Bistane," she admitted
reluctantly.

"But you can?"

"Upon occasion."

A fleeting expression passed through the deeps of his
brilliant blue eyes. He made an almost imperceptible
move toward her saying, "It would be a pity to have in-
herited our eyes and not our powers, although there's
that in you, as many have said, which is not altogether
Vaelinar. . . ."

Sevryn turned slightly, blocking Bistane's path, saying,
"Have a care, lord."

He drew himself up. "No offense meant, milady Rivergrace." He turned away from both of them, hiding
his face as he repeated his question mildly, "Then what
might you see on a day like today?"

She looked beyond the yards, beyond the paths and
graveled roads fencing off the manor from the lands,
and across the fields and groves as far as she could see,
cloud-laden mountains on the far horizon. What she observed cut her to the bone, and she would not have spo-

ken it aloud, but something compelled her. "I see," she said slowly, "a dark and tangled net lowering over us."

A stunned silence followed her words and then Bistane forced a laugh. "That will remind me not to seek answers which I should not have!" He turned back, with an easy grin on his keen features. "You have your jest, milady, and well done. Someone has already told you that it is Tressandre ild Fallyn who rides in, no doubt. I'll leave you two to chuckle at me while I go see if there's anything left in the kitchens for a second breakfasting." Smiling yet, he moved past them and away.

Sevryn's hand unclenched from her shoulder and slid down her back where he rested it. "He is a Vantane for a reason," he remarked quietly.

"I wasn't making fun of him."

He turned her about so he could look down into her face. "It lightens my heart to see you. Forgive me for not being with you these past few days."

"And I should not be here now."

"I didn't say that."

"It's not often that I see fear in your face." She put her hand up and cupped the side of his bruised jaw.

"Perhaps it is reflected from yours." He covered her hand with his, cold from the shower water and rough from his training.

"We're both bothered. You begged me to come to you, and now you're staying away. Were there consequences? Did Lara find out? Does she send you out every day to get beaten like this?"

"If she has, and I imagine she did, this is her house, after all, she's said nothing. It's not her will that keeps me in the arena." His jaw tightened under her touch. "This is something I must do."

"I'll admit I know little of training for war. It's not the apple picking I was raised to do . . . but I do know that, if you're picking apples, you don't do it by climbing the ladder and throwing yourself to the ground as hard as you can, over and over."

Sevryn chuckled in spite of himself. "I'll try to keep that in mind." He released her hand.

"Keep this in mind as well. I have three brothers. I remember well that when one was bothered, he'd nudge the others until a brawl erupted. Hosmer always says there's nothing like a fight in the dirt to clear the mind."

"I should remember that you are a font of Farbranch wisdom. I'll ask you to remember that there are things I must deal with, in my own way."

His solemn gray eyes watched her face closely. "We're together then, and yet alone." She withdrew her hand from his face slowly.

"It's best that way." He took a step back from her, and she thought she could not bear that, the distance he wanted to put between them. They had come from places so far apart to find one another, and now he seemed to hesitate. "Can I give you a warning without hitting your Dweller stubborn streak?"

"It's a streak that's served me well, but Tolby raised no fools."

He nodded. "Stay clear of Tressandre. She's not coming here on Lara's bidding, and that alone will have the two of them at odds. I can't say why she is here, only that it is likely not to serve anyone's interests but her own."

"Why open the border to her, then?"

"Lariel can't afford to shut out an ally, even one as unpredictable as the Stronghold ild Fallyn. You were fortunate that she didn't notice you at the Concords last summer, but now she knows of you and little good can come of that. You are a puzzle to the Vaelinars, and they have little patience with enigmas. You don't want to be caught in a power struggle between the two of them."

"Surely she isn't coming for me."

"I doubt it's for that reason alone, but . . ." he paused and shifted his weight.

Rivergrace caught a hint of intuition. "She knows you."

He did not answer for a very long moment, and then said quietly, "Yes."

It struck her. She didn't mean it to, but it did, and she caught her breath for a moment after finding it rough in her throat. She could not be like a child in this; she had known Sevryn had a life far beyond hers, and some of it had been very rough indeed. He would not speak of those years locked away in his memories when he had been imprisoned by Quendius, but she knew those years would haunt him forever. He did not stand now with Tressandre, but with her, and that should be enough. She made a slight gesture as if wiping away a sign written in the air between them. "That is past. I understand that."

"She may not."

"I trust you."

His gaze slid away from her briefly. She found that more chilling, more deadly, than the embrace of the River Goddess. She touched his face. Bruises lined his eyes, physical proof of the burdens he already carried. She didn't want to tell him, but she had to. "I have to tell you this, then," she said, unsure if he would heed her. "A warning, if you will take it, because I don't know what else to call it. The River Goddess haunts me, from the rivers I once found safe to my very dreams. She implores me to return something I've stolen from her. I have nothing, nothing, I swear to you, but she threatens you and all the others I hold dear. Believe me, if you can, and stay clear of fresh water. Stay out of her reach. She touches me when nothing else can, and I don't know what I can do yet. Please believe me and keep yourself safe." She tucked one arm about herself, like a shield, preparing for his rebuttal.

"Is this a threat from her . . . or from you?"

"Sevryn, how can you say that to me? Why would I threaten you?"

"Because I haven't pressed Lara to do what's right."

"Wasn't it you who told me we have what we have with or without her?"

His gray eyes looked hard as granite and as unmovable. "I might have said something to that effect."

"And you meant it."

"As much as you mean it when you say you love me."

She pulled her other arm over her first, doubling her shield. "You sound as if love is a weapon."

"It can be." He touched the back of her wrist. "Or it can be a better shield than flesh and bone, steel and stone."

"Against what? Disbelief? It seems not."

He took a short breath. "Forgive me, aderro. I am not . . . myself."

"Listen to me, then. A Goddess hunts us both. I can't do what she asks of me because I don't know how."

He looked her in the eyes again and gave a bitter laugh. "Then you know why I can't be around you. The Gods conspire, it seems. Cerat whispers in my soul, and he wants blood, a lot of blood, and most of all he wants yours." Sevryn turned half away. "I hoped it was only a nightmare. It seems we are God-and-Demon-touched, Grace, our souls pitted against their power, and I can't tell you if we have a hope of standing against them."

"Not alone," she whispered.

"No. Not alone, we don't." He reached out again to grasp her hand tightly for a moment before letting go harshly. "I'll send word to you later." He broke away from her, shoulders bent, moving away briskly, and he did not look back.

Chapter
Twenty-Two

THE WIND BROUGHT in the late morning storm, along with a thunder of hoofbeats and shrill whistles punctuated by sharp cracks of a whip. Riderless horses ran with the grace of those who know they are fleet of foot and admirable of beauty, their ears pricked high and their nostrils flared to drink deeply of the wind. They galloped down the lane, scattering waterfowl and farmer boys ahead of them who had come to gawk or been caught asleep at the edge of the pastures, and they snorted with amusement, their forelocks, manes, and tails flying as they ran. Behind them, standing in her stirrups, long hair bannered behind her as wild as any mane, rode Tressandre ild Fallyn, her arm brandishing the whip which she cracked now and then to keep the herd on the main lane, her colors of black and silver flowing about her as she drove the band ahead of her. Behind her cantered lancers and cavalry and bowmen, all in the colors of Stronghold ild Fallyn, all of them looking as if they drew the storm with them like a cloak swirling down upon the estate.

Jeredon rocked back a little in his cart with a muttered word that neither Rivergrace nor Nutmeg caught. Nutmeg stared as though entranced, and Grace thought of their Dweller brothers and how they had fallen under Tressandre's spell on one spring fair day. That was the day raiders hit the small village of Stonesend and Nutmeg nearly died.

"Does she know how beautiful she is?" Nutmeg murmured.

"Oh, she knows. She's had her hooks in all of us at one time or another, I'll wager." Jeredon watched the ensemble clatter into the yard, the free horses pounding and stamping to a halt, milling about with their heads thrown up and the whites of their eyes showing a touch, their hooves gleaming, as if they, and not the front, were the storm before the rain.

Rivergrace glanced to him. "Sevryn . . ."

Jeredon's attention came about. He frowned at her a moment before leaning out of his cart and sweeping a rock off the garden wall at his elbow. He tossed it to her. "That is a rock," he said. "Hundreds of years older than you . . . perhaps thousands, if rocks are what we think they are. Yours is not the first hand to hold it. Can you blame it for the hands of others who might first have picked it up, shaped it, built with it, or cast it aside when it had no way of knowing about you or that your hand might cup it more fairly, more lovingly, than any other?"

"Are you saying a man is as blameless as a rock?"

"Somewhat. And most of us are as clueless." His gaze swept over Nutmeg casually before Jeredon swiveled his cart about to face Tressandre as she curbed her horse to a prancing walk, the mount blowing a little with exertion as it sidestepped toward them, one wary eye on the man in his contraption. Nutmeg's hand dropped to the back of the cart behind Jeredon where she gripped it, knuckles whitening.

Rivergrace replaced the rock into its niche in the garden wall and dusted off her hands on her skirts as the beautiful Vaelinar rode near, and reined to a halt. Her vibrant green eyes seemed to take no notice of anyone but Jeredon. She tucked a long strand of wild honey hair behind a curved ear.

"Good day, Jeredon Eladar. You look well. Your hair is wet. Has the rain hit here before us for a while?"

"Good day as well, Lady Tressandre, and no, although I think the storm rides your heels. A little rain would be refreshing. I've been swimming for exercising."

Tressandre laughed at him, her voice full of promise more than that of merriment, and her green upon green eyes held a knowing glitter. "A better man than I! Any creek hereabouts will be too cold for my blood." She assessed Grace then quickly, but her gaze lingered on Nutmeg for quite a long while as Jeredon explained about a mineral pool with heated waters. Tress removed her attention and coiled her whip with neat, graceful movements. "As you describe it, then, a swim would be quite refreshing. Perhaps I might be invited next time?"

"Most assuredly. What have you brought us? Green-broken horses?"

"Only the best from our lands but far from wild. These riderless are archer-trained, for the queen's bowmen. I heard your force was cut down and that you were training new men. We thought this humble gift from our Stronghold would help in your endeavors while my brother Alton answers the muster as we ild Fallyn were directed." She gave Jeredon a look through slightly lowered, thick eyelashes.

"If only armies marched as fast as rumors fly," said Jeredon dryly, "then we would have Diort surrounded within the day."

"Rumor only, then? My apologies if my spies were so poorly informed."

"Not misinformed at all, to my misfortune. I sent off a troop of lads I thought well-trained, and they might have been on an open field with battle lines, and not shot at from behind the nearest tree. They were too bold and forgot that they exposed themselves every time they set themselves for a good shot. I've been trying to make amends."

Tressandre tied her whip to her saddle as she gave her reins over to one of her lancers. "Amends are not necessary," she began, "We only thought to lend our aid." Her voice faded as one of Lariel's stable lads dropped a corral pole, and with a sharp whistle, headed her horses into pasture. They responded with snorts and kicks and tails flying, dashed into the grass enclosure where winter's bitter touch had barely grazed the greenery. Expressionless, she watched her charges sprinting away, letting her finely chiseled features show only her beauty and not her thoughts. When the eager whickers and whinnying died away, a new voice cut through the air.

"Tressandre ild Fallyn. I thought I heard the sound of spurs and whips."

She looked back over her shoulder idly; one hand twitched as she dropped it to her thigh where her fingers stroked the haft of a sheathed dagger. "Bistane Vantane. I thought I smelled the stable yards. Or is it the middens?"

"If anyone would know the smell of human *velk*, it would be you."

"I missed your escort at the border." Tressandre did not turn further, continuing to watch Vantane over her shoulder, her gaze veiled by the fall of her dark honey-colored hair over her brow and down her shoulder and back. Disdain outlined her brow.

"I turned back in disappointment when I saw that the only ild Fallyn who could fight was not among your group."

"True if you look for the only one who fights on your level. Alton has gone east, as ordered." Tressandre turned on her heel, then, her gaze sharp upon Bistane. "He would have preferred the chance to even old scores, as no one wishes to ride into battle with more enemies at your back than before you."

"He would know the proper placement of traitorous enemies, that is certain."

"Tell me, Bistane, does such bitterness damage your singing voice? It surely must."

Bistane made a dismissive gesture. "I sing well enough when there is no blade in my flank."

"That must be difficult since your back is usually turned as you run away."

"A Vantane is generally too busy on the field to run or to notice whose back is turned which way, something a coward must do at a distance." Bistane's words dropped coldly. They stared at one another.

Jeredon coughed. "Truce, the two of you." He put his hands up, leaning forward in his carriage chair.

Bistane's lip curled into a half smile as he took a step back from Tressandre, and when he spoke, his tone had become light again. "Why, it has been truce for a century or so, has it not, fair Tressandre? How the seasons scatter before a beauty such as yours." Bistane leaned upon Jeredon's cart. "Have a care with this instructress, Jeredon. Her prowess with a bow is indeed without match. She cheats, of course, but that does not make her or any of the Stronghold less effective an archer."

"Cheats? How?"

Bistane smiled thinly at Nutmeg's outburst, as though all of them had overlooked her for the moment. "By virtue of her Vaelinar Talents. Perhaps she will demonstate for you, Mistress Farbranch."

Tressandre's nostrils flared ever so slightly as she looked down on Nutmeg. Her lips parted a little as if she considered an answer and dismissed it, saying instead,

"Jeredon and his nursemaid will get ample evidence as we move to join the muster."

"My orders," Jeredon said tightly, "are to remain at Larandaril."

Her eyebrows flew up in surprise in what, Rivergrace thought, might be the first natural expression she'd seen on the woman in the past moments.

"The queen doubtless has her reasons." Bistane thumped a hand on Jeredon's shoulder in sympathy.

"The queen wishes to keep a guard here."

Tressandre's face settled into a mask of hard beauty. "Perhaps she needs a demonstration, as well, of my particular Talents." She reached to her back and withdrew an arrow. She dropped it, but it did not fall. It hovered in the air in front of her. "The Stronghold of ild Fallyn can will an arrow stronger, harder, and truer than any other. So, too, I can drive the queen's infirm brother." And she looked to Jeredon who began to rise without his stirring a muscle. "I can bring a king to his feet."

Nutmeg gasped as Jeredon thrust his hands out to steady himself, inadvertently thrusting her away from him unnoticed as Tressandre brought him effortlessly to his feet without laying a hand upon him. He let out a low groan as he straightened. Rivergrace caught Nutmeg by the arm to steady her as they watched Jeredon stand. It seemed effortless from the Vaelinar, but Grace saw the cords of Tressandre's neck tighten and the edges of her eyes narrow in concentration. The finest of lines flawed her beautiful face. Nutmeg put her fist to her mouth as Jeredon's face lightened, and an expression of hope passed over his features before he cleared his throat and his eyes went neutral.

Lariel Anderieon's voice cut through the sudden quiet. "Well done, Tressandre ild Fallyn, but as Lord Bistane noted, perhaps the queen does have plans. Those plans might include a man who can think whether on his feet or not. While the handful of you greet each other in the stable yards, Tranta Istlanthir has come in by my front door, and he brings dire news which I would wish all of you to know."

Tranta Istlanthir came from a family which held perhaps the most distinctive marking of any Vaelinar who had come to Kerith, his hair of dark, brillantine blue unchanged down through generations, eyes of dark green upon light green, and skin so fair it held a faint blue reflection of his hair. Rivergrace liked him for his self-deprecating way, sure of himself but not displaying it as many of the Vaelinars did. Although his family's and his own skills were strong and varied, one still could not imagine him far from his roots, and it was true that one would find him mostly near the cliffs of Tomarq and on the great bay where the city of Hawthorne reigned, overlooking the vast western ocean. While it was true that he held an indisputable affinity for salt water and its shores, he did not often sail. They plied a small fleet for coastal fishing only, and some minor trade from port to port, but the Istlanthirs did not wander far, it being an unspoken law that the salted waters held mysteries which the Vaelinars were loath to explore, and enemies whose attention had strayed for the moment and whom they did not wish to attract. It was also equally true that he was smitten by his Warrior Queen, and that he would do anything for her although she seldom even looked upon him, something Rivergrace could not understand. Tranta was intelligent and held a good sense of humor, his tone usually light unlike the fate-weighted sensibilities of the Stronghold of the ild Fallyn or the House Vantane. Perhaps Lara did not take him seriously, as he did not seem to take himself. He remained one of Grace's favorite people since their first meetings, and as he saw her approach through the manor's main hallway, his eyes lit as well, and he made a half bow toward her. He'd given up the cane he'd been using when she saw him last, which meant that his injuries from his great fall off the cliffs of Tomarq while attending the Jewel had healed. The ocean had cradled him when she could have smashed him asunder, but still his injuries had been considerable for a fall from that height.

Or perhaps he had merely decided a cane was too cumbersome, and a limp would be merely an acceptable character trait. Rivergrace found her face lighting up as she dipped a curtsy to him, Nutmeg on her heels. He had offered once to trade secrets with her on the vagaries of salted water versus fresh and the Goddesses and Gods thereof, but they'd never had the opportunity. She'd thought him half-joking anyway, as his Talent lay in the fire of the great Jewel which shielded the coast with its fierce eye which reflected the heat and fire of the heavens to scour the oceans of any offenders as they tried to close upon the shore. Still, she thought he held a love for the sea. With hair and eyes like that, how could he not?

"Mistresses Farbranch," he noted, as Nutmeg joined Rivergrace in a quick bob. "It takes the weariness from my labors away to see you both. Nutmeg, I hear you have tamed our Warrior Prince and that he is healing admirably under your touch."

Nutmeg's face warmed into a blush, but she pinched her full lips shut and would not say a word as Jeredon wheeled past her, Tressandre at his right arm. Tranta watched them go by, and raised an eyebrow. Then he inclined his head to the girls. "Whoever said that man's nature was as inconstant as the sea and tide, certainly knew what he was talking about. Sit with me, so that I can swear I have never had a pair of prettier guards?"

Lara stopped by them. "They will not be attending, Tranta, as sorry as I am to disappoint you. I'm certain Nutmeg has duties elsewhere, and I need Grace to find Sevryn as it seems that he is the only one not here yet."

Dismissed, Rivergrace could only let Tranta press his hand upon her forearm as she gathered up Nutmeg and left the conference room. Uncharacteristically quiet, Nutmeg let herself be shepherded down the hall and into the downstairs wing before she took a great, long sobbing breath and stopped, putting her back to the wall. Rivergrace bent down to her sister and saw her eyes glistening with unshed tears.

"Meg. What is it?"

"He pushed me away. He never looked back, Grace." And Nutmeg tilted her face up, sorrow beginning to cascade down her cheeks. She put her hands out and lifted them slowly. *"I can't do that for him."*

"You know, and I know, and Lara knows . . . there's isn't an arrow let fly that won't fall to earth sooner or later. He can't depend upon her."

"But he will."

"The queen won't let him. Not for long, anyway."

"He's headstrong as an old billy goat, and he wants to go with the men. He has no intention of staying if he can help it, legs or no legs, cart or no cart."

"And can you blame him?"

Nutmeg took the square of linen Grace fished out of her skirt pocket and noisily blew her nose before answering. "No." She inhaled, hiccuped, then swallowed tightly. "It's what we've been working for."

"Then his intentions have little to do with Tressandre. He means to go, one way or another, don't you see? And when his eyes clear a bit, he'll see, too."

"D'you think?"

Rivergrace put her hands on Nutmeg's shoulders and shook her, just a little. "We've brothers. We know what idiotic and wonderful beasts they are."

"And we can run circles about any one of them." Nutmeg tried to make a smile, it came out crooked and damp. "The trouble is . . . the trouble is, I love him."

It struck her then, the implication of Meg's words, and what Grace had brought to their family. It was her fault, all of it, the terrible disruption of their lives. Losing their home to raiders and Ravers who came looking for her strange blood, to their forced migration to the city of Calcort where her father ran a winery and cider house. Even beyond that to the very Silverwing River

where Nutmeg had pulled her from the waters. It was
she who'd brought the Vaelinars to her Dweller family
doorstep, and there was nowhere that this love would not
be difficult and frowned upon. Yet she knew Nutmeg's
heart and that she had not planned or schemed for this,
and that her sister could no more deny it than she could
deny bringing breath into her body. It was her fault and
how could she undo it without damaging Meg?

"I know you do. I know." She drew Nutmeg to her
and held her very close and tight for long moments. She
had no powers of foretelling, no magical talent for seeing the future, nor did Nutmeg, but both of them knew
that it could come to no good end. Yet, here it was, and
couldn't be changed, and they'd have to deal with it.
She wondered only if her love for Sevryn could be as
misled.

Nutmeg said fiercely, "She would not have dismissed
me like that if I'd been somebody."

"You are somebody."

"A nursemaid. If I had more familiarity with being a
queen and having a household, I could figure how low
that was, but I think it might be lower than a rotten apple
in a barrel." Nutmeg's mouth twisted.

Grace smoothed her hair back from her face. Nutmeg's
rosy cheeks had gotten even rosier, but the pinch lines
about her mouth grew pale. "Don't say such things."

"How can you not? How can you not think them?
Grace, she sent you away, too. Any one of th' guards
could have gone to find Sevryn. She didn't want you
there either. I'm just a nursemaid, but . . . what are you?"
Nutmeg's gaze searched Rivergrace's face. "Lariel hasn't
let Sevryn declare for you."

"Sssssh." Grace steadied her, afraid that even here
in this alcove, the walls might have ears, and she had
already heard much in an alcove herself. "War changes
everything."

"Not friendships. Does it?"

"I don't know. But it won't change mine, and it won't

change yours, and that's what counts, isn't it? We have deep roots, remember? And we don't forget them."

Nutmeg sucked in a quavering breath. "Never."

She pulled back and kissed Nutmeg on the top of her head. "I've got to go fetch Sevryn. Will you be all right?"

"I will be. Upstairs, cleaning and tidying up, and maybe working on a new pattern for Mother. I've been neglecting things and need to put a hand to them again. Mayhap I might even find time to short sheet the bed of a certain unwelcome guest." Nutmeg put her chin up. She spun around in a cloud of amber hair and fled down the hallway before Grace could give her another hug.

Outside, a gentle rain had begun to fall, its patter so tentative it could scarcely be felt or heard. It would have to rain like this for a handful of days to make its presence felt by the earth, she thought, hardly more than a mist yet the storm brewing overhead and upon the hills foretold a more substantial rainfall. Would it come? Or did the River Goddess meddle in waters that were not of her domain, and withhold what she could as punishment? Or was it only that these lands were in cycle for a drought, as simple and unwanted as that? She moved through it without even bothering to put a cloak on, headed for the arena, hearing by shouts and the clash of wood upon wood that the men drilled and fought regardless of the impending weather. Clusters of men let her through, their bodies dusty and muddy and bloodied, their scent strong upon the damp air, their eyes lingering on her briefly as she came around the wooden structure whose high walls seemed to shake with unseen but heard blows.

She went through one of the gateways and stood in the shadow, watching men as they struggled against one another and wondered how this could be compared to war. It was brutal and yet, she knew, not as brutal as what Queen Lariel planned. There were no war machines here.

No trenches to be lined with tar and dried tinder. No pits with stakes. No catapults that could throw smashing boulders. Here, you saw the face of your enemy. Saw the sweat slick his body. Saw the blood when you split his skin. Heard the grunt when you bruised flesh or bone. Felt an echo of his pain in your own body. This was worse and yet ... and yet, it was not, because it was accountable. It was not senseless violence where victory would be counted in numbers of the faceless fallen.

She knotted her hands in her skirt.

Sevryn stood as the solo in the middle of a two-on-one melee. The odds, even then, might not have been fair. A third man rolled on the ground, groaning, and a fourth stood with his back to the other side of the arena wall, his hand to his nose which bled copiously. Sevryn turned suddenly, lashing with his foot out and high, catching one of his opponents to the jaw that snapped his head back and dropped the soldier. He took a blow to his exposed flank, but rolled from it and came up with his fist to the other's gut. The man doubled over with a groan and went to his knees. Sevryn merely reached out and pushed him over, saying, "Enough."

He looked past Grace as though she were not there, beckoning to another group of four who had been watching with their elbows hooked over a side railing. She called out, "The queen commands your presence."

Sevryn stopped in mid-gesture, and blinked. He wiped the back of his hand across his forehead as though just now realizing she stood there. Everyone milled to a stop, a few of them looking to the sky overhead, where rain began to solidify a little and tumble down, wetting their heads.

"Another time," he said, and grabbed a rag from the rails to scrub his face as he crossed the arena to Rivergrace. He stopped there for a long moment, his sides heaving as he caught his breath, and cleaned his face, and in all that time he did not look into her eyes once until finally he dropped the rag into the dust.

When he did, she took a half step back. A light gleamed in his gray eyes, a witch light, like one off a swamp at night, a greenish glow that her brothers Garner and Hosmer used to tease them about with scary tales. A Demon light, they'd said.

They had been teasing her and Nutmeg, but as she looked up into Sevryn's battered face, she realized that their old wives' tale had been based, once, upon truth.

He passed his hand over his eyes as if he could clear them that way. It helped a bit, the light dimming until she could almost tell herself she hadn't seen it, but it lingered in the darkness of his pupils as though it watched her from that depth. "You shouldn't be here."

"Then tell me where I should be."

"Not here. Not now. I wouldn't have you see . . . this."

She examined the arena and the men helping each other stand, as they took stock of their injuries, and spoke to one another in low, wary tones. "You don't fight them. You fight yourself."

He considered her face. "Yes." He gave a dry, mocking laugh.

"Can't Lariel help you? Or Jeredon?"

He closed the ground between them. "They can't know."

"They're your friends."

"This part of me has no friends. If I cannot control it, if I cannot excise it, then I'm dangerous to everyone. She will exile me."

"Do you wish to control it?"

He did not quite look at her, but at someplace beyond her when he answered quietly, "It gives me power. It fills me with a passion, a heat, that makes me able to do things I can't do otherwise. It might keep me alive if I can learn to use it."

"What if it uses you?"

He lowered his voice. "There is no such thing as being Demon touched. One touch, and it wants nothing less than possession. And nothing comes without a price."

"Do you think you're the only one who would be paying it? Is that how you make the bargain with yourself, that Cerat touches no one but you? It's not a matter of control if you would trade yourself, bits of yourself, moment by moment. It will betray you. I carried Cerat, too. I know the echo of its voice."

"But he didn't stay with you." Sevryn's gray gaze flickered over her face.

"No."

"If I can't excise it, then I must control it. Trust me, Grace, to do what I can do." He touched a tangle of her hair to smooth it back behind her ear. He traced the curve of her cheekbone, and it felt like both fire and ice upon her skin. She wanted to grab his hand and press her face to his palm but did not. "I can't be near you like this until I do." He took a deep breath. "Where is she?"

"In the conference room."

"I take it the ild Fallyn is here, then."

"And Tranta as well."

"Him, too?" Sevryn frowned. A bit of blood leaked from the corner of his mouth, and he rubbed at the fleck with the ball of his thumb. "Tell her I'll be up as soon as I clean myself."

"She'll wait impatiently. I'm not to be there."

"No?" He looked as though he might be searching for something and could not quite grasp it. Finally, he tilted his head back and said, "It's drizzling."

"Only a little. It will pass." She gathered her skirt slightly to step away from him, adding, "Only it will pass too soon and too easily. This storm is one we need." She felt his stare as she left, crossing the yards which had begun to muddy slightly, his stare which held a heat and an intensity that made the hair rise at the nape of her neck, a frisson that ran through her entire body before she moved out of his sight and reached the safety of the back kitchen doors.

Quendius watched Narskap as he crouched to the ground, one hand stirring the marks of many hoofprints, the dirt and leaves stirred up, as the wind held the smell of rain growing near. There were those who said water had no smell, but he thought it only a defect on the part of human flesh to be unable to scent it. Animals certainly could. He'd seen them migrate across continents in search of it, dig in the ground in hopes of finding it in sandy bottoms, and race in front of pounding storms in search of shelter. This would be no pounding storm when it hit. Barely enough, perhaps, to satisfy the earth. Larandaril suffered as the rest of the provinces of First Home did. A dry winter did no one any good except those like himself who trafficked in misery and ill times.

Narskap finally stood. "Too far ahead of us for the border to still be open."

"Pity. Still, I should be able to get us through."

Narskap unbound the horses' reins from a small shrub where he'd tied them, saying only, "It isn't far in front of us."

"I want you ahead of me. No sense in alerting them that we are here if I blunder into it."

Narskap nodded and moved past him, his ragged, spare body looking as though a strong wind might cut him down, but it would not. He was steel under his skin, not sinew like others but steel and bone. Nor did he say what both of the two knew was obvious: Narskap would see and sense the border while Quendius could not, not until he had triggered its alarm and its repellent ward which might be strong enough to drop him on his ass. Narskap could see, well, Quendius was not sure what Narskap could see. The man had never tried to explain it to him nor had Quendius asked. Others had. One he had tortured until the explanation came gushing out like the blood and vomit he was spewing, but it had made no sense. He was blind when it came to seeing the threads and elements that wove the world together. What he did see was the abyss which hung through those threads, a complete and total darkness which he found quite absolute and threatening. He did not think, from the few Vaelinar magic workers who had talked with him that they saw it. There was a bleakness to the world, yes, there was always balance. Night for day, evil for good, disease for health, and so on. Quendius had never met anyone who had seen the fathomless, the null, the absolute absence of the universe as he did between all those brightly promising threads others observed. It was more than death. It was nothingness. Death gave rise to life all the time. One only had to look at the natural world to see it. This took everything and returned nothing. He feared it as little else he had ever experienced. It was not a flaw in himself. It was a reality he used.

He watched as Narskap stopped and put his hand out, almost as if sifting through a current in the air. A damp wind stirred around them. One of the horses lifted its head, ears flicking back and forth, but did not whicker. Narskap had trained them well, a man who could do much when he put the shreds of his mind to it. Quendius had come to depend upon him. Perhaps too much. Perhaps this was the time to make utmost use of him.

Narskap tilted his head and looked back at him, an unreadable expression on his face, and said quietly, "We are close. Stay here."

Quendius stayed, shifting his weight, feeling the bow upon his back as the leather quiver moved and settled a bit between his shoulders. He watched Narskap take two more cautious steps forward before stopping abruptly. "Here. Do you wish to cross here or have me follow along the border?"

"Here is as good as anywhere. They will be after us once the wards alert the Anderieon rabble." There was timber upon these hills, which would give him cover until he got closer. Once upon a time he had been in the eastern range, where he made an altar that desecrated the font of the sacred river Andredia. That altar had been built to bless the forges he erected in the mountain holding, the slag of mining and processing the ore, corrupting the Andredia further. He wondered if rivers could remember such a thing, and if it would shriek out at his presence to betray them. He decided that if it had been possible, it would have happened when he first befouled it, not decades later when its corruption was finally halted.

He joined Narskap and reached for the woman who sat slackly on his horse. A small string of drool glistened on her chin as her mouth hung to one side, but a fierce light fired in her eyes and then died out. It seemed for a moment that Tiiva knew him and might even think of fighting him. The coppery stink of old blood and putrefying flesh rose fully from her, in a suggestive aura. He dragged her down by her injured arm and a sharp cry came from her misshapen mouth.

He stroked her lank and greasy hair. "The border knows her. It should let us pass." Quendius released her and gave her a sharp shove to the small of her back. Tiiva stumbled down the rest of the rough foothill, weaving and wavering as she walked. She dragged one foot slowly after the other, the hem of her long, luxurious dress torn and filthy.

She moaned and shambled to a stop and fell to one knee. She undoubtedly felt, as he did and Narskap did, the scalp-crawling assessment of the warded border though it let them through. He had heard, though it had never been proven, that the wards could slay a trespasser. More likely it would be the quick response of the armed rangers patrolling here. He did not doubt, however, that the unwanted might be stunned, stupefied, and made easy targets.

Quendius waited until Narskap passed him, horses trailing after him. He drew his sword. He circled around Tiiva until he confronted her. He lifted her chin with a fisted hand until her dull face looked up. The sword caught a ray of sun. He took her head off.

Then, with three more slaps of the sword, he topped

a young sapling and sharpened its trunk into a crude
stake. A last swing of the sword and Quendius slapped
an arm, silken-sleeved with a lacy cuff, onto its new
perch, slender hand pointing down into Larandaril. He
laughed.

Chapter
Twenty-Three

COULD HE SAY THAT the sparse timber shivered as he approached, that the land seemed to buckle under his footfall, that he could hear the scurry of small animals running, that the air itself seemed to thicken and yet quiver? It was said that once a year there would be a presentation ceremony where all those newly birthed or newly married into the kingdom would be introduced to that magic so that it could recognize and accept them. He did not know the truth of that. It seemed an inefficient and unlikely way to manage a border with or without enchantment, and he thought it more likely that the border was closed to all and only opened by force of will when necessary for the lower classes and only those immediately in Lara's inner circle would have been initiated otherwise.

Tiiva's body would serve as notice of what forged steel thought of magic. He dropped her head into a crude burlap sack that slapped at his horse's withers as they moved.

He thought he could feel what Narskap warned of, a thickening of the air, a resistance to his very being, and then he punched through, Narskap following at his heels, and it became easier to breathe.

His hound drew in a hissing breath through his teeth. "So easy," he said.

"Yes," murmured Quendius. "Good." He took the reins for his horse from Narskap's hand and swung up. "I suggest we hurry. We'll have cover most of the way, if the maps I have are true."

"Have you a target?"

"Oh, yes. One which shall bring that old fox Bistel Vantane out of his hole, I believe."

Narskap's head snapped around, his gaze bright and hard. "Vantane?"

"He has something I want." Quendius' mouth thinned. "And I shall have it." Without further explanation, he heeled his mount downslope leaving his hound to follow and wonder.

The room fell silent as Sevryn entered, although he did not feel he had interrupted any great argument, as Osten Drebukar sat next to Tranta Istlanthir, their Houses sharing the burden of the great Jewel and Shield of Tomarq, and Osten's face which had near been cleaved in two looked both thoughtful and distressed. His heavy hand drummed on the table in front of him, belying his seemingly relaxed, burly form slouched back into his chair. He nodded gravely at Sevryn who apologized before taking his seat. A map of the First Home of Kerith was upon the table, the same map he'd looked upon every day that Lariel had held talks upon the war and how she planned to carry it out, and that map had never changed. Sevryn wondered what the Mageborn had thought when they sat about planning their warfare and how their deeds would inextricably change the face of their lands, the very foundation and seas of the continent forever recarved.

Jeredon put out a fist and bumped it against Sevryn's shoulder.

"Beg pardon for my lateness, Highness."

Lariel considered him only briefly, her attention dropping back to the map and the pieces she had placed upon it, although her massive general continued to consider him with a frown. "I had thought," Osten finally rumbled, "that you were a dagger man and one of finesse. Trained by Gilgarran and all. Yet I hear that you are out in the arena daily, pounding down my men as though they were clay poppets to be remolded at will."

"It seems wise," Sevryn told him, "to hone whatever abilities I can." He pointed to Lara's helm which sat on an end table at the wall behind her chair, and the fetish which dangled down from it. "The Raymy are not likely to ask what my strengths are before they attack."

Tranta's jaw dropped. He stared at the helm for a moment. "Is that—I'd heard but I did not know for sure. Where did they come ashore?"

"South at the old salt bay."

"In force?"

"A few handful made it to land, but we've no idea how many boats lay out to sea."

Istlanthir ran a hand as pale as marble through his sea-blue hair. "Then it makes my news all the worse, which is why I came to deliver it in person. There is a flaw in the Jewel since the attack against it. I've been unable to repair it. Think of it as a . . . blind spot . . . in its sweep which clouds its view."

"How vast a blind spot?"

"I had not thought it significant, since it sweeps side to side . . ." Tranta paused, gathering his words. "This discovery changes my perception. The Shield faltered and let them through. It's a slender gate, like the eye of a needle, and I thought we could close it. It was not the blind spot which brought me here, however. I've been trying to discern and calculate it, but I cannot, yet the problem exists and can't be ignored any longer."

"It gets worse?" Jeredon dropped his chin to his chest with a low mutter.

"It does. The Shield is a Way, as you all know. The gem and the cradle which rocks it are the result of will melded with engineering. The Jewel holds a charge which it focuses. Anything which trespasses in its sight is incinerated. Sigils to reflect her beams are few and expensive and extremely well regulated."

"Tree's blood, man, get to it." Bistane shoved his chair back and stood, his entire body vibrating with unspent agitation.

"She is losing her charge. She is constructed so as to gain it back, day by day, on her own with very little interference from the Istlanthir who guardian her. The sun, even the fire of the stars, feeds her. But now she weakens. There is no other word or explanation for it and I can't replace what she is losing. The Shield is failing, every day, slowly but surely, and as it does, the fracture within the Jewel grows and so does the blind spot. When she fails ultimately, the bay and Hawthorne and our coast will be cracked wide open. The smugglers will learn of it first, but then—" Tranta stopped, with a hard swallow.

"You're certain there is no repair?"

Tranta faced Lariel. "We haven't found one yet."

She tilted her head slightly as she did when she thought deeply. "The sweep of her vision hardly reaches as far south as the old salt bay. It's the treacherous storms and reefs which keep it clear of friend or foe there."

"Possibly. Unless the Raymy came along our coast, probing for a weak spot in our observations and finally found it turning south. You've a trophy dangling from that helm. Who gained it for you? Were they scouts or a fighting force?"

"Daravan found them," Sevryn told him. "If they were scouts, Gods help us when the fighters come ashore."

"The old stories do them justice?"

"And then some," he answered solemnly.

They all looked to Lariel then. "Why are we fighting east if the Raymy lie to the west?"

"Because I know what I know and if Diort is not laid down in his tracks, we'll be sandwiched between them. It's a dry winter. I want to take him now before the warm currents from the sea bring the Raymy in with them in the spring season. Our shipbuilders and traders tell me that is the most propitious time to come in from the western sea. I *will* see Diort dead or bowed before his people. We will all starve when this dry winter turns to a dry spring and we must face the Raymy with empty bellies and broken vows." Lara stood. She leaned on her hands. "We don't know if the Raymy seek alliances, or if they are even an enemy which would consider such a thing, but we do know Abayan Diort. He has shattered villages which would not submit to him and cajoled the others. He may know what we know of them and think he can deal with them in his delusions. For now, he is the enemy. My enemy. Beat him, and we will enfold his fighters and his people, and then face what we have to face. It's the only thing we can do."

"You don't know his intent."

"I have seen his actions. They speak for his intent."

"Lara, he's not come into the lands outside of the old domains of the Mageborn. Not with force."

"He's been so close to the old boundaries that if he breathed, he breached them."

"But not crossed them."

"He will."

Bistane paced the length of the room. He stopped long enough to trade looks with Osten, then returned to pacing. "We muster. It could be he is moving into place only to keep an eye on us, to see what we are doing."

"It could be," Jeredon said quietly, "that she is baiting him to do what he normally would not." He wouldn't look upon his sister's face as he spoke.

Lara slapped her hands upon the table. "It takes days upon days to move an infantry into place. I won't waste energy and valuable supplies toying with Diort. We've already divisions where I want them."

"Then what?"

She looked down at the map. "We muster at Ashenbrook. We go to war where Kanako won before falling."

"And we hope history does not repeat itself?" Jeredon's dry words fell on them, but Osten held up a hand, his face creasing even more deeply than its scarred visage. "A moment." He rubbed his hand across his brow. He looked to Lara. "Time, my queen."

She took a deep breath, then straightened and stepped back from the table. "All right, then. Another subject, one closer at hand. Tiiva crossed the wards into Larandaril about a candlemark ago."

"What?"

Osten nodded heavily. "We've not had a sighting, but her presence is unmistakable."

"Where did she cross?"

"We think from the low hills, northwest, by the Drebukar border."

"She's a hunter," Jeredon remarked. "She knows these lands as well as I do, and if she wants to come upon us relatively quietly, she can do it."

"She's a traitor."

"She may be a traitor with news or an offering," Lara said flatly. The silver in her blue eyes glinted. "I don't want our hand tipped to her."

Bistane stopped. "As if any of us would do that."

They stared at one another across the table for a very long moment, then a bit of color blossomed on Lariel's face before she dropped her gaze and said, "I did not mean to suggest any of you would."

"You suggest much these days, my queen, and we only ask that you take us into consideration before you do." Bistane made a half bow in her direction.

Her mouth twisted. "You sound more like your father every day. He disapproves of what I plan to lead."

"Yet he stands ready to help when asked, and a division from our House has joined your muster," Bistane reminded her gently.

Osten shoved back from the tabletop, his thick hands on the edge of the map. He took one of the markers and lifted it, turned it about and about in his callused fingers. "We're a little shy of troops, Lara, if you wish to accomplish what you want to." He set the marker down, near the Rivers Revela and Ashenbrook. He said it as if it were a new revelation, when they had been arguing about it for days, but Lara did not react as she had in the past. "We have ild Fallyn, Istlanthir, Drebukar, Vantane, Arsmyth, Caranthe, and Ferstanthe, Naimilith, the lines of Igart, DeCadil, Elath, Inamatran, Sastrina, Briban, and Garanth. And then we have the unnamed but the followers of the Strongholds, Houses, and lines."

Lara's mouth curved into a disagreeing moue. "Then we'll have what we need, when the time comes."

"If you say so. I would give my life upon your word, but I owe the troops more consideration."

"We've discussed this before, Osten."

"And you've not been forthcoming either. Even if we bring in cavalry, we can't do it quickly enough to give them the support they're going to be needing. I know the House of Anderieon holds magic that you don't reveal, but a feat of that sort would be nothing less than miraculous." He cleared his throat, looking at her from under heavy, bifurcated brows. "I knew your grandfather well, and he never relied on miracles for battle."

"Nor shall I. But I don't intend to tip my hand. Not now and not here. If Tiiva taught me but one thing, it's that there is no safety anywhere."

Bistane eyed the faces of Lariel and Osten as words flew between them before commenting softly, "What expectations do either of you have? Are we looking to a pitched battle or a sortie that is likely to change Diort's mind and send him retreating? Are we entrenching there for the winter?"

Osten shifted his massive legs. He tightened his jaw on whatever answer he might have made. Sevryn leaned forward. "We can, but I sense the thinking is to hit him hard, so hard it rocks him back on his heels and makes him retreat to where he can be comfortable and safe—and negotiate."

"That would be preferable, yes," Lara agreed.

"We can't negotiate in strength if we're the ones retreating."

She looked to her brother. "I don't intend to be in that position."

"Lara, no one goes to war intending to lose, but there is usually only one victor."

"Thank you for pointing out what I had not considered," she told Jeredon flatly. Sevryn wished for the old days when she might have thrown a pillow at him when the only enmity between them came from natural sibling rivalry. Jeredon's face creased slightly as if he shared the same thought.

Tressandre ild Fallyn had kept her silence, one hand on the arm of Jeredon's carriage chair, her wind-tousled hair framing her beautifully guarded face. "It seems to me that it is possible one might already have been negotiating with Diort, if only to see if Galdarkans bend or if they are as stiff-necked as they are arrogant." Her full mouth curved slightly. "You could offer me in marriage, but that would scarcely give you the safe alliance you wish."

Her self-mocking words brought a chuckle about the table, bleeding tension away. "Barring that, you have other options. We can offer teachers and apprentices in craftsmanship even the Galdarkan can't yet approach. And, there are others about your House which might bring the kind of marital partnership you wish. If our lovely, returning Tiiva weren't a base traitor, she would have been a good offering. What is the worst we can expect of such a mating? Impossible for children, but what if there were a miracle? What do you fear, my queen?"

"I fear the Raymy and the return of the Mageborn." Lara's response fell into silence.

Tressandre recovered first. "Mageborn? You can't be serious. The Gods of Kerith wiped out those bloodlines centuries ago. We've no rivals here when it comes to working magic."

"Tressandre, you know more than most how lost bloodlines can be recouped. Is that not a specialty of your Stronghold now? Finding those with mixed blood and bringing back the Vaelinar strains in them through careful breeding? What makes you think that every last drop of Mageborn blood has been excised by Gods who were careless to begin with? It's only a matter of time until one of two things happen: the Gods of Kerith deal with us as invaders directly or they raise the Mageborn again to do so." Lara took a breath. "The Raymy may well be their opening gambit. We are the *Suldarran*, the lost, and there is no way home that we've found. Yes, we guard against ourselves, but we most stringently guard against an alien land which can never quite be home to us." Her words fell into a sudden silence. They shifted uneasily in their chairs, and Bistane ceased his pacing, his slender body taut.

"We're indeed lost if we throw everything we have at Diort and the Raymy hit our back."

Her gaze flicked to Bistane. "Would you have me split forces and face both without enough to prevail?"

Osten looked into Lara's face a moment, then shook his head heavily, answering in Bistane's stead. "Of course not. We're caught between the rock and the hard place." He pushed himself forward and drew the map toward him. "Let's see what we can do to make sure this becomes our advantage and not our defeat."

They drew together and bowed their heads over the map and the small game pieces scattered upon it.

Rivergrace leaned upon the hallway wall, her small

mirror cupped in her hand, her thoughts still lingering on the words she had overheard, as she withdrew a few steps, quietly, so as not to hit the boards that would invariably creak. She slipped her mirror quickly into a pocket before her shaking hand could drop it. A faint flush of guilt for having eavesdropped warmed her face, replaced by uneasy confirmation of what she had feared, that the talk might touch upon her and the queen's treatment. Had Tressandre suggested that she might be offered? Was she no more than one of those tiny clay pieces they pushed about upon their map?

She knew, of course, that in Lara's eyes she was not. She also knew the distrust and uneasiness she saw whenever Lariel looked her in the face since those moments by the river, a happening she could not quite remember other than as a heated and desperate power that surged through her. Something which, in Lariel's eyes, kept her from being accepted and embraced into their society. Not one of them, and not ever to be one of them, not even to be married to a half-breed whom Lara *had* embraced. She knotted her fingers in her pocket. Grace could either ride upon the current of this river or she could defy it, and use it to take her where she willed. She was, she reminded herself, a Farbranch if nothing else, one of a family which Tolby Farbranch had often, and proudly, declared was so stubborn that if they fell in a river, they would float upstream.

Before she made that move, she would talk to Sevryn again, and Nutmeg. That seemed the wisest course.

Grace dropped a shoulder to turn quietly in the hallway, and hands as hard as steel caught her, and a voice that sounded as if it were rarely used and broken as a shattered reed spoke low in her ear.

"Do not move. Or cry out."

Chapter
Twenty-Four

GRACE FROZE. THE SMELL of old sweat and fresh rain, woodsmoke and horses rose from her captor, along with leather and weapon oil, and something herbal that he chewed, perhaps for a toothache, perhaps just to chew something. He drew her against his body, retreating, forcing her a few steps back from the conference room, away from the voices sharp and conciliatory, argumentative and suggestive, away from whatever help she might have cried out for. Another man moved past her, even as her captor forced her to the bend in the corridors. She recognized Quendius in his long vest of curly white wool and his regal soot-colored skin as he took an arrow from the quiver on his back and nocked it. Her breath caught. The arrowhead glinted like a crimson jewel, catching the fire of the light, and she wondered how it was no one in the conference room could see him in the doorway, bow in hand, fiery arrow aimed toward them. The man who held her tightened his grip in anticipation.

She fell limply in surrender to his pull. His weight twisted in surprise at her move, and she wrenched free, crying, "Attack!" Something loud clanged behind her with Nutmeg's triumphant exclamation. "Tree's blood! That should settle you!"

The conference room erupted with shouts, the scraping of chairs, and the table being overthrown. Quendius loosed his arrow as the immense form of Osten filled the doorway charging outward. The great man staggered back a step, his hand grasping at the shaft in his barrel chest as he let out a grunt of pain. But the arrow did not give to his pull and his body blocked the doorway as Quendius lowered his bow. Osten grappled with the shaft. Two daggers flew past the bulk of the general's body toward Quendius. He dodged them nimbly, and they clattered to the floor as Osten roared in frustration. A great font of blood spewed from his mouth as the arrow drilled its way deeper into his chest, burrowing. Dropping his sword, he wrestled with it as if it were a mighty beast fastened upon his throat. He spewed blood with every cry of anger, and then sheer pain and panic filled his voice. The arrow shaft wiggled its way deep into Osten, and the gory wound swallowed even the flights. He dropped to his knees with a low moan. A greedy light filled Quendius' face and he stood, one hand outstretched. The arrow fought its way out of Osten's back and then, still in flight as if freshly loosed, returned to Quendius' hand. He replaced it in the quiver and nocked a fresh arrow, aiming at the chaos before him, as Osten toppled over with a last gasping cry of shock and anger.

Grace threw herself at Quendius. A hot sting skimmed her ear as she blundered into him, but he'd already loosed the arrow and it flew, straight and clean through the air, at Lariel.

Sevryn threw her a glance, the briefest of looks, before he dropped his shoulder to fling himself across Lara and the arrow sank into the meat of his shoulder.

He grunted in pain as he flung an arm back, clawing at the shaft. Grace kicked and punched and she heard the clang again, and saw a dented chamber pot being swung by its bail as the two men buffeting her fell back. Nutmeg charged them again, chamber pot resounding as it caught Quendius on the side of his jaw. Grace kicked her way free. She saw Sevryn pull the arrow shaft free and drop it. It made a sound . . . how wood could have a voice she didn't know, but it did . . . a sound of yowling and rending that pierced the eardrums to hear it. Quendius barked out a word, and the thing returned to his hand. Both men turned in the corridor and took to their heels, leaving Nutmeg staggering in their wake, blistering their heels with Dweller curses upon themselves, their family, and every tree and root in their home. The chamber pot swung from her hand.

Then she rounded upon Grace and hugged her, holding her upright, both of them shaking. Grace only had eyes for Sevryn, as he got to his feet, his wound already staunched, and they traded looks. She recognized then the voice of the weapon: Cerat. Why had the demon not killed him as it had Osten? What further power had it awakened in Sevryn? She feared the answers as he bent over Lariel and gave his hand to help her to her feet and to Osten's side. His face paled as the blood drained from it. Everyone else in the room began to stir, righting the table once more and getting to their own feet, moving to pull Osten from the doorway and lay his body out straight just in case, in hopes, that he was not dead.

If she thought to see love and concern in Sevryn's face, she did not. Instead, his eyes narrowed and a fearsome, hard gleam that looked like a flame shone at the back of his pupils. She put her hand back to Nutmeg, stepping away. Like a stranger, he hadn't come to her aid. Like a Demon, he'd gone to where blood was promised even though his action had saved Lariel. Had he intended to? More than she feared not knowing herself, she worried that neither did he.

Nutmeg dropped her mangled chamber pot. "What do we do now?"

"We leave," Rivergrace told her and withdrew from the scene of Vaelinars mourning their dead and their loss.

LARA STOOD OUTSIDE HER CHAMBERS for a moment, wiping her hands on a cloth although she had already washed and dried them several times over. The healers had finally sent her away, saying that they would finish dressing Osten's body for the memorial services. She put her forehead to the satiny wood of her threshold. Now she had no choice but to call upon Bistel. He would answer; Bistane had already assured her as they laid out Osten. There was no question of his answering.

It was Bistel's faith in her that would be called to the fore. If Quendius had hoped to disrupt her plans by taking out the general in charge of her forces, he had erred grossly. The warlord Vantane had been her first general, but he had disagreed with her, firmly, about her battle plans. "It is folly," he'd said, "to depend upon the undependable. A Way cannot be the linchpin of your victory." And he had resigned from his duties.

But he would know, intimately, of her plans and would

step into Osten's place smoothly, if disapprovingly. Not a single one of the troops under his command, indeed, not even his own son, would know of the real reasons he and Lara had disagreed. He would, to his death, follow the strategy she had laid down.

Only, she thought, if he believed, it would not lead to the deaths of most of them. Or so she hoped.

She wiped her hands one more time as if they still held the stain of Osten's blood and then opened the door to her apartments. Tiiva's head stared at her from her desk, blood pooled at the stump of its neck. A step carried her inside and the smell hit her. She flung a hand to her mouth to stifle her cry.

She held no safe ground anywhere. Her guards had not kept him from her innermost sanctuary. The living as well as the dead betrayed her.

Dear Mom and Da,
A quick note before I dash off into an adventure of my own. I beg your forgiveness if I embarrass my family, but it seems I have to let my heart rule this time, even if it sends my head over my heels! Don't be worrying about me. Weather watchers on the estate grounds say that the drought is everywhere, and I worry about your vines, Da. I have sent you some of my coin, by the Oxfort guild banker who rides through here, to help pay for the water being drawn for irrigation. The banker also told me of the news through the cities that the Gods are bending down again to talk and listen to us. I told him, silly Kernan, that the Gods never stopped talking to us, that Their Voice is in every root and leaf of everything that grows! He accused me of blasphemy, but he took my money anyway! I send you all my love wrapped in this hasty bundle! ~ Nutmeg

Neither dawn nor Nutmeg had stirred within her rooms when Rivergrace awoke and quietly slid from bed. She took as few things as she could gather quickly without waking her sister, and then slipped out the door. A plan had crept into her dreams, rising as softly and ethereally as mist off a river, until the fog lay over her even as she began to awaken. Only this fog, instead of obscuring the landscape, seemed to sharpen and detail it for her. She needed answers she would never get by asking directly, for any information she got from a Vaelinar would be wrapped in machinations and obligation. There was only one place and one person she could go to, and she packed accordingly.

Outside the door, she wrote a few lines of farewell and reassurance on a scrap of paper and slipped it back under. Then she capped her pen and placed it with her writing things and paper in her pack, along with the other items she carried. The back stairs of the manor would be busy even this early in the morning with the laundresses and downstairs the cooks and helpers, so she took the main staircase, staying well to the shadowed side of it. Rivergrace moved as stealthily as she could despite the murmur of the wood beneath her feet.

Yesterday, the manor had been in a furor over Osten's death until Lara's fury had descended into grief. Grace and Nutmeg had stayed in their apartment and dined there. Grace had been scolded by her sister for stepping into harm's way where only her own brisk use of an empty chamber pot could have saved her. Never mind that Nutmeg had just as stealthily followed Grace down to the conference rooms to spy on her, just as Rivergrace had been spying on the gathering. Whatever the reason, Grace could not argue with Meg, for she had indeed been saved by the lusty wielding of one chamber pot. After scolding one another and then consoling each other, the two had finally fallen into bed where Rivergrace had lain awake for a very long time and Nutmeg had fallen into a fitful sleep where she murmured Jeredon's name now and again, and thoughts she could no longer deny crept into Rivergrace's mind. No one skulked about the hallways today to stop her, although she breathed shallowly and stepped lightly just in case. Once outside, she took a deep breath before heading to the stables.

Outside, a predawn chill lay on the ground, with clouds simmering on the crest of the mountains beyond the forests. It might clear today or it might rain or sleet. She pulled the hood up on her cloak and drew the ties close. The hem of the cloak swirled along with bits of frost and fog as it swept along the ground. Inside the stable yard she could see gusts of breath from the warmer horses as the stable lads turned them out for the morning, even before their hooves and eyes flashed as they frisked into the briskness of the day, and loped into the pastures awaiting them. She watched them as they charged from the barn at a controlled speed, their ears up, their luxurious manes and tails cascading about them as they plunged from the barn door to the whistles and chirps of the lads who cared for them. It occurred to her that she'd outsmarted herself, for there wouldn't be a horse left in the barn for her to take. She slowed as she neared the yard.

Her fear lessened as she saw the farrier stoking up his small fire and forge, and sharpening his hoof cutters. He looked up and gave her a wave, his heavy leather apron protecting him from the cold of the wintery morning, its hide scarred with teeth marks and even hoofprints.

One of the stable lads came out with a barrel of muck and stopped. His face curved in a smile. "Fair mornin', m'lady Rivergrace. Out for a ride this early?"

"Before all the talking and the memorial begins seems the best time to go. Have you anyone for me that isn't turned out?"

"Oh, I've a handful or so still in their stalls, impatient and stamping the ground." He appraised her. "I imagine you want a sweet-tempered sort, with a good gait and stamina. You're not the kind to go racing after the hounds and hawks."

She smiled. "That would do me just fine."

"I'll get Long Shanks, then. Be back in just a bit." He muscled his steaming cartload of pungent muck off to the far side of the yards, to be spread and herbed and dried before it would be turned into the fallow fields. The stink lingered after him and Rivergrace rubbed at her nose, trying to stave off a sneeze.

She was not expecting an elegant-lined tashya horse to be led out to her, but when the lad reappeared, he had a tawny, black-pointed gelding by the halter, with head held high and ears flicking back and forth as though deciding what to make of her. Long-legged and groomed within an inch of his life, his hide shone like a newly minted gold coin. His forelock was so long, the gelding had to tilt his head a little to eye her, and he did it with a slightly vain cast that reminded her so much of the handsome Lord Bistane that Grace had to put her hand over her mouth to keep from laughing at her thought. The sun, peeking in and out of the clouds, set his tawny hide to looking like bronze, well polished and rich. The lad brought out the tack, finished his grooming quickly, and began to equip the horse for riding.

"Quite right not to laugh at him," the lad said, his hands moving in fast, efficient blurs. "He's a pretty one and he knows it, but it's not his fault. We've all been telling him that for all of his years, and he listened. He's got the smoothest stride of any horse in the queen's stable, and he'll take you as far as you want to go."

"Oh, I'm not going far," Rivergrace said. She tried to hide her daypack somewhat behind her riding skirt.

"I would, iffen it were me. The lords and ladies will come pouring in here soon enough, and their demands and airs and such, looking for a hard ride to chase away the grief. We've seen 'em all before. Begging your pardon if you're friends with any of 'em," he added, with a slight blush, as he tightened the girth and began to check the strength of the stirrups and other bindings. He both soothed with his hands and straightened, and the gelding leaned against him a little in affection, lipping at his sleeve.

"You can't be calling him Long Shanks." A name like that belonged to a Dweller or Kernan mount, not befitting one of the sleek tashyas.

The lad chuckled. "No, m'lady, indeed not. His name is Barad, meaning in the Vaelinar tongue, well-struck."

He translated easily for her as if she did not look Vaelinar enough to know the language, although the word was one she wasn't familiar with. Even he could not tell her lineage other than she was a favorite of the Warrior Queen. Her cheeks stung a little as the lad pressed the horse's reins into her hand.

"Shall I be tellin' 'em where you're off to?"

Rivergrace shook her head. "I'll be back soon enough, and today is not a day for merrymaking, is it?"

"Indeed not, ma'am. Osten Drebukar left a mighty hole to be filled, that's to be sure. The hunters came back from the hills late, their horses worn and blowin' hard, but not a sign of th' murderers had they found. So don't be riding off far, now." The lad looked vindicated as she swung up and slung her daypack from her shoulders. She fit her boots into the stirrups and let him shorten them a bit more for her and inspect them, making sure she would be comfortable. He patted Barad on the withers. "He'll take you as fast as you want to go. He'll run his heart out for you, but don't be letting him, aye?" He cocked an eyebrow at her.

"I won't."

Satisfied, the lad slapped a hand on Barad's rump, sending them clattering out of the stable yard and onto the open road. What he did not tell her was that he had sent Lord Sevryn out even earlier, when the dark purple cloak of night still hung heavily upon the skies, and he'd ridden out much quieter, and took a different road out of the stable yard. The lad watched her go much as he had the other, none the wiser for their missions nor even particularly curious as to what drove them on their way. Such curiosity, he'd learned, did not befit a mere lad of the stables.

Rivergrace deliberately did not take the lanes. She turned Barad's head to follow the Andredia and so the gelding did, with a spring in his long-striding walk, and curious ears flipping back and forth as they startled birds and small animals from their path. He did not startle when they flushed and scurried out of the way, but he did let out a whicker now and then, or a chuff, as if to acknowledge they had both been surprised. The brief rain of the day before had left dew sparkling in the grass and the gelding's hooves struck and scattered the drops like diamonds as he took her along the riverbed, the holdings of the Warrior Queen falling farther and farther behind them.

A flight of river birds took to the air at her back, and Grace turned in her saddle, watching them with a slight frown in the hazy sunlight. They were not the alna of her years along the Silverwing River, but a small, tender bird which sat in the reeds and bank grasses to eat the fat bugs along the muddy shores and hated to fly if it did not have to. Something akin to her and the gelding had set them off. She pulled rein and turned Barad into a stand of sturdy shrubs to wait and see what might be following.

In a handful of moments, she could see a beribboned straw hat, glossy amber hair tied back, and hear the trot of a stout mountain pony headed her way. A smile tugged at the corners of Rivergrace's mouth. She waited until Nutmeg and her pony had clearly breasted the reeds nearby, dented chamber pot and saddlebags bouncing on the pony's withers with every trotting step before pulling Barad out of hiding.

"And where is it you think you're going?"

Nutmeg hauled back on her reins. "Wherever it is you are. Did you think I'd let you go without me?" Her pony plowed to a stop and promptly dropped its head to lip and chew on whatever flowers and blades of grass it could find, opportunities of this sort never to be neglected. Mountain ponies held different equine priorities than did the hot bloods.

"What about your nursing charge?"

"Him?" Nutmeg curled her lip. "If he was a fledgling, I'd have kicked him out of the nest long ago. Besides, he has another nurse now and one that will be far tougher than I on his sorry hide. She carries a whip. So where is it we're going?"

"North," said Rivergrace shortly, after gazing for just a moment at Nutmeg. "To Ferstanthe."

Nutmeg seemed to let that sink in. "The library, eh," she answered slowly. She pursed her lips in thought a moment before remarking, "I don't understand it. You've got that look on your face, and you ride after a pile of books and scrolls."

"That look?"

"Aye. The face you always made when Hosmer grabbed your hair ribbons off one time too many or Garner tricked us into doing chores and we found out too late we'd been taken. That look that says you've had enough and you're ready to fight back. So, I ask myself, what's in a book of Ferstanthe?"

The chill that had been inside Grace for days since nearly drowning in the embrace of the River Goddess felt as though it had finally begun to melt. She hadn't quite known for sure what she intended from Azel d'Stanthe of Ferstanthe. Sanctuary maybe. A good listener with a bit of advice. Or, perhaps, something more. She straightened the reins in her hand. "I've lost the queen's trust. Or maybe I never really had it. Perhaps queens take a good deal longer to decide on friendship."

"Lariel wouldn't know a prize apple if it fell on her head."

"Be that true, I must find a way to convince her. She doesn't think I'm Vaelinar, Nutmeg."

"What? Is she blind? Do pointed ears grow everywhere like leaves on trees?"

"It's more than the ears, I'm certain."

"You've the eyes and you can make sweet water out of th' most poisoned brew. What more does she want?"

"I don't know." Rivergrace shook her head a little. Her movement made her horse restive, and he pawed at the ground. "I have to know who I am, where I start and where I want to finish. I was unraveled, Meg, and then rewoven, but I have to know . . . I have to know what threads I've knotted within me, what soul is *mine*. And then, to fight, I have to know what I want. From her, from Sevryn . . ."

"He's gone daft, aye."

Not a question but a statement coached in confident Dweller tones. She looked up to meet her sister's cinnamon eyes. "In a way," Grace agreed. "They haunt us, Cerat and the River Goddess. They have their claws sunk in us, and they want . . . I don't know. I thought we were done with them, but they aren't done with us."

"Touched by a God or Demon—it leaves its mark the way a dousing with pig slop leaves its stink, even after you wipe it away."

Her nose wrinkled a bit as she knew from her childhood days on the farm and in the orchards just what Nutmeg meant, even as she forged ahead, adding, "But don't you be thinkin', Grace, that you haven't got powers of your own. That Goddess wouldn't have sunk herself into you, hiding behind you, if you hadn't already been able to find sweet water and draw the poisons from it, and love the rivers the way you did. She didn't bring that to you, you already had it. *You were born with it.* She couldn't have survived in you without that."

"I have to know who I am, to fight her. And to help Sevryn, if there's any way to help. There has to be an answer somewhere."

"In the books."

"Why not? We live, we dream, we think, we die.

Sometimes we take a moment to put all this down on a page, to puzzle it out or leave a map for those who follow behind us, to show them the way and the traps. Don't you think?"

" 'Twould be the wisest thing to do, but in my mood, I'm not about to admit there's a man with a lick of common sense anywhere, let alone in a library. Still." Nutmeg straightened her straw hat. "This cannot be the first time a Dweller and a Vaelinar have fallen in love, and I'd like to read the tales. I'm not all that sure a pretty word or two will help us in a fight, but it's a place to start, and I'm right behind you if there's a chance to set things right." She put a heel to her pony and reined it close to Barad who snorted at the fuzz-hided beast all shaggy in his winter coat.

Grace smiled down at her. "He'll be sorry, you know."

"Tree's root, he will! Who got to th' villains first yesterday, eh? Me and my pot or that woman and her whip? He'll be in a sorry state, and it'll be his own doing." Nutmeg settled herself in her stirrups and clucked to her pony to keep up as Rivergrace headed her horse out. They rode to the border and ridges of Larandaril, Nutmeg's voice chattering in merry counterpoint to the thud of their mounts' hooves. She had much more to say about dull-witted men who let their eyes be blinded with gilt and sparkles, be they Vaelinar, Kernan, Dweller, or Galdarkan, as her short-legged mount snorted and huffed to keep up with the longer-striding Barad.

Quendius halted his horse. "It's time we parted ways for a bit."

Narskap, blood clotted thickly over one ear, and with a sizable lump on his head, looked as if he wished to say something, but his thin lips remained shut.

Quendius touched his quiver of arrows. "One failed. Why is that?"

"I don't know."

"Call up Cerat and ask him."

Narskap did not hold his words this time. "No," he returned. "That I will not do. To invoke him, I will draw the attention of those we don't want, and it might well loose the Demon beyond my control."

"So you would trade a small failure for a great one."

"I deem it the wiser course. You had two successes."

Quendius regarded his hound for a long moment, flint-black eyes sparked with a great darkness. "I did, and I shall remember that."

"I know."

"Ride, then. I shall catch up with you."

"They will be on the border, right behind us."

"And this, I know. But they won't find me, and they had better not find you. No, I want to sit in camp a bit and see what kind of hornet's nest we've stirred up. Allow me my amusement."

Narskap dropped his chin in agreement and turned his horse to the northeast. Quendius watched him go before he dismounted and then led his mount along the stony ridges, stopping now and then to brush away his tracks with a tree branch, and to scent the wind as if he, and not Narskap, were the hound. He camped in stealth and watched as hunting troops passed by, not catching sign or spoor of his passage and as they circled in frustration before heading back into the cloistered land of Larandaril. He preferred to be behind his troubles rather than in front of them, he thought, as he crossed the rugged land that made it near impossible to approach the favored country by more than single file, and on foot. It was naturally extremely difficult to invade except by the single broad pass at the river's end, and that, of course, was always guarded. Yes, the Anderieon family had known well what it had done when it had taken up this country and made it theirs, defensible against not only those of the world they'd trespassed on but also easily held against those of their own kind. They had taken the spoils of their occupation and made a homeland for themselves.

It was during his slow and deliberate journey overland, looking for weaknesses, that two passed him on horse and pony, alert to their surroundings yet unaware of his presence as he pulled aside and pinched his horse's nostrils to keep him quiet, and he gathered a destination from their chatter. That road would take him north, as he needed, and then he could turn east and south again to his own badlands. As they passed him by, speaking earnestly of their plans and hopes, it occurred to him that he had not been to Ferstanthe in many, many decades and that he might find some useful knowledge there, or even that what the library contained might well be as dangerous as one of the Demon-imbued weapons Narskap so carefully crafted for him. He should look into it.

Chapter
Twenty-Six

"BAD WEATHER, AND EVERYWHERE, it sounds like." Tolby Farbranch eyed this end of Calcort, where vineyards and nut orchards and fruit groves abounded, before the rugged rock wall and ridge that protected the city gave way to even rougher scapement that any army would hesitate to boil over. The soft side of the city had gates and walls, thick and tall and brawny but they were beyond the city limits of that, and as a Dweller who liked his horizons far flung, it pleased him to live here on the outskirts. This was his vineyard and his cider house down below, with his small home, and while it was not the spread he'd held on the Silverwing, he could still be proud of it. Proud and worried.

"It all comes round, doesn't it."

Tolby patted his youngest son on the shoulder as he straightened, and dusted the soil from his hands. It drifted on the wind, fine and dry, as he would wish it didn't. Soil should be rich and moist. He squinted at the horizon where only the faint wisps of clouds looked like they bore any rain at all. Row after row of trimmed-back vines spun away from him like spokes on a wheel. They'd be all right, for now. They were dormant till the earliest of spring, but like all life, they wouldn't thrive on just a moment of rain or a quick answer when there were thousands of questions or one meal when a lifetime stretched far ahead of one. No, nurturing was ever ongoing and cumulative.

Keldan said, "I'll finish with these rows. I think I heard Garner and Hosmer scuffling in the house."

"Did you now? Over what?"

"Hard to tell. It's not like Hosmer to be off duty so early, so it might be something important." Keldan, the youngest, the one with the farthest to go when he decided to leave, just smiled faintly and went back to turning minerals into the rows with his hoe, one step at a time, his mind far away on whatever it was Keldan thought about.

Tolby got to the main house, at town's end, in time to see Hosmer swing up on his horse and trot off in a huff, his left hand to his jaw. The boys had been tumbling around a bit, it seemed, and Garner looked up with a guilty start as Tolby stomped the dust off his boots at the doorjamb and came in. Tolby's gaze swept the room and saw the pack and traveling clothes and raised his eyebrows.

"Where do you think it is you might be going?"

"Like father, like son," grumbled Garner. "This is just the same discussion I ended with Hosmer." He blew on his bruised knuckles.

"It's never ended. One battle breeds another. Is it something that will bring a tear to your mother's eye?"

"No, sir, never that."

"So what is it, then, you're heading out the door to do?"

"Word on the street is that the Oxforts are hiring caravan guards. Hosmer has been leaned on to go and join up, by way of spying on the traders and see what they're up to. I talked him out of it, for to do that, he'd have to abandon his post with the Town Guard and his reputation, and he's worked far too hard for that."

"You talked him into disobeying orders."

"No, Da. 'Twasn't his commanding officer who did the leaning, but a fellow who was just curious and thought they could earn some extra merit by having an adventure. Not wise, I told him. Not wise at all."

"I tend to agree with you on that. Why is it better you go instead?"

"Now this part you won't be liking at all, but you asked," Garner said solemnly, giving him a look from under a lock of hair hanging low across his brows, reminding Tolby not a little of their recalcitrant little mountain stallion, Bumblebee. "I gamble a bit, and have gambled with him, and have even been into him for some coin." He held his hand up before Tolby could bite off a gruff word. "You asked, Da, so now listen. I'm not proud of it, but there it is, and that's the way it is with gamblers. I learned. Most don't. I gamble, but I stop when I've lost what I can afford, which is very little. But Bregan Oxfort has a sharp memory, swift as a trap on a fur line, and he'll think that my wanting to get out of town quickly and with a bit of muscle around me and money in my pocket to solve my troubles will be the right of it. He'll never suspect me of spying on him."

"Sound thinking."

"I thought so. Hosmer disagreed with me a bit, but I persuaded him." Garner bent to pick up his pack. "I'm off, then. I left a note for Mom, and now this talk with you, and I'm done."

"You'll be back when?"

"When I know enough to be of some help to the City Guard and Sevryn."

"Sevryn?"

Garner cleared his throat. "Well, now, I might have forgot to mention that he came through to put the bug in Hosmer's ear."

"That's some forgetting. Did he carry word from Meg and Grace?"

"Nothing on paper. He said only that the queen is knotted up in plans and that we should be hearing from the girls soon."

"Ah." Tolby rocked back on his heels, visibly disappointed. He had hoped for more, and his work-worn wife would be far more disappointed than he. He stuck a thumb in his belt to gather other thoughts. "He's going with you, then?"

"Sevryn? Not him. If you believe in being Demonridden, he is. He has other missions, elsewhere, and scarce took enough time to stop and talk with us. Aymaran stood tied to the rails, and blowin' hard but Sevryn barely took notice of him. He had somewhere else to be, and quickly."

"And I keep you from your destiny, too, it seems."

"I am going, Da."

"I know. I guess I canna say no. You're grown and you've full memory that I used to be a caravan guard myself, once. Not a misspent youth but a hard one, with hard teachers and long lessons."

"I know that." Garner gave him an honest smile, reminding Tolby of the long-ago days when all his sons were just knee-high lads. He stood in the doorway, both impatient to be off and just as patient to listen to his father. Tolby would be lying to himself if he hadn't known his son spent a lot of nights gambling, for there were days when the money Garner slipped into the family earnings were all that had kept the vineyards and cider house going in the early seasons.

"So what lesson did you learn, son?" asked Tolby quietly.

Garner paused, and then answered, "Don't be catching me upside the head for this one, Da, but I learned that Bregan Oxfort is a cheat and if I'm going to play him, I need to be a bigger cheat than he is." He gave a wink before ducking hastily out the door.

Tolby considered the rough wooden planks before patting down his vest and finding his pipe. Smoking instrument in hand, he went out the door as well, good slow paces so as not to see his son riding down the road, and headed to his cider press. He had a bit of work to do before starting another crush; as he stepped into the building, the scent of apples overwhelmed him, beautiful crisp apples in all their hues of red and gold and even a flushed pink, waiting to be pressed and made into a drink that Tolby Farbranch could boast about. He sat on an overturned empty barrel and tamped down a bit of toback in the bowl of his pipe, lit it, and then enjoyed a deep draft or two while considering what he would tell his wife about their son. It was likely, he conceded, that she probably already knew as much about the affair as he did, with the exception of Garner's actually leaving, for Lily was as wise about the children and family as any woman he had ever known. He smiled about the stem of his pipe. He couldn't have married a finer lass, and the wonder of it was that she loved him as much as he loved and adored her. Hard as some of the years had been, still, he would not have had his life any other way.

He smoked a bit more, thinking, and then let his pipe go cold, before putting it away and rising to work on the presses. With his whittling knife, he stooped over the workings, trying to smooth out a piece that stubbornly refused to mesh its gears with the others as well as it could, nothing that would stop it from doing its duty but still brought a clenching to his teeth when he heard it during the crush. Some time later, with the winter sun gleaming through the windows, and himself covered in fine shavings, he could hear a bit of commotion out on the streets. Curiously, he walked to the doors of the great cider house and peered out as a strident voice hawking wares reached him.

"Gods awaken! Gods be a-listenin' again. Buy your altars here! Prepare to hear Their guidance. Great portents and omens begin to stir! Be ready!"

Tolby snorted as he saw the man, a priest, bedecked with poles like any street vendor, staggering a bit under the weight of his relics, children trailing him and occasionally poking sticks at his thin ankles in hopes of tripping him to raise an even greater excitement. Tolby emerged as he saw that and flapped his arms at the younguns, scolding them for their treatment of a priest, for all that he himself did not put much stock in the Kernan strain. Sandals flapping and robe dusty, the Kernan came to a halt, his poles swaying and gave him a grateful smile. "Thankee, Master, these children do be curious and feisty these days."

"You're a bit away from the temples, yourself, and decked out like a spring garland for the fairs."

"Ah, but that's my lot," the priest said, and drew his sleeved arm over his forehead which glistened with sweat despite the chill of the winter day. "When the Gods speak again, all should hear!"

"Aye? After all these centuries, what seems to be the rush?" Tolby eyed the pottery which looked like miniature water wells and statue nooks, shaped by hand and fired hastily from the crackled glaze on them.

"That's the point, in't it, Master? All these years without divine guidance, but we never gave up, did we? And now the signs point that the Gods have examined us closely, found us worthy again, and lean close to speak!"

"Indeed?" Tolby took a moment to knock the fine shavings off his clothes before meeting the priest's eyes again. A-course, that was the Kernan way of things. Dwellers had never conversed directly with the Gods, so never felt the lack of communication when the Kernans were cut off. Dwellers knew well the deep voices and workings of the Gods in the world about them, and were never bereft of guidance and judgment. Kernans, though, they were a nervous and insecure folk.

"Buy one, good master, for I would hate to think a fine fellow like you could be left behind when the Gods speak again. Only a silver bit, although if you wished a grander one, I could bring one by later when it's painted and such."

"Exactly what is it?"

"A listening altar. A bit of incense, a little wine or hard cider, a sprinkling of petals or herbs here."

"And I would hear through it . . . how exactly?"

"Why, with your ears, good sir! With your ears? How else?"

Tolby scratched one. "I already have ears, good priest, and I don't see an extra pair among your relics."

"Indeed not! No, no, these altars and alcoves attest to your faith and your readiness, so that Their Voices reach you when the time comes! This is your testament that you are prepared." The priest beamed at him, a flight of wrinkles spreading across his worn face, an earnest gleam in his eyes.

"Ah." Tolby patted his vest unconsciously to remind himself that his pipe had been cold when he'd placed it there. He'd only put a still-lit pipe in his clothes once, but the smoldering and burning that had ensued was enough to keep him wary even decades after the event. "Good man, I'll bring you a cup of cider and send you on your way while I think about it and discuss it with my wife. You understand how wives are, no doubt, and if she desires one, why then I'll find you at the temples."

The priest flapped his mouth wordlessly for a moment as if unsure whether he'd been rejected or accepted, but then finally nodded. "A drink would be appreciated. This is my third load today." He lowered his voice so that the scattered children, who'd stayed nearby to see what might be made of this priest, could not hear him so easily. " 'Tis said even the Oxforts at Hawthorne have ordered a custom altar for their manors."

More like the Oxforts had something to do with the selling of them, Tolby thought, and made a noncommittal sound appropriate to the gossip. With a duck of his head, Tolby took to his heels and fetched a nice draw of cider. He patted the Kernan on one shoulder, being careful not to upset the poles balanced there, and sent the priest on his way. He watched him go, children trailing at a distance and throwing glances at him to see if he would interfere with their fun again. He shook his fist and growled at one who skittered away.

Priests selling goods like common street vendors. Not that the temples didn't do a fair business of selling things, oh no, Tolby was not so naïve as that. Still, the sight of the Kernan struck him as both odd and unnerving. On the heels of so many other things changing in his world, he did not like the idea of the Gods springing back to life and stirring the pot, as it were. He didn't like the idea at all.

"THE COLUMNS ARE MARCHING," Tiforan said solemnly, as he gave a kneeling bow before Abayan Diort. Diort looked on him coolly. Tiforan was not his choice as a second-in-command, but as third or fourth, he might do. Thus, he would be left behind as Diort moved on to Ashenbrook. His tattoos, deeply etched into his cheekbones, twitched as if he sensed the small disapproval Diort felt when looking upon him. Weathered by the badland sun, his golden-bronze skin had darkened to a warm brown, and the corners of his eyes were etched near as deep as the knife-carved tattoos, though those markings were not the august ones worn by Diort.

"Good. Tell Hefort I want the sands cast."

"Today, Warlord? After the men have already marched?"

"It's not for my army, Tif. Their fate is already set. The Warrior Queen of the Vaelinars wants a quick battle, I wager, a handful of days at the most, to achieve her

point. I read the sands for another answer. Now go."
Diort watched the man get to his feet and leave in haste,
and thought again that this was someone he would not
willingly leave in charge, for he did not wish to be questioned over something so trivial as an oracle. Now, if
he were to argue battle tactics instead of minor occur-
rences, that might give Abayan hope. He sat down and
pondered his chain of command, trying to decide if he
wished to make changes.

The oracle came soon enough, crawling on her knees.
She had claimed, when the mantle of prophecy had been
passed to her, that the weight of the world was too great
for her to bear standing, and so regressed to creeping
about on hands and knees. It was an affectation that
gave her credence among shallow Galdarkans and kept
her from being hauled about here and there by minor
lords who wished to use her gifts, but despite her show,
she actually held a gift that Diort could perceive and
admire. So he tolerated her histrionics much as he tolerated Tiforan's minor rebellions. Hefort, however, had
proved far more valuable to him.

She looked up at him, yellow-green eyes shrewd, her
young face lined about her mouth as though she held
bad opinions in her teeth and chewed on them all the
long days. As well she might, knowing what she did.
"You sent for me."

"I did, Hefort. I would like the sands cast, if you are
able."

She snorted. "I'm able. It is yourself that must be
ready and willing to accept my read."

Diort shifted in his chair to lean down toward her. "I
do not ask for that which I do not want."

"Good that it is you know that. Very well, then." She
reached inside her cloak lined with pockets, each filled
with a small glass vial of brightly colored sand. The vials
alone were worth a small fortune, each shaped and cut
brilliantly, small decanters of the sand of prophecy, their
mouths gilt in gold and their handles set with gems.

There were times when Hefort physically cast the sands and others when she merely spread the vials before her in a pattern and mused upon their meaning before intoning her message. He had no idea what she would do today.

She plucked a single vial out, filled with a gray-white powder. She uncorked it and shook a bit out on the back of her hand, then inhaled it deeply. Hefort recorked the bottle as her eyes rolled back in her head a moment and her body quaked. She sat back on her haunches like an animal, her hands moving independently of her reaction to the inhalant, stowing the vial back from whence it had come and pulling a second out and spilling its crimson sand upon the floor before his feet. Then she began to draw in it with one finger, symbols and movements that he could scarce grasp in his own vision before she wiped it out and drew another, over and over, a parade of symbols and pictographs springing from her artistry only to be wiped out as she spoke to herself, trying to grasp what she saw. Hand trembling, she capped the vial of crimson sand and put it also in her cloak. She looked up, and her eyes were both seeing him and half blind at the same time. The war hammer at his back vibrated in agitation as if the minor Demon inside it had been awakened.

"Your spies are slow. There should be word arriving that the great warlord of the queen is dead, assassinated, and Osten Drebukar will not face you in battle." She held her hand palm up as Diort let out a word in surprise, stopping him. "The outcome of the battle is not foretold to me, nor is that your question. His death does not assure your victory." The oracle did not wait for him to answer her or to ask his question. She licked dry lips and continued, "That which the Gods themselves have said would never happen again, is already stirring and coming about. Old masters will return, and you must choose. I cannot tell you which is the right, only you can know what you must do. The fate of many, however, will rest upon your decision. Bow your knee only after great thought, Warlord, for you are the Guardian of these lands."

Hefort stopped. She took a deep breath as if fighting for it. Abayan half rose to help her, but she shook her head. "Listen! There is one who would use Kerith as a stepping stone to the Heavens, and his heel will grind us to dust if we allow that. You are one of those few who can stay his madness. Not the only one, but your allies have not yet become aware. Enemies today may be the brothers you need at your back tomorrow." Hefort gulped down another breath. Shiny sweat covered her brow in a slick sheen. Her hand trembled as she held it in the air between them, her fingers stained with crimson powder. "Look to the pathways for the answer to your question."

With that last, Hefort dropped her hand and her body prone in front of him. She began to weep quietly as if overcome, and he did not move, afraid of disturbing her and her vision if there were more to be said.

So they remained until the sun lowered and the sands became as ice in the night and her sobbing finally ceased. Only then did he put out his hand to cup her head and thank her, and send for blankets to comfort her, and warm stew to nourish her. But first, as he stood, he scrubbed out the last marking of the crimson dust in front of his feet, not liking the symbol he saw there.

It was the marking the nomad clans of Galdarkans used to warn all who might trespass that chaos and death lay in the countryside ahead.

Diort slept in another tent, leaving the exhausted woman to rest and rise on her own. Tiforan met him in the morning with his horse, cloak, and pack as instructed, his face tilted in curiosity. He held back for only a moment as Abayan filled his hands.

"Do you ride because of the oracle?"

"No. Did I not tell you I would leave this morning?"

"Yes, Warlord, but I thought ... she seemed distraught. She filled the night with her weeping. It's being said about the camp that she inhaled the dust of graves. All know that brings the most powerful visions."

"Really. What else is said in the camps?"

"That you are driven by her words."

Abayan let himself laugh softly. It seemed only to knot up Tiforan even more. "She gave you a dire quest."

"She did not. Puzzling, yes, and informative, yes, but not dire."

"Still you ride."

"I've things to do before I join my army. I didn't ask her to predict a victory, but she gave a good accounting on that. You can repeat those words and those words only in the camp." He shouldered his packs as he took up the reins to his horse. "You have nothing to fear, Tiforan—but me." With that, he swung up and kicked the horse into movement, leaving his third-in-command behind, jaw hanging. He did not mention that Hefort was weeping again in the morning when he went to reward her and say good-bye, nor that she remembered not a word she'd uttered. It was the crimson stain upon her fingers that set her off again, her hands shaking and inconsolable, and so he left the oracle alone in his tent to recover, not convinced one way or another of the truthfulness of the night. He thought omens fragile things, broken by one wrong step of the men who tried to follow them and could not. So, they might be like a lantern hung in a tent on a dark night, a hazy beacon homeward or a wisp of moonlight off a glass-light patch of sand. Reality or mirage, he could only count on his own wits and sense of direction in the end.

Look to the pathways, she'd said to him. He knew she had not spoken of the Elven Ways, those damned but necessary nets that tied Kerith together, but rather those roads taken by the guardians when all haste had been needed to defend their Mageborn. He knew the secret

passages, they'd been ingrained in him, but no one he
knew had trod them in centuries. It was said some were
haunted by the angry specters of Mageborn who'd per-
ished at the hands of their rivals and the Gods despite
the efforts of their Galdarkans to save them. It was said
that foul things ran the tunnels of others. That stone and
water had twisted and destroyed some of them. That
nothing remained as it had been intended centuries
past. It would fall upon him to see what was true. But
did he not have a war hammer which could break stone?
Turn earth? Could shake the very foundations of the pil-
lars of the world if he struck it at the base of them? Who
better to see what the pathways still held?

Diort turned his horse's head toward the base of the
melted hills on his southern hand. When he reached his
destination, he murmured the passwords given unto his
guardianship and horse and rider vanished into the tunnels where time and distance seemed not to exist under
the earth.

Bregan Oxfort loosened his brace a little as he settled
down by his campfire. Recruiting in Calcort had been
profitable and enthusiastic, creating a fervor which he
felt certain would sweep through the other cities. He'd
left that in charge of one of his father's apprentices, a
dour, wizened old Kernan by the name of Garfin, returning to Hawthorne to supervise the new relic industry.
His body protested the hard ride. He preferred not to
travel by elaborate trader carriage when he could help
it, though in the last few years, he could feel the pain of
riding astride. That damned Ferryman. He would take
him on again, if he thought he'd survive the encounter,
and this time bring the being down, annihilate him, rend
him forever from the daylight of Kerith. Boatmen on
the Nylara had survived before, they would again, just as
they did on any river which swelled with rain and melt-

ing snows. Barges and ferries were better built, rudders stronger, cables and pulleys better anchored. It would be no loss to anyone but the purses of the Vaelinars. That might be a good exercise for his new regiment of caravan guards, a coordinated attack on the blight of the river. There ought to be some underlying, compelling excuse he could arrange....

Pain lanced through his thigh. Bregan glanced down in surprise to find his hand knotted into his trouser, darkened fingers gouging into half-numb flesh. The clever brace curled about his leg carried a glow as if newly forged and yet uncooled from the fires, its heat burning its way through his clothing even as its warmth subsided. He uncurled his hand slowly, catching his lip in his teeth in concentration as he fought the shooting agony and the effort necessary to unclench his stiff hand. Each tiny movement wrought havoc that echoed through his entire frame, aches he had not had in years as though the very thought of attacking the Ferryman again brought punishment. He watched as each digit straightened with a spasm of more pain, the base of his nails pale, blood welling from his mouth. Decorative runes upon his brace flared once and then went out, darkened.

Bregan pushed his leg out in front of him, hating it, cursing his flesh for living only enough to bring him pain every day. His breath hissed from between his teeth as everything subsided except for the slow trickle of blood from his bitten lip, and that he finally wiped away with the back of his hand. As the tide of pain ebbed, he became aware that his heart had been pounding, beating in his ears, and it, too, began to slow into a measured drumming, pulse by pulse. The brace felt cool to his hand when he brushed his left hand across it, as though it had never held a heat threatening to scorch through the fabric of his trousers and neither had it left a mark upon him. Dare he trust his senses? Was he losing not only his body but the threads of his mind, and all of it to the machinations of the Vaelinars? How long could

he endure it? How long must any of them endure what
the wretched invaders wrung from them day by day?
He sat and stared into the fire, unseeing, until the flames
guttered into low, glowing embers. Then a twig cracked
loudly as something or someone trod upon it carelessly.
Oxfort reached for his sword and stood up with effort.
Once on his feet, he was no cripple, and the sword fit
his left hand admirably. Beyond the sparse illumination of the fire as he stirred it, a shadow solidified in the
darkness.

Bregan tightened his hold on his sword as the shadow
separated itself from the night and stepped into the firelight. It loomed larger and larger until the tattoos on his
face and the headpiece which held back his hair flashed
in the illumination, and Bregan knew without doubt
who accosted him. He did not lower his blade.

"Lord Diort. Either you are far afield, or I am."

Abayan spread his hands to show they were empty.
The fire glazed his skin like fresh-forged bronze, and his
jade eyes glinted in the shadows with a catlike sheen.
The great war hammer he always carried stayed at his
back. Dust glinted on his clothing, a rusty tear or two
in his sleeves showed the tinge of dried blood, and his
boots carried heavy gouges and scuff marks as though,
for all his composure, he had been in a scuffle. "In all
fairness," the Galdarkan said, in his slightly stilted way,
"I think we are both off our normal paths. It is welcome
to see you, however."

"Me?"

Abayan ignored the distrust in Bregan's voice. "May I
sit?" He gestured at the fireside.

"I think it best if both of us stay on our feet. My pardon, Lord Diort, but things are not always as they seem,
and I wonder if it's even you I talk with."

"As you command." Diort's face twisted slightly, and
then he rolled his shoulders as if to flex a stiffness and
soreness out of them. "I am in hopes we can share some
information."

"I thought Quendius kept you on a leash and as well-informed as he wished."

"The same thought could be said of you."

Bregan lowered his sword point a bit, so that Diort could not see it shake in his hand, not out of weakness, but a spate of anger. "No one leashes me."

"Good to know. I have sprung mine, but not without a great deal of effort. Taxing. Quendius is a man who knows the weaknesses of others, and exploits them."

"So do many other men."

"True." Diort turned his face briefly, revealing the sharp outline of his profile, his hooked nose and proud brow, as he listened for something outside the firelight of the small camp. When he turned back, he said quietly, "I did not expect to find you here, but having found you, I think we should speak. If you cannot or will not talk with me, give me the courtesy of that acknowledgment and I will leave."

"I would never be so discourteous to a former business partner." Bregan sat down, and indicated the stump across from him. He opened his pack and took out several cloth-wrapped parcels, the aroma of which filled the air with goodness: fresh bread, cheese, a delicately spiced and salted meat, and some good red apples. "Share my dinner?"

And they ate quietly before they began to speak earnestly of many things.

IF BREGAN OXFORT HAD BEEN THE ANSWER the oracle spoke of, Diort could not begin to fathom the question posed. He left the trader at his campfire, curled in sleep in a still night-dark morning, and made his way back to the pathway where he'd left his horse on a grazing tie. A feeling of discomfort crawled down his back as he did so, strangely not wanting to leave the Kernan alone although he knew Bregan's prowess with the sword and his ability to take care of himself despite appearances. It felt as though an obligation had been laid on his shoulders, a beholding he could not shrug off though Abayan knew he neither held nor could fulfill it. No rhyme or reason lay behind this sense of obligation, and he gritted his teeth as he walked away from it. It seemed that the farther he got from it, however, the more it compelled him to return to Bregan's side, until he took up his horse's reins and led him back on a pathway. Then it disappeared with a *snap!* as if a taut line had broken.

His horse walked wearily after him, brown-and-yellow
stems of grass hanging from his lips as he still chewed.
The pathways he remembered from his youth still existed, although roots choked them now and gravel falls,
and nests of ferocious rodents the size of his torso. He
had cleaned and cleared what he could, and the branch
he chose now should take him all the way to the shores
of Hawthorne in far less time than it would take him to
ride there. Time did not exist in the tunnels as it did elsewhere. How its string was knotted up by the magic of the
Mageborn, he could not tell, for he was not a Mageborn,
only the son of generations created to protect them.
It was not a magic like those worked by the strangers,
that he knew. This came from Kerith, from within its
very being, and did not have the twisted sense to it that
anything made by the Vaelinars had when he touched
upon it. Abayan could not declare that Vaelinar magic
was unclean but only different. As different as clay from
water, neither being good nor bad on their own till used
or misused.

He had ridden through many of the paths and had
to lead his horse through still more, but as fast as they
moved him, and as powerful as they were, they were for
him alone. He could not move an army through, even
one by one, if he wished. Perhaps a handful of guardian Galdarkans might be suffered, but he doubted the
pathways would allow more. If they could be enlarged
or remade . . . Rakka growled at his back as if sensing his
thoughts. But Abayan would not wield the war hammer
unless a rockfall impeded his way, for the weapon was
not a maker, it was an unmaker. To use it unwisely on
the pathway would be to bring the whole thing collaps-
ing upon him, burying the tunnel and himself forever.
Rakka, earthmover Demon, did not care. It was its way
to find the flaw in stone and bring it shivering, quaking,
down to nothing more than gravel. It held no care or
thought other than to destroy. Diort was more than a
Demon, or so he prayed. He moved toward the ocean,

toward a faraway light that was now no more than a
spark in the twilight of the pathway's gloom, knowing that when he got there, he would do no more than
look and then return the way he had come, no answer
in hand other than that his duty as a guardian had been
performed as foretold.

Or had it been?

"My bottom hurts," Nutmeg announced, "and this is
boring." She threw one leg over the saddle and bounced
a moment sideways on her trotting pony. "Three days on
the trail and nothing."

Rivergrace reined up. "Would you rather," she asked,
the corner of her mouth turning up a little, "be practic-
ing in the arena?"

"Don't have to practice. Jeredon said my talent was in
fisticuffs, and my brothers had already taught me well.
That, and the branch club."

"I suppose chamber pot swinging would be an off-
shoot of your club prowess."

Nutmeg grinned. "It had better be." She pushed her
straw hat back off her head. "Do you suppose he even
noticed?"

She undoubtedly meant Jeredon. "I rather doubt it,"
Grace answered sadly. "I imagine all their thoughts were
on Osten. Losing him is a great blow to all of us. I can't
think of what it will be like to have him gone."

"I can't either. Word on the back stairs was that Bistel
Vantane will come to replace him, and all the servants
are shaking in their boots. Bistel is a hard man, they say,
and gives no quarter to any under him, from the lowest
to the highest."

"Would you rather have a man command who gives
favors to the high and frowns on the rest of us?"

"No, but . . . he is stern. Not like Bistane."

"I think he's very like Bistane, from when we met

him last high summer. He doesn't sing, of course, but he notices everything and forgets nothing. His eyes are like the war falcons their House is named for, I think. Bistane can let his humor show because he doesn't have to command yet, but he never forgets he's his father's son for all that."

"How could you forget that?"

"Perhaps if you don't know who your father is."

Nutmeg's face went red. "Grace, I didn't mean—you don't think I meant . . ."

"What? Oh, never! How could I forget my own family? Pull your hat back on, Meg, I think the wind is whistling straight through your ears!" Grace put her boot toe out to jostle her sister's boot with a small laugh.

"Oh, well, I suppose that's better than having a head thicker than wood!"

"At least wood floats." She sobered a bit, as she gave rein to her horse, listening to Nutmeg snort as she tugged her hat back in place and followed.

Nutmeg had said only once that she could not believe with all Grace had gone through, that she had not been given her father's name when she died . . . her true father. The River Goddess had revealed her mother, Lindala, to her, but nothing of her father or her lineage. Not a one of the Vaelinars queried later on her behalf could report a Lindala in their bloodline. She might as well not have existed among a people who clung to their Houses and Strongholds and family lines as if they were ropes thrown to a drowning person. Even now, with half-breeds and more thinning down the Vaelinar heritage, names were told, and known, and remembered. Stigma, yes, for going outside their boundary but remembered. An errant talent here and there might yet be recovered. Sevryn had told her some of the Houses were recruiting and even abducting mixed breeds and trying to refine the Vaelinar in them. Pride no longer stood in their way. So, then, why did no one claim Lindala? Why did no one know her? Why wasn't anyone able to name the man who'd courted and won her, and then lost them both to slavery?

Yet, as he'd also said to her. "No one claims Quendius either and his Vaelinar heritage is indisputable."

Grace held her Dweller raising deep inside her, a core around which the rest of her existed. She knew she'd be a different person if anyone else had found her on the Silverwing River, and she thanked the fates for the loving family who had. She would not carry shame for it. But it seemed she needed proof and more of who she might have been so that the Warrior Queen Lariel Anderieon could also trust who she might become, and for that she knew of no other place to turn than the historian and scholar Azel d'Stanthe of Ferstanthe. There were answers buried in his library to questions no one could dare to ask, and she would beg his permission to seach for the information she needed. More than that, she hoped to find her true self. She'd had enough of Lara telling her what she could and could not say or could and could not do with the magic that did course through her veins. How could she not help if she held the means within her to do so? How could the Vaelinars look at the other peoples of Kerith as nothing more than beggars? It was not a matter of fearing Lara's wrath. It was a matter of not being able to look within herself and see what she wished to. She did not remember her mother or know her father, but she knew herself. That, she would not let anyone take away from her, be it a Warrior Queen or a Goddess of the Rivers, even though she knew now that her hold upon it was frail. She needed an anchor. Once she had thought that anchor would be Sevryn. Now, she didn't know. But Azel held the key to knowledge and knowledge would give her answers she needed.

And, as she'd found in the past, possibly answers she had not hoped for, or wanted, but would have to deal with. So be it.

Chapter
Twenty-Nine

B ISTEL BROUGHT HIS ARM DOWN, stroking the falcon which bobbed his head to rub his hooked beak against a proffered finger, before ripping into a strip of bloodied meat that Bistel held. The bird made small sounds of warning off as it ate and Bistel heeded its cries. No mere messenger bird, this was a proud vantane who had been trained to fight his way through the skies and across enemies, if need be. The bird had flown far and hard, and his message had been difficult indeed. Osten, dead. His services asked for. She dared not demand, not after the disagreement over warfare they'd had, but she asked. His life turned, in a way which he had hoped to avoid for a few decades longer. *How do I count my sins, O God of War, or will they be counted for me?* He watched the bird devour its reward, bloody gobbets of flesh that had moments ago been a small coney which also had no doubt wished for a few more moments of life. Such was the way. He handed off the vantane to one of his falconers, stripped off his glove, and headed back to his house to make ready. He would meet Lariel Anderieon at the appointed place but not before his time. He had a few arrangements to make, first. He would honor his pledge— but in his own way.

He walked through his manor, lingering a moment here and there. Matters had been settled for Bistane who knew every corner of this home as well as he did. He also had in writing what he needed for Verdayne. Those papers he had placed in two sets of trusted hands, and would place in a third, lest there be any argument. War could take any of them. He paused in his bedroom long enough to pluck a cloak pin out of a carved box on a side table, fingering it a long while before pinning it in place. Created with a distinctly female craftsmanship, he had no real idea who had smithed it. Bistel gave a thin smile. He liked to think his wife had done it, although he had no idea who his wife could have been, that life torn away from him many, many years ago. He was young then, barely more than a stripling lord, a very young, knee-high squire. He and his father, whom he'd served, had been the lone survivors of their immediate line when the world exploded and Vaelinars found themselves on Kerith. There were others close enough in blood and temperament that they'd formed a House and kept a front against the ilk of those who became known as the ild Fallyn.

They had all had an affinity for one another then, those who grouped into Houses and Strongholds. Bistane walked as if he had been born to step into his footsteps without a single falter. He had his own mind, for which Bistel was grateful, for he had never intended to rear an exact replica for himself ... Gods forbid his same mistakes would be repeated endlessly on Kerith.

Bistel placed his palm over his cloak pin and then left his room. He pored over ledgers and books in his study, called in a scribe to make a few changes and notes and then, when the last page had dried, he closed his journal solemnly and told his scribe good-bye. The wizened Kernan corked his ink bottle, gathered up his kit of pens and whittling knives and his sheaves of paper, and backed out of the study after a deep bow and an even deeper sniff to hold back what looked suspiciously like tears in his eyes.

Bistel waited until the house had emptied before packing his kit and leaving himself. He paused by a silver-backed mirror near the main doors. His sharp nose, his bristle of close-cut now shock-white hair, his eyes that blazed blue upon blue, this face was not likely to look upon itself again in these halls. He knew that even if the mirror, once storied to be an oracle of the Vaelinar, did not.

When he rode his horse out, his warhorse on a lead behind him, he did not look back although he could hear the stir of stableboys and men scrambling out to look, and falconers, and cooks, and tailors, and gardeners, and smiths, and their wives and children, all watching their lord ride out to his last war. They could not know what he knew in his heart, that when he went down if he went down, it would not be in defeat but victory. That was part of his pledge to Lara.

Verdayne walked out with him, striding at his mount's shoulder, as far as the gates at the lane's edge, beyond the earshot and view of the holding. He wrapped his hand about Bistel's boot and squeezed the foot as hard as he could.

"No," said Bistel to him, and dismounted, and took his second son in a hug and held him for a very long time. "I loved your mother as much as I have ever loved anyone, and you and Bistel still hold my heart. Never forget that as long as you live, which will be by anyone's standards, a long and full life."

He kissed Verdayne's cheek, tasted tears, got back on his horse, and rode off, his heart full.

"You seem vexed." Tressandre ran her hand through her hair, tilting her head to one side as she looked up at Jeredon. She sat at his feet, her slender legs crossed, as the archers he'd been instructing took a break for water and fresh bread and cheese laid out for them. "They're doing well."

"Very well. It's not them I have a complaint with. I haven't seen Nutmeg for a day or two."

"Your little nursemaid? Should I be insulted, that I haven't taken care of you?" She let her voice be light.

He put his hand on her shoulder. "Never, Tressandre. I just realized I hadn't seen her."

"She is a country lass, is she not?"

"Raised on her family's ranch and orchards, yes, although they now own a fine cider house in Calcort, and her mother's tailoring skills have made her mistress of a good shop."

Tressandre could not catch his gaze. Jeredon searched the archery field and the open lands beyond it as though he hoped to see the object of his thoughts. She stirred, putting her legs out in front of her to stretch them, showing a good bit of flesh, and knowing that, finally, had drawn his attention. The wind held a cold, nasty touch to it, but her ultimate goal made momentary discomfort bearable. "One of my men said that he saw her leave on her pony, with hat and packs and what might have been a fishing pole. Perhaps she took a day or two off. It is difficult work being a caretaker."

Jeredon made a noise at the back of his throat. "I'm not the easiest of patients either."

She searched his profile. One did not supplant a rival with ill words, she decided. Not this one, at any rate, though she could scarcely believe a Dweller could rival her. "She has worked hard, m'lord Eladar. Without her diligence, you would not be what you are today, with muscles still strong and willing so that I could bring you to your feet. Let her go for a day or two and find some peace. She deserves that, I think."

He let his breath out slowly. "Yes, yes, I imagine she does." Jeredon looked at her then. "You surprise me, Tressandre."

She let her mouth curve slightly. "In good ways, I should hope."

"Very good." His hand on her shoulder tightened. "I'm seeing substance I've overlooked before."

"You surprise me as well. What my family counts as base, you seem to prize. I'm not afraid to show my true self before you." She put her head against his knee, a gesture she hoped he would see as tender and not designed to hide the expression on her face. Jeredon had not seen the true side of her. Most never would. He would, well and good, but only when it was time and he was bound to her with ties that would be unbreakable. Perhaps even an heir from the endangered bloodline. Until then, she played at this charade to get what she wished from him. "After a day in this wind, it'll be welcome to swim at the hot pools. Good for you, m'lord Jeredon, as well."

His hand dropped from her shoulder to her back, massaging her lightly. "I'm looking forward to it."

Oh, yes. She would make certain that their visit was unforgettable and that he would look forward to it, day after day, until the battlefield drew them. He had a chink in his armor, the arrogant Eladar, and she knew exactly where it was now. She would conquer him first, as surely as she was female and an ild Fallyn. A genuine smile flushed her lips.

The cheerful prattling fell at last into blessed silence. Quendius dropped into a crouch to watch the girls as they approached a sharp-banked brook, surging high with runoff from a highland snow. They halted with their backs to him, their horse and pony swinging their tails slowly from side to side, while the tall one seemed to

have a concern about crossing. This time of year, they
were fortunate they weren't up to their mounts' hocks
in snow and ice, so why would a little high water bother
them? His mouth curled as he watched. He did not know
how the two of them had lived thus far. He had trailed
them for the better part of two days and neither had the
slightest notion. He could have slipped into their camp
at any time and slit their throats. After listening to the
little one talk endlessly, he was almost ready to, except
that did not fit his plans for the moment. He did not
think the tall one would go on without her companion if
something untoward happened.

After long moments of watching, he realized they had
fallen into complete silence and were waiting. For what?
To rest their mounts? Then why not build a fire and do
something reasonable like dismount and let them graze
a bit as well? What were these soft, silly creatures thinking? Behind him, his own mount stamped as if reading
his impatience.

An image wavered on the white-cresting river. He
watched as it coalesced into the hooded form of the Ferryman, wading toward them. The tall girl leaned out of
her saddle to drop a coin into his palm and Quendius
watched with narrowed eyes as the specter took both
horse and pony by the headstall and walked them into
the river with him. His thoughts spun furiously. Why had
she summoned him and how had she even thought the
Ferryman, anchored to the Nylara River, would come to
her? And how had he twisted his binding to do so? Yet
here he was, giving them safe passage across the frothing mountain river, far from his own station and ferry.
Quendius watched closely, intently, and then, just before
emerging on the far shore, the Ferryman and his charges
disappeared from his sight.

He watched and waited, but they never appeared on
the far shore of the river.

Quendius sat back on his heels with a disgusted grunt.
He did not know what had just happened. He scrubbed

the heel of his hand over his face before standing and
grabbing the reins of his horse who jerked his head
back, startled. Quendius growled at him, and the beast
subsided immediately. Relenting, Quendius rubbed his
knuckles along the horse's jaw. He, at least, had some
sense and training drilled into him. He clucked to the
horse and led him to the water's edge for a drink. As the
horse dropped his head to lip at the icy waters, a pounding hit Quendius in the temple.

He dropped one shoulder slightly, turning about, his
back to the river. Not a pounding, exactly but . . . a heavy
buzz. Yes. And more. His own sword made a *chitta* sound
at his back. Lesser Demon that imbued it, it was nothing
articulate, not as the great sword Cerat had been, but
its talent for seeking blood and biting deep into whatever target Quendius swung it at made it invaluable. It
responded now to whatever it was that had assailed his
senses. Then, as he let those same senses course over the
area about him, from the stone, he heard Rakka's voice.

He knew the earthmover's voice well. Narskap had
crafted the weapon for him, in addition to Cerat, but
the war hammer had refused to bond to him. No matter, it had served to bind great Diort to Quendius, for a
while. Now Diort carried it, free of Quendius although
not free of the Demon. Rakka would demand a price
someday. Quendius knew it. Narskap had smithed it for
that. Diort would learn, to his dismay.

Quendius scuffed the toe of his boot on the riverbank.
In the meantime, Rakka sounded near. Very near. He
pulled his horse away from the river and went in search
of the Demon's growl.

He trailed the low rumble to a rocky overhang, pausing
for a moment before stepping into its shadow. He found
himself in a tunnel, scarce wide enough for more than one
to pass through, although high enough for that one to ride.
Quendius put out his hand. It had been carved through
the rock like a hot knife cuts through butter and cheese,
and he knew the sign—the black fabric—of magic when

he saw it. He dropped the reins in a ground-tie, moving forward quietly. The tunnel was not recently made, so he knew that Rakka had not done it, although the war hammer growled here and there in the passage ahead of him, and sounded at least once, its vibration buffeting his hearing. He could hear the slide of gravel and rock. Someone used the hammer to clear the tunnel, and that someone could only be Abayan Diort.

What have we here, my friend? thought Quendius as he followed cautiously. The rock itself held a low light, emanating from tiles placed at frequent intervals. They burned steadily, unlike an oil lamp, although their illumination stayed low. He paused once to see chalking under one of the tiles. It gave direction, as well as a time of arrival. The chalk marks were new, untouched by moisture or lichen or the vagaries of deep tunneling into stone. Quendius examined them a moment in wonder. An echo came to him, uttering words that sank heavily into his soul, words of ancient Galdarkan, words of Mageborn command. He knew them as soon as he heard them, he, a Vaelinar without a bit of magic in his blood, knew he listened to legends of old. More, he remembered what he heard, and he knew what it was. It etched indelibly into his being, his flawed, needy being, and filled him. He knew where he stood and how he would move and what he could do with this knowledge to destroy his enemies.

For this alone, he might let his old ally live when they met again.

Time and distance did not matter here, where the Mageborn had plied their trade. He could move at will, and so could any army which would follow him, as long as they were content to march in single file. Like ants, he thought. Steady but determined ants. Swarming when they reached their destination. He put back his head and let out a howl.

Abayan Diort had shown him how to walk on the old pathways of the Galdarkan high guardians.

SEVRYN CROSSED ONE OF THE SEVEN SISTERS into Hawthorne after two days of hard riding and one crossing aided by the Dark Ferryman without incident. Wooden planks reverberated under hoof falls, and kites cried as they rode the sea wind over the city. Ahead of him on the right, he could see the high cliffs of Tomarq and the dazzle that was the precious Jewel and Shield. The cliffs buffered the harbor around which Hawthorne sat, and the winds that reached here were far less than those which whipped out on the open ocean. This was a natural harbor, a safe harbor, as long as no one thought to trespass into it. The capital, as Gilgarran had often told him, was a city of import because men made it so. But why was that? What was it about certain places that men felt made them important? Perhaps it was because, even in their petty bones, they could sense the natural alliances of the elements and their world into a fortuitous crossing, even as they could sense those places which were cursed by negative and evil alliances.

Hawthorne was one of the good spots, a fitting capital; a sound place to center and begin things. Just so, Gilgarran had lectured Sevryn.

As he passed through the city walls, a frisson of worry danced down the back of his neck. This was one of those moments when his whole life, and those of the people around him, would change. He did not often have those feelings of being at a crossroads, but when he did, he was never wrong. Only this time, he could not see the way to go. He often didn't, only that the moment had arrived. He supposed that would have to be enough. How many, after all, knew exactly when they held their fate in their own hands, exclusive of the actions of others? The moment held him longer, imprinting him, tasting as he acknowledged it, before it let him go and faded from his thought. But it had been there, and he had not imagined it, and now he had only to seize it. His fate.

He headed into the trade quarter, searching the side streets for a barely remembered alleyway and shop. He rode by it three times before he found it, but when he did, it leaped into his mind so clearly that he wondered how he had not seen it from the very first. The storefront was bannered: Feldari and Son. Gilgarran's business had been with the son, who, no doubt, was now the father or perhaps even grandfather of this establishment. He handed Aymaran off to a lad who stood by the front door, waiting for customers, and gave him a coin to keep the horse comfortable. It took a moment to note the shops and storerooms on either side, the alley opening onto the streets, the height of the buildings, the ease or difficulty of gaining the rooftops and the traffic on the main street in general before he entered. This was how Gilgarran had taught him to view the world and this was how he served the queen. No matter what she thought of him.

"You don't serve me at all doing this," Lara said sharply. "You waste time, precious time, at a crucial moment. You can't abandon me now." Her apartment looked as though she had not allowed any of the maids in, her bed tossed and torn in the room behind her as she sat at her desk, her face half-turned to him as though she might deny he even existed if she blinked. Lamps and candles guttered low, running out of oil or having burned down to mere stubs.

"Osten is dead. Nothing brings him back, and Bistel will go as you appointed him, despite his disagreement with your plans. I'll be gone but a few days, and you, Lariel, have to learn patience."

Heat flooded her face, highlighting her cheekbones. "Only my brother dares to talk to me like that."

"And so he would, if the moon hadn't gotten into his eyes and blinded him to everything but Tressandre."

She slapped a rolled map upon her desk. The candles flickered. The hour was so early that black night still curtained the skies, and she looked to him as though she had not slept at all, which was likely. She reached back and knotted her hair at the nape of her neck to get it out of her way, which only served to the accent the anger in her expression. "You are going."

"I intend to."

"I won't call guards on you, but don't expect to be forgiven."

"There is nothing to forgive. I'm not betraying you in any way, and all you have to suffer in my absence for a few days. I can even carry messages to Hawthorne if you wish."

Neck stiff, she refused to look openly at him. "Tranta stays, and he'll send out whatever I need to convey."

"I'll be back long before the appointed moment."

"You do this for yourself."

"For myself and for Rivergrace." His voice softened a bit. "Osten fell and your life was endangered, and even though Narskap held a knife to Grace's neck, it was you my body shielded. She saw that. He didn't harm her, but he might as well have put that knife into her heart."

"She knows your duty. Perhaps better than you do."

He cut the air with his hand.

"He would have killed her if he had intended to." Lara pressed him.

"I won't bandy his intent with you. We both know they might have wanted a hostage they could dispose of later, and that we are lucky to have only lost Osten. That arrow . . ." He put a hand to where it had bitten into him and then left as if repelled. He had no understanding of that particular miracle. "That was a diabolical weapon."

"Which did not work on you. Why not?"

"One of many answers I don't have."

"Your answers won't plot out a successful war for me. I need my best men here."

"I think I can contribute more by doing this first. Tiiva brought them across the border and died for it—" He paused at the thought of the grisly signpost Quendius and Narskap had left behind them, flaunting the wards which had once kept Larandaril safe and inviolate. She obviously held no further use for him. Rivergrace would have joined the remains if they'd taken her. He added more gently, "Quendius has only emphasized the point you already knew, that we have no safe harbor here."

Lariel toyed with the map she had flattened on her desktop. "What do you hope to accomplish?"

"That is between me and Gilgarran." He smiled thinly.

"An even older loyalty."

"Yes. I don't relinquish them lightly, my pledges and loyalties."

"I'll hold you to that. Go, then. With my anger and need behind you."

"May it spur me to do my work all the faster," he said, bowed, and left her. He had walked but two or three steps down the hall when the door slammed shut behind him as though it had been kicked in frustration.

He could still feel her cold disapproval about him, or perhaps it was just the winter wind off the sea. It might not whip him or billow his cloak as if it were a sail, but it chilled him nonetheless. He read the bannered sign again. Feldari and Son. Gilgarran had trusted him to keep all the contacts secret, to hold close to his chest the network that Gilgarran had spent a lifetime building. His whole teaching with that gentleman existed upon and within secrecy. But if that network were not to be used, why build it? He took a deep breath and entered.

A Kernan, his dark hair peppered with gray and white, his apron rolled about an expanding waist, stopped his sweeping. He wore cuffs over his sleeves to protect them from ink stains. "May I help you, my lord?"

Sevryn recognized him, even if he hadn't been recognized in turn, although the last time they had met, this Feldari had been perhaps fifteen years of age and now he looked to be in the last of his middle years, heading into the august years of seniorhood. He swept the hood of his cloak from his head to speak the passwords. "Greetings to you, as have been given to your father and your father's father and his father before that, and as I hope to live to give to your sons and your sons' sons some day."

Feldari paled. His dark brown eyes squinted hard at Sevryn as he stumbled a step backward to be both stopped and supported by the high countertop behind him. His broom clattered to the floor.

Sevryn stepped forward quickly to take his elbow. Feldari could not tear his gaze away, his eyes now as wide as if he saw Death itself coming for him. "Have a care, Master," Sevryn said. "One would think something unusual is happening."

Feldari clasped his hands together to keep them from shaking as he tried to recover. "Quite right, right indeed. It's cold outside. We have spiced wine warming on the back hearth. One moment, and I'll have it fetched for you." He paused after gulping down another breath.

"We . . . I . . . heard he was dead. No word about you nor had your name ever been given. I can't believe my eyes. You haven't aged a day since I saw you when I was a knee-high stock boy. Well, perhaps a day or even a year or two, but not . . . not . . ."

"I understand, Master Feldari. That wine would go well about now, don't you think?"

"Yes. Yes." He raised his voice. "Alani, two mugs of that mulled wine, and quickly. I have business." He looked at Sevryn. "Don't I?"

"You do."

Some time later, he found himself seated in a quiet vault below ground, tapers lit, with two wooden coffers left on a polished table in front of him. The Feldaris were scribes, record keepers, and contractors; and more than that, they were depositories. Gilgarran had owned several homes, but he did not assume they would remain inviolate while he traveled and plied his trade, so he counted on the discretion of a few businessmen about the lands to hold the goods he wished kept safe. Sevryn wasn't at all sure what he'd find inside the chests or if it would help him at all with some of the questions for which he knew he had to find answers. If not here, then another day in another city. Sevryn stripped off his riding gloves, put his cloak behind the hilt of his sword, drew a taper close, and opened the first coffer after a bit of tinkering with its lock.

The lid fell back with an aroma of fine wood and pressed herbs drifting up, herbs that killed insects that might find their way inside to feast upon whatever treasures the coffer held. He brushed them off a few sealed purses, their leather strings still supple, their insides still bulging with coins and jewels and whatever else Gilgarran had placed inside. He sorted through the papers at the bottom, an assortment of maps and copies of contracts . . . he paused at that, wondering why, then saw Gilgarran had been keeping a somewhat surreptitious watch on the Oxfort trading empire. The map he wished for, he did not find.

That might make interesting and necessary reading later. What he needed now were the reports based upon which Gilgarran decided to raid the forge above the Silverwing and Andredia Rivers, the forge run in secret by Quendius until the two of them had raided it, causing Gilgarran's death and Sevryn's enslavement for nigh on to twenty years. He found a note or two on weapons deals and barters, but nothing upon which Gilgarran would act. His eyes scanned the other missives quickly, including a report speculating on the accession of young Lariel Anderieon to the position of Warrior Queen over the suit of her brother, Jeredon Eladar, and what Talents she might hold that would qualify her. It remained inconclusive, acknowledging that her grandfather had kept her gifts very secret and that only he knew what qualities he searched for in his heir. It had predicted correctly, however, that he would indeed pick Lariel over the more favored Jeredon.

Sevryn made an unhappy noise as he opened the second trunk. More maps and purses of gems and gold coins, money which he had not wanted traced for one reason or another, obviously not trusting the traders' guild banks with all his goods. He sifted through the paper goods and found no word on the forges at all, no notes on the weaponsmith or the smithy slave working for him who knew how to imbue Demons into metal, let alone how to unbind and free them. What news or intelligence had set Gilgarran at Quendius' throat? Who had sent him word on Demons? He shuffled carefully through relics without finding what he needed. No hint at all about who might have been so incredibly strong of will as to be able call forth Cerat and bring him into this world to wreak havoc—and who had left him to possess whoever and whatever he could. Or, most pressing, how to get Cerat to quit his possessions.

He could, he supposed, go to any temple and tell them
he was Demon-ridden and see what sort of exorcism they
proposed, but he knew he did not trust the Kernan priests
any more than he would trust Quendius himself with his
life and soul. Nor could he endanger Lariel's position
with a tale of his possession for rumors of that would run
like wildfire through the lands, and whatever dislike the
people already held for Vaelinars, it would be double-fold.
They had been here for centuries: distrusted, disliked, and
finally allied and somewhat accepted, but the news of a
devil at her side would sweep much of that good away.
No, not for himself or Rivergrace would he destroy the
frail balance of power the Vaelinars had achieved. No answers here, none that he needed. He would have to keep
searching the depositories for Gilgarran that he knew of,
and his stomach clenched a bit because he knew that his
mentor had revealed much, but not all, to him.

He was going to close the second trunk when a bundle
drew his interest.

It was a single folded letter, bound to a small leather
book by a faded ribbon, that he reached for and drew
out carefully.

He slid the letter free and opened it, paper crinkling
faintly. He knew Gilgarran's handwriting, although this
was penned most carefully and legibly, as if intentionally
leaving a record.

My Dear Lad,
  *If you are reading this letter, then I am dead. Un-
original but true. As I know what it says, it stands to
reason I won't be reading it again. If you have waited
years to retrieve this, to protect the integrity of our
friends, my hat off to you, and I am long dead.*
  *You are correct if you have suspected that the mys-
tery of your antecedents has intrigued me, and I have
combined the investigation of your missing parents
with other explorations of my own. You've been an
apt apprentice and pupil to me, and it was no hard-*

*ship taking you on. I fear that I can report little suc-
cess other than to tell you that your mother did not
abandon you intending never to return. It seems she
met with an accidental death upon her travels, as it is
sometimes the ill fortune to do so. As for your father,
I have nothing but the barest suspicion, nothing I
should tell you yet, and so cannot leave you anything
but this barest of crumbs as my bequest to you.*

*There is a book herein. Keep it close if you carry
it with you. Not a few have died for it over the years.
I have obtained it in my chase for the Old Deceiver
and though I have but lightly reviewed it, I have
hopes. There is one or more among us who came not
on that great day but before and who are not listed
in our numbers. It has long been rumored among
certain Dwellers and Kernans and in their oral tradition that some of us walked Kerith before the great
invasion. If so, who were they? Do they yet live?
Did they lay the ground for our being here and if so,
how? And for what purpose do they remain among
us, if not as trickster or deceiver? I have long suspected that there is a singular one who moves behind us, stirring trouble, breaking treaties, spreading
lies, quietly but effectively to restrain us. If there is
such a one, he is deadly and will not hesitate to strike
mortally to keep his secret. Therefore, be cautious,
Sevryn. It is not only your life you may risk.*

*Remember yourself and your teachings, and may
they lead you on a long road indeed.*

Yours, Gilgarran

Sevryn fought not to crumple the paper in frustration.
Barest crumb? Not even that. Where did his mother
die? Who gave that information to Gilgarran? How did
he come by it? He clenched one hand, knuckles bled
to white. As for suspicions, they were more than Sevryn
had. Why not tell him so the truth could be found? Why
not tell him, at last? Why?

And worse, a traitor buried within them. Gilgarran had worried at the revelation for centuries, if Sevryn knew him. How could Sevryn deal with what Gilgarran could not? What evidence Gilgarran might have had of these treacheries were not found in this casket. Had they died with his teacher? Or were they buried elsewhere?

The letter slipped from his numb fingers. He stared at it until his eyes went dry and he finally blinked. Then he opened his hand, reached out, and carefully folded it up, returning it to the coffer. He knew Gilgarran well. He knew the flowery script but not the flowery manner of his writing. Gilgarran was nothing if not direct. There might be more than he could see, and if he knew his old teacher, there would be a world hidden within that short missive. He would wait until he could think clearer, until he could puzzle his way in and out of the letter.

The small book, leather-bound, slipped out of the ribbon easily onto his palm. It held no title, handmade it seemed, and quite probably one of a kind. Perhaps Gilgarran had even been the bookbinder. It was aged but still supple, and it looked as if it had been carried and read for quite a while before it had been archived. He opened it carefully.

List of the First Days

Sevryn read the title page twice. As he turned it, a small scrap of paper fell out, and he recognized this handwriting as more characteristically Gilgarran's, hastily but carefully done. *Daravan also searches for this book. Why? Keep it from him.*

Sevryn closed the book on his finger to think.

Daravan. Another who delved into many secrets and shared few of them. Had they competed for this book? What knowledge did it hold that was not already on record in the great library of Ferstanthe? Did it hold truth or rumor, findings Gilgarran dared not repeat until he could confirm them, but he had diaries copied. What, then? Had chasing down the illegal weaponsmith and forges of Quendius cut short substantiating this book?

Had he been in quest of the Old Deceiver? Gilgarran was not a man who doubted what he knew. What he knew, he knew well.

Sevryn glanced upward, wondering if he should give the book to Feldari to be copied or if that would endanger the Kernan. How could Daravan know if he did so?

Because Daravan seemed, as Gilgarran had, to be nearly everywhere and know nearly everything. He was a shadow without needing a sun to make himself appear.

Sevryn chewed on the corner of his lip a moment before paging past the opening and beginning to read. As his fingers held the book close, he felt a roughness along the binding. Turning it over, he spied a rougher edge on the inside leaf. He took his dagger out and carefully eased it open. A slim and folded piece of paper slid out. He opened it with the blade's tip and saw a map. Answers he needed. He glanced back at the book. There were more answers within, if he knew Gilgarran. Perhaps even the code to reading the map properly, for he would wrap puzzles about puzzles.

He put the map aside and bent to read once more as if his life—no, his and that of Rivergrace—depended upon it.

Chapter
Thirty-One

AZEL D'STANTHE STOOD BY THE GATE to
his small domain as if he waited for them, his burly
figure swathed in voluminous robes against the now bitter cold of the forested north. A wind whistled through
the great trees, ruffling their needled branches with a
roar like that of the ocean, Meg told Rivergrace who
had never been to the sea. The aroma of their sap and
scent swirled around them, crisp and refreshing. Nutmeg freed one hand from holding the reins to wave in
welcome.

"How did he know?"

"I'm not sure," Grace answered. "He knows many
things." They rode up slowly, where she could see surprised delight on the historian's face.

"Welcome, welcome, Lady Rivergrace and Mistress
Farbranch!" he boomed, and held his arms out to help
them from their mounts. "My library shall be full indeed
this evening! What a wonderful surprise for an old man."
He wasn't that old for a Vaelinar though doubtless gen-

erations old for a Dweller, but he carried his prime years in a body that looked experienced. He beamed as he set them on the ground. "I shall tell my lads to lay down a second fire and warm the chilly old place up a bit. What brings the two of you here?"

"Reading and to ask your advice," Grace told him. "As usual."

"Alas, my last advice to you wasn't that accurate, I fear."

"You meant well, and you were right in most ways."

Azel shifted inside his robes. "And wrong in the most important one. I told you that you were nothing more than a vessel to hold a magic not of this world. That is an error I'm glad was untrue. You have a life of your own and you're most definitely meant to be yourself!" He whistled, and one of his young scholar apprentices came flying out of the library door, robes billowing behind and sandals slapping upon the ground, to take the horses to the stables. A second apprentice hung in the doorway to see if he was needed, and Azel bellowed at him, "More fires! More rooms! More cider to warm!"

"Yessir, m'lord," the youth relayed the order back as he disappeared into the great building.

"Now," Azel said, as he hugged both of him. "I await the bidding of Lord Bistel who had sent word he was on his way this day, but you two go inside and eat and have a hot drink . . . I insist, and so I will brook no argument!"

He took their hands and led them toward his doors, laughing as he did. He left them inside the great stone arches. The building looked more like one of the great temples of Calcort rather than a home or manor, for there were only alcoves and no real sign of welcome until the apprentice led them to a side wing where fires roared and the stone warmed, and rugs appeared on the flooring, with chairs and small tables grouped by the firesides. In that room, they could smell the scent of a kitchen: coal and wood burning, and bread baking, and meat sizzling on a spit filling the air with its appetizing scent. The apprentice said nothing, but a wide grin flashed across his young, freckled face as he bowed and promised to bring them food back as soon as possible. He took to his heels.

Nutmeg sat and primly tucked her legs under her chair. "I hope he's right about hurrying. I swear I could eat a book."

"A book! I doubt if that would taste any good."

"No, but chewing all that paper would keep me busy for a while." She sighed. "And it has to be better than dried fish."

Rivergrace circled the room before picking a spot by the fire and warming herself for a while. Her sister's humor and chatter had begun to thin, and an uncharacteristic frown line deepened between her amber eyes, letting Grace know that something profound worried at her, like a street dog at an old bone. She would talk more about it when she was ready, but Grace knew she wanted to find proof that she loved the right person and that it could work. For herself, she already knew the answer to that when the daughter of ild Fallyn turned Jeredon's head so easily. Yet it was a realization that would have to come to Nutmeg when it came, and Rivergrace also knew that things could change and she could be wrong. No one could tell her how her destiny would be with Sevryn; that was something that would have to be forged between the two of them, and so it would be with Nutmeg. Or, as Tolby Farbranch would say, the seed is far from the sprig and farther still from the sapling which grows into the tree.

The apprentice and a kitchen maid interrupted her thoughts just as the fire had toasted the icy wind from her bones very nicely. They each bore a tray of piping hot bread, slices of juicy meat, fresh fruits and cheese, and a mug of steaming cider. They pulled the small tables together to make a bigger dining table, tucked large napkins about each of the girls, and left them to enjoy their feast.

Nutmeg put down a sandwich and a half before mopping her mouth and chin and sitting back. "Now, what is our plan of attack?"

Grace who could eat as much as any hearty Dweller although she always did so at a much slower pace, raised her eyebrows in surprise, her mouth and hands full of food. "Attack?" she managed between chews.

"Azel will want to know what it is we want to know, and do we tell him or do we come armed with a well-placed distraction."

"Lie to him?"

"Put it that way, aye. Shall we lie to him? Iffen we do, what shall we say?" Nutmeg took up a small plum and polished it on her sleeve before biting into it.

"I don't know that we have to do that." Rivergrace finished her bite and swallowed slowly, considering. "He's always been truthful with me, even bluntly so."

"That he has. A-course, his job here is to preserve the truth, isn't it?" Nutmeg looked across the table at her. "A different job from that of a Warrior Queen."

"I know. She does things for a deeper purpose than you or I can guess. She has centuries of history behind her and ahead of her, and she has been trained for all that. I don't want to try and doubt her reasoning."

"She is flat-out wrong about you and Sevryn. That I know," declared Nutmeg, sitting back in conviction that was only a little marred by the fruit juice dribbling down her chin.

"She might see something in the pattern of the weave we can't." Rivergrace ate the last bite of her sandwich, chewing as though it were the problem before them. "It's like your mother at the loom, but Lariel has decades and decades of time to choose the threads."

"She can be as wrong as anybody. And, seems as if I have to be the one to say it, Azel is a Vaelinar and she is a Vaelinar."

"As am I."

"No," Nutmeg told her. "You're my sister, and

something more than Vaelinar, that's what they all think, an' a few have said it—they don't know what, and it scares them." She punctuated the air with a poking finger. "You've seen it, though you've not said much to me, and I've seen and heard it. Lara doesn't know what to do with you. I imagine she's had Azel lookin' through all the piled-up words here trying to help her decide. So, is the twig going to be bent or straight?"

Rivergrace opened her mouth to answer, when a quiet footfall sounded behind their chairs, and a commanding voice noted, "It is a poor guest who comes to a host for aid and lies about what help they wish, intending to steal what cannot be offered." She snapped her lips shut as Bistel Vantane stopped beside their table. "Are there leavings for me?"

Nutmeg hopped up and made a plate for the warlord, her face flushed and her own mouth pinched, but she said as she gave it to him, "That doesn't deny the fact that's behind us and brought us here."

Bistel sat down heavily, smelling of horse and leather and the evergreens. He balanced the plate on his knee. "And I won't deny it either. Lariel is more like her grandfather than many know, following in his footsteps. He was always a quiet man, keeping much that he knew and wished to know to himself, for voicing either answers or questions would leave a trail that he didn't want anyone following but himself. She has that caution in her. As for fearing you, Rivergrace, can you blame her? When the two of you met, you feared yourself. As for now, well." He took a hearty bite, chewed and swallowed before finishing. "If you've come to Azel for help, let him give it as fully as he can. Otherwise, you've made a fool's journey to do a fool's task."

"Trust in Azel."

"You cannot trust halfway. Either you do, or you don't. Either you trust, or you distrust and deal with caution." He shrugged. He finished off the sandwich Nutmeg had made him in two more bites, then leaned forward to the table and made himself a second, a massive sandwich larger than his hands, and placed it on his plate while stabbing a slab of cheese.

"And what do you do here?" Nutmeg asked pointedly, refusing to give way before the warlord.

He examined her closely. "I've come to do a ritual."

Rivergrace found her hands shaking and dropped them quickly into her lap to hide it. His statement had a finality about it that scared her. "Before you go to war?"

"Before I go to this war, yes, m'lady Rivergrace. I doubt I will have time to do it elsewhen. I've promised Queen Lariel to meet her, so I leave as soon as I've done."

"Where is Azel?" Rivergrace picked up her mug of still warm cider and held it tightly.

"Out with a few guards looking at the border of this small corner of the lands. I thought I saw the lean and hungry man who shadows Quendius on my heels as I rode through. Now there is a man whose story I would like to see in the Books. He might have much to tell us."

"Narskap."

"That's the one." He nibbled on his crust.

Rivergrace and Nutmeg traded looks. Had he followed them there, trailing them without the girls knowing it? The thought made her cold in spite of the warm drink in her hands, and she took a hasty gulp of it. "He was with Quendius when he . . . they . . . killed Osten."

"I know, lass. War falcons flew fast and hard to carry that sad news. I would be after Quendius even now, but the queen is determined to put Abayan Diort in his place. She has some reason for her stubbornness, but she hasn't enlightened me. Still, I am here, on my way to the battle."

"Because of trust."

"Trust and honor and loyalty." Bistel nodded, the light in his blue eyes fierce. He paused, then added, "I wish I could say I knew your father and mother, lass, but I can't.

Yet that doesn't mean you don't have a rightful place among us. What it means is that their names were forgotten, obliterated, or never brought to light." He thought a moment, then said, "In the old days, those of us who had no lands or titles risked the anathema of creating Ways to gain those things. Ways were made and sometimes unleashed such terrible power that, so we would not end up like the Mageborn, they were outlawed. Still, some would try. They usually failed. A Way is a feat of great magic and most of us aren't capable of it, or if we open one, we can't control it. Bloodlines which broke those laws were subject to death. One might hide their children from that sort of justice if they knew they were going to take the risk." He looked squarely at Rivergrace. "Your name may not have been known except in the records of those death sentences. It would not be written anywhere else, but here, in those cases."

His words stunned her, and it fell to Nutmeg to stammer faintly, "Thank you, Lord Bistel," in Rivergrace's stead.

"It's little enough help." He finished his supper and stood, putting his metal plate back on the table. "Perhaps I will see you later this evening, when Azel breaks out the good liquor." He winked and left with the confident long stride and straight shoulders of a leader of men, his white hair looking like a torch of light as he disappeared into the depths of the library.

Chapter
Thirty-Two

A GREAT WIND RACED through the night. Narskap bent in it, perched upon the tiles of the high roof of the library. He would have shivered, but that might have given him away, and so he found a stillness and wrapped it about himself and endured. It would be daylight soon, with hopefully a bit of sunlight to thaw the winter a little, and he would live to see it.

He had doubled back to keep a watch on his master and found him watching prey, and so trailed the tracker. A nagging worry about the true intentions of Quendius proved well-founded when Narskap caught him after Rivergrace and Nutmeg. Where Quendius had lost them and turned back only to disappear himself, Narskap chose to follow Rivergrace and her short sister for reasons he did not entirely know. Perhaps he followed in place of his master, perhaps he followed because as a hound, keeping to the trail was required of him. He found the Ferryman waiting for him on the bank of the small river. The phantom took him without query or coin to the other side where he quickly caught up, staying to cover as the forests grew thicker and greener and colder until they reached Ferstanthe.

Then, and only then, Narskap left them, tethering his horse in a small dell outside where the beast could crop grass and find water, and yet still be waiting for him when he returned. He slipped past the guards and the vigilant Azel, and heard of the visitations expected and unexpected, and made his way to safety upon the roof-tops. From there, he would take whatever opportunities presented themselves to him, to slip through whatever cracks the enemy might leave open to him. He slept, fit-fully, on the roof, his ear pressed to the tile as if he lis-tened to a better life within. Then, as the first of the sun tried to crack open clouds that curtained it, he crept to the wing where chimneys puffed out thin, gray columns of smoke, and found an eave and a window. He shin-nied down to test the window and slipped, his hands and body still half numb from the cold, and banged against the closed shutter. The sound it uttered was not all that great, but he scuttled back to the shadows and clung, holding his breath, to see what he might have roused.

Nutmeg woke. Soft mattress and blankets surrounded her, warm with her body heat and that of Rivergrace, and of the still glowing coals in the nearby fireplace, and as she rubbed at her eyes, she could feel sleep falling away. She closed her eyes again, determinedly, but her mind filled with thoughts that tumbled around like a pile of puppies. A bit of breakfast might quiet her, she thought. Her stomach woke then and it was not about to let her sleep until she had a morsel or two to fill it. Not about to stop grumbling and rumbling like a cranky old man until she paid it attention. Better than thinking overmuch, though.

She got up carefully and dressed, getting her soft boots

on as quickly as she could, for the flagstone flooring held the night's chill in it, and she shivered as it tried to sink into her. She opened the bedroom shutters and looked out into the shank of the morning, early but undoubtedly dawn. She closed the shutters but not carefully, in a hurry to get out of the room before she might awaken Rivergrace who lay on her side, auburn hair trailing upon her pillow, her eyes peacefully closed but with dark bruises of fatigue and worry still marking her face. She did not hear the rustle and quiet step behind her as something entered the room from the outside window and joined the deep shadows of its corners as she left it.

Once outside the bedroom, the halls lay steeped in nighttime yet, although she could see the barest first light of dawn filtering through the shutters and covering drapes. A shadow fluttered behind her. Meg rubbed her eyes, still crusted with sleep, and turned back for a moment, listening and watching. An eerie feeling of not being alone crawled down her neck, but she couldn't see anything in the draperied halls to prove it. She could smell the very faint aroma of baking bread and headed toward it, her thoughts filled with mornings with her family, tussling with her brothers for the first crust of fresh bread to fill with cheese and smoked meat. To her surprise, she found Lord Bistel perched upon a humble three-legged kitchen stool, carving bits of meat for himself.

She dipped a curtsy. "Good morning, Lord Bistel."

"Come join me before the cook discovers we are stealing her most tender bites and kicks us both out."

Nutmeg hid her grin and climbed onto a tall stool herself. He served her quickly with a trencher of fresh bread, sprinkling it with meat still sizzling and pink in its juices, and pushed a wheel of cheese her way, and a crock of what looked to be sweetened berries to join it. A feast, all in all. She settled down to eating. They ate for a while in silence, enjoying the fare.

She licked some juice from the corner of her mouth.

"Is it true that you all have to write in the *Books of All Truth*? Is that the ritual you came to do?"

"It is true that the historians and librarians of Ferstanthe hope we will. I'm not sure that many of us are up to the task. It is secret, although I can see that it's not much of one," he added wryly. He sliced a very thin sliver of cheese, so transparent she could almost see clearly through it as he held it up to sniff before he devoured it.

"Why?"

"Truth is a very wiggly fish, hard to catch barehanded, and harder to hold onto without choking the life out of it."

"But you can write anything."

"Not in these journals. They are a Way, if you understand what I mean."

"Really?"

He nodded. "Really, but if you tell anyone I told you, I'll deny it, and you'll be in a great deal of trouble all by yourself."

"Then why tell me?"

He neatly sliced a piece of cheese for her. "Because it seems to me that you and your sister should know this. I've seen a great deal, young Farbranch, and the time of my seeing is drawing to a close. I leave here to go to the appointment that Lariel Anderieon made for me, and beyond that, I doubt I'll see much more."

Nutmeg swallowed tightly. "Perhaps not."

"Indeed. So, my visit here, is to write the Truth as I saw and remember it."

"So others can read it?"

"That's the strange thing about this part of the library. No one reads the books that have been left there."

"Then why do it?"

"Why, indeed? Because there may be a day when nothing else can stand but these truths, and they must be borne no matter how heavy a burden, or else the walls of the world will collapse entirely."

"A last stand."

"Yes."

"Against what?"

He shook his head. "I don't know, and I'm not sure the House of Ferstanthe knows. There aren't many prophets among us nor would we trust them if there were. We are contentious enough that we are our own doom, I think."

"Still, it seems to me," and she tilted her head, unsure if she could match words with Bistel, but trying anyway, "it seems to me that truth is probably the most powerful weapon there could be, next to love."

Bistel smiled suddenly, his bright blue eyes crackling with the warmth of it. "Well said."

Pleased, she added, "How long does it take to write in your journal?" thinking that a lifetime could well take weeks, if not seasons. Grace had grumbled often about the intricacies of writing in Vaelinar script. She wondered if her quick scraps of letters to her family might be in the same vein.

"I'm finished."

"So soon?"

"Yes, it makes you wonder if I had that much truth inside me, eh? But it came out like a flood, and it was like riding tidewaters to keep up with it. I spent the night tidying up. I have kept an accounting with me and there was only a bit left to add to it before I put it on the shelves."

"And you wrote everything?"

"I hope so. If not, perhaps next time."

"Can you tell me something?"

He looked at her, as if weighing his response. "What is it?"

"The aryn trees. Is it true they sprang from one tree, from a greenwood staff you planted when you came?"

"Yes. And no. We had seeds, too, later."

"How did a warrior become a farmer?"

The corner of his mouth twitched. "How, indeed. In

the early days, we fought among ourselves, and it was bitter, and I took the only thing living that I had from the time before we were Lost and thrown to Kerith, and I drove it into the ground as if it could anchor me and shelter me from all that we were bringing down upon ourselves."

"But a staff. How could you know it was living wood?"

"It had budded once or twice, just the smallest eye, and I had carved it off, and when it did so a third time, I realized that there was life inside that staff of greenwood that I could not, and should not, deny. My career was war, ensuring death, yet here was ... was this bit of wood that I leaned upon, and it held life. So I planted it. Watered it. And this great tree sprang forth. Not all at once, mind you, it grew as any tree grows, at its own pace and taking seasons, but it undeniably grew." He leaned back a moment, one expression chasing another across his face as if he decided something.

Bistel took something from an inside pocket of his richly embroidered leather vest, and dropped it next to Nutmeg's trencher. "I'd like you to have this."

A tiny gold key, on a beautiful gold link chain, sparkled at her. "What is it?"

"My key to the closet holding the *Books of All Truth*. I am perhaps the oldest left of the Vaelinar, and like a tree, I know it can be better to bend rather than break. Some laws are meant to be ... bent."

Her mouth opened and closed several times, seeking words. He stopped it with a finger lightly across her lips. "Lady Rivergrace will, I believe, need it. And, perhaps, yourself. Dwellers have a stock of wisdom all their own, and I'm fond of your people, but sometimes a bit of knowledge outside the boundary is needed, too. Not a word of this to anyone, or I'll have betrayed my trust."

She nodded, both bewildered and thrilled by Bistel's demand of her. He stood and gave her a brief bow, taking up his saddlebags which he'd stowed under the small table, and left without a backward glance. She watched him go, thinking that her da would have liked to have met him, to talk of trees and destiny.

She yawned, her stomach full, and made her way back to their room where Rivergrace still slept, although the shutter had been thrown open by the wind somehow and the room grown cold. She latched the shutter this time and crept carefully back under the blankets to sleep until the day dawned warmer.

Rivergrace sneezed and dust motes flew like tiny spores of feather grass through the air, drifting down from the upward shelf and ladder where she perched, swirling in the beam of sunlight angling down from the high arched windows, until they landed nearly unseen on the stone floor. Her sister gave a pealing laugh.

"Easy for you to laugh, I nearly fell off the ladder."

Nutmeg tossed her head from her sitting position at the bottom shelf, her lap full of scrolls. "A hearty sneeze, like a good laugh, shows the passion of a person. Everyone says that!"

"Oh, they do?" Rivergrace slid a book out carefully to look at it more closely before returning it to its position.

"They do! There's a lady at Larandaril, I won't be givin' out her name, but all the maids talk about her. When she sneezes, it's the most delicate little mffft of noise. So, they say, can you imagine what she does in bed with her gentleman pleasuring her? Are you enjoying yourself, milady, he'd ask and she'd go mffft and tell him, thank you, milord, I'm well satisfied now."

Rivergrace laughed at that, holding onto the top of the ladder tightly for fear she would topple from it, and when she'd caught her breath, she asked, "Honestly, Nutmeg, how do you think of such things?"

"Not me! It's those saucy maids." Nutmeg rolled her eyes. "But at least it made you smile."

"That, and more. What you must hear."

"Oh, I'm up to my neck in gossip about the higher-ups. They think of me as one of them, you know, a servant."

Rivergrace looked down to see a shadow flicker across Meg's face, as she picked up a scroll to examine it, and replace it in its bin. She scratched her eyebrows in thought, all merriment fled from her expression, and did not notice Grace's scrutiny. She peered upward. "I'm not finding much on Kerith Gods," she complained.

"I didn't expect to." Grace descended the ladder with an armful of books and sat down next to her. "I'd probably have more luck on Temple Row, buying an old woman's fetish to drive the River Goddess away." She sighed, and scrubbed off a dusty book with the hem of her sleeve.

"What about your other problem?"

Rivergrace opened her book, not seeing its words, but thinking of Nutmeg's question. Finally she answered, "I can't ask Azel. From the way the apprentices spoke among themselves this morning, it's under lock and key and forbidden to all but himself."

Something sparked in Nutmeg's eyes. "Perhaps Lord Bistel could help."

"Our lord might well be the person to behead us, if we tried to get in." Grace dusted her sleeve as she frowned.

"He gave me a key at breakfast this morning before you woke."

"He what?"

Nutmeg just stared at her, knowing she'd heard what was said.

"I ate breakfast with you and he was nowhere about."

"Second breakfast," Nutmeg corrected her firmly. "I was up at sunrise, being a bit hungry and all, and ate a touch earlier, too."

She hadn't even noticed her leaving the bed. Rivergrace blushed a bit at having slept so soundly. "But why? Why would he do such a thing?"

Nutmeg tilted her head as thoughts seemed to run through it. Finally, she repeated what the warlord told her. "He said he was the eldest of the eld, but he was also a grower of trees and knew that it was better to bend than to break."

They considered each other. Rivergrace said, "A sound thought."

"I thought so." She lifted her wrist, where a chain and key were wound about it, and tucked into the hem of her sleeve so they would not jangle. "Should we try it?"

Rivergrace pushed the library ladder to one side, and took a calming breath. "It's what we came for, isn't it?" She followed Nutmeg through the labyrinth of rooms, ducking twice when they passed an apprentice scribe or librarian hurrying through the myriad of rooms and halls. Azel kept them busy it seemed, their hands ink stained and their arms filled with journals as they moved throughout the wings of the library, in such a hurry they never saw Grace and Meg approaching the banned rooms. The air in the wing hung heavily as they drew near, as though seldom stirred by living bodies, although sconces burned here where windows did not break the solid walls. A heavy grille, locked and forbidding, shut away the final room.

Nutmeg looked about quickly, then took her key and put it in the tiny, intricate lock. A twist and the gate fell open, moving on well-oiled hinges despite the fact it looked as though it was rarely used. They moved inside quickly and shut it behind them, and the lock snicked smoothly into place. Rivergrace swung about, but Nutmeg took her by the hand. "It'll open," she said reassuringly.

They moved through the stacks. The journals here were all slim, and bound in leather with gilt lettering upon their spine, each shelf arranged by familiar House and Stronghold names as they scanned them. Vaelinars past and present, most of them now past, had evidently written in these books . . . or had been meant to. Grace

paused by the books marked ild Fallyn, then walked
past. These were secrets she was not meant to know, or
they would not be locked away. What purpose they had
been foreseen for, she didn't know, but she wouldn't
tempt fate by riffling through these pages. She came to
look for mention of herself and no more.

She trailed her fingers along the shelves as she walked
by slowly, reading each shelf and each title, not knowing what she should search, and hoping that she would
know when she saw it. Nutmeg plopped down on the
floor just inside the grille, one shoulder to the first bookcase, and took out a slender book marked *Treatise on the
Natives of Kerith*. As Grace slanted a look toward her,
she said defiantly, "It's a book about me, and I ought to
be able to read it."

Her sister had a point, so she merely nodded and
pressed deeper into the room, feeling the air itself draw
close about her as if it was a curtain seeking to hide
the contents of the shelves and bar them from her. She
pushed each step forward as it grew more and more difficult to move, and finally stopped when it seemed she
could go no farther even though the back of the room
lay shadowed beyond her. She put a hand out to a shelf
to steady herself. With great effort, she turned her head
to look at the titles.

All but one was blank, or the gilt letters so ornate they
blurred before her vision, making them unreadable. The
sole spine she could read wavered before her sight and
then, as she narrowed her eyes, the title solidified before
her: *Violations of the Ways and Judgments Thereof*. A
dry title only a historian could love, she thought, as she
reached for it, thinking of Bistel's advice. She touched it
and a tide rose in her, a tide of shock and awe and fear
and eagerness, that surged through her being so that she
could scarcely hold the book in her shaking hands. She
opened it carefully and began to read of the dreadful
deeds of misguided Vaelinars and ambition and magic,
of revenge and greed and justice, and of love and ha-

tred. To succeed in building a Way built your line into a House or Stronghold or Fort. To fail was to be executed summarily—not only the perpetrator but all of his or her immediate bloodline. As precious as Vaelinar blood with its magical abilities could be, they did not hesitate to annihilate it if their Law was violated.

She could understand that, in a way. Taking the bright threads of the world and entangling them in a new way, spinning out webs and knots where none had existed before, yes, she could understand the heavy judgment on those who did so and those who did so badly. To make and unmake the fabric of life itself carried a heavy responsibility. She closed the book and put it back on the shelf. Had her mother and father attempted to break that Law and fled the consequences? She had not seen their names among the judgments. If they were the descendants of lawbreakers, she would have to know names that she did not. Rivergrace had no idea who her grandparents might be. She rubbed eyes growing weary.

Her elbow knocked a book off a shelf. She fumbled for it and caught it just as it hit the floor and fell open in her hands.

Warring Gods read the title page. She turned it.

A Kernan priest had written this treatise. Thin, it hardly seemed more than a document of rambling speculation, but someone had thought it of enough import to bind it and place it here, in Ferstanthe's inner library. She leafed the page over and began to read:

It has been surmised that our sleeping Gods have little knowledge of the events which brought the Vaelinars to our lands. Of course, debates on the veracity of that can be heard on any temple corner, from the youngest acolyte to the most esteemed scholar. How can an arrival which sent a blast through the northwestern lands and laid low an entire forest go unnoticed, even to an omnipotent eye closed in slumber? It could not. What I propose then is to examine the evidence that the event was noticed and that our Gods, although in quietude, are pondering their response.

It may be noted that when Vaelinars died in the first centuries of their occupation that their souls were taken in a ceremony dubbed "Returning." A ritual kept private (and rightly so) lends itself to few witnesses outside those of Vaelinar heritage. We do have, however, two or three letters (see below) which relate the unusual circumstances of such a Returning. The body of the dead appears to grow translucent and the soul, seen as a gossamer aura, the beauty of which is attested to many times over, is drawn away from the planes of Kerith, both physical and spiritual, and Returned to the hands of its own rightful Gods.

My argument, however, begins with recent testimonials of a much more horrific Returning in which the dying is torn asunder as if the soul itself were involved in a tug-of-war between two vastly different spiritual planes ... as if the Gods themselves were warring over the dead. In at least two cases, the suffering Vaelinar had not even passed into death before such a battle took place, the suffering a dreadful thing to behold. The testimonials are quoted verbatim in the text of this pamphlet, but I warn the reader that the matter is difficult to read. Before digressing into the testimonials, I repeat my assertion that the Gods are indeed awake, and their attention upon all of us will be dreadful when it is focused. Gods are nothing if not jealous of the powers of creation and the world which They have brought to life. Their anger is likely to be dropped upon us all when we catch their eyes again. A God can only be banished by another God and likewise the world of Demons mirrors that plane, although on a much lesser level, and mortals have been known to defeat Demons only with the help of Gods. Therefore, we must live

*circumspectly and with reverence lest we be caught
between warring armies of Immortals.*

Rivergrace closed the book on her finger, trying to decide if she wished to read further. A draft found the side
of her cheek and played upon it, as if a cold, still hand ca-
ressed her. Once touched, always touched, even beyond
death. Herself, Sevryn, even the River Goddess, did not
lie beyond Cerat's corruption. Gods, and Demons, were
not to be crossed. It lay in her hands to find the way to
quiet them, if such a resolution existed. Silently, she replaced the slim tome into its place on the shelf.

Grace found Nutmeg asleep, her head back against
the hard wood of the bookcase, her lap and hands empty
as if she'd long ago finished the journal she'd started.
She tapped her sister gently on the head. Nutmeg stirred
and gathered her feet under her.

"Find anything?"

"History," she answered. "History of being Suldarran,
the Lost, without a beginning or knowing the end."

Nutmeg rubbed her eyes as she rose. "That makes no
sense."

"And now you know what I found." Grace smiled
sadly. "Let's go before we're found here."

They left quietly, listening for footsteps in the wing,
staying in shadows when they could. When the key shimmered on Nutmeg's wrist, catching a glint from the sun's
low slanting rays, Rivergrace looked at it and tried to remember if she had locked the vault doors when she left,
and could not. "Go on," she said, giving Nutmeg a loving
push. "I have to check the gate and see if it's locked. I'll
catch up."

"Wait! You'll need this, silly beans." Nutmeg undid
her bracelet and wound it around Grace's slender arm.
The key swung back and forth in a golden glimmer.

She retraced her steps quickly as she made her way
back through the labyrinth of rooms and shelves, and
then saw the final door ajar. She put her hand on the lock,

ready to close the door shut as it should have been, when she heard a sound inside. Quietly, she lifted the latch and stepped inside.

Narskap turned to face her, hand in the air, caught in the act of placing a book upon the shelf. Gaunt beyond knowing, in riding leathers of brown and gray, his hair pulled back in a tight queue, and his face bruised from Nutmeg's attack. They stared at one another for the most fleeting of moments before he said softly, "Do not call out." His broken voice cut the air into whispered shards. His words fell like shattered stone.

Fear rippled through her, and anger followed in its wake. She stood frozen with her hand on the door, his gaze on her face, and then she felt a calmness flowing from him. Of all the things she associated with the Hound of Quendius, serenity was not one. Curiosity piqued her. "What are you doing here?"

"I could ask you the same." Narskap shifted his gaze, scanned the shelves of the small, enclosed room, before looking back to meet her eyes. "Ferstanthe keeps these memories forbidden, but there are things I need to know. I presume you also search." He slid the book in his hand back into place. "Have you found what you needed?"

Why should she tell him anything? Yet, the difference in his voice, even his posture, told her that this was and was not the same man who'd held a knife to her throat days ago. How had he changed and why? "No."

"Nor I." He turned slightly to face her, holding both hands at his sides palm out, unarmed. "Give me a moment?"

She gathered her thoughts warily. "To do what?"

"Talk with you. I'm sane now. I don't know how long it will last, but as I stand here, I'm not the man that Quendius calls to heel. For the time being, I'm myself."

This was the man who could entrap Gods. What did she risk talking to him? And yet, if he could trap Gods, what chance did that leave for her? She balanced her weight so that she could slam the door and move quickly if needed, the very slightest change of balance, but he caught it. Awareness flickered through his eyes. "Don't run," he asked of her.

"What choice do you give me?"

"To listen first. If I begin to . . . lose myself . . . you'll know it, and then, close the door, lock it, and find Azel d'Stanthe. Until then, give me a chance and listen."

"How do I know that you don't use words as quickly as you use a knife?"

"You don't. I'd give my word, but I doubt you'd take that, nor should you. My word is only good as long as my mind is sound." Narskap tucked a loose string of hair behind one ear, a nervous, quick gesture. She thought she could almost see the man he might have been once, behind the face which now was skeletally thin.

Grace took a slow breath. She tapped the power that rippled just under her skin, the power of her birthright and that remnant of the River Goddess, and held it as she might a skittish horse on a tight rein, waiting for her command. To do what, she did not know. "All right. I'll listen."

A smile broke on that stony face as quickly as a raindrop hitting parched ground to be soaked in, so quickly come and gone that she thought she might have imagined it. He turned his face quickly to hide any further emotion which could betray him. "I'm here because you are and because Quendius has long desired to break into these rooms. I've a standing order, if you want to call it that, to seize the opportunity."

"You followed us here."

"Yes."

He admitted that he would do mischief here, if he could, and only she stood between him and that deed, but need tugged at her before she would decide on her actions. "Do you hope to capture me again?"

"If I did, you would be under rope and chain."

"Then why? What do you care what I do?" She would not tell him of her search and why, because it struck her that the knowledge would be as sharp to him as any sword he could carry. Yet his next words struck her.

"Because you hold yourself like your mother did, and you've her eyes, and because you could take Cerat from me and carry it."

"Don't talk to me about my mother. I don't want to hear about her from you. I don't want to know what . . . what she might have gone through." Her eyes stung and her throat threatened to close. She blinked fiercely.

His right hand clenched and opened as if still thirsting to hold the Demon sword she'd taken from him. The movement distracted her.

"Sometimes," Grace said carefully, "it still burns my hand."

"It didn't burn mine. It came to me as if I called it. As for your mother, she wasn't my slave . . . I was hers." He dropped his shoulder as if he might turn away to avoid meeting her eyes again. "The Warrior Queen won't give you your legacy."

"Not yet."

"Why?"

"She doubts me." And why not, Grace told herself. Here she stood, talking with the enemy. Perhaps she deserved that doubt and more.

"What I'm telling you won't ease her mind, but it's all I can offer you. I loved Lindala more than life itself, but little good it did her. I called Gods and Demons for her sake and she paid the price." He took a breath that sounded like stone grinding upon stone. " I'm what's left of your father. Fyrvae . . ." He stopped, as his eyes glittered brightly, and then he began again. "I was once known as Fyrvae. When you took the sword from me, and carried it, I should have known. I think Quendius recognized it. Only I or one of my blood could even touch Cerat."

"You lie."

"To what purpose? To estrange you from your queen? From your man? You're here, alone, already. And I can see the strength in you, a cord of blue and a cord of gold, from your mother's gift of water and mine of fire, and they're braided strongly in you."

Fire. She shrank back on one heel. Was it both he and Cerat that burned inside of her? Yet another reason for Lariel to turn her away. Rivergrace turned her face, unable to bear another word, but he filled the air with them, hoarse and grating.

"I can't cage you, lady called Rivergrace, even if I tried. I can't promise you that Quendius can't, or Lariel or another of the high Vaelinars. But I can't. Nor do I want to. Seeing you fills me with pride and shame."

"Fyrvae." She almost sighed the name.

"My blood, if it's listed in here anywhere, is listed so briefly you might see it only as a mist between the pages. Trying to open a Way had become illegal, and yet there were those who would still attempt it, to become a House with standing and land and fortune ... and my father's attempt and failure brought the full brunt of punishment down upon us. We were DeCadil and he wanted a House for us. I fled, with Lindala, ahead of the extermination of our line. We had no place to go. Quendius took us in, and then he enslaved us. Gods forgive me that you were born in darkness and lived in the mines where no child should ever have hoped to flourish, but you did. I think it was because of your mother that you grew with love and hope. And the river. I worked in the forges to either please Quendius enough so that he might yet release us or make a weapon so powerful I could kill him and escape. I did both, and neither freed me, but broke me and killed my love." His voice wavered, and a strange light came and went through his eyes. He shook all over. Rivergrace knew that whatever moments of sanity he had left would be fleeting. He stared over her shoulder then, beyond the threshold where she stood.

He would bolt. She saw a tremor run through him. She had so much she needed to know. "You called Gods to your weapons."

"I made a Way. The God followed it into my forging. Gods," he said, "are like catching the wind and the sun and the rain. They know little of the earth which is where we come from when we begin and return when we end." He opened and closed his eyes fitfully. He shook his head violently, twice, before speaking again, his voice rasping, nearly choking. "The one you cradled within you . . . She lies to you, Daughter. Cerat has a bridge to the Goddess. You've stolen nothing of hers. What you have, you nurtured. It came from the same great being which begat all of us, even the Gods, and it stays with you because there it flourishes, to become what it was meant to be. Do you understand me? You stole nothing."

"But how can I—"

His body jerked violently and hunched over, cutting her question off, and she flung herself to the side as he let out a howl and burst past her, and was gone. Not even an echo from his running footsteps reached her. The Hound of Quendius had returned and fled.

Chapter Thirty-Three

AZEL SAT ENJOYING THE HOT CUP in his hands and watched Rivergrace over its wide rim. "You found nothing with the name Lindala, then, is what you're telling me."

She shook her head. "It's as if she didn't exist."

He lowered his cup to lean forward and pat her knee. "We know that she must have, you're living proof of it. My suggestion then, is to leave the stacks of histories, since she has been expunged, and go to the boring, muddled stacks of wills and levies."

"Wills and levies?" echoed Nutmeg.

"Aye, little one. When Lily, may it be many years from now, goes, does she not have a record of who gets what pot, and who gets the loom, and who gets the spinning wheel, and so on?"

"Of course she does!"

"Those things are oft filed with the levies every two-year, I believe, despite good health and hope, especially

among those who live in the country, where rough
weather, disease, and raiders make life uneasy."

Rivergrace straightened in her chair. "Even among
the Vaelinars?"

"Especially among the Vaelinars who do not have a
House or a Stronghold to shelter them. I have found in
my studies that it is most often the women who file such
wills, as the main inheritance goes through the paternal
branch, so the land and outbuildings or business would go
to a son or sons, undisputed. But a woman's things, ah, she
would want to place those quite specifically and did so."

"I get the good dishes and the shop," stated Nutmeg.
"To share with Rivergrace."

"My point." Azel lifted his cup again.

"A will might have been overlooked," Grace murmured. "But not filed by Lindala but perhaps left to her
before she was excised. Something recorded, often for
taxation purposes, but rarely amended might be overlooked when her name was removed."

"Yes. Also," and Azel stared off into the dust motes
dancing in a ray of sunlight for a moment. "An odd
thought, but possibly a useful one. Check the registra-
tion books for the hounds and falcons. The breeders
are noted as diligently as the animals themselves, and
if your mother was involved with either, it's possible
her name would have been overlooked there as well.
Many of our young women breed dogs and horses and
the birds."

"Then," said Nutmeg briskly as she rose and dusted
off her skirts. "It's back to the books."

"Today?"

"We've still reading light left?"

"For a candlemark, at the most. Then, I fear the
sconces aren't strong enough for my old eyes although
they might be for yours."

Rivergrace stood as well. "We'll make do." Gold glittered at her wrist as she did before she quickly pulled
her sleeve down into place.

Azel pursed his lips and let out a piercing whistle. His answer came in the form of running footsteps. "I'll have one of the apprentices take you to the documents section." He appraised Rivergrace. "I think I would go back about 120 years or so, 150 at the most, to begin looking."

The apprentice appeared, hair sticking out of her tight braids, her face flushed from her run to answer. She dipped a response to Azel's clipped order and beckoned for the girls to follow her. They angled off into a different wing altogether, where the windows gave most of the illumination, and clouds winging overhead sent shadows skittering through the bookcases. There they were left. Rivergrace watched Nutmeg as she ran her hand over the great, flat-bound books, where the edges of the documents held inside of them looked like ruffled sleeve cuffs. She had her answer, which she had no intention of sharing with either Azel or her sister, until she'd turned it over and over inside of herself, searching. Searching for what, she wasn't sure. The truth of it? Did she trust Narskap to be able to utter the truth? Not sharing with Meg pinched at her a bit and, yet, she knew that they had both reached the age where they were withholding part of their lives from one another. They had grown.

She found a ledger book from a decade suggested and took it down to flip through it gently, not really seeing the entries, her mind tussling with what she already knew.

"Listen to this," said Nutmeg quietly. "To my daughter, Lisan, currently the bedslave of a Vaelinar craftsman, if she returns as a free woman, I will my first good set of cooking pots with lids and my set of metal needles and the quilt of my grandmother and feather mattress." She took a breath. "And we thought slavery ended long ago."

"It was supposed to have." Rivergrace rubbed the scar on one arm absently. "We know better."

Nutmeg looked up at her. Then she put her finger to the entry. "This is from a Dweller family, the Mintleafs."

"Are you thinking of what people might say about your being a nurse for Jeredon?"

Her rosy cheeks paled. "No."

"It's not the same, not at all. And who knows if the woman who wrote that was not mean-spirited and angry, and this was her way of calling her daughter a name which would reach her even from beyond death?"

"Some people are like that."

"To our sorrow, yes." She reached over and closed Nutmeg's ledger carefully. "What we need isn't in that book. Find a new one?"

They worked quietly for the next candlemark, now and then lifting their chins to read softly to the other some point they'd uncovered, feeling the weight of decades upon them until Rivergrace finally closed her ledger with a sigh.

"We won't find it in here either."

"Not without years of searching."

She ran her hand through her tangle of hair, pushing it back from her face and over her shoulder. "I've learned that I have to deal with this on my own."

"With Farbranch help."

"Aye, always with the help of my family." Rivergrace smiled gently at Nutmeg. "It's time to go back."

"Good!" Nutmeg bounded to her feet. "I don't want to be left out of things."

"That would never happen."

Nutmeg flashed a grin. "Not if I can help it!"

They left the libraries of Ferstanthe in the morning after a hearty breakfast and a rib-cracking hug from Azel. Their mounts, frisky in the brisk morning air, took to their heels with a squeal as if they could outrun the winter wind with the promise of ice in its sting.

Abayan Diort pored over his maps one last time, and then sent for Tiforan. His third-in-command arrived promptly, his eyes alert despite the faintly puzzled expression on his face. "Warlord?" The tent flaps framing him showed the campfires burning low on the browned hillsides, the thinned evergreens of the region, the closeness of his army to their ultimate destination.

"Scouting reports detail the same amount of force."

"Smaller than expected, but no doubt their elite and strongest. They think to subdue us in one fell blow."

"So it seems to me as well." Abayan clicked his tongue against his teeth in thought before adding, "I am entrusting you with a delicate matter but one of import to me." He detailed his plan to Tiforan who punctuated with sharp nods to show he understood at various points before standing still. He answered when Diort finally fell silent, "Thank you for giving me this."

"Don't thank me yet. Fail at any step along the way and it could cost lives. Wander upon the pathways, and you will never be found. I give you passage for this and only this."

"I will go only the way you've given me, and say only the password you've revealed to me. I won't fail you, Diort."

Diort waved a hand at him as he looked back over his maps. Outside, a horse whinnied in the late night. He stopped, listened, heard nothing more, and returned to his scrutiny.

"We are nearly in place," Tiforan remarked.

"Yes. Scouts report that Lord Bistel arrived just before sunset to take charge. His presence lends more confirmation that these are their elite forces, their best and bravest. It won't be long now. Are you ready for war?"

"Ready and eager."

Diort gave a dry chuckle. He tapped the map with one fingernail. "There is a trap here. Between the Ashenbrook and the Revela Rivers. Queen Lariel perhaps thinks I don't know of it, and hopes to capitalize on that. She's forgotten I have Rakka. Or has she? The Vaelinars have fought this battle before. I'm as capable of learning from their history as they are. Or does she count on that? And, if so, what is the real trap?"

"Answers of that sort don't come until we're on the battlefield."

"Yes. And that is why I send you out. If you succeed, I will have an advantage they can't possibly foresee."

Tiforan touched his forefingers to his brow in respect. "Thank you for the honor. When do I leave?"

"Tomorrow at noon. Any sooner, since armies crawl, and my hand will be tipped." Abayan saluted him in return before turning his attention back to his map. Was the Warrior Queen brilliant or young, untried, and naïve? And would either lead to the death of his plans?

Chapter Thirty-Four

THE KNOCK, SOFT AS IT WAS, still awakened
her. Lariel rolled out of bed and onto her feet in one
movement and in the next was in full stride, grabbing
her dagger as she crossed her rooms. She opened it with
caution, using the door itself as a partial shield, thinking to see her guard lean quietly in to speak with her,
but Daravan stood framed by soft moonlight and tapers
burning down to fragrant pools of wax in the hallway.
He took her hand, dagger and all, and drew himself inward as he closed his fingers about hers. His other hand
went to her lips, fingers upon her mouth to silence her.

"Do not scold your guard. I sent him off for a pitcher
of mulled wine."

He needed it, from the icy coldness in his hands. Lara
toed the door nearly shut as she felt her mouth curve
into a smile under his touch. He dropped his hand as she
did, his thumb brushing along her jaw.

"Your devotion to your duty is remarkable."

"You," he breathed softly, "are not my duty." He bent his head and kissed the side of her neck.

"You presume much."

He chuckled, a warm gust of breath against her skin. "I presume nothing but fond memories of the past. We were like this once, you and I, and I'm asking for nothing more than reminiscence. Send me away if you wish."

She held still in his arms a moment, deciding, and when she couldn't find a protest, he drew her closer. She managed a coherent thought finally. "Then you have no urgent news which brings you so late to my side?"

"I always have news." He kept his mouth to her neck, nibbling, inhaling her scent, his words a tickling whisper upon her skin.

"What if I do not wish to entertain your . . . news?"

Daravan laughed softly. "No news at all until you entertain *this*." With that, he drew her close, sinking his teeth into a bite and molding her body to his, leaving little doubt as to his intentions. He released his bite and kissed away the sting, working now across the shoulder he bared while he brought his hand up along her ribs to firmly circle her breast.

She felt heat surge from the center of her being and turned her face to meet his mouth, pressing upward to him, tasting him in answer, until they broke off when neither seemed able to breathe.

A muted voice at the door said, "Wine, as ordered, m'lord, m'lady," and a booted foot slid a tray inward before the door fully closed and shut them away.

"Will you have me tonight?" Daravan asked of her, before bending to her mouth again, taking her answer in other ways than words until she put her hand up in protest between them.

"Of the few I trust, you're the only one I desire," Lara told him. He buried his free hand in her hair, and his other hand stayed upon her breast, thumb circling her nipple through her thin gown until she thought she would cry out with the aching sensation he brought to her.

"Excellent." He cupped the back of her head to bring her to his kisses again, hot and hungry and devouring until her senses swam and all curiosity about his news fled, and she was only Lara with no thought of the Warrior Queen.

A very long time later, she awoke to his breathing in the bed beside her, blankets fragrant with the musk of their lovemaking, her body spooned against Daravan's, her nipples still tender and rosy, and she wondered what had brought him to Larandaril. She let out a lingering sigh to have such thoughts pushing insistently back into her mind. She had not been a lover to Daravan for a very long time, and even then it had been brief when she was still a young and uncertain Warrior Queen. This evening had been sweeter than she remembered, but she could not forget herself forever. She put her hand on his shoulder. Like the wary man he was, it awakened him immediately. He stirred in the covers.

"Again?" he asked softly, a laugh in his voice.

"Again? What ego you have!"

He turned on his back to pull her against his shoulder. "And what appetite you have."

She dodged his kiss but could not avoid the hand that reached for her still so tender breast. Her breath hissed inward involuntarily as he evoked sensations through her. Finally she put her hand over his to stay him. "Not now, not yet."

"No?"

"No." Lara let out a shaky exhale. "We have business."

He clucked his tongue but relaxed under her hand, his still upon her warm flesh but no longer exciting her. "And if I don't obey you, you'll set Jeredon upon me in the morning?"

"I would, but he's already gone to Ashenbrook with Tressandre."

"I thought you meant to keep him here?" He turned his head to look at her face. "Is that wise?"

"I'm not sure, but the ild Fallyn Talent is keeping him on his feet, and that is all he wants for the moment."

"Tressandre will exact a price for that."

"I think he knows, although I'm not sure he really understands the extent of it."

"Better that he had stayed with the little Dweller lass taking care of him. She would not have plotted slitting throats in the dark if she grew weary."

Lara turned a little in the hollow of the bed to face him and rest her head more securely on his shoulder. "I think danger lies even in that path for him."

"Really? Interesting." Daravan lay still a moment before murmuring, "You have no heir."

"No."

"If both of you fall, we Vaelinars may turn on each other."

"No. That is part of my deal with Bistel, to have him step into Osten's place. Bistane will hold the reins until an Anderieon warrior is found. If not . . ." she pressed her cheek against his warmth. "Then he will hold both lands."

"The ild Fallyns won't take kindly to it, but there's not much you can do if you've documents."

"I've documents." She pushed her thumb into his rib cage. "Now tell me what it is you came to tell me."

"So impatient. The Anderieon blood runs strong in you. Is there none of your mother to balance it? I remember her as a sweet-tempered woman of hidden but indomitable will, rather like robes woven of the most gossamer spidersilk only to be ribbed with steel stays."

"Don't speak of my mother to me."

"Still? You still deny her? That isn't wise or good for you, Lara."

She answered fiercely, "Not a word of her."

He kissed her temple in gentle admonishment. "That isn't right. Blood is blood, my young queen, even if you fight against it. She did what she thought was right, after marrying wrong twice."

"Eladar was a good man. My brother proves it."

"But not the man he needed to be, and he died before he could prove it upon her body with a second, more Anderieon child, true? As for her second husband, he found the grave before you had even quickened in her womb."

"Stop it," said Lara, softly and urgently. "No more."

"If it can't be said here, then where? It's never been proved that your mother seduced your grandfather for a child. He might well have seduced her. She was always his most loving daughter. He wanted Anderieon blood and Talent in his line. Had to have it. Who is to say that it isn't him you should hate instead of her?"

"He raised me!" she answered fiercely. "She bled herself out instead of facing life, and it was he who raised me! If not from guilt, then why? If not from shame, why?"

"Perhaps, my dear," he told her, and kissed her brow again, "because he told her to, even as he told her to carry you. You can't know. I can't know, and she is too long dead to tell us."

"No one knows. Don't speak of it again. Not to me, not to anyone."

His large hand framed her face a moment, his skin warm and smelling of her essence, his touch was both rough and tender. "You know I've kept my word these many years."

"Then why talk about it now!" She would have turned her face away, but he held her close.

"Because I need to remind you of the confidence you have in me. The news I have is that someone has carried a pact to Abayan Diort. My spies tell me that it will be said I did so. You cannot believe that. What you can believe is that m'lady Rivergrace has offered herself in marriage to Diort, for terms to be negotiated."

"What? She has no House or Fortress, no standing—why would he even consider it?"

"Because, as we've discussed, she does have magic within her veins, even if we're not sure of her bloodlines and her Talents. He desires that. She or her advisers have shrewdly guessed you won't willingly offer an alliance with him, so they put her out there. And, it seems, he is interested."

Lara grew very still for long moments. "Would he negotiate peace?"

"My spies weren't in the tent with Diort and the man who brought a deal to his table, but he has marched to Ashenbrook and will arrive there in a handful of days, so it doesn't seem likely. She has power, my dear, power that he thinks he can use."

Lara's lip curled briefly. "*She* can hardly use it."

"Perhaps." Daravan paused. "Have you ever considered that she might carry the long missing heritage of the Mageborn in her? That she is both of us and them?"

Her long silence before answering told him that she had considered just that. "They are all dead. They were gone centuries before we were lost upon Kerith."

"I think, if a God were determined to wipe out myself and my family, I would find a way to stay very, very hidden. Wouldn't you?"

"It's not possible."

He waited for her to stir restlessly before adding, "Why else would a River Goddess of Kerith choose her as sanctuary? There are much more suitable fleshes to take as Her vessel, unless that Goddess saw and recognized something in Grace that you and I can't."

"The Goddess is a minor deity, anchored to the Silverwing, as near as I can tell, although Grace seems to be able to call her up in other waters. The only deity I fear is Andredia. The river and font we guard is the anchor to her being on Kerith, and she calls herself one of the main elements in the making of this world. We have Gods of our own, but she's not one to be ignored or crossed in any way." Lara paused a long moment before continuing. "Rivergrace hasn't the guile to bargain with Diort."

"She hid successfully among the Dwellers from all her enemies for years. Do you think an innocent can do that?" He released his hold upon her, and Lara sat.

"I think what I know. If you had word that Tiiva had done this, hoping to supplant me, or the ild Fallyn, then it would be believable."

"Tressandre has tried a number of times over the years to supplant you and failed. She thinks Jeredon is her key now."

"She'll fail there, too. Jeredon wants to be whole to help me, not to replace me." Lara combed her heavy hair back from her face, its gold-and-platinum strands cascading through her fingers onto her neck and shoulders.

"You're certain of him."

"Yes." She could feel Daravan watching and measuring her, but she did know Jeredon's heart, didn't she? As well as she knew her own. From her first days walking, he'd been there for her, teasing and teaching, and he had been relieved when it was soon apparent that she was the heir their grandfather hoped for, and would mentor, and would appoint. He'd have the freedom to be what he wanted. He did as all expected and vied with her for the title, but no one thought he would be chosen and he wasn't. Never had he expressed disappointment or envy. She would know if he had, wouldn't she?

Just as she would have known if Rivergrace had carried an ambition inside of her. If not Grace herself, then who might manipulate her? Sevryn was Lara's right hand. He'd put his life before her many a time, the latest when Quendius had aimed his arrows at them. Did he resent her for not endorsing Rivergrace? Yes, but he'd made that known. He had done nothing underhanded. Rivergrace was his heart. He'd never give her over to Abayan Diort. Or offer her as bait.

Lara closed her hand tightly. She knew the few she

trusted well. Did she not? As Jeredon the hunter studied
the signs of his prey, she the queen studied the signs of
her people. This was part of the power of her Anderieon
blood, the blood her grandfather so coveted that he'd
committed incest to ensure its continuation. But even
her heritage couldn't sift through Rivergrace. Who could
know what rested inside a woman of unknown lineage
and who had sheltered a Goddess? She couldn't afford
to be wrong or ignorant.

She murmured a word not meant for his ears, but he,
trained to the silence of forests as well as stealthy men
heard it: traitor. She reached for her gown. He put his
hand on her shoulder.

"Stay in bed with me."

Her back stiffened, but his other hand moved there,
powerful, seeking out and rubbing knots of tension and
worry until she returned quietly, then willingly to his
arms. He made love to her again, and she drifted away
to sleep. And dreams.

It was the dream she feared above all others. A battlefield that left her people annihilated and their future in bloody ruins. Hounds howled in distress, horses
wandered, bloodied and heads down, limping lamely
among litters of bodies. Moans rose from the dying and
filled her ears, tore at her heart as she stood, both hands
wrapped about her sword, almost too weary to lift it
a final time. She'd had this vision before but never so
complete, so real, so devastating. She wavered upon her
feet when the unmistakable feeling of power and weaving ran over her. Someone within their ranks plucked
at the threads of creation, plucked and chose elements,
and began weaving a Way. The survivors rallied behind
her. She could hear those whole of body picking up the
wounded as the Way gathered strength and then opened
in front of her.

Trevilara. The Way home. She saw into the gap as
plain as any sight she'd ever had, and knew the land of
green and gold that met her eyes was real, and waiting

for her, and was her birthright. It was their escape and their destiny and she called for her people, the survivors, to follow her into it.

An answering call challenged her, and Abayan Diort stood between her and the Way, weapon in hand, blocking her. The Way to Trevilara framed his head in golden flame and the Guardian stood unrelenting. His troops flanked her, kept her from retreat, and now he stood between her and the desire of all their hearts.

Lara woke in a sweat. She put her palm over her mouth to still her cry of despair. Daravan stirred faintly beside her. The cords of her throat strained as she swallowed tightly, holding back her vision, her omen, and her sobs. Then she managed a breath and sat, swinging her legs out of bed.

Daravan rolled over and murmured a quiet protest.

"It's almost dawn. I have things to do. You rest. I'll have some food sent up from the kitchen." She rose and drew curtains about her bed, shutting it out of her sight and mind while she prepared for the day.

Azel opened the gate to the inner cabinet, enjoying the smell of paper and leather, and the satisfaction of having gotten Bistel Vantane's memoirs in his collection at long last. It was not a rite of death although many of his brethren had made it so. He had Vaelinar, though, who came in every few decades to update their writings in case memory faded or life took them unexpectedly. He knew what Bistel thought he faced and felt the old warlord to be wrong. Few could hope to best the man in strength or strategy and, barring treachery, Azel thought the head of the Vantanes would live for many decades more.

As a historian, he itched to read what Bistel had written but that was not allowed in the *Books of All Truth*. They were to stay inviolate once written and completed.

He would not even read the partial compilations. He did not totally understand the destiny intended for the books, but there was one, and his understanding—or not—of it did not make it any less real. It only made a thorn in his side which would both pinch and itch because of his interest and passion for knowledge. At night, sometimes, he would muse if he himself would live long enough to see that destiny reached and he could at last quench his desire for the books.

He checked the shelves for dust, and the mites that hid almost invisibly within, and for other pests that he had the apprentices smoke out of the various wings of the library on a regular basis. All seemed to be in order. His robes billowed about him as he savored the moment, his chest swelling in a bit of pride that he allowed himself. Spring would bring him a new handful of apprentices, in answer to his plea, to be trained for other libraries, perhaps one in Hawthorne and one to the east among the Galdarkan lands, knowledge being taken to be used and disseminated, as he'd always argued it should be. There would be no *Books of All Truth* in those libraries, but that would be his next crusade. Memory could be a fragile thing, as fragile as truth, and he wanted to encourage his people and other peoples to document their lives. That, he told himself, was what lifted them above animals, the tales to be told to educate and illuminate. Knowledge.

Azel brushed his fingertips across a shelf. A very, very faint sheeting of dust met his touch. He lifted his hand and saw not the gray dun of ordinary dust, but a rusty, near-black soot. It had a greasy feel as he rubbed his fingers against one another. A nasty, evil feel. He sniffed at it. The odor, so faint he could not detect it until held to his nose, permeated his senses. A rotting smell. A wrong, destructive stink.

Azel wiped his hand against his robes before turning to run out of the room, yelling for his apprentices.

When he finished concocting a defense, he would

have to send a message to Lariel Anderieon and tell her that corruption had been brought to the library of Ferstanthe, and an enemy had struck at the heart of the Way of the *Books of All Truth*. He would have to name those who had most recently been there, even though he quailed at the thought of doing so. He watched as a handful of his best came running in, faces flushed and hair wild, tugging their robes and tunics into place.

"We've mold in the books. Not any mold, but a corruption of epic possibility. We could lose every book in here. They must be separated and treated, as quickly as possible. There may be a handful which will need to be copied. If there are, they are to be treated and put aside for me. Your vows hold you even against this dire circumstance, am I clear?"

Six faces, complexion paling, three white, one ash, one copper, and one bronze, nodded at him. He clapped his hands together. "Now move!"

The senior apprentice pointed at two juniors. "Prepare isolation rooms. Set wards. A sitting table per book. You, Isargth, go get the pots to boiling, I want mold rot potion in gallons readied. The rest of us remove one book at a time. Wash your hands in herbal antiseptics before you touch another. Clear? Lord Azel, I presume you will do your work, if necessary, in the Star west room?"

He dipped his head in confirmation.

"Done, then." The apprentices turned and dashed in their assigned directions.

Azel could feel his heart pounding in his chest. His library was a Way, the Way which had built the House of Ferstanthe, and now it felt as though it had begun to tumble down around him. He looked at the volume in his hand. It seemed to be at the heart of the contagion, and he knew he would have to treat it and then copy and replace needed pages. This Book had been written by the founder of House Pantoreth, of which Tiiva had been the last direct descendant. "I'll be in my room. Send the disinfectant and potion there immediately, whatever

we have on hand while the large vats are being brewed."
Afraid to touch shelves or even his other hand with the
contaminated memoir, he made his way out of the cabinets of All Truth. He brushed shoulders with Lonniset,
the youngest and most promising of his apprentices. He
looked at her wide eyes.

"We've been through worse," he said reassuringly to
her. "We'll weather this." He did not believe his own
words as he passed her by.

Lonniset finished pulling on her gloves as Azel left
the cabinets. She pivoted, looking at all the volumes,
most of them small, delicate journals, the truthful and
priceless recollections of the dead. A faint odor hung
in the air, beyond that of leather and the mustiness of
aging paper. She took a hesitant step forward, uncertain
of where to start, but she could feel the darkness which
had struck at the library, feel it like a black arrowhead
in her chest, expanding with each breath. As she took
another step, trying to decide where Azel had swept the
first volume off the shelves for that should be her beginning place, her elbow smacked painfully at the end of
the rack. She sucked her breath in at the smart of it as a
journal tumbled to her feet. She picked it up and turned
it over in her hands, not recognizing the item. The apprentices knew all the books, even though they rarely
touched them, but they knew the look and title of each
and every one, emblazoned into their fiber. It was not
only part of their job, it was the Way which braided itself
into them when they were inducted. She did not know
this one. She ran a gloved finger over the title, punched
into the leather.

Fyrvae of DeCadil Forgotten.

It was clean. Worn and the leather aged, but clean.
She pocketed it to both take it to the decontagion area
and to show Lord Azel. As she did so, and put her head
back up, the odor lingering in the air intensified. Lonniset turned her head slowly as her body went rigid. The
smell of putrid flesh, of rotting stench, filled her nostrils.

She gagged and brought her hand up to cover her nose, even as she examined the nearby shelves closely. Here, centered here . . . her free hand came up, palm down, as if she would grasp something with it and yet she did not, only brushed the air above the cabinet and then, her hand went icy cold, all the way to the elbow. A dark oiliness coated the back of her throat, despite her gloved hand. She tried to swallow it down and could not, her whole mouth filling with bitterness. Then her searching hand, fiery numb with the aching cold, plunged down on an object wedged between two books and came up with a hard, round ball which stabbed into the fabric protecting her flesh.

A pomander filled her palm. Lonniset stared at it in wonder. Not a fragrant sachet of herbs studding a small fruit meant for a ladies' drawer or purse, this thing had been built of the most vile Kernan witchery she'd ever seen—or tasted—in her young years. She had a small strain of Kernan blood in her, the embarrassment of her family, two generations back, but now it pricked her like the sharpest of thorns and she thanked it. Without it, the object might have gone unnoticed for most of the day until the shelves were emptied. Azel himself hadn't sensed it as the heart of the attack. She let out a sharp whistle signaling, *Found it,* to the others, for she'd no doubt that this abomination was the source of their problems. Finding it, however, gave no promise that its influence could be stopped or reversed. She stepped out of the cabinets as Silman the senior apprentice and then Lord Azel himself answered her whistle and they all stared in shock at the pomander.

The words of Fyrvae went forgotten in her pocket.

Nutmeg stood in her saddle and bounced for a few strides of her pony, her nose wrinkled, and her hat flouncing off to be held only by the ribbon firmly tied under her chin.

The wind had chilled her nose to an apple red, matching her cheeks. "I am not wading across this river."

"I agree, it's too cold." Grace brought her mount to a halt and peered at the body of water cutting across their path. Cold but not deep, certainly not deep enough to make it dangerous to ford. Runoff from the hills and mountains had not hit to swell the rivers and brooks they'd come across. Too dry. Where had all the winter rain and snow gone? She wiped one eye with the back of her hand. She wanted to be with Sevryn, to tell him what she'd learned and what she feared. Would she be able to read an expression on his face, a face he had schooled to keep his emotions silent, a face that he had schooled in the service of Lariel? Would he accept her? Could he? He had suffered the worst degradations a man could endure under Quendius and Narskap. If he left her the slightest hope, she would fight for him, fight for both of them. But only if he could give her the faintest glimmer of hope. She needed that, as the most stubborn blade of grass needed the slightest drop of rainwater and hint of sunlight.

"Grace? Grace, are you in there?" Nutmeg squinted up into her face as she pulled her recalcitrant hat back onto her head.

"I am. Just thinking."

"That library gave us a bushel to think about, didn't it?"

"It gave me a whole cartload, I think." Grace smiled briefly at Meg. "I'm sorry I've been thinking too much."

"You've always been the quiet one," she answered. "I'm used to that."

"You've been quiet a lot lately, too."

"I have thoughts running around in my head like two squirrels fighting over a nut." Nutmeg fussed a moment with her thick and lustrous hair, trying to tame it under her hat without much success. It had started out the morning braided, but with every bouncing step of her mount, it had slowly come unwound.

"Jeredon."

"Aye. Am I so foolish, Rivergrace?"

"Maybe." She looked away for a moment, not wanting to see any hurt in her sister's eyes before looking back again. "You can't love him."

"But I do, and I thought he loved me, too."

"Oh, Meg."

"I used to think it was meant to be." It was Nutmeg who looked away then, unable to meet her gaze. "And when we . . . whenever he made love to me . . . I thought the world had stopped and started again."

"Meg . . ."

"No. Don't be disappointed in me. I couldn't bear it if you were, or Da or Mom." She sighed. "I couldn't bear it. And now he won't even look at me, and I should have known, I should have, that it couldn't be. He tried t'be telling me. I wasn't for accepting. But it was in the books, Grace. In all the books and scrolls. Vaelinars have never taken a Dweller to wife. Never. *Never.*" Her voice trailed off.

"It has nothing to do with you. He's Vaelinar, and I've begun to learn that has meaning far deeper than any of us could know unless we were born and raised as one."

"You're an outsider, too."

"Yes."

"But not Sevryn."

"Oh, he is. Just not at Lariel's side. She raised him up, and she can cast him down, too, if she wishes. But he's a half-breed, and the others don't forget that."

"We picked a fine pair, didn't we?"

"They *are* a fine pair. I'm just not sure if we can hold onto our dreams with them."

Nutmeg looked to her then. "You wouldn't leave Sevryn."

"I would if he didn't try. It's like a pony and cart, I think. It's a partnership, or neither goes anywhere. I won't do all the work. I'll walk away first because part of love is respect, and if he doesn't have it for me, I won't hang on and hope he finds it somehow. I can't give him all my strength for what faces us if he doesn't value it and give back his."

"Respect," echoed Nutmeg. She nodded. She pointed at the river. "That's settled, then, I think we should get our respectable butts home."

Chapter
Thirty-Five

SEVRYN OPENED HIS MAP AGAIN, carefully, the paper protesting with a crackle as he did so. Years had made it ever more brittle and even with care it would not last long as he used it, but he hadn't taken time to have it copied. Nor, he reflected, would he want it scribed by someone else. The slightest bit of error or straying or overlook would give him an entirely different document than the one Gilgarran had secreted. A fast horse and the peculiar work of the Ferryman had brought him here and quickly. Aymaran lifted a hoof as if to stomp in protest against the skirling wind and icy mist that gusted off the escarpment, but he put it down in silence as Sevryn used his Voice to soothe and quiet him. Carefully, he returned the map to its original folds and stowed it away. He kneed the horse down off the ridge a little, getting as close to the weathered structures he'd found as he dared without encountering a sentry.

This then, was where Quendius had withdrawn. A thin curl of blue-gray smoke rose from the main fortress building and a large outbuilding to the rear. One would be for the kitchen chimney and the other, unless he was greatly mistaken, would be the forge. The fires in the forge would be banked, coals only, kept going mainly for minor repair work and to avoid having to lay an entirely new fire if needed. He could see a lone man pass by every now and then, bent against the stinging wind, cloak wrapped tightly about his body. On occasion it would be a Bolger. But as Sevryn assessed the area keenly, he could see that whatever forces Quendius had held here had been moved out. This had been a training facility and barracks as well as forge. He could see the working arenas, the targets, the trenches. He knew what he looked down upon. The only thing he did not know was where Quendius had taken his men, but he thought that obvious.

Both the Vaelinar and the Galdarkan armies would have their backs to his raiders. Both would be equally vulnerable in the aftermath of their battle.

Sevryn turned his horse off the ridge and dug his heels into Aymaran's flanks, hard as Time spurred him. If sentries spied him, they'd still have to catch him.

At the first hard-flowing river he could find to cross, he reined up, steam rising from Aymaran's warm body and his. He dismounted to stand with the toe of his boots in the water and he called for the Ferryman. He knew that, if the Ferryman had taken him from the banks of the Nylara to another river, the Ferryman would also show up to return him, as if the trip were a circle and must be completed. So had the journey Daravan taken him on worked. Summoned and crossed, then he was there to summon again for a return crossing. But Sevryn was not at all certain how Daravan could order up the Ferryman otherwise or if the phantom would obey anyone else. There had been payment promised between the two and when the specter had thought to garner the same from Sevryn, Daravan had denied the Ferryman. Would there be a payment required now, if the Ferryman appeared, and could he afford the price?

His arm ached. He rubbed it through his cloak and shirt. The wound healed quickly, as if the dire arrow of Quendius had barely struck him, but it had drilled deeply before rejecting his flesh. He couldn't call it anything else. The arrow had rejected him, denied itself the taking of him as prey as its brethren had taken Osten. He could only be happy that it did, but he knew Cerat's voice when he heard it, knew the Demon's touch when he felt it. Quendius had imbued the Demon into his arrows. Why, then, had Cerat not killed him? He knew the sliver of Cerat he carried inside himself called for anger and rage, blood and death. Would he not have been the desired target? The meat that Cerat could not resist? Would he not?

Or, perhaps, like bards and toback shop tale-tellers liked to posit, there is a time and a season for all things, even death.

If the Ferryman would take a chunk of Cerat as his toll, he would gladly pay.

Sevryn's mouth eased into a thin, dry smile. He kicked at the lip of the river. "I've no caravan or goods, all I have is need, Ferryman. Come, and take me across."

He waited. A falcon winged high overhead, its cry swallowed by the wind. Trees sounded like a restless tide on both sides of the river. The water itself rushed and gurgled and spun away from him. Aymaran lowered his head to drink, slowly, wise horse not to drink too fast or too deep after a hard ride but unable to resist a drink at all. He squatted and cupped the freezing water for a drink himself.

A vision stabbed through his eyes, a lightning moment, a view of Rivergrace and Nutmeg at water's edge. He felt her as keenly as he felt the stabbing cold of the river he touched.

But how and why did she ride as he did? Why wasn't

she back at Larandaril's hold, safe for the moment where he'd left her? He cupped the river again, thrusting his arm fully into the whitecaps meeting the shoreline but no other sight came to his eyes. Had the two been alone or riding with Lariel? Did the queen hasten her way to war and to join Bistel?

He pushed both hands into the water, making Aymaran throw his head up with a snort and back away as he cried out, "Aderro! Rivergrace!" The illusion had no answer for him.

A dry voice over his shoulder said, " Aderro? That is how you cry for me?"

Sevryn pivoted in a spray of icy water and the Dark Ferryman stood waiting with his cowled head lowered to look upon him. Did the being have a sense of humor or need? Had it ever been part of the living world? Sevryn would have sworn not, but he'd just been greeted by a voice filled with irony. He looked into the abyss of the cowl and saw nothing.

The Ferryman held out his hand to seek payment. "Who will you die for?"

A chill danced upon Sevryn's neck, as the Ferryman eerily echoed what Daravan had said only so many days ago to him. He answered, "For my lady Rivergrace. And for my queen."

With a nod and a beckon to follow, the specter moved past him, into the river. Sevryn caught at his arm as he did. "Wait!" The shock of contact rocked him onto his heels, but he did not let go as the being looked down at him again. Sparks flew along his sleeve and the robes of the Ferryman as he held him. But the being paused.

"The Andredia. Can you take me to the Andredia River?" Sevryn was not, could not be sure, that the Ferryman even existed in the same time and place that he did, for all its actions and reactions. A Way of the Vaelinar, yet not a Way that any one admitted to creating or directing, the Ferryman did what he did.

The abyss of its face looked into his for a very long

moment. "Payment will be rendered," the Ferryman said flatly. He shook off Sevryn's hand and waded back into the river. Sevryn grabbed for Aymaran's reins and hurried to follow. A deal seemed to have been struck. He did not know the payment or when it would be collected. Too late to worry about the consequences, he strode in the Ferryman's wake.

The river rose before them like a wall, a tidal wave coming in from the sea, and its silty bottom grabbed at his steps as if it were quicksand. Aymaran whickered in alarm as Sevryn bent his head low, forcing himself into the spray as water threatened to curl over them, wiping them all out. Yet it never engulfed the Ferryman. Every step he took, the wave retreated, still towering, still undulating, still threatening, but never crashing down upon them. Icy water soaked him to the bone, and his horse slogged behind, moaning in pain. Sevryn put his hand to the chin strap, rubbing Aymaran, encouraging him with a hope the river's bank lay only a few more strides away.

The water assailed not only his body but his will. The river threatened to drag him down and swirl him away in its current, never to surface. It promised to suck the air from his lungs and rush into its place, drowning him. It railed at his intrusion against its natural place in the world. Sevryn put his arm up to shield his face as the spray and wind all but tore his cloak from his body. The ragged cloth flapped about him like shredded, sodden wings. Aymaran staggered and went to his knees behind him, squealing as the river inundated him. Sevryn put his shoulder to the horse's and urged him up, back on his hooves, both of them shaking with the winter ice of the water, their teeth rattling, and the implacable figure of the Ferryman barely seen ahead of them.

Sevryn realized he could not lose the phantom. He dragged on Aymaran's bridle to hurry the frightened horse. He could lose his mount if he had to, but he dare not lose the Ferryman.

The tide rising against them, the tremendous wave towering over them, began to curl further, whitecapped froth crowning it. Sevryn looked into it, blinking, his face drenched. He thought of the Andredia as his horse tugged desperately on the bridle, balking at being led any farther. The simple river they had faced had become a torrential ocean, and they seemed no closer to crossing it than they had been when they started, but the Ferryman did not falter.

It was he who held them back. Sevryn scrubbed a hand across his face. The insurmountable barrier was himself! The Andredia knew him. Its priestess Lariel had given him free passage across its waters and into its valley kingdom. He knew well the river in its seasons, in its sweetness and in its bitterness when Quendius had poisoned it. He knew the river as well as he knew Rivergrace's voice and touch. And it was the Andredia whose shore he desired to trespass on now.

The wave broke over them. But it died before it did, shrinking down upon itself until it was but a frothy veil of water that curled over their heads and then receded to the riverbank. The Ferryman emerged, turned, and waited for Sevryn to urge Aymaran from the riverbed. The horse put his head out and shook vigorously, like a dog, shedding drops everywhere. Sevryn patted the beast in apology. "I nearly drowned us, lad. Sorry for that."

The Ferryman held his hand up in farewell and in a swirl of his ebony veils and robes, disappeared into a darkling mist on the shore. Sevryn wiped his eyes, and looked again onto the swift-flowing and no longer angry sacred River Andredia. Now he had only to find both his love and his queen.

"WHAT IS IT?"

Rivergrace paused, one boot in the water and one boot out. How could she possibly explain what she'd just felt, that Sevryn had been at a crossing, too, and they'd seen each other for the smallest flash of a moment. Would her sister think she was daft? She pursed her lips a moment to find the words. "Did you ever get a feeling you see our family? When you know you couldn't have, but you get a flash of him at the cider press or her at her tailoring table?"

Nutmeg peered up at her from under the brim of her now somewhat battered looking hat. "You mean, as if they were thinking of you at the same moment you were thinking of them, and you just knew what they were doing and if they were all right or not?"

"Yes! That's it, exactly."

"No."

Grace shoved at her shoulder. "No?"

"Aye, no. Keldan gets those feelings, time to time, but

never me. I'm thick, I suppose. Ghosts don't care to be teasing me because I can't see them." Nutmeg wrinkled her nose and fluffed her sleeve back out. "A-course, you've always been strange that way." She walked briskly past Rivergrace, her boots sending up a trough of water.

With a mild snort of protest, Rivergrace moved to catch up. Nutmeg's voice trailed after her cheerfully, teasing, words that Grace couldn't quite hear. And then, in a flash, Nutmeg disappeared.

In the blink of an eye, the river had swallowed her up. "Meg!" Rivergrace screamed. The pony reared, tossing his head, the whites of his eyes showing in wild fear. She grabbed at his bridle to keep him from bolting off. "Nutmeg!"

She saw nothing but a whirlpool of water being sucked down by the scared pony's rigid legs. Wrapping both pairs of reins to the pony's saddle, she waded forward. Nothing met her eyes, nothing. It was as though Nutmeg had stepped into a bottomless hole and disappeared. She dug at the water. A scrap of cloth met her touch. She grabbed at it, almost had it, before the river or perhaps Nutmeg's thrashing movements tore it out of her grasp.

With a gulping breath, she plunged after it. The water tore at her, but she caught an arm, a hand, felt fingers tighten on her and she pulled upward, the two of them. It was her nightmare come to life, for something dragged Nutmeg downward, ever downward into an impossible watery world. She found an angry strength inside and pulled Nutmeg up with her, standing, drawing her sodden sister out of the raging current and embracing her for a moment. Then she threw Nutmeg sputtering over her pony.

Cold hands wrapped about her legs.

"Hang on," she managed. "Don't come after me. She'll kill you." And then, like that, she was pulled under and whatever else she might have said burst in a string of bubbles from her lips as the deep blue kingdom and the River Goddess claimed her. What had been a simple river churned into a seemingly bottomless lake.

She fought this time, kicked and clawed at the hold. This was no embrace she would allow. If she went down, the Goddess would have to fight her every bit of the way. They fell in a tumult of white water. She could see the woman thrashing with her, silvery blue hair and fair skin, a countenance of sheer beauty except for the hatred that contorted her features. One of the fairest of the fair, born of living water and light and life, and she roiled, a darkness coming out of her in an inky mist, enveloping the two of them.

In her dream, Rivergrace had breathed. Now, she could not. The water pressed against her nostrils and mouth, and she knew she would drown. The being which had enticed her to surrender once now gave her no chance. Death was the only gift being offered. She kicked and twisted against the other's hold, her layered winter clothes sodden and weighing her down like an anchor, her movements slowed by the water's pressure. She would die here. The Goddess would snuff out her life with no more regard than a waning candle. No bargains, no cajoling, no offering from the Immortals. Rivergrace felt her lungs cry for air and gashes open up on her arms and legs as the other flailed at her, and she looked through an ever-growing cloud of stained water and could feel the poison in it.

She grew weary. There would be no ending to the struggle until she gave up what the other demanded, and there was no way she could do that, for it had become an integral part of herself, such a part that she wondered if it had even come from this being or had merely been awakened by her. She had no way of knowing, but she did know that when she let go of her life, it would be ended. Unless the Goddess in her fury struck out at those she loved anyway. Unless . . .

Her lips parted involuntarily with the need to suck in

air although her throat would fill with water. She could
taste the foul poisoning upon them that the Goddess
rained into the water from every pore of her being. Immortal corruption wrapped around the two of them as
they wrestled and danced their way into the depths.

No.

She couldn't give up. The sheer wrongness of it struck
every cord in her body, as desperate as the need for air.
Water should be *life*. If not hers, then the lives of all who
touched fresh water upon the land as it fell upon it and
flowed through and under it. Sweet water, good water,
life-bringing and sustaining water. Wind and storm might
drive into flood and fury but that would be transitory.
What should remain always should be a font of good.
She could not allow the madness of this Immortal to destroy that. But she struggled to no avail, and her heart
thumped loudly in her ears and her chest swelled almost
to breaking, and Rivergrace knew she couldn't do what
she had to do alone. The River Goddess pushed against
her, mouth yawning, teeth sharp and pointed as a spined
eel, going for her throat. She wrapped her hands about
the other and sent the last of her thoughts spiraling outward, to the sky, to the wind and sun, with a call to the
one being she could think of who might help her.

She felt something shatter as she pushed her plea out.
A wall perhaps, holding thoughts back from ordinary
flesh such as hers, she couldn't know. But it broke and
she felt her thoughts arrowing to a destination even as
the Goddess pierced the skin of her throat, and then
strove again for a deeper, tearing, bite. Grace's senses
whirled, and her sight grew dimmer. She would breathe
in another moment, gulping in the inky water, and that
would begin her ending.

Between one heartbeat and the next, he appeared.

The only being she knew who could tame a river,
the Ferryman appeared in a swirl of his dark cloak and
robes, almost indistinguishable from the inky mist of
corruption surrounding the Goddess. He reached out

and ripped Rivergrace from her hold. He thrust her upward, catapulting her toward the surface and the sky, where sunlight danced upon the curtain of water. She broke into the open just as her body gave out and she gulped, but it was air she took in. Air and spray, and she coughed and choked and her temples pounded and her lungs cramped, but she breathed.

"Grace!" Nutmeg reached down with a sob to grasp her forearm and braced her against the pony's stalwart body, rooted firmly in the river. Water thrashed around his hooves and their bodies.

The Ferryman rose as the river began to still. He folded his arms across his chest and came out of the water straight and quiet, but she could feel his gaze scorching over her.

Rivergrace shivered as he began to turn away from them. "Wait."

The phantom paused. She let go of Nutmeg and took a quaking step toward him, her hand out.

"I can't leave the river poisoned," she said. "Even if the Goddess intends it. It's not right. This is what I *do*."

The cowl dipped in acknowledgment. He took her hand in his, a hand not of flesh yet solid and with feeling, and he anchored her as she sank into the river once more. She could not sense the Goddess, but corruption lay in her wake, oily and deadly. Had he destroyed her or had she merely fled, her vengeance delayed for another time? It did not matter now, it could not. Rivergrace had one thing she could do, and do well, and she bent her thoughts to it as the Ferryman held her safe with one hand.

But she did not touch the waters as she always had. As her hand dipped into them, they burst into flame. She could feel their heat, although not wicked hot, and see them spread, golden-orange and red, licking through the blue-and-gray river, as the fire devoured the staining in the water. She shook as fire poured out of her until her face burned from its heat and her hair rose about her, borne on wings of dry air lifting off the surface. The Ferryman made a noise at her side, and his hand tightened painfully on hers even as she combed the river. How could she summon a fire like this, that burned even the river?

When she broke the surface again, the water sparkled clear and clean about her. The Ferryman kept her hand in his as he took the pony by the headstall and led all of them across to the other shore. They emerged, drenched, horses stamping with squeals of relief upon solid ground. Fire rained from her as well, licking upon the grasses on the bank and she stomped the sparks out as it finally quelled.

The Dark Ferryman released his hold on her. The cowl dipped toward her as if he searched her face.

"I owe you payment for crossing. Our lives . . . I thank you for our lives."

"No payment needed. You have already given." He added, "The darkest Demon holds light, and the lightest God casts shadow."

She wondered at the humanity of him, and whoever had cast and bound him as the Ferryman, an enigma even among the Vaelinars. No one knew who he had been before, only what he endured now. "What would you do if you were free?" Rivergrace touched the sleeve of the phantom. "Is there one who might have called you as my love calls to me?"

"One needs a heart to be called."

"You must have one, you answered me. The ties which bind me to my family and Sevryn aren't chains but rays of light which flow both ways." Even as she said it to him, she felt it and something heavy fell away from her. Loving Sevryn could never burden her. The ties didn't weigh her down or she them. They were light, even if they carried shadow behind them as all light did, and they illuminated her life. "May you find such rays in every river you cross."

The specter towered over her but did not pull away

from her touch. He stretched out his hand as if he would grasp hers a last time, and then stopped, motionless. A low sigh escaped from within his deep hood.

Rivergrace removed her hand, saying, "My thanks to you again, one I call friend." She gathered her reins to mount, Nutmeg already back in her saddle, face pale white with the dread of their encounter, and for once with nothing to say.

She looked back once to the river and saw the Dark Ferryman standing there, a still dark shadow cast across the water, watching after them.

Chapter
Thirty-Seven

BACK IN THE DAYS when Hosmer wanted to be a member of the Guard more than anything, he'd drilled all of them in the fine arts of defense and offense and, Garner reflected, he'd learned what he had because he had to. There was no placating Hosmer otherwise. Never was a Dweller more determined to grow a tree from a rock, as the saying went. They'd spent hours in the dusty rows of the orchard, dodging trees heavy with bud or fruit, even his sisters involved, all to make Hosmer happy ... and give him a target. Bruises and skinned limbs, pulled hair and sore jaws, they'd learned the finer arts of warfare, according to some arcane book of guardery (was that even a word, Garner wondered) that Hosmer had obtained from Trader Robin Greathouse. At the time, he would have bet against it that he would ever need to dredge up those skills, but he would have lost. And he would have lost spectacularly, but not his life the way the Barrel brothers had when raiders and Ravers attacked on the fringe of their lands. Hosmer had fought back; he had fought back. His sisters and mother and father and younger brother Keldan had fought back, and they'd all won. They'd lost their lands but kept their lives. In the game of warfare, that made them winners.

Sweat dappled his brow despite the gloomy skies and the chill, wintry, wind that swirled about constantly without a hint of rain. A squint upward confirmed that. In the way of a Dweller, he shrugged uneasily at that. Dry, too dry, and even though he hadn't the heart for the land and growing things that his father had, it still worried him greatly. He took a swig from his waterskin and watched as the Bolger clansman circled his pony about, readying to head back Garner's way. Bolgers did not scare him. Raiders or nomads, craftsmen or trappers, he knew them in all their roles. Bolgers were a part of the country life he'd been raised in. Not Ravers. Ravers were wraiths of evil and murder wrapped in rags of black cloth who rode or bounded along on stilt legs, hounds of death. It had been a Raver who'd carved a hole in Garner's rib cage, just below his heart, digging for that same heart, and it was Ravers he feared.

He slung his waterskin back on his belt and shifted his weight, and then waited along with a handful of other caravan guards wearing the Oxfort tunic. His hand slid inside his shirt where a strange object hung from a thong about his neck, an amulet of some sort he'd taken off the Raver who'd tried to kill him and died in the effort, and rubbed his thumb over it. The scar along his ribs ached now and then. It didn't ache today. He couldn't tell if it would ache tomorrow. But it could, and would, as if some sliver off the thing's carapace had lodged into his bones like some worrisome thorn that he'd never shed until life carved him up for good.

The Bolger let out a whoop as he dug his heels into the side of his mountain pony and came at them. Never mind that raiders or Ravers rarely whooped a warning when they charged on you. It was the silent ambush that killed. This was practice. Garner waved his fellows aside, yelling, "Spread out, he can't target us all that way. Let him fix on one of us, then circle him!"

They didn't listen. Four of them scattered to their right, being right-handed and right-footed, and the clansman bore down on them. Garner gave the thumbs-up to the one who went his way, though staying a respectable distance apart, and they flanked their drill instructor even as the Bolger swung his rock-weighted bolo and brought down two men, and kicked a third as he loped past, taking him down to his knees with a gasp. The clansman let out a shout of surprise, however, as Garner and his man came up behind, with a thumping of their own that hit him square in the back.

Winners. Two alive, three eating dust, and one dead in his stirrups. That was war in this game.

Garner danced back into place as he waited for the Bolger to straighten and ride back to them. The two entangled in the bolo spat grit out of their mouths and reached for their water as soon as they could stand, while the one with a boot put to his gut sucked air in greedily with wheeze after wheeze.

His instructor came back, bailing out of his saddle with a grin that stretched his leathery face ear to ear, revealing his tusks. "Gud, gud," he told them. "Kilt me." He pushed his pony aside and then pointed at them. "You, you, you, wrestle."

Paired up, they waited until their defeated brothers had caught their breath, and did as told.

Wrestling now, a Dweller's stock in trade nearly, at least in a large boisterous family like Garner's. He put down every man standing, before he retreated, and waited. Garner expected their instructor to take him on last, and braced himself for it, though it would hardly be a fair contest. Bolgers had far more strength in their arms and bowed legs than any Dweller or Kernan could hope to have, but before the final bout of their day could take place, their training camp had a visitor.

He saw a look of dislike crawl across the Bolger's face, and turned to see what he watched. A lone horseman rode into camp, reining toward the caravan where Bregan stayed when he was about, and he was about on this day. Garner recognized the man known as Quendius from a brief but fateful encounter one day as the hair on the back of his neck prickled. His instructor jerked a thumb at Garner. The Bolger could not whistle because of his tusks, but Garner could, and let out a long, piercing blast for the horse line boys to come running, and they answered, panting, in front of the Oxfort caravan before Quendius swung off his lathered and dusty tashya mount.

Garner turned away as if disinterested. But he wasn't. This was why Sevryn had asked him to join the Oxfort ranks, and this was one of the men most specifically Sevryn had needed followed. He would not find out now, but he would watch and listen.

Quendius did not leave the caravan all that long afternoon or evening, and his mount was still tied at the horse line, being massaged and groomed and given grain, when Garner woke in the morning and uncurled from his blankets on the ground.

What had the trader and weaponsmith met about? What was their game?

A low, misty fog hung over the training camp, blown straight off the bay, and even the Jewel couldn't be seen through it, although he would bet his day's wages that it would burn off by the time the sun was halfway up in the sky. While they sat hunkered over their skillets of hash, he debated sending word to Sevryn. But what word? He knew little or less. He could report a meeting, nothing more. That would only worry Sevryn, and the man was already worried; that was why he'd put Garner in place. Garner scraped his pan clean before taking it over to the boiling cauldron for a quick dunk of cleaning. He had more to learn; he had only to find a way to do it.

The Way found him first. Bregan emerged from his

caravan dressed not in his trader finery but for a ride. "I need four men," he announced. He pointed at the Bolger instructor, Garner, and two of the other trainees.

Quendius came out behind him, a dark shirt that matched the sooty color of his skin under his long, white woolly vest, and frowned. "Not the Bolger," he said. "I need men."

Garner's pulse thumped heavily in his chest at the sight of the weaponsmith.

The Bolger lifted his upper lip in disdain as he turned away from the Vaelinar.

"Mount up, field gear." Bregan pointed at a fourth, a young Kernan who had shown some promise in training although he was greener than a summer apple.

They were in their stirrups and ready before the horse boys held mounts for the trader and the weaponsmith. As he watched, Garner scratched at his chin where a smudge of a beard had taken root. Oxfort caravan guards trained close to a hundred men in this camp and the ones staying behind were quickly formed into drilling units by the tough Bolger and a scar-faced Kernan, Stickle by name, who had far better guard sense than gambling sense. He rode out after Bregan and Quendius with his Bolger instructor uttering another long, scornful hiss after them. He cast another glance at the sky where a pale winter sun fought to beat down at them through thinning clouds and fog.

Of all the places where he thought Bregan and Quendius might lead them, he would never have bet on the rear gate to Temple Row in Hawthorne. The horses moved restively in the close quarters of the alley, their hooves loud on the clay tiles that paved the way. The temples of Hawthorne were grander than those of Calcort and far more than the simple houses in Stonesend, but they were not opulent by any means. The tiles had been broken by time and wear and relaid with new mortaring, rather than replaced, so that whatever pattern they'd once held had been scattered and rearranged, and the glazing over their surface long faded from sun and salt air. A priest had come out to greet them, the wind even under the sheltering eaves of the temple finding him to ruffle thinning brown curls about his head as he spoke in a flustered manner.

"Master Oxfort! Is there a problem at the counting-house? I deposited the sales as per your command, and they had told me that all was in order. I trust I have not offended you in any way!"

"I've heard nothing amiss. Collect yourself, good priest, and take a deep breath." Bregan swung down, the only finery glittering about him the metal brace upon his leg, curling metalwork done by the most cunning of Vaelinar and holding him steady. "I am glad our people have taken your sermons seriously and purchased the listeners for their households. We don't want to miss the words of the Gods when They speak to us again."

The priest bobbed. "No, indeed not. Never. Yet, here you are. How may I help you, Master Oxfort?"

"A grave situation has come to my attention, which only you can help me solve. What I propose to you now has been brought to me by great effort and through a long meditation of what to do about what I have learned." Bregan frowned, and brushed his hair back from his forehead, a gesture that seemed almost boyish. The Kernan priest's eyes never left his face. Oxfort lowered his voice a little. "What I will suggest to you is near treasonous. Have I your confidence?"

"Absolutely, my son, as any who come to a temple must have!"

"Good, then. I've been brought information which tells me that our efforts, so hard worked upon and so needed, will come to nothing."

The priest sucked in his breath sharply. "Tell me not."

"Yes, and yet there is a glimmer of hope. All these centuries," and Bregan paused until he was certain the priest, and the two boys hanging back in his shadow, listened closely. "All these centuries of punishment for our sins and the arrogance of the Mageborn we took because we felt it our lot to do so. We have hope now that the Gods are about to speak to us again, but their efforts will be futile, as they have been for many, many decades. It is not our failure. We've proved our humility and our love. No. Those who would rule us have blocked the voices of the Gods."

The priest wrung his hands. "Who would do such a thing? And how could they?"

Bregan pointed, away from the temple, over the rooftops of the city, across Hawthorne and the bay, his finger aimed at the great Jewel of Tomarq which, like the sunlight, had finally broken through the haze and shone like a faraway ruby on the cliffs. "That," he told them, "is a Shield not only for the bay and our coast but a Shield from the Gods who would deal with the Vaelinars. So I have been told, and so I have come to believe."

The priest swung about to follow the line of Bregan's hand. He swallowed down a gulp or perhaps it was a tremor, for Garner saw the man shake from head to toe. When he turned about, it was to say in a quailing voice, "But you ride with one of them." His gaze fastened upon Quendius and slid away.

"Not all wish to rule. Some quest for the truth. This man came to me after many years of finding evidence of his suspicions, and now I am come to you."

The priest put his chin up. "What, if anything, can we do?"

"I intend, with your help, to confront them. To demand they put their Shield down and let us live as the Gods command us to."

The priest managed a quick look at Quendius. "You stood in the temple with me. You said you wanted to know how we worshiped."

"I did." The Vaelinar's deep voice rolled out with the tenor of thunder coming from far away. "I wanted to see if the people I was willing to risk my life for were worth it. I came to the conclusion you are."

The priest bowed deeply. "Tell me what you would have me do."

"I want robes for the six of us, and we will go with you and your most devoted priests, up to the Gate of the Jewel."

"Today?"

"Now," said Bregan firmly.

The priest spun about on his heel. "Quick, quick, then! Robes, you heard the master!" He scurried into the depths of his sanctuary, leaving behind only the echo of his running footsteps.

Quendius looked to Bregan. "Selling merchandise with the temple? Is there an agreement I should perhaps have a part of?"

"That agreement pays for the guards you use and I recruit, feed, train, clothe, equip, and board. I think we are quits on this deal." Bregan's jawline hardened, and Quendius only chuckled.

Garner sat quietly, feeling the heat of his horse's flanks warm the inside of his legs. He had become part of something he could neither stop nor warn Sevryn about. He tried not to let the thoughts running through his mind show in his expression. They had not brought him along to think. Yet that's what he was, a man who thought, wasn't he, and he'd be a fool not to be one; and did they think that they were just going to ride up to the Gate where the Istlanthir kept guard over the great Way their House and the House of Drebukar had made, and did they also think the Vaelinars were going to say, "Come right in and, of course, we'll undo the Way so that your Gods can talk to you?" If they thought that, they had another think coming. But he kept his musing under tight wraps, all the long ride out of Hawthorne and up to the cliffs of Tomarq where they picked out the trail cautiously until they came to the great abyss known as the Gate of the Jewel where a barracks house blocked the trail. He expected the Vaelinars to come boiling out like hornets from a fallen nest but only one came forth.

They sat on horseback. Woven robes covered their bodies and great, floppy hoods hid their faces. The Vaelinar who stepped out had the distinctive faintly blue skin and hair the color of the ocean that he warded, so Garner knew it must be either Tranta or the younger of the two guardians, Kever. He hadn't met either although Nutmeg might have, being part of Lariel's entourage, so he could not say who they faced. Whoever he was, his dark green upon lighter green eyes gave them all the once-over before seeking out the priest who rode in front.

"Greetings, my friends, on a dry and gloomy winter's day. What can I do for you?"

"We come on a mission for our Gods," the priest answered. The wind pushed his hood back on his head, revealing him, and a tremor ran through him as if he feared the sudden exposure.

Istlanthir smiled thinly. "Gods and sorrow are in attendance aplenty down the trail at House Drebukar, if you're looking for the memorial of Osten Drebukar. Here, only the sun, wind, and sea can sway a man." His dark blue hair fanned out about his shoulders, and the great jewel sat turning slowly in its cradle behind him, almost as if it rode his shoulder.

"Our mission," said the priest, "is the Jewel. Would you put down the Gate so we can approach?"

The Vaelinar tilted his head slightly. He waved a hand through the air. "Even with the Gate down, you can't cross the chasm from here. The only way to get truly close to the Jewel is to climb the cliff."

The priest's hand shook violently. He stilled it by grabbing onto his saddle, startling his rough-maned horse as he did so. "It . . . it has become known to us that the Shield is blocking us from our Gods, that it stills their

Voices so that we cannot hear them and we implore you, to drop that barrier."

"What are you babbling about?" The thin veil of weary humor about Istlanthir dropped immediately. He took a step back as if to widen his view of all of them. Garner saw shrewdness spark in his eyes.

"It is a wish, a plea, milord Istlanthir, for you to stop the Jewel in its Way, so that we may hear our Gods, as is our right and hope."

Garner watched the priest as he literally shook in his stirrups, but the man would not give ground.

"This Way, this gem, has protected Hawthorne and the bay for centuries. The entire coast for all of that time. And you wish me to topple it from its cradle?"

"Yes, milord, you have the right of it."

Istlanthir shook his head slowly. "Turn back on the trail and ride down the way you came. Your faces will be forgotten as soon as you leave."

Garner wondered if his face could be seen through the shadow of the hood pulled around it. Surely not. The guard riding next to him shifted in his saddle slightly, as if he pondered the same.

The priest sucked in a great breath. "It is you who should leave. All of you who exploded into our lands and never left, and take the bounty of it by force, and have no right to rule it or us. You who should worry if I will remember your face when I count those misdeeds done against me and my people and my followers. You who should fear to be standing here on this cliff at this time!"

"Old man." Istlanthir had his hands on his cross-strapped sword hilts but had not drawn them. "I commend your loyalty to your worship and worshipers. If you worry about the Shield, petition the next Council two years hence, and gather your evidence to present then. There is no truth to your fears, but I invite you to investigate them until the hair falls from your head and the teeth from your mouth. In the meantime, the Jewel will stand and do what it was created to do, and that is to protect both of us and thousands more."

"Lies, and you hide behind them."

"I have no reason to lie to you, Priest, but neither do I have any great reason to give you further regard. Turn around and ride back the way you came."

"Not as long as the Jewel stands!" With that, the priest threw back his robe and sprang from his horse, pulling his knobby wooden staff from its saddle strap.

Garner and his fellows bailed as well, springing apart, and freeing themselves from their robes, swords and staves filling their hands. The Istlanthir whipped about, his hands blurs of motion and the man next to Garner fell, two daggers protruding from his chest, as he coughed and cried out in a pink froth. Garner brought his horse down in front of him as a barrier and unfastened the bolo from his belt. The Istlanthir whirled about and took another man down before stepping back, not winded or dismayed, and called out, "It is not too late to leave, Priest."

Quendius dropped his robe and drew his bow off his shoulder, and nocked an arrow to it. "I think it is."

They stood facing one another over the heads and shoulders of the Kernans and others, Bregan Oxfort on one knee, his head cleared of the hood but motionless inside his borrowed robes, watching both of them.

"You're a fool. Even with the Gate down, you can't cross the final chasm to the Jewel. The only way is to climb from the seaside. It's the final defense. Even my brother has to climb."

"And fall," Quendius remarked.

Istlanthir's skin paled to a ghostly white. He gripped a sword as he would a spear. "You will have to go through me to get to the Jewel."

"Oh, I'm well prepared to do that." Quendius smiled, and let the arrow fly.

Time slowed. Garner could only watch as the arrow

arced across the distance, centered on Istlanthir who heeled in and threw his sword, shoulder muscles rippling. The two weapons passed one another, the arrow far nearer its target than the sword which would fall short of Quendius. Garner let loose his bolo.

The arrow struck Istlanthir in the chest, driving him back, drilling through him as his voice cried out, but he did not fall. He put his hands to the arrow, but it did not thunk home in his flesh. It went through him, like an animal eating through the sweet meats of its fallen prey, and when the arrow came clear of his body, it flew onward. Garner's bolo twisted across the span and tangled about the sword, bringing it clattering down just short of Bregan Oxfort's throat. Istlanthir faltered and went to his knees. Turned, his chest destroyed and gaping, and watched the arrow fly onward. It gained speed, blood and gore dripping from its shaft and arrowhead which sparkled like a smaller ruby eye of the main Jewel ... a splinter going home ... and it hit.

The Jewel shattered. The cradle let out a groan of metal and shards and ground to a halt, covered in ruby dust and debris. The arrow lay in its midst, head glittering. Then it rose and returned to the outstretched hand of Quendius.

That was when time caught up. Istlanthir toppled with a groan, and his body shimmered, then danced and twitched upon the ground and his flesh began to grow translucent before rending from his bones and he not yet dead but certainly dying. He let out a last, heartbreaking scream. Bregan staggered to his feet. Quendius caught him by the collar.

"Behold the Returning of a Vaelinar where two worlds fight for his dying soul and his dying flesh."

Garner's breakfast rose bitter in his throat to choke him. He spewed it out about the ground as what had been a man, a brave and fighting man, disintegrated into ribbons of bloody flesh and broken bone, even the weapons and clothing upon him torn to such a degree that nothing remained recognizable. Kites coasting on the sea winds dipped down with strident cries to the kill and began to fight over it, squawking and flapping at one another. No one who hadn't seen it could tell who died there. The priest made an incoherent choking noise in his throat. Quendius clapped him on the shoulder.

"Brace yourself, old man. The Gods will come calling soon." He pointed out to the sea, where small sparkles on the waves bobbed up and down, drawing ever nearer and Garner gulped a sour swallow downward as he saw what Quendius revealed. Sea craft, coming in on the tide, an armada. "My army will bring the Gods back to you, I vow. Never will you pray so hard." He laughed as he threw himself back on his horse and left them to their small destinies on the cliff.

Chapter
Thirty-Eight

SEVRYN FOUND TRANTA Istlanthir in the far pasture working one of the ild Fallyn tashya horses as he rode down into Andredia's river valley. The two made quite a pair as the wind whipped about them, and the horse cantered so close to Tranta who lunged at him on foot that his mane and tail whipped about the man, veiling him from sight in a swirl of flaxen hair. It would be difficult to judge which of them was the most colorful: the horse with the gold-dappled chestnut hide and flaxen hair or the Vaelinar lord with his dark blue hair and clothes of green and sea blue and gold. Neither, Sevryn mused, would be difficult to pick out of a crowd. He watched Tranta pivot smoothly as the horse cantered round and round him, seeing that his friend moved as easily in his gait as the tashya. After his fall from the high sea cliffs of Tomarq, that had been in doubt. But, as tales told, the Vaelinars healed well. What should have been fatal and had, indeed, nearly killed him was now only a memory in his scars and aching bones.

As, nearly, his own wound was puckering down to be, although his healing skills were more attributable to the ability of the queen's healers. He could not begrudge the full-blooded the advantage he didn't hold. If it weren't for that, Jeredon might never have a chance to heal and walk again, and that seemed to still be a distinct possibility in his case. He could not see Jeredon restrained to a cart the rest of his undoubtedly long life. Although Tressandre might have gotten him to his feet for now, who knew what toll that was taking on the natural healing process? It was a risk Jeredon had eagerly accepted. Sevryn could not blame him, although he would not have suffered either hurt or healing at Tressandre's hands if he could help it. Not again.

Tranta saw him and waved a hand as Sevryn trotted downwind and past. He hoped the queen would be as welcoming. The information he had might soothe her as a balm, or ...

The border alarm cut across the shriek of the winter wind with its own screeching blast. Leaves shivered and fell from twisting branches. Aymaran tossed his head and danced to one side, his black-tipped ears flicking forward and back at the sound of the trumpeting. Sevryn urged him forward. Trumpets cut the air again, and Aymaran whinnied back in defiance. He looked back to Tranta and saw him falter, dropping the horse's long rein line and staggering back, one hand to his chest as if the alarm cut through to his very heart. He went to one knee with a strangled cry and then toppled onto his face.

Sevryn flung himself out of the saddle and vaulted the fence post as the horse in training did an awkward bucking jump over the body now in his pathway. Tranta lay with his back heaving as he fought for breath. He groaned as Sevryn took him in his arms and turned him over. A string of spittle hung from his lips as he gasped for air and his pale skin went gray but he lived and there wasn't, to Sevryn's questing fingers, a mark on him. Sevryn opened his winter vest to loosen his collar. He feared the worst. He had, once or twice, seen head injuries come back a year or two or even a handful of years later, bursting inside the head and felling an otherwise seemingly healthy man. He brushed his hand over Tranta's brow. "What is it?"

Tranta's breath rattled in his throat. Sevryn wiped his mouth and then hoisted Tranta to his feet. "Can you stand? Walk? Just to my horse."

Tranta's eyes rolled back in their sockets and then he blinked, trying to focus upon Sevryn's face. He fixed his gaze upon Sevryn as a drowning man hangs onto a rope. But he stayed on his feet.

Sevryn walked him, step by wavering step to the fence, found a gate, and fumbled it open while Tranta hung on a post by his elbows, swaying back and forth as if the merest gust of wind would bring him down again. Color rose over his skin, though, like the faintest of blushes while Sevryn brought his horse over.

"Can you manage a leg up?"

"Think . . . so." Tranta wiped his mouth with the back of his hand again, dazed, but he tracked the horse and latched his hands over the saddle's pommel. He went up like a sack of meal, but he stayed up while Sevryn mounted behind him and put one arm about his rib cage.

"What is it? What happened?"

Tranta coughed. "World," he husked. "Exploded. My brother . . ."

Fearing the worst, Sevryn closed his legs hard upon Aymaran's flanks and whistled him to the wind.

Chapter Thirty-Nine

"WHY DID YOU DO IT?"

"I saw the path of the sword. I knew it wouldn't bring down its intended target. It's no different than sighting a sapling and knowing which way it will grow." Garner answered Bregan reluctantly. He pulled apart a piece of bread from its crust, both still warm in his fingers, and stuffed it in his mouth. He'd moved aside from his fellow caravan guards to take his meal, watching the sea in its flood tide and pondering what he saw: a sight that dug down and bored its way into him where it stayed as a bloody fearsome thing. He wanted no company while he weighed his actions, but the trader had sought him out anyway. He shrugged as if he'd said enough. He didn't want to talk, and he hoped that the trader would catch the hint, but Bregan Oxfort merely sat and watched him, his eyebrows knitted low over his eyes. A scarred and muscle-bound Bolger nearby glanced over at them, before grimacing as if in distaste and looking away. Quendius kept watch on them, one way or another. Garner shifted as Bregan prodded him, uncaring that they were being observed. The Bolger got up with a bored yawn and moved away, leaving them alone.

"You joined to pay off gambling debts. If the sword had hit true, you would be freed of your obligation. The holder of your chits would be dead. But you swung your bolo and stopped it."

"There are many things I won't do to be free of a debt."

"A true Farbranch, then."

Garner's hands stilled in the act of cutting a sliver of meat from his rations. He'd been found out. Or rather, had been known about all along. Garner resumed cutting his meat before putting his knife aside. He let the juices sop into his bread without eating. "What are we discussing here, Master Oxfort?"

Bregan tapped the side of his leg brace with his fingertips. Garner observed and thought that might be a tell, a giveaway on his emotions. He'd have to watch for it when next he faced Bregan, if ever there would be such a time in the future. Sitting where he sat now, he could hardly imagine being in another time. Bregan continued, "Did you think that I would ever forget the face of a man who gambled across a table from me? Particularly one who usually won? Debts you may have, but I doubt they're from your gambling habits."

"I have obligations also," Bregan told him quietly. "And because of them, I made sure you were accepted as a recruit, because I desired to have the Hand of the Queen know what I might be up to. He would, if he wanted to, would he not, the lover of your sister? So what you have now is my gratitude, for one, and a problem we share, for the other." Oxfort drummed against his brace. "Whatever debt you claimed, a purse of twenty-five crowns is put to your name. My life is worth far more to me than that, but it's a fair reward, I think."

"More than fair." Garner watched the trader's face.

He might be rewarded, but he thought he was also being bought.

Bregan leaned forward, pitching his voice into a whisper, although it seemed unlikely any would hear the two of them, for he'd already had the area cleared when he crossed the ground to talk to Garner. "Our problem is that we saw a Vaelinar noble murdered."

"Scant little trace of that deed left." Garner did not think that sight would ever leave him, it would stay in his mind forever: a greasy, bloody smear and gobbets of unrecognizable flesh that drew the kites from the skies immediately to pick it over until nothing but a few scraps of cloth remained. Gods who warred over a death both body and soul. A coldness shivered down the back of his neck before slithering away.

"I know. I don't know what it is Quendius plans . . . still, I know what he does is scarcely for the good of my people. Get word to Sevryn what you witnessed. Tell him of the death of Lord Istlanthir. Kever, I think, the younger brother, although I can't be certain of that. You'll have set up a way to communicate to the Queen's Hand, I wager."

"We should have, if I am what you think I am."

"Yes. Well, I do make assumptions from time to time. Call it a good gamble." Bregan paused. "Sevryn's knowing is the only thing that may get the two of us out of here alive."

"As one of your guard, I'd hate to disappoint you." He paused. "I'll need a distraction."

Bregan smiled thinly. "I will be providing one, then." He reached out to shake Garner's hand.

Garner grasped his firm grip, and the trader left him to finish his dinner. And take care of other matters.

He mulled it over. The trader had waited till high tide. Therefore, the trader had weighed matters before talking with him before deciding the risk would be worth it. Oxfort wanted something done and Garner to be the doer of it. If he was caught, it would be on his head and his head alone. That would be a sure bet. Yet this was a thing he dared not to leave undone. He turned his head, catching the Bolger's eye yet again, but they both looked to the sea. Ships came in, dozens of them, small and agile, with the tide and wind behind them.

He finished up his dinner which, despite the juices soaked in and the tenderness of the roast meat, seemed to have gone dry and hard to swallow. He watched as other lads finished up, came over and clapped him on the shoulder, and asked him what Bregan's life was worth. He quipped, "A few crowns."

His fellow hoisted two bottles of applejack. "And a round of drinks, thanks t'Master Oxfort," at which they all cheered. He allowed as how he'd be right after joining them in a bit. The guard who'd been watching them lumbered to his feet and followed after, grumbling for a pull at the brandy.

Bregan Oxfort and he had much in common, as gambling men went.

He hoped so, as this would mean their lives and many others, for he feared Quendius and his army as he had never feared anything before.

Chapter Forty

LARA SAT QUIETLY, with Tranta's hand in hers, watching the rise and fall of his chest as he slept or . . . whatever it was his body did, to recover from what had befallen him. She could feel the chill in his fingers as he lay in what her healers diagnosed as profound shock. Something had struck at him through his soul, and his body still reeled from the blow. He would recover, she thought, if she had to find a gateway to his spirit. Even quiet like this, even after working with the horses, he still smelled faintly of the ocean. His hair lay across the sheets like waves of a warm and inviting seashore. Her other hand strayed to touch it gently. His strength had always been a quiet but steady force, unlike that of Bistane who had a temper which could flare like a battle's rage. Two strong men, one who courted her openly and the other who stayed silent, waiting patiently. Osten Drebukar had extolled Tranta's virtues for him as a proud uncle would brag of his nephew, and no wonder, for their houses were inextricably tied together. Losses faced her. She knew that. But she would lose no one in this way, if she could help it. Especially not Tranta.

She pressed both of her hands about the one she held as if she could will warmth and her strength into him. No response answered her. Lara bowed her head over their hands. An emotion ran through her, one she scarcely recognized, the realization that she could not afford to lose him, not for any reason. She knew that her life was not her own, that she had been and would always be used for bargaining, for alliances, for diplomacy. Yet there was something here that she had just discovered and didn't want to let go although she doubted she would ever be able to explore it. She wanted to. Her night with Daravan had given her two things: a temporary warmth and the knowledge that she no longer wanted to settle for temporary. Make that three: she also knew that Daravan did not hold a future for her. Did she resent what Sevryn and Rivergrace had? What Jeredon had held with Nutmeg and turned away from? Would it make her bitter to watch others moving toward a soulmate she knew she could never have? She would be forever wandering, one of the Suldarran, lost on Kerith. She had but one goal to accomplish in her lifetime and that was to bring her people back to Trevilara. Was it so close to her that she could see it truly in her visions with only Abayan Diort blocking her way? If she stepped past or over him, would she accomplish her goal and leave herself able to be fulfilled fully in all ways?

Hope and fear entwined themselves inseparably within her.

Tranta's fingers fluttered in her grip. Lifting her chin, she removed one of her hands from her hold on his and watched him. Expressions raced across his face and disappeared, like tides rising and ebbing so quickly she almost could not catch them, and then his breathing altered. He fought to rouse. She leaned closer, urging him silently in his battle to stay alive.

* * *

"We can't say what it is," Bistane told Sevryn. He leaned against the stairway railing, his keen blue eyes unrevealing. He did not have to say much because it was enough that he had come down to talk to Sevryn rather than Lara. The queen had few words for him, it seemed.

"The head injury?"

"The healers don't seem to think so, but whatever it was, it nearly killed him. He stays in shock. Fortunate for all of us you were there."

"I wasn't there for fortune's sake. When you see the queen, tell her I have intelligence for her." Sevryn turned abruptly and headed for the back stairs and the kitchen doors to wash at the racks outside and fill his lungs with fresh air that did not have the stink of disapproval in it.

A yard lad from the mews came running as soon as Sevryn stepped outside to the bite of air growing ever colder and drier. He puffed to a stop. "Milord, milord, one of your birds came in from Hawthorne way." A message pellet filled his hand and he dropped it into Sevryn's palm. "Urgent, we thought."

He flicked the lad a coin which the other caught as it flashed through the air. He twisted open the capsule and read, in cramped yet careful lettering signed with a G, "Shield & Kever destroyed by Q. Ships landing by Tomarq."

He read it again and yet a third time as if he could have misread or misinterpreted the message. He threw his head back as the wind howled down with a frigid blast to his face.

Tranta had been right. Their world had exploded.

He ran for the stairs. The queen would see him whether she wished it or not.

It was said that the silvery streaks in her blue-and-gold eyes had come from lightning. He believed it when he saw true fury flooding them as he faced her. It was the smoke and steel from her grandfather, the anger which could be wielded like a weapon if it could be honed, and her eyes narrowed as if she did that very thing. The main window of her apartments framed her, a stormy blue-and-green vista at her back. She had insisted on speaking with him there, rather than in Tranta's rooms. For that, he couldn't blame her. They would have raised voices and they did so now. Or spoken in tight words so that any warrior would hear the steel they held. Bistane had followed on his heels and the room seemed crowded with just the three of them.

"Give me leave to go after Quendius now."

One eyebrow rose. "This time you ask permission?"

Warmth flooded Sevryn. From the pit of his gut where Cerat resided to the hollow of his throat upward to dash upon his cheeks. For all he knew, the red heat settled at last in his eyes, glowing and demonic. He would hide it from her if he could, but he didn't need to. She turned away from him. Her maimed hand clenched and unclenched in the folds of her skirt. "If I have to kill every last standing Galdarkan, I will *not* leave our flanks and backs open for Quendius to savage. He will not feast on the leavings of our battlefield!"

"As for your offer," Bistane murmured, "how close do you think you can get if he heads an army of his own?"

"I received information from inside those same forces. I think I can get as close as I need." He closed his teeth on his own anger and felt it recede inside, a tide ebbing. "Before he closes on us, I should move."

"Gilgarran had reasons for leaving him in place. So, too, did Daravan. I argued with them. I saw . . ." She rubbed her forehead as if clearing away a cobweb. "No, Sevryn. I do not give you leave. We have a plan in place."

From that, he had deduced a trap whose springing depended on absolute surprise and so no one else had been privy to its formulation. He opened his mouth to protest when an alarm sounded, the border trumpets winding yet again and he went to the window to look out upon Larandaril as if he could see the trouble from there.

Perhaps he could. Or perhaps it was only meant for Lariel. He saw a shimmer upon the glass of this broad window, a view that seemed impossibly detailed and clear, the rolling hills of the far boundaries as close as the nearby groves. The view rippled and distorted even as he looked out and Lara brushed him aside, blocking him as she leaned upon the windowsill. The long-range view blurred for him. He had no idea such a thing had existed for Lara, for anyone.

But he'd already seen the trespassers as she viewed them now, and they both uttered in one voice, "Rivergrace."

Lara added flatly, "Get a detail."

"You'd think," Nutmeg said wearily, her brandy-colored eyes frowning, "that all this wind would bring clouds."

"And rain." Rivergrace shrugged into the hood of her cloak, tied snugly under her chin and yet it would be torn away every handful of minutes until she could tug it back into place.

"Definitely rain. If not snow 'n' ice." Her hat long ago eaten by river waters, she had only a small scarf wrapped about her hair and down over her ears for warmth. Her nose matched her cheeks in redness and Grace doubted the color came from her cheerfulness and bouncy attitude. "Something good out of this bitter blow." She wrinkled her nose at the sky as if she could intimidate it. Her pony broke into a stiff-legged trot as they crested a hill. "We have to be near," she added, her voice rising up and down with her pony's gait.

"We passed the border, that much I know. Didn't you feel it? Like a window drape that didn't want to be opened but finally gave way. And a prickling at the back of your neck as though something unfriendly is watching."

"I've had *that* since we left," declared Nutmeg. "If

we're that close, we should be in time for early supper." She bounced to a sudden halt as Grace pulled up her mount and her pony instinctively did the same.

"I don't think I want to ride in."

"What?" Nutmeg's head snapped around.

"I went to the library for help. What I found was ... entirely different." She could not meet her sister's eyes. "I found more questions than answers."

"Da would say that life never grows us a tree so tall we can't climb it, but I've decided he's likely wrong on that one." Nutmeg brushed a finger against one eye that had grown a bit misty. "You can't save someone from themselves, Grace. You can only be there to help them if they ask. You can help who you love if you want to, only I don't want to. I figured that out, sometime after I found myself buried up to my chin in scrolls and books."

"It sounds like you have the right of it. Still, I don't think I belong down there. Not now."

Nutmeg said quietly, "I need you. And Sevryn does, even if he won't tell you so. You give him the spine he needs to fight for you!"

Rivergrace shook her head slowly. It wasn't spine Sevryn needed. He was not afraid to fight for her. He was afraid that once he began to fight, he would not be able to stop himself until Cerat's bloodlust had been slaked, and who knew what bloodletting and souldrinking that would take? She knew that now. He was afraid of himself. She knew what that felt like. She took a breath chilled with indecision and then a sight met her eyes. "The choice has been made for me, it seems."

"What?"

"They're coming for us." Grace pointed downslope, where a body of horsemen rode toward them, and angling alongside, a single horseman charged, his chestnut mount moving like a flame licking up the hillside.

"Sevryn, that one'll be," Nutmeg observed. "Not on Aymaran, but I can tell by the way he sits a horse."

"Yes." Her heart did a funny little beat in her chest,

and she put her hand up, over the cloak, as if she could hold it steady by placing her palm over it. Would he be furious that she had left without telling him? And when she told him that she carried the blood of the enemy, what would he think? Was it possible he had known, deep inside himself, since those days when Cerat had swallowed his soul into the great sword? Buried inside the metal, had he known who had forged it and caged the Souldrinker into it, and how only one of his blood could even think to master and wield the blade? Had he known it and kept that from her, or perhaps sensed it deep within the threads of his soul so that when he was rewoven into life again, if she told him, it would be like plucking a cord and he would remember it? Would he hate her for it? Or had he, possibly, shielded her from the truth he'd learned?

And how would that affect the Demon he wrestled? Did Fyrvae tame Demons or only give them license to come into this world and wreak their havoc? Did she have it in her to help, or would she undermine what little control Sevryn had?

She could not even guess. She watched the riders stream out of the valley pasture, surging uphill toward them.

"Nutmeg—"

"No, by the blood of the trees and the stones of the stars, I will not be ridin' off and leaving you."

"You didn't let me finish."

"Wasn't intending to let you," Nutmeg said sternly. "We're family. If that's trouble, we're both in it. Only thing is, how can books cause this much fuss?"

"It all depends upon what's written in them." Rivergrace straightened her back and watched the horsemen draw clear.

Nutmeg muttered lowly, "This one must've been on how t' avoid taxes. They look awfully keen to greet us." She shoved her booted feet firmly into her stirrups.

Fresh air flowed over Tiforan's face. He inhaled deeply despite the cold biting into his lungs when he did. He did not like dark, closed-in places, but he had taken the pathways as he had been told to do, and now he was here beyond the borders of Larandaril. The leathery Bolger riding next to him flexed his shoulders, and jumped off his mount, checking the ground around them. "Tracks," he said. "Heat still in them."

How the beastman could feel anything through those heavily callused and scarred hands, Tiforan had no idea, but he nodded. He flicked his fingers at Lyat, his junior. "I want a note made. The borders of Larandaril are warded, that much is true. But the wards cannot tell one intrusion from another. We've crossed on the heels of another, and so we are through. An interesting flaw to remember."

Hastily, Lyat pulled instruments from his pack and made notes in his odd scribe notehand, to be more fully detailed later. Tiforan sat as the Bolger coursed about on foot, rather like a hound, taking in those who'd ridden before them. He went to one knee for a long time, then, silent except for a slight grunt every once in a while as if debating with himself, although what deep thoughts such a being could hold Tiforan could not imagine.

Other than the icy wind, winter seemed to have little grip on this lush valley as a dwindling sun gleamed over it fitfully as useless clouds veiled it now and again. Trees still held coppery and yellow leaves, though thinning, and the evergreens were almost blue in their vivid greenery. Grass blades still peppered the landscape everywhere, untouched by nighttime frost. A paradise, he thought, held by those who deserved nothing of it. Soon, it would be stripped from them, and he would aid in the doing of it. That gave him great satisfaction. Finally, the Bolger put his hand flat to the ground, and said, "Horses. Coming fast and hard. After othersss, I think."

"Are we in sight?"

The Bolger shook his head.

"We stay here then, in cover. No need to let them know we are here. Yet." Tiforan patted his horse's neck in satisfaction. The mount quieted under his touch. He could hear then, the dull thunder of horse hooves and the cracking of leaves and twigs snapping under them. They were close. Very close.

Sevryn reached them first, lying low over his horse's neck and lashing the reins as he raced uphill. The tashya responded, pulling out ahead of the others by many lengths, nostrils flared as he snorted to a plunging halt next to them. "Grace! Get out of here!"

She thought her heart failed her. "Don't do this—"

"Ride. As hard as you can." The lines of his face tightened as she searched it for any sign of hope. Anything.

Had he given her up to his queen? Fear rose in her chest. "What did you tell them?"

"Ride. *Now.*"

That was not an answer she could accept. She put her hand out. He grasped hers tightly and she felt a thrill run through her, an energy from himself to her, filled with love and desperation. It drove the one fear out of her, replacing it with another. He turned to Meg.

"Nutmeg, take her and run. Don't turn back, for anything. Find a haven. Send for Tolby."

She found her breath again. Something wrong yes, but not between them. Not now, not yet. "What's wrong?"

"Hold!" Lariel's voice cut through his answer like a sharpened sword. Guards on horseback, led by Lara and Bistane, wheeled around them in flashes of mane and tail and flying hooves. "Take them. I want them both under arrest until the one known as Rivergrace can be tried as a traitor."

Tension leaped through their handclasp. Grace saw

Sevryn flex his free wrist as a red spark lit his eyes. She threw her appeal to Bistane whose horse jostled flank to flank with Sevryn's chestnut mount. "Don't let him fight!" she pled. "Don't let him do this."

Bistane swiftly drew his dagger, reversed it, and struck before Sevryn could land a blow of his own. Only his dagger hilt hit Sevryn hard just behind the ear, and he fell from his horse, his hand torn from her hold.

Rivergrace ripped her gaze from his limp form and found the queen's eyes fixed upon her.

"Traitor," repeated Lariel.

Chapter
Forty-One

RUFUS LET OUT A LOW GROWL. Much as Tifo-ran hated touching him, even with riding gloves, he did so. The shoulder he grabbed bunched tightly. "Leave them. We're close but not close enough." He watched the horsemen wheel about. Someone dismounted long enough to sling the fallen body over his mount. He knew only two by sight: Bistane Vantane whose hawklike pro-file was a copy of his warlord father's, and the Warrior Queen Lariel who looked better than the miniature painting he'd been shown. He let go of the Bolger in distaste. "Bring us down behind them. I don't want to be seen. We'll make shelter for the night."

Rufus grunted then, in acknowledgment. He got to his feet with a heavy shrug.

Tiforan had no doubt his mission would be successful because he willed it so. Still, there were intrigues inside the idyllic borders of Larandaril. He would have to re-member all that he saw and surmised when he reported

to Diort. Lariel's reign seemed far more troubled than
they had known.

"It would be a grave mistake," Lara said softly, "to have
me question your loyalties now."

"Then do not do it." Sevryn stood, a trifle wobbly on
his feet, but he stood. A small trickle of blood down the
side of his neck had dried. Bistane flanked him in case
he needed to be held up ... or restrained.

"I'd be a fool if I didn't understand a little about love."
She opened her hand, exposing two folded letters in it.
"Drebukar and one of our traders have both sent word
about the Shield of Tomarq. The Jewel is destroyed,
and Kever missing. There are signs of a struggle." That
same hand cut the air as Sevryn opened his mouth to
interrupt. "I choose to believe your informant about the
loss of Kever. Not only because you've always obtained
good intelligence for us, but also because of Tranta's reaction. The Istlanthir have always had a very close bond.
It's part of their family's trait, as inbred in them as hair
the color of the sea." Her fingers rubbed the letters. "But
don't mistake my understanding for anything other than
it is. I am debating having you put in the same cellar to
await court-martial. There is no doubt you have shown
true colors the years you have served me, but ..." She
raised her eyes. "And I want you to listen carefully. Because of our long lives, we have long memories. Memories of friendship and betrayal, of hatred as well as love.
I know that plans for vengeance can be decades in the
making and even centuries in being carried out. It is not
beyond reason to think you could be a pawn."

Sevryn got out a sound before Lara's gesture stifled
him once again, but she said to Bistane, "Gag him if necessary. He *will* hear me out."

Bistane gave a short bow.

She put her shoulders back. "If anyone put you into motion, it was Gilgarran. I trusted his advice when he would give it to me, but there was much he left unsaid. Whether he trusted in me, I'll never know, or whether he thought to let me go my own way and make my own mistakes. He whispered in my ear, when they made me Warrior Queen, that he would mark my steps. I can't think of any harm he'd want to bring to the Anderieons, but he was vain in his wisdom. He often thought no one knew better than he did, and he could be impetuous in his decisions. It's possible that someone directed him even though Gilgarran had no idea of it. And through him, you." Lara leveled her gaze on Sevryn who made no move other than to allow the side of his mouth to twitch. "If he guessed he was being used, he let no one know of his suspicions, not even you."

To that, she seemed to expect a response, for she waited silently, with one eyebrow raised. He let the silence linger a little longer before answering, "No, Highness, he did not. Although Quendius ... Quendius is a man Gilgarran let live. We could have had him once or twice, and he let the opportunity slip. I always thought that, although Quendius is undoubtedly an enemy we need to bring down, Gilgarran thought someone stood behind him. Someone that he would let Quendius lead him to, eventually. He might have been wrong."

"Error or deliberate decision, it cost him his life. I suggest you defer from following that example. You will not see Rivergrace tonight, I forbid that, but I've no doubt you will come to her defense tomorrow. She is set for court-martial."

Sevryn swayed a little in spite of his rigid stance. Bistane put a hand on his elbow. "On what charges?"

"Two, of high treason. You'll know more tomorrow. Don't give me reason to jail you with her tonight, Sevryn, for at the moment you seem to be her only defense."

"Osten is dead and Bistel is gone. How can you think to put anyone on trial?"

"Bistane stands in his father's stead, and although I would rather be mourning both Osten and Kever, betrayal gives me no choice but to hold a trial." She jerked her head at Bistane. "See that he makes it to his quarters." She turned her back on them both.

Hand still on Sevryn's elbow, Bistane led him gently away.

The tiny nub of candle left to them had burned out and the old cellar, empty of everything but dust and old barrels and themselves, had gone nearly pitch-black. They had each upended a seat before the taper had pooled into nothing but a small bit of melted wax, and Rivergrace sat with her back to an empty wine rack. Something scuttled past their boot toes in the dark.

"I wonder if they're trying to put a scare into us and they'll be coming to get us later."

"I wonder where Sevryn is," shot back Nutmeg. "I thought he'd tear the place down to get you."

She might have thought so, too, but now she worried only that Bistane had hit him too hard. She would not have thought anything could keep him from freeing them. She did not have an answer for Meg.

That thing, little beastie or whatever it was, scampered past their feet again. Grace thought of lifting her legs and curling up on the barrel top, but Nutmeg merely growled at it. Her voice sounded precociously fierce in their cell.

"What do you think the queen meant by traitor?"

"I'm not sure."

"Oh."

Rivergrace tucked her hair behind her ear, felt its pointed curve, so different from her sister's. "It may be something I know or something I am."

"Tell me."

"I don't want to . . . I don't want you to look at me as if I were a monster."

"Grace, if you had two left feet and your head on backward, you'd still be the sister I pulled out of the river! My sister, brought to me! The sister I always wanted, and the one I'll always love, no matter what." This time, her voice sounded indisputably fierce and firm.

"I think I'd better tell you, then." And, in a darkness so dense and heavy that she could not see anything at all, let alone Nutmeg's face, Rivergrace told her haltingly of what she had learned. The story felt as if it took forever to spin out. Then, she waited for Nutmeg's reaction. The silence seemed endless.

"Well," said Nutmeg slowly. "Is that all?"

"It would be enough, don't you think?"

"I think you don't remember our orchards very well. If you graft a tree, it bears the fruit of th' graft. It doesn't suddenly sprout weeds or hairs from a boar's chin, or even the fruit of the stump which first nurtured the graft. And you, Rivergrace, as I keep telling you and whose thick head is even more proof, are grafted onto the Farbranch family! If the queen had half a wit left after worrying about this war of hers, she'd see that, too." Nutmeg made a huffy sound. Then, much more quietly, she said in a worried note, "I don't think they've remembered to bring us dinner, have they?"

Chapter
Forty-Two

MORNING CREPT IN SLUGGISHLY. An icy mist hung drearily over the plains that promised no rain and yet no sun either. Bistel walked through his troops, rousing various commanders and leaving instructions with those who had water Talent to keep the mist cloaking them as long as they could. As he strode by the various campfires which had been banked to little more than glowing coals, he could hear the start of drums. Jeredon rose as he paused, getting to his feet and starting after Bistel with an awkward, scissor-legged gait. He finally gave up and let Tressandre levitate him across the uneven ground as he followed in the other man's wake. He looked alert, but Tressandre's smoke-green eyes stayed heavy with sleep, her dark honey-colored hair tumbled about her shoulders as though she had not had time to comb or tie it back before hurrying after Jeredon.

Bistel let Jeredon draw even with him. "Why the drums?"

"Because," Bistel answered him, "it is a reminder that

he is primitive, compared to us, and we are alien compared to him. Also, in this fog, it's his best way of getting his troops into position. He is warning us that he will attack today."

"That'll be a relief, then, after days of staring down his gullet."

"What do you expect from him?" Bistel fixed his gaze on Jeredon, his shock-white hair mirroring the heavy fog about them.

"I rather think this will be a test sortee. He's not fought us. He'll want to draw us out as much as he can, see what our strengths and weaknesses are."

Bistel nodded his agreement to Jeredon. "I think so, as well. Still, dead is dead, for those who fight poorly today."

"I'll have to tell our troops to fight poorly as little as possible." In his shadow, Tressandre's mouth curved in an ironic smile in response to Jeredon's remark.

"You do that. Rouse everyone, but do so quietly. Diort may choose thunder to announce his presence, but I rather like the stealth of the mist."

"Yes, sir," Jeredon responded. Putting his hand on Tressandre's ready forearm, he turned in his glide and made his way to the commanders who still slept in the cold and forbidding morning. Only a few had been awakened by their passage, but more began to stir to the drumming, shaking awake their companions and getting quickly to their feet. He and Tressandre wove among them, speaking softly and steadily, putting them on alert without alarm. They were seasoned although none had been involved in a conflict like this. They reached for their gear, which had been repaired, honed, and oiled, all in readiness as mounts on the horse lines lifted their heads and whickered inquiringly, pricked ears flicking back and forth. Collared dogs shook themselves awake, spikes rattling. Vantanes in their jesses lifted their leather-hooded heads high alertly, knowing the time when they would be loosed to the skies must be near.

"Your troops," began Jeredon, but Tressandre cut him off with a shake of her unbound hair.

"Alton will tend to them. My place is at your side."

"I won't drain your strength for my vanity, Tress. I'll be using my cart when Bistel orders us off."

"Till then, is it not easier on you to do this?" And she gestured, indicating his glide by her side.

"Magic makes many things possible, but not all are easy or wise."

Tressandre laughed. "Jeredon, you sound like a stodgy old librarian! You must have had Azel for a teacher."

He rarely heard Tressandre laugh, but he reflected that he preferred the sound of Nutmeg laughing, fresh, happy, and open without artifice or without the meanness of someone laughing at him rather than with him, even when he knew well she laughed at him. He gave a rueful smile, instead of letting the emotion he felt, that of missing Nutmeg, show on his face. After weaving their way through the camps, they returned to the hillock that Bistel had designated as his post. It held higher ground, for observation, though it was highly unlikely the warlord would spend much time there. He preferred to be among the fighters himself, where he could gauge the tempo of the battle and the strength of the weapons as well as the men using them, and test the strategy of those he faced. Other commanders joined Jeredon and Tressandre as he got his cart. Alton brushed his sister's cheekbone with a light kiss of greeting and her eyes flashed in surly discontent as he did. The others came far more quietly, some with banners in their hands, from times beyond which any of them remembered, for the beginning of the Vaelinars lay before they had been lost. The names and symbols on those replicated banners had but one meaning: home and honor.

And then the waiting began.

The drums stopped. Bistel lifted his head and faced into the slight wind that hung over the river plains as if scenting it like a hound. He lifted a hand.

"Tressandre, Alton!"

They swung about, faces alert.

"The wind has shifted. The fog is lifting unless we expend a great deal of energy to hold it, but we won't. Diort knows that as well. He'll be attacking. I want three of your best archers, with ild Fallyn Talent, up on that ridge to knock down whatever scouts he will send high. I don't want anyone overlooking the battlefield but us. Understand? As for your other fighters on the ground, tell them to hit and hit hard but not to expend themselves or their ammunition. He's testing us. We'll show him we're tough but just not how tough. Not yet. Don't give way, but hold your own. Understood?"

"Why not just take them out today? Why wait?" Alton's stormy green eyes fixed on Bistel's face.

"Because we're not strong enough. Not yet. We're strong enough to meet him and bow his back, but not to plow him under. We need the Warrior Queen and her contingent to do that . . . and perhaps even then it is not wise to grind him into the dust. I don't want him taken out, do the two of you understand? Even if you can. I won't make a martyr and rallying flag out of him for generations of nomadic blood feuds."

Tressandre's lip curled. "If we grind them into dust, no one will remember him."

"Someone always remembers. Always. Are my orders understood?" Bistel stared Alton in the face until the young man had to look away, ducking his chin. "As ordered, Warlord Vantane."

Tressandre said nothing but turned about with a toss of her head. She looked back over her shoulder. "What if Diort himself goes up to scout?"

"He won't. He doesn't know, yet, that his life is not forfeit. But if he perceives it and goes up on the ridge, then he'll know that we've dammed the Revela and certain of our plans will have to be changed."

"He is still to be held inviolate."

"He is untouchable."

She licked her lips. "Would Osten Drebukar have planned it so?"

"That we cannot know. I will tell you this, Tressandre. If I have to spend as much time fighting the Stronghold ild Fallyn as I do the enemy, I'll relieve you of your command and turn your fighters over to someone else. Is that clear?"

"As you command. One only wonders, Warlord." She nodded to Alton and strode off with him to set up their archers as directed.

Bistel sat down on a dew-covered hillock. Below the slight rise, he could see the blankets of fighters forming into a front. They would clash inevitably. He didn't know what Osten Drebukar would have done, although he had a good guess, having sat at the table and done a good deal of planning with him and Lariel. But in moments like this, strategy had to be flexible and responsive. He could not know who would hold and who would break until it happened. Osten might well have gone into this attempting to shatter the Galdarkans from the very first skirmish. He might have been that aggressive, knowing that Lara's intention was to put down Diort and any thought he might have of progressing his actions into the west. Of making sure that Diort would have to bow to her and whatever alliance she proposed.

But then Osten might not have. He certainly hadn't pursued Quendius with any vigor over the years, although there was at least one time or two when that weaponsmith could have been squashed like an ugly bug. Perhaps he had never felt that Quendius needed to be dealt with. Or, perhaps, like many of the older ones, he had muttered to himself, "Sooty skin, the color of kings." Quendius had come out of nowhere, like all of them, but his roots might have run deep in the old homeland. They were Suldarran, lost, so who could know except the old superstitions, the old muttered tales less than half remembered? As for that, who could know now what stayed Osten's hand? Bistel only knew what he would do against Diort and as he had tried, more than once, to do against Quendius.

Bistel spat to one side as if clearing his mouth of a bad taste. He stood, and motioned to a young Vaelinar waiting quietly at his right hand, a Vaelinar who did not hold the surname of Vantane but who certainly echoed Bistel's and Bistane's features. "Get my horse. Pass the word down. When the drums start again, they will strike, and strike hard."

He had scarcely mounted when the rhythmic beating began again. He stood in his saddle. "Signal Jeredon to bring his men up and attack the right flank." Another lad took to his heels as though scalded. Bistel watched him run to the flagmen and the signal went up. He stayed standing a moment longer, to assess the sea of moving men and women downwind and slightly below him. For a moment he thought of a field of wheat, still green and growing, shifting and swaying in a slight wind as every shoot searched for the sun. Fleetingly he saw himself as a harvester of men, saddened that he would be cutting them down before their prime, their ripeness. He too, might well be cut down, by the battle plans of an uncertain Warrior Queen, although he could scarcely say that he was not ripe for it. His shock of white hair would give that the lie. He took up the helm hanging off his saddle by its strap, shook it out, and put it on. The moment passed as he knew it had to.

As he rode down to his company, he saw the sky fill with arrows and could hear the dull thunder of Diort's shield men putting up their wall. Arrowheads hit covers with a rattling like hail and before quiet could fall and the shield men could see around their protection, Bistel brought his cavalrymen in to flank them, and the fighting started in earnest.

Horses cried shrilly and war dogs barked and snarled and howled, all dimmed and barely heard over the clash of sword, shield, pike, and mace. He fought with sword, and a dagger in his off-hand, forgoing a shield on his arm, using only the plated protection on his leg armor, with chain-link beneath, lined with raw spidersilk under that which even arrowheads could not penetrate well. Two Galdarkans toppled from the stony ridge where ild Fallyn pushed arrows found them. No one else dared to make the climb, and so Diort fought a little more blind than he would have liked. The response of his companies showed caution.

Bistel spearheaded his own offenses. He swung till both forearms and shoulders ached and blood smeared his mail from head to toe and his horse wore a coat of lather and blood spray, though none of it his. He cut his way steadily through the Galdarkan line, sectioning off a portion of it, footmen abandoned by their brethren. On any other day, he would have signaled that putting down their arms sufficed but on this day, he did not. There would be no winners on this day, but he wished to leave an impression in Diort's mind. This was not an exercise. If he entered into war against the Vaelinars, he would pay, and pay dearly.

Bistel would leave no illusions behind him.

Across the dry ground now muddying with spilled blood and sweat, he looked up with a swing as a cavalryman and his mount fell away from him, and saw Diort only a charge away. Their eyes met. The ground between them lay bare, though littered with wood splinters and broken bodies and fallen banners.

Bistel lifted his reins and shifted to touch his boots to his horse's flank.

The ild Fallyn could not have Diort. But he himself was another matter. Taking the Galdarkan alive might solve much.

In one smooth move, as Bistel's horse dug in his hooves and lunged forward, Abayan Diort dropped his sword and drew the great war hammer at his back. He threw himself off his horse and swung it at the ground, slamming it upon the rapidly disappearing distance between them.

A thunderclap sounded, and *rakka* murmured low in its wake, as the earth split and the ground shivered. Stone shattered. Dust and gravel flew as an abyss opened. Bistel's horse came to a sliding stop on his hindquarters. They halted at the edge of the crevice. He could have forced the horse into a jump as his mount regained its balance, but he decided against it. They faced each other again, he and Diort, over the yawning gap. Bistel put a finger to the brow of his helm and saluted, before spinning his mount around and spurring him back the way he had come, out of archer range and regrouping the attack on the rear flank.

Message sent, and delivered, on both sides. No quarter would be asked or given.

Chapter
Forty-Three

TRANTA WOKE AT MORNING'S THIN, REEDY LIGHT. The ghostly cast of winter through the windows of the sickroom added to his pallor. But wake he did, and his stirring woke Lara sitting at his side. He blinked as if he could not quite focus. She laid the back of her hand on his forehead. He reached up and held it there briefly.

"You're back."

"I felt called." He turned his head slightly and winced as he did so.

"We need you. Can you tell me what happened?"

"The world shattered. Now you tell me." He licked cracked lips and his voice sounded thin, no stronger than fog along the sea.

She didn't want to tell him. She fussed with her dress, which had wrinkled during the night's vigil, before turning even as she turned her eyes away. "Sevryn . . ." Her words failed her.

Tranta raised himself on his elbow. He flinched and

cradled his head as if it had been cracked. "Not Sevryn. I saw him when I fell."

Lara cleared her throat. "He received a message after you were struck unconscious. Tranta. The Jewel of Tomarq is no more."

He grabbed her shoulder with a hand that bit into her flesh but she made no sound. "My brother?"

"Died defending it. But we ... we have no body. We can't be certain."

His fingers gripped her harder. "No." He let go of her suddenly as he fell back onto the bed cushions. "I couldn't have felt it."

She looked upon him. "We both know better. You felt something, and the force of it nearly killed you."

He put both of his hands to his head as if he could hold himself together. "Falling," he whispered hoarsely. "I'm falling!"

She put her hands over his. "Listen to me. You are here. You're more than the Jewel and separate from your brother. Hold on to me, and don't let go."

"I am tied to the Jewel. My brother ..."

"I know. I know. But you're also tied to me. I'm your Warrior Queen, Tranta, and I am," she gripped him harder, "I'm ordering you to obey and stay with me. The Jewel is only the eye of the Way your blood built there. It's blinded now, but it is not destroyed. Can't you feel it?"

"What I feel is," and she could feel him cold and shaking under her touch, "I feel myself falling again. Climbing the air uselessly. Hanging over the ocean forever, knowing that when I hit, I can't live through it again. Not a second time."

"You won't hit. And you're not falling. Hold onto me!"

"I failed in my trust." Tranta looked at her, his eyes the color now of a sea pounded by winter storm, dark blue and cold blue-gray, hopeless, under assault. "I saw the flaw. I never thought it would shatter."

"You've failed nothing, nor has Kever. Do you understand me? The Jewel was attacked. You've failed only if you give up."

He shuddered. He slid his hands out from under hers, slowly, and then grasped each in his own, and hung on for dear life. She could feel his existence fraying, threads breaking, as if he were the Way itself, the Shield of Tomarq, shredding to nothing but wisps of bright element to be lost forever. But she also found that the Way sensed her, sensed them both as if it were a living being, and it sought for wholeness through them. It would plunder them both if she let it, as a drowning man might drown his rescuer in panic, and she retreated from it carefully, leaving it only a bit of her energy upon which to cling. He felt it, too. Sweat dappled his face.

"It can be repaired," she told him. "It waits for you. Do you feel it?"

"I . . . can't."

"Not today. But time doesn't exist for it. And I promise you, we will find the means to weave it whole again. Just stay with me, stay with us, the Vaelinar, and you'll be whole again."

He took a deep breath. Then he kissed each of her hands. "I'll do whatever you ask of me."

"Then I ask you to rest a bit, and come help deliver judgment at a trial." Her smile went bittersweet. "I'll tell you more after you rest."

He closed his eyes and she didn't leave until his grasp of her went slack. Then she slipped away to become the queen she had to be for the task ahead.

"I think it's morning," Rivergrace said quietly.

By the sound of it, Nutmeg rolled to a sitting position. "How can you tell? Can you see anything? Hear anything?"

"Nothing but the growling of your stomach. Not that mine is any quieter." They had, indeed, been forgotten at dinnertime. Rivergrace tucked her riding skirt closer about her.

"If that thing skitters by me one more time," Nutmeg muttered darkly, "I'm eating it!"

"But you don't know what it is."

"I don't care. Serves it right."

Rivergrace reached out and touched her sister's sleeve, then found her hand and squeezed it tightly before letting go. Her sister felt warm to her own ice-cold hand. She opened her eyes to find herself still enveloped in the suffocating darkness, and she swallowed a bitter taste at the back of her mouth, trying to calm the near panicked thumping of her heart. She hated closed-in places where she could not see, the nearly forgotten memories of her childhood wrapping tight around her as if choking the air as well as the light away from her. No sound of dank and dripping water surrounded her, or endless trails of grit and stone and gravel, or the farther away rush of an underground river. It often stank with sludge from the mining operations and the forge, but it also ran clearly now and again and those were the times when her mother would take her to its banks to get drinking water and to bathe. The river could be seen, its waters eerily phosphorescent green on top of a deep, nearly black blueness as it ribboned away into rock-sharp canyons, cut under the mountain by hundreds of years of wear. The river was the only place in all the mines, caverns, and tunnels where she had not felt as if the mountain could crush her at any minute.

She took a deep breath. Nutmeg whispered, "Are you all right? I . . . I forgot how you hate this."

"I'm all right. Just . . . waiting." She leaned her head back against a cupboard or a wall, she couldn't be sure which although she knew it was wooden, and then she thought she heard something. "Meg."

"What?"

"I think I hear footsteps."

"Probably the cooks and maids getting food out to

the tables," said Nutmeg with just a touch of sulkiness to her voice.

The footfalls grew closer and heavier. Rivergrace got to her feet, trying to straighten out her riding skirts and dust herself off. "Soldiers," she and Nutmeg noted together.

The door opened abruptly for all that they knew it was going to, and Nutmeg jumped a little at Grace's elbow. They both squinted at the gray morning light as it flooded in, silhouetting bodies standing in the doorway.

"Have you come to execute us?" Nutmeg asked.

"Not yet, little one, but the morning has just begun." As a guardsman took Nutmeg and pulled her out of the room, Rivergrace followed, trying to see who had come for them. The guard she knew only well enough to nod at, but his stern face showed no warming.

"What have we done?"

None of them answered her, nor did they seem as if they would. Head down, thinking, she followed. If Sevryn, or anyone else, had revealed his suspicions of her parentage, would the queen have reacted this way? She did not know Lariel well enough to guess. But had she led them false in any way? She could not think. She knew she had to, to muster some sort of understanding and perhaps even a defense but her thoughts flew about in her head like a wild bird which had gotten itself caged. She thought of her beloved alna birds, fisher birds on the freshwater rivers, particularly her home river the Silverwing, and that thought gave her a moment of calm. She would not know what she faced until she faced it, and it would be useless to fear it until then. If only she could fly as free as one of her alna! Yet, she could think of nowhere she might go other than to Sevryn or back to Tolby and Lily. What kind of coward was she? She walked beside a man and guards who were readying for war, who had already suffered loss beyond imagining, and she had to think beyond herself. She had to protect Nutmeg, if she could, and still see the truth through because she must trust herself, if no one else. Fire and water fought within her. She felt as if she were a weapon being forged and tempered between the two elements.

Rivergrace put her head back and straightened her shoulders and lengthened her stride, so the others found themselves hurrying to keep up with her. The guards paused in the hallway as Tranta Istlanthir lifted a weary hand to stop them and they stood aside. Solemn lines marked his face and dark circles bruised his eyes. He looked as if it took great effort for him to stay on his feet.

"Tranta!" she said anyway, feeling some joy to see a friend. She looked behind him for Sevryn and, not seeing him, returned her gaze to Tranta.

"The queen forbid his coming," Istlanthir told her. "He is well enough, except for that bump Bistane gave him. You'll see him later."

"Thank you for telling me."

"There is little I can say. We aren't friends here, Rivergrace, under Lara's orders. There are grave matters to be decided and nothing more I can tell you than that. We're to take you out to use the conveniences, see that you are fed, and then you will be brought to trial."

"Thank the lucky stars for *that,*" Nutmeg exulted. She hurried past the guardsmen showing her the way through the crowded storage cellar up to the kitchen stairs. Rivergrace made to follow, but Tranta stopped her with one hand lightly on her shoulder. Nutmeg kept up a bright chatter, all the more she thought, so that she and Tranta could speak quietly without being overheard.

"I need to ask you something, though Her Highness was explicit I keep silent. But this I must do." The sunlight from a high window did not illuminate his face kindly, but rather sharpened the shadow and sadness upon it. He looked as if he had aged decades since the last time she'd seen him and, although she knew it could be like that for Vaelinar, he was too young to have it happen to him.

"I'll answer if I can. What is it?"

"What do you know of Kever?"

"Once, I would have said he is the more handsome of the Istlanthir brothers, but this doesn't seem like the time to joke."

"No." He shook his head slowly. "He is gone, missing from his post at the Jewel of Tomarq. Sevryn tells me his sources say that he is dead, but there is no body to know for sure."

"Oh, Tranta." She could understand now the sorrow that rippled through him. Rivergrace tripped, and it was only Tranta's hold that kept her steady. Her voice, though, she could not keep from quavering in her shock. "Gone? Did he fall from the cliff? If there's no body, Sevryn could be wrong, couldn't he? There's a chance, isn't there?"

"I trust Sevryn with my life. Do you?"

Without hesitation, she answered, "Yes."

Tranta wavered. He closed his eyes and then swallowed, a hard, tight noise. He opened his eyes to look down upon her. "Then I must trust him with my brother's death."

She said nothing more after searching his face and seeing the resolution there. He had given up hope for Kever, based on his trust in Sevryn and Sevryn's word. So much given up for something so ... frail. Yet she understood, because if her love had told her much the same thing, she would believe in him. Still, to give up another's life ...

Tranta removed his hand from her shoulder. "I can't say any more to you until the trial convenes, and even then, there may not be anything I can say. Do you understand what I'm telling you?"

She shook her head slowly as they trailed after Nutmeg and the guardsmen. "I don't understand any of this."

"You will soon enough." He rubbed his eyes, eyes the color of many seas and storms, wearily. "I have to warn you, the evidence is compelling."

"But of what? What have I done?"

"High treason," he said, then shut his mouth firmly. The muscles in his jaws moved, and she knew he would not say another word, as he had told her would happen.

Tiforan knelt behind the Bolger's crouching form, intent on the outbuildings in the heart of Larandaril. He had to admit that Rufus had brought them far closer, and more easily, than he would have deemed possible. It helped that much of the guard power of the estate was gone, mustered for the war, but it did not help that the troopers remaining behind seemed to be Queen Lariel's elite. He could only wonder why the queen had not yet left for battle and why she tarried, but it served his purpose to know that the prize Diort had sent him for remained at hand. He knew the troops had already skirmished. More than that, his warlord had not revealed to him. Diort would not send word of victory based on an initial testing of their forces; he was far too canny a soldier for that. As for the queen, Tiforan could only suppose that she had boats ready to ferry her up the Ashenbrook, the only weak spot he could see in the battlefield as described to him by his commander and the scouting maps. Such a maneuver might get her there within a handful of days. He would send word, as soon as he completed his mission and got clear of Larandaril, to warn Diort of the coming of the elite force. If they still moved after the chaos Tiforan planned to cause.

"What do you think?"

Rufus made a noise deep in his throat. "They gather," he rasped.

"I know they gather, they're readying to move out." Tiforan's impatience colored his words heavily.

Rufus turned his head slowly to look back at him over his shoulder. The Bolger jabbed a thumb at the second floor of the building. "They gather."

Tiforan narrowed his gaze and then saw the numbers of Vaelinars, barely visible through narrow, high windows, coming into what must be a room large enough to encompass much of that second floor's wing. "Why," he muttered, not expecting an answer and not getting one except for a shrug from Rufus.

"We go." Rufus got to his feet and began to shamble closer to the main manor, Lyat at his heels. Tiforan waited only a moment to weigh the dangers of such a movement before getting to his feet and following after. Rufus had shown an innate instinct for Larandaril as well as what Tiforan thought to be a knowledge of the valley kingdom. It could not be luck which made Diort assign the obstinate Bolger to his mission.

Nor did he think it was luck when the Bolger shouldered open a small, stubborn door near the laundry works, and led them inside. Webs hung down from the narrow corridor's ceiling, and the air smelled heavily of smoke and soap. It seemed to be a fire door, advisable for the many lit cauldrons of the laundry, and no one had used it for many a year, if ever, yet it opened when Rufus put his heavy-shouldered weight to it, and Tiforan found himself on the verge of acquiring the prize his king and warlord desired. The nearness of victory on a mission both he and Diort had deemed near impossible lay so close he could taste it. He moved into the bowels of the manor, close on the Bolger's heels.

Nutmeg was still dusting crumbs from a hasty sandwich off her cheeks and her clothing as the guards ushered the two of them into a vast room which Rivergrace had never been in before, although she knew it was a ballroom for gatherings the Warrior Queen had never held in the few seasons Grace had been by her side. Vaelinars lined it now, but not in the costumes of celebration. They wore their field gear, their leathers and silks and armor, and she could see the scars upon the leathers and the pounded-out and repaired dents on the breastplates and the helms they carried tucked under their arms, and the harnesses upon their torsos held weapons stowed. The armor glinted as a gray sunlight slanted through the narrow, arched panes of the windows, but they were not ceremonial and they showed the brunt of warfare.

Tranta rubbed his eyes, eyes the color of many seas and storms, wearily. Solemn expressions rode faces as those assembled turned to watch Rivergrace enter. Tranta left them, as he had warned her he would, and went to Lariel's side.

Grace could not decipher Lara's gaze as their eyes met across the room. This was not the friend who had defended her upon the mountain ridges as they rode to the font of the Andredia River, nor the woman who had worked a magic of her own and cut off a finger to do so, and not even the Warrior Queen whose life they had saved at the Midsummer Council. This was a ruler and one whose friendship could not be claimed by Rivergrace. An arm's length away stood Sevryn and Bistane. She could not mistake the look on Sevryn's face.

His lips moved slightly and she heard, clear across the wide room, his Voice sent to her and her alone by the talent he had honed: "Whatever happens, do not lie. I will be here for you, aderro."

Lara shot him a sharp look as if she could hear him, and his only response was to step backward, Bistane putting his chin up alertly.

The guards left them standing at the room's center. The wooden floor, richly waxed, creaked slightly as Nutmeg moved closer to her. She could feel heated indignation rolling off Nutmeg.

"As queen of the lands of the valley known as Larandaril, I hereby convene this trial and court-martial of the woman known as Rivergrace, held and placed under charges of high treason. The Dweller known as Nutmeg

Farbranch is of no consequence in these proceedings and should be removed." Lara began to lift a hand.

Nutmeg boiled over. "I won't be leaving my sister."

"You have no right to stay."

"I'm of no consequence! No consequence! Who are you, Lariel Anderieon to tell me I don't matter? No right? These lands were ours long before you came here, and they'll be ours again long after you leave. So if there's any authority in this room at all, it's mine!" She took a gulping breath before rushing on.

"If you think to try Rivergrace without me, then you'll need to go to the courts of the Gods themselves," declared Nutmeg, pulling herself to stand as tall as she could among those who towered over her. She flung her hand to gesture at them, light bursting from her finger-tips and showering down on the assembly in a curtain of sparks that danced and bounced upon the marble floor as they hit and fell into dimness. Her mouth gaped open a moment in surprise, then clapped shut.

Tranta bent close to Sevryn, his blue hair sweeping along his shoulder, veiling his mouth as he commented dryly, "Pardon the theatrics, but I deemed her words deserved them."

And Nutmeg crossed her arms over her chest, glaring at any who might take another step closer to her. Lara paused, her gaze sweeping over the assembly as if weighing their reaction, and then her mouth quirked slightly.

"Are you prepared to face whatever decision may be found and punishment dealt out?"

"She's my sister. That means share and share alike."

"So be it, then." She nodded toward the only person in the room sitting, papers and writing instrument at hand at a small desk behind her. "And so note it." She glanced at Tranta. "May it also be noted that the use of magic and Talents in this room is, for the duration of the trial, prohibited? This will be for the benefit of all."

Rivergrace felt a small lessening of tension drain from

her neck and shoulders as she heard Lara's proclamation and Nutmeg made a small sound of satisfaction.

"In addition, there will be no admissible statements allowed from any who are not full-blooded Vaelinar."

Sevryn's head jerked about. "What?"

"It is the rule of this court."

"Don't do this, Lariel. Don't cut me out."

She did not look at Sevryn though his eyes must have bored hotly into her. "These are not my rules, these are the rules of those who came before us, and knew what they did."

"This is not justice, then."

"Sometimes truth has little to do with justice. If you cannot hold your silence, you'll be removed. Bistane?"

A very long pause before Bistane answered reluctantly, "As you wish, Your Highness."

Lara waited a moment or two before saying, "The two main accusers are not present, but I have their sworn statements before me. The charges are high treason against the Vaelinars and the first accusation comes from Azel d'Stanthe of Ferstanthe. Following a visitation from Rivergrace to the library, he let it be known that the *Books of All Truth* have been corrupted with an unknown and deadly mold that has begun to destroy the works at an unprecedented rate. He and his apprentices are fighting the corruption with all at their disposal and have, as of this morning, finally attained some small degree of success. The damage done, however, to the Books diseased is incalculable."

"Although Lord Bistel was also a visitor to the library at this time, he left before Rivergrace. Azel has made a determination, according to the extent and speed of the corrupting agent, that Bistel could not have spread the mold. Upon seizing Rivergrace at the borders, guards removed from her wrist a bracelet which contains a key to the cabinets of the *Books of All Truth*, and the accusation falls upon her shoulders." Lara looked to the scribe to see if her words had been taken down. After a moment, the scribe nodded to her.

"The second accusation comes from Lord Daravan. He has reported to me that the Galdarkan warlord Abayan Diort was approached by an ambassador offering to negotiate terms of peace with an alliance by marriage. This negotiation was done in secret, the offer sent by Lady Rivergrace with herself as the bride price. Other terms of the contract remain unknown. The ambassador posed as Daravan himself, which was how he discovered the proposition. We can only surmise that this alliance would have included the overthrow of all that we know as Vaelinar." Lara paused as a ripple of sound ran around the room, but Rivergrace's gaze fixed on Sevryn and stayed there, as if she could read from his eyes what his thoughts might be. Chills ran down Grace's back as she heard the charges, things she had no idea had happened nor how they could have happened, yet she was supposed to have been the perpetrator of the deeds. How dare she hope to defend herself against that of which she was totally ignorant?

Nutmeg swayed against her briefly, their riding skirts brushing against each other.

Lara tilted her head slightly, her eyes dark and unreadable. "How do you plead, Rivergrace of the Farbranches?"

She took a deep breath. Feeling as if the River Goddess had grabbed her yet again to drag her down into chilly and unbreathable depths, she answered, "Guilty to the charge of having a key. It was given to me, and I used it, and if that is a crime, then I'm guilty of it. I had a need to search for information and the friend that passed me the key knew so and did it out of our friendship. I wouldn't harm the books if I could, but no, I did nothing to them, nor had Lord Bistel."

Bistane commented dryly, "Lord Bistel is not on trial here."

Her hand fluttered at her side for an instant. "No. I . . . I understand that." She tried to recapture her thoughts. "The second charge. I have but one man I wish to spend my life with, and that is Sevryn Dardanon. There is nothing I can add to that." Her mouth had grown dry and she had to lick her lips to say what she was going to say next.

Lara interrupted. "What proof do you offer?"

"Proof? None except all that I have said and done in my life. All of which you knew before those charges were brought to you, and you decided you believed them." Rivergrace's hand moved again, helplessly. "You move in centuries. I live in moments, moments given to me by my Dweller family and their teaching. They taught me that life is to be lived now, and suffered and triumphed now. I've been accused of not being wholly Vaelinar, and there is truth in that. I won't wait decade upon decade to live. As to the rest, I am not guilty with one exception. I went to the library in search of who I might really be. Part of the answer was given to me, and this may well be the treason you so dearly wish to hang upon me." She faltered a moment.

"I am the daughter of the man once known as Fyrvae, smith to Quendius, and who now exists as his hound, Narskap. He is a broken being, but I believe what he told me at Ferstanthe. He may be the one who poisoned the books, but I've no proof, and I won't accuse him of it. If I am guilty of my bloodline, then so be it." Her words fell into a deadly quiet.

A Drebukan, a son or nephew of the murdered Osten, cried out. "Murderer!" Steel filled his hand, and he lunged. Both Bistane and Sevryn reacted, and the open floor of the ballroom filled with surging bodies. Nutmeg took her arm and swirled her away from the fray, dragging her toward the open doors, but crossed swords blocked them. Lariel held one of them. Their eyes met across the gleaming steel.

"You will never go to Abayan Diort. Never. Not as long as I stand."

"This is madness," Sevryn yelled to her. He held the Drebukan at bay, swords crossed with daggers between them. "This is no trial but a vendetta, Lara. We have other enemies, close at hand, we should be striking at!"

"And she would bind them together, Narskap to Diort." Lara's hand knuckled whitely on her sword's hilt. The guard standing with her kept his hand steady, the sinews on his forearm standing out with the strain. His blade crossed hers, but it not only blocked the door—it blocked the blow she might have struck—and held her constrained. The two swords murmured together, steel singing briefly. "I will not be questioned."

"You must be," Bistane said, not unkindly. "Or else you would be the very tyrant you would oppose. Even your grandfather bent himself to be questioned."

"I know what I know, and what I have seen."

Loud words began to buffet them, and Rivergrace shrank back a little against Nutmeg, her ears ringing with the anger and strife of the many voices talking at once.

"Proof," grated out Tranta as the voices began to die down. "What proof? Upon my dead brother's soul, you've not shown us enough to convict Rivergrace."

"Proof?" Lara pulled her sword back and sheathed it, her movements slow and deliberate. Her mouth twisted to one side. "If I said I was Anderieon, would you doubt me?"

"Of course not. You are the heir of the Anderieons as certain as the sun rises in the sky."

"And if I tell you that I know who my enemies are, and why, would you doubt me?"

No one in the ballroom seemed to wish to answer her, although several shifted their weight uneasily, and the wood of the flooring creaked with their movement as if giving voice to their hesitation.

"In the interest of justice, we would all have to doubt you until evidence proved you right. How dare you forget that?" Bistane answered her with sorrow.

She ran her hand through her hair, brushing it back from her face. "I don't forget it. I weigh what I know with what I am given to see, every day. I put aside alliances, friendship, even love, to make that accounting." She looked over Rivergrace quickly, before turning away.

"Prophecy," said Sevryn quietly. Yet his voice carried over all the murmurs, all the conferrings, and Lara faced him.

"It is not reliable." One of the Drebukar spoke up, his face a whole and thin image of his kinsman Osten, his brow knotted in disapproval.

"It is reliable. When it occurs. When it can be deciphered. It's not a way to rule a people from day to day. Still, I know what I have seen." The cords in Lara's throat stood out as if her very throat tightened about her words, trying to stifle them, yet still she spoke.

Tranta made a gesture of disdain, turning away from her, his blue hair falling across his shoulders like a barrier. He faltered as if the life within his body were too heavy for him to carry.

"Do you want to know what I see, then? Do you?" Lara cried. She put her hands up and they shook. "I see a Way opening. I see our home beyond it, lost Trevilara, in all its splendor and beauty and wildness, calling for us, and it is he—he who stands between us and the Way home, Abayan Diort, with his war hammer in hand and there is no way on this or any other God-given earth that we can go home without going through him, and *he will not let us pass*! I know it is our home because it calls for me, for you, for all of us, and its beauty is like a cutting edge and like nothing that can be seen anywhere on Kerith. Its need for us is as sharp as our need for it, and the Way has opened. How can any of you wonder, then, why I am telling you to make war against Abayan Diort?"

"Trevilara!" cried Bistane.

"No longer the Suldarran."

Rivergrace could hear the longing. *No longer lost.* The need to be home, to have a home, was almost palpable in the room, but not in her. Nutmeg's fingers laced through hers as if instinctively knowing what Rivergrace felt.

A riot of questions broke out, probing, challenging, pleading, burying the queen.

Lara's shout cut across the commotion. "Silence!"

Instead of silence, the room fell into absolute darkness.

Chapter
Forty-Four

A VICIOUS YANK out of the abyss of darkness grabbed up Rivergrace. It tore her away from Nutmeg and propelled her, slamming her into a doorway and then into openness. The entire manor appeared to have been plunged into deepest night. No lamps had been lit for it was morning, and so nothing could be seen beyond the end of her nose. It was as though she were still locked up, awaiting trial, and she might awaken from the nightmare. But the rough hand on her arm bruised into her flesh, and she knew she would not. And she could tell that it was Lara who had her, for the hand only had three long digits and a thumb, not four.

"Who comes to rescue you?"

"A rescue? I thought we were being attacked again."

"Answer me!" Lara shook her lightly.

"No one that I know of, I swear."

Lara pushed and pulled her stumbling down the corridor. Raised in this manor, the Warrior Queen no doubt knew where she guided them, but Grace had no such memory and she tripped and staggered to the other's impatient tugs. Her knuckles skinned as they rapped against one rough wall, drawing her breath in with a hiss, but Lariel did not slow. They rattled down a back stair which Grace knew had to have been the servants' stair because of its narrow familiarity, and then into another hallway and light flared as Lara thrust a hand out to bring a wall lamp into flickering life.

"Grace, by my life, how could you do this to us?"

"I don't know. How would I know?" Rivergrace stammered in answer.

Lara stared into her face.

"You don't believe me."

She did not answer.

"How can you think this of me?"

"I think you could be misled. I've seen you with a sword in your hand—a sword that only one or two others could hold—so I know what you are capable of, when you need to be. With Narskap as a father . . ." Lara's words trailed off.

"He's not my father. Narskap is a broken thing that remembers only now and then what he was, what he did, what he might have been meant to do. My father is all but dead, and the only thing he holds for me is proof that I am Vaelinar. Not more and not less as many of you reckon me."

"Blood runs deeper than any river. You may find that you can't dismiss him as easily as that."

"Easy? It's not easy. He's all I have left of myself, and yet he is nothing of myself! How can that be easy?" Temper ate through her fear, and she shook off Lara's hand.

Lara moved as if to slap her, and Rivergrace moved as quickly, catching the other by the wrist and holding her. Surprise raced across Lariel's face. "You have strength you don't even know you have. I can't let you go as you are. I was blind not to have seen it, you for Sevryn and

he for you. He has been very guarded this past season.
Gods, how could I have missed it? You are both possessed. I fought the Demon-Gods of Kerith in the Secret
Wars, I thought never to see the like again. I can't leave
you like this, to be used as a weapon against yourself
and us. I will let you live, if I can." She twisted in Grace's
hold, turning about, slamming Rivergrace against the
wall and knocking the breath out of her. "Forgive me,"
she whispered as she leaned close and thrust her mind
into Grace's.

In a dizzying moment, Rivergrace lost the sense of
herself captive in a rough-hewn corridor, hemmed in
by inky darkness with only a small lamp illuminating
the two of them. She felt the rush of the wind against
her face, under her wings, and saw the treetops as they
dropped below her flight and she was free, but she was
not. She was Lara and a war falcon, she was a wisp of
cloud holding the merest promise of rain, and she was
winter with the sun trying to chisel away at her icy back,
and she was an abyss of memory which Lara began to
stir. She could feel herself falling through Lara's fingers,
slipping away, as the other made a noise of determination low in her throat.

She had been violated like this before when the Goddess had unwoven her life and soul down to nothingness
before reweaving her threads, but that had been done
with a ruthless gentleness and this . . . this was like being
chopped at. Uprooted. Having her heart pulled out of
her by a hand thrust down her throat. She struggled
and fought, gagged and spit. Then she felt the thread at
which Lara pulled.

It was that which made her Vaelinar, which gave her
eyes like seas and lakes, which gave her the power to
know water and fire and summon them, it was that which
was etched into every bit of her, and Lara's touch was
like a firebrand which sought to cauterize every morsel of her that held that power. She fought back as only

she could. Fire here, then she brought water to quench it. Burning embers there, then she brought up a cooling mist. Lara entwined their powers, seeking to yank Rivergrace's out, and she became as insubstantial as the dew, slipping out of Lara's hold.

"No!"

Did that cry erupt from her throat or Lara's? She could not tell. She could feel her body again, forehead to the wall, arm bent behind her, Lara's breath hot against her cheek. She would not give up herself. Not any part of her, not even that which she feared and hated. She could feel Lara draw in a deep breath and steel her body and knew that the next attack would either succeed . . . or kill her.

"Surrender, Grace. Give in. Or what you will become will destroy all you love on Kerith, your Dweller family, your Kernan friends, everyone. *Trust me. I know what the Demon-Gods are able to do.* Give in, and it will hurt as little as possible. . . ."

She would not give up that which she had fought so hard to win. Not her beloved family or Sevryn or even the friendship which Lara burned to ashes now. Not a moment of it. As much as the gift of the River Goddess had betrayed it, it was nothing like this, and she turned to it, made herself as the mist, the dew, the light rain that favors spring, the fog that blesses the sun-torched ground, the small puddles which nurture the smallest drinkers of the forests and plains, and Lara could not uproot her for she was everywhere, in a million droplets. In that moment, Lara was as she was, not the steel hand in a glove digging out her soul, but the freshness of sweet water, and she felt both her resolve and her regret, her love and her sorrow and the extreme loneliness that was the Warrior Queen's heritage. Rivergrace tasted her, and knew that her own taste lay open to Lara, if she would but drink.

And then, her cheek turned to grind against the

harshness of the wall's planking, and her eyes focused. She saw a gathering in the darkness that swallowed them both, a tall being coalesce out of the nothingness, hooded cloak and vast presence and it reached for her, tearing them apart, and Rivergrace felt herself being Taken.

Chapter
Forty-Five

WINTER CHURNED THE SEA waters to an icy gray, yet even that angry tide did not slow the landing of boats from the great ships anchored just outside the harbor, nor could fog entirely hide the troops as they made shore.

Bregan bumped a shoulder against Garner. "They cannot be men," the trader murmured.

Under any other circumstances, Garner would have wondered why the trader had made an ally, a confidant of him, but what they'd seen together had bonded them. And each realized that he needed a good fighter to guard his back. Two of them increased their odds of living through what lay ahead. He nodded his head. "No. They don't move like men."

"I'd hoped for smugglers. Pirates. Thieves."

"There are Ravers among them, the smaller ones wrapped in black cloth. I don't know the others."

Bregan shot him a look. "You know Ravers?"

"Fought them, a few times."

"And lived to tell about it."

Garner could see his worth had gone up in the trader's eyes. "For the moment, aye. But the big ones. They're the commandin' types, and I've not seen their likes anywhere."

"Nor I. We'll be marching in front of them, I've been told."

"But will we be leadin' them, or are we bait?" Garner's jaw tightened as he watched the troops assemble, black shapes moving indistinctly through freezing sea mists.

"We can only pray. I'm told the Gods are listening now. Let us hope so," Bregan answered dryly. "What happened to the boat that smashed on the rocks? Where are the dead?"

Garner reached out with a green stick to stir the coals at the very small fire he had warming their booted feet. He took a breath. "This may be the most efficient army ever assembled," he told Bregan. "There are no dead because the officers ate their foot soldiers where they fell."

"They what? They ate them?"

"Every last scrap, except for the armor and weapons. If you can call the carapaces armor. More like shells, licked clean."

"They eat their own," the other repeated, as if he could not quite comprehend that.

"They do."

The color drained from Bregan's face. "May the Gods have mercy on us."

"If They're listening, amen," Garner said. He got to his feet as a ripple of movement began, both in the mists where the unknown army gathered, and among the caravan guards. The muted noise of hundreds getting to their feet, the leather and armor moving, boots stamping with weapons clanking dully as they did, the sound of an army getting ready to mobilize, hung in the heavy air. It made the hair rise on the back of his neck. He had never thought to hear such a noise, let alone be immersed in it. He had grown things for most of his life, killing only out of necessity, and tipped his hand in gambling for fun and levity. He had no place in war. There were reasons to go to war. To protect the innocent. To defend yourself. To face that which only you could face, whether it be fear or bullying or hatred. But he had only one reason to be where he was now. He put his hand on Bregan Oxfort's forearm.

"This is not right."

Oxfort looked into his face, mouth thinning, saying nothing at first, and then, quietly, "Hawthorne has closed the Seven Sisters. The city is safe enough for now, but they're ready for a siege. Indications are that Quendius and this army will not hit them until . . . after. I have no love for the Vaelinars, everyone knows that, but I will not turn my people over to an enemy that eats their own."

"I will do whatever I can to stop them."

"And I. Watch your back, though, Farbranch, for I doubt many will stand with us. Fear is a powerful whip."

Garner nodded his understanding. Bregan moved away from him then, and his voice could be heard powerfully cutting through the noise of the caravan guards as they geared up. "Find your units. Stand ready!"

He could hear the command passed down, and feel the thinning sun try to beat down on his head. He pulled on an old hat, one he and his brother had made years ago, when they were plying their trade to earn extra money by selling goods to Mistress Greathouse. He had been young, only a lad then. Now he was a man. He doubted he would get much older. His chest burned at the thought, and something stung the corners of his eyes.

He shouldered his pack and moved into step with his command.

Quendius alone stood out of the fog, surprisingly, for his white vest should have mingled, and his sooty skin

taken on the aspect of the shadows but he had found a
patch of newly risen sunlight and thrust himself into it
as he stood on a rocky platform overlooking all of them.
Narskap squatted at his heels, more skeleton than man,
in battered leathers, his eyes burning hollowly in their
sockets as he watched Quendius.

"We march!" Quendius declared, and swung his hand
about, and a cave mouth which Garner had not discerned
before, yawned out of the mist and shadows and tumbled
rock. "Only death and scavengers are triumphant on a
battlefield, and we follow those footsteps. Keep up," he
added, his obsidian gaze sweeping the humans close to
him. "You won't like it if you fall behind."

A chill lanced through Garner. Quendius was not a
particularly truthful man, but he uttered it then.

Quendius spoke a word, and the mountainside shuddered open even wider, as he shattered the safeguards
on the Pathways of the Guardians, and his army stepped
inside.

Garner did not have to duck at the mouth's overhang
as so many did, but once inside, he saw that the slick tunnels had been carved for much taller folk. The tunneling
was wide, enough for eight to march abreast. Gravel underneath gave way to a patterned grooving, rather like
tile, and he eyed it as he trod over it. His horse tugged at
the reins, not liking the sound of its own hoof falls, nor
could Garner blame the creature. It was as if a living
mountain had swallowed them, and they would be eaten
or spit out. Neither fate sounded desirable. Turning back
was not an option, not with the army of Ravers and their
even more dire masters on their heels. Something fluttered in his pack. He opened the flap and took out the
small bird he had wrapped gently inside. It shook its
wings faintly, and he could feel its quivering fear. He had
no message for it to carry, for he knew nothing he had not
already sent on, but he felt . . . he felt horrible this tiny
thing was under the stone with him. He removed it from
its wrappings and let the alna go. It took to wing swiftly,

flitting one way and another, back over the heads of the army, escaping swipes of arms and surprised shouts until its silhouette cut across the faraway mouth of sunlight at the tunnel's beginning and it found freedom with one last visible wing stroke.

That tiny movement gave Garner a flicker of hope. He closed his pack and turned to go on, and found Narskap squinting at him. "Dinner," he grumbled, "but not enough to share nor worth th' trouble." He shrugged as he moved past the one called the Hound of Quendius as if it made no matter to him that he'd been observed or frowned at. He waited to see if his bluff would be called, but no action followed him. He could feel time move along with him as if he strode into a sluggish river, unseen but felt, with every stride he took. He could not explain what he sensed, nor was there anyone he dared to ask. He heard murmurs around him. The Mageborn had carved these tunnels, and they'd done it to move an army quickly and unseen.

Sevryn and Nutmeg reached Lara first, as the inky cloud which enveloped the manor slowly began to dissolve away. Eyes dazed, her hair in a cloud of disorder about her pale face, Lara sat up carefully as Nutmeg went to her knees beside her. "Where is Rivergrace?"

"Here, isn't she?" Lara put a hand to her brow, wincing. "I had her . . ." She withdrew her hand, looking at it as if she could not believe that Grace had eluded her grasp. She made a fist.

"She's gone," Sevryn said. "Did you give her over?"

"No. Rivergrace is mine, and mine alone to deal with." Lara scrambled to her feet with Sevryn's help, and pushed her hair from her face, as the last of the darkness spun out of existence. "She's been taken. Unless you took part in it," and she stared, her eyes narrowing, into Sevryn's face.

"Not I. Although I would have." His jaw tightened and his words sounded like stone.

"We'll go after," declared Nutmeg.

"No. No one is to go after her. I have to get my troops to Ashenbrook." And she let her hard gaze bear down on Sevryn until he seemed to crumple under it as if all the strength had left his bones and he swayed back against the wall, putting a hand behind him for support.

Nutmeg drew herself up. Whatever the queen had done to Sevryn, she could not fear. "Beggin' your pardon, Your Highness and all, but you keep overlookin' me. You're not the queen of me, and although I count you as a friend, I don't think much of what's been going on."

"There are matters about which you have no concept. If I were going to grow a tree, I'd ask your advice, but there are destinies here beyond you."

"Destiny is just another word for high and mighty ambitions which us common people are supposed to be too stupid to consider. You think to turn the world like it's on your spinning wheel, but you forget that it's th' likes of me who live within that cloth! Well, I won't be forgotten. Who I love and what I intend to do with my life is just as important as any great fates you've been imagining! I'm going, and I'll be finding her!" With that, Nutmeg darted off, Dweller nimble and quick, and even Lara whirling around to halt her, could not do so. She had disappeared into thin air, much as Rivergrace had.

"Let me go after," Sevryn begged.

"You go now and even if you find her, you will never have a moment's peace on Kerith. I will make it so."

Heat flared in Sevryn's face and in his storm-gray eyes, the eyes that marked him as less than Vaelinar pureblood for their singular rather than dual color, as powerless, although magic did course in his veins.

Lara cried out to him. "*I will be obeyed!*"

Cerat rose in him, heated and flushed with anger and power. He ground his jaws together, trying to swallow down the fiery surge that filled him. He would kill his own queen and friend if not. He clenched his hands, fighting down the Demon, and sank to his knees on the floor to keep himself from lunging at her in fury. He would not, would not, give way!

The corridor filled even as the murk dissipated. Bistane reached them first, a handful of guards at his heels, sword in one hand, dagger in the other. He sheathed them as he reached Lara's side. "Are you all right?"

"I am. Rivergrace is gone."

"Do you want her followed?"

"No. I want her killed on sight, if we are fortunate enough to see her, otherwise, I can no longer afford the distraction. Get my regiment ready to move out." Lara made as if to stride past, before looking down on Sevryn. "He goes with us."

She signaled then for the others to accompany her, leaving Bistane to give Sevryn a hand up. He bent over to offer it, and Sevryn did not respond.

"Let me go after her."

"I have orders. We have orders," Bistane amended. His blue-on-blue eyes sparkled sharply.

"I can't follow them."

"We have little choice now. When you made your pledge to her, as you did to Gilgarran, you knew there would be difficult times."

Sevryn managed to get to his feet, leaning heavily against the wall. "Do you trust your father?"

The corner of Bistane's mouth pulled. "He is a difficult and demanding man, but, yes, I trust him with my life and soul."

"And does he trust Lariel?"

Bistane hesitated even longer, unable to meet Sevryn's eyes for a moment, before answering. "He has his own lands and his own life. He has seen the queen from her birthing to her leadership."

"But does he trust her?"

Bistane stayed silent.

"Do you know?"

Bistane shook his head. "I am my father's son, but I don't share his mind. Remember that I have feelings for Lara and would be at her side, if she allows it. You ask me to say that which I don't know and that which I can't say, as well as much that we both know, because he is at Ashenbrook as she asked."

"That is doubt enough to let me go."

"And have her think she is beset with treason?"

Sevryn cleared his throat. With that one movement, he regained his balance and knew instantly where his weapons were on his body and which ones he could gain first. A calm and icy sense of purpose replaced the rage and fury. "There is someone who moves among us, and has from the very first days, one whose name is not written down, one pursued by both Gilgarran and Daravan. He blinds us when we should see and confuses us when the truth is clear, and we don't know his name. *Not yet.*"

"You think he turns us around here?"

"I think it's more than possible, but I can't say it's certain. Lara is beset with doubt and anger. Does it cloud her decisions? I fear that, but I can't say. I do know that if this enemy wishes to do anything, he must first turn us against each other. Let me go, Bistane, and know that it's not because I want to betray Lariel but because I must go after Rivergrace."

Bistane put his hand out, and Sevryn clasped it for a long moment. "Go then, because I understand the heart."

"May we meet next as the friends we have always been."

Chapter
Forty-Six

HER SENSES OVERWHELMED, IT CARRIED HER. She could not feel or see anything but a swirl of nothingness about her, yet whatever it was had body enough to hold her aloft. She feared a minion of the River Goddess, but this was nothing made of water, although it carried the deepest chill of snow and ice throughout it. She could not hear breathing, but she could hear evidence of their passage through the manor and out a door as it banged shut behind them. The wind rose as they emerged outside, and she felt as if a whirl-wind had hold of her, she spinning around and around inside the funnel as she had seen once in her life before they had all been hustled down to the cellar. The wind sucked air out of her lungs every time she fought a breath down. She tried to focus her eyes and could not as everything spun around her. The cold sank into her bones, making her teeth chatter uncontrollably. The force that contained her clasped her tighter as her body shook in violent tremors. Fear made the cold worse, the shaking worse, and she couldn't find a way to drive it off. The only thing she could tell for certain was that this thing was not a Raver, for she knew the stink of them, and that they were solid: shell and pincer, mandible and antenna, razorlike stick arms hidden by wisps of rags. She knew Ravers by how they fought and how they died.

This being of force had a familiar feel to it. She put her hand out to thrust herself from its suffocating hold on her and a small shock ran up her arm. She did not slow it; but it loosened its grip on her somewhat, and she inhaled a long gulp that did not feel as if it left ice crystals in its wake. The bitter coppery taste at the back of her throat stayed. She could not see clearly, if there were anything to see, but she was buffeted as if her carrier ran. Twigs broke and stones skittered away from their passage. Branches whipped by her though she could only hear and smell their evergreen aroma. She closed her eyes against the dizziness that threatened her senses, and that helped a bit. Then she heard the slosh of water as they crossed a stream or river. A heartbeat or two later, and gravel crackled under them. It moved with a speed that she could not match to the lands of Larandaril, as though it could hurtle whole pastures and groves with one stride. What was it that held her?

And, as Lariel had asked of her, was it rescue or attack?

It slowed. She could only measure the time by her own heartbeats but she sensed that it, whatever it was, had tired. It swung her to her feet, one hard grasp still on her forearm and waited until she steadied. She could see they had made it to the mountains, the blue-green evergreen boughs rustled about them and russet needles lay strewn about the forest floor, and whatever creatures were here had been stilled by their appearance. With a purpose she could not decipher, it pulled her roughly after it as it headed toward a sharp, cutting mountain peak and the rockfall at its base. Scrub brush ruffled the rocks, sere and yet managing to live still among the stone they had split with their determination to grow. She could feel the need for rain everywhere; it touched her like a crowd of children on the streets of Calcort, begging for food and water, for life itself. The need drained her.

A twisted root caught the toe of her boot, and she fell to one knee. The being holding her yanked her back to her feet as it uttered a hissing sigh that might have been either sympathy or disgust at her clumsiness. Her shoulder aching, Rivergrace clambered after the thing as it found a crevice in the foot of the peak and drew her inside. Cobwebs fell about her shoulders like a shawl, bits of rock quartz caught in them like diamonds which sparkled only briefly until they lost all daylight as they moved deeper into the mountain. Her throat began to close.

"No. No farther. Not here." She pulled back. Despite the chill surrounding her, her forehead felt clammy with sweat. Not the mines, not the shafts and tunnels, she could face anything but them, the stoneworks that had taken her family from her.

A light flared. It dazzled her for a blink or two. The being thrust a torch into her hand, a small wandlike object whose light settled to a soft blue white as she took it. She felt the being itself flicker as though the light fed from it, was fueled by it, was eating it away.

Its implacable hold on her faded.

"Don't. You can't leave me here!"

She tottered back a step and whirled about to go the other way, to find the way out. The mountain shimmered, and stirred, and then a soft curtain of gravel and dust began to fall from its side, obscuring her exit altogether, blocking the only way out. Dust and noise hung in the air taking its time to subside as she covered her face with her sleeve.

The thing lifted a hand and pointed down the cavern. "Go," it said. Then it wavered within its veils of darkness, growing strong, then weak, then disappearing altogether.

In that last moment of sight, she realized it had been the Dark Ferryman who'd snatched her from Lara's clutch.

She moved forward the only way which had been left to her, her steps echoing loudly over the broken stone. Then a sound came to her, a multitude of footsteps over the stone. It drummed from far away as though a secret heartbeat of the mountain but she heard it, and it sent a deep chill into her being.

Nutmeg grabbed a horse from one of the archers who'd been out on practice from the looks of it, and had come in for water and a bite to eat. She could not mount the tall beast on her own, but she got a boot into the stirrup and held onto the saddle as the startled animal flung its head up and bolted away. She held on for dear life, unable to pull herself into the saddle, her body bumping alongside the beast as it ran. The horse slowed by the pasture fencing as if puzzled by her odd position, and her hand knotted in the reins, trying to pull it about. It sidled up against a fence post in a wary halt. That was all she needed. Weak in the knees but determined, Nutmeg scrambled onto the fence post. She snubbed the horse securely and got the stirrup on the near side shortened, slapped the tashya gelding on its rump to turn it, and got the stirrup on the far side adjusted. Then she climbed into the saddle and set her feet.

The horse put his head up with a snort, one ear flicking back, as if to acknowledge he finally had a proper rider in place. "That's right," Nutmeg told him grimly. She reined him off the fence and eyed the hills stretching along Larandaril's border. A dark cloud moved against the leaden sky, not in the direction of the wind, but along the ground as if it had a singular destination in mind. She had no idea who had taken Grace or where she might have gone, but that caught her sight by dint of its menace and strangeness. That was the way she would begin her search.

She put a heel to the horse's flank. "Show me what you've got," she called to him, and stretched out low against the horse's neck, her hand laced in its mane and the reins. The horse flew at her command, lean body stretching out and long strides eating up the countryside as they went after the whirlwind. As she hung on tightly, her heart racing in time to the horse's flight, she thought of a tale the miller used to tell at the Stonesend toback shop, a story of the perils of harnessing the wind. She felt as though she had caught this windstorm by the tail and could only pray to hold on long enough to find her sister. The wind caught her hair and tore at her blouse, sending shivers down her spine. It howled dark things in her ears, but she kept her eyes on the storm cloud ahead, a cloud that seemed to have arisen from the ground and flowed upon it like a dire presence.

Her horse ran as if his hooves were on fire.

He found Aymaran and saddled him quickly, pulling blanket and leathers into position, listening to the confusion of the stable yard as he did so, as the queen's orders were shouted down the ranks and no one paid attention to him. He swung up and rode out quickly. At a small freshet that ran across the upper meadows, he dismounted long enough to kneel in the water, praying that he could sense Rivergrace through its touch. The chance of that, he knew, would be little, but it was the only way he had to track her, and it failed him as he knew it probably would.

Sevryn's chin dropped to his chest while he thought. Larandaril's border stretched far and away but only a fourth of it was passable, even without wards upon the boundaries. Forbidding ridges and peaks cut across much of the river valley and although they could be assayed, it could only be done by someone who had scouted it carefully and laid out a trail. An attack such as they had suffered precluded that. It had been done too swiftly for much detail in planning. It struck him as opportunistic. As someone who might have breached the border by coming in on Nutmeg's and Rivergrace's entry, following them closely and lying in wait until they could pierce the wards themselves.

Aymaran tossed his head impatiently as Sevryn mounted up again, and turned him toward the hills where his love had been arrested for treason. Along the way, he could see fresh sign of a running horse. He slowed Aymaran to a walk while he leaned out, looking at the prints closely, seeing the barred shoe of the ild Fallyn Stronghold, as distinctive as a tattoo upon one of their tashya horse's ears. He didn't know who rode that horse, but that alone boded ill, and so he turned Aymaran slightly to follow, even as storm made the gray clouds grow ink-dark and ominous on the hills and mountains. He could taste rain on the air, but none ever fell. It might as well have, for the hoofprints he tracked disappeared into thin air, as if washed away.

Sevryn dismounted. He walked the rough ground slowly, looking for sign.

A low whinny greeted them as they crossed a rockfall, Aymaran's hooves clicking and kicking loose stone. The horse stood quietly, pulling at scant bits of winter grass, his ears flicking back and forth in welcome to their presence. Sevryn thought he recognized the horse. He scanned the peak of the cliff, and a shadow of granite upon stone stepped out to greet him. When Daravan moved, he revealed an opening slit into the ridge.

"You ride point for Lara?"

"Not this day."

"You're after Rivergrace, then." Daravan smiled ruefully, his gray upon gray eyes crinkling at the edge, lines etched by sadness rather than laughter.

"Have you seen her?"

"I have. A dubious rescuer brought her this way and took her into the mountain." Daravan stood, one hand upon the opening, not to reveal it but as if he blocked it. "You can't pass. She was taken inside and let free. It's not her day to die, although I cannot say the same about you."

He would not be stopped, only delayed. He surveyed his chances, his position, even as he answered. "You saw her led in there? She's afraid of dying under stone, of being trapped in it forever. How could you leave her to that?"

"What she fears, and what she deserves to fear, are two different things. She'll do better than most of us lost in there, and it will keep her safe while the rest of us face what tomorrow brings."

"Then put all of us in a grave today, to ensure that we'll be safe tomorrow. Who put you in a position to judge the future of any of us?"

Daravan looked at him mildly. His brow arched slightly as he did, and he dropped one shoulder as if anticipating exactly what Sevryn did next, to bring his sword blade up.

The blades met and crossed in a lightning movement. Daravan stared at Sevryn through them. He said quietly, over the high, keening sound of the two steels rubbing against one another, "She was meant to die. Be thankful enough that Rivergrace did not, nor will, at least not this day."

"And are you deaf? What you have sent her into is, to her, worse than death. Do you think she fears dying? She has done it before, well aware of the frailty of her nature, and she will face it again. She knows that better than any of us, or any other living thing I've ever met. But there is a dark side to life that tortures her, and I won't leave her to face that alone!" Sevryn surged against the swords, breaking their stalemate, kicking sharply at Daravan's ankle as he did so, and whirling about with his sword now free. Daravan swung only to be parried. They closed on each other. Sevryn flexed his wrist, freeing his wrist dagger to be carried as a shield. They fought silently, with only the swords sounding above their grunts and sighs of effort, and the shuffle of their boots in the dirt and grass.

He caught Daravan in the upper arm, a slashing cut that would do little but bleed him, a wound that would weaken him in time if they fought long enough, but he knew Daravan would never allow their duel to drag out. Nor could he afford to either. He had to reach River-grace before the mountain swallowed her whole, with its twists, turns, and—Gods forbid—abysses.

He did what he swore to himself he would not willingly do, but he could not afford to be kept dallying here. He called upon Cerat and felt the white-hot rage rise within him. It roared along his veins, filling him. Daravan's eyes widened as he saw it reflected in Sevryn's eyes.

"My Gods," Daravan got out, as he brought both hands up to parry Sevryn's blow that nearly drove him to his knees and he staggered back to gather himself for the next. "I've loosed the wrong Demon."

His ears hot as molten steel, his arms moving of their own volition, Sevryn drove in after Daravan. Cerat wanted to taste his blood, to see the hot, crimson fountain, to smell the coppery scent, to taste the metallic bittersweet flavor, to hear the wetness splash, and most of all, to know the frightened leap of the opponent's heart and flutter of his soul as if it knew it was being hunted.

Steel rang. Sevryn twisted his right arm, bringing the blade in a circle and Daravan's sword went flying away from his hand, clattering to the ground. Daravan kicked at him, inside his dagger hand, and Sevryn fell back a step but only a step as Daravan lunged for his dropped sword.

"Leave it." His Voice shivered through his command, and Daravan hesitated.

His arm out for the weapon, Daravan looked up at him, frozen in motion. His jaws clenched, his teeth gritted, the man forced his words out. "What father gave you that Talent and the Demon?"

"No father gave me the Demon. An enemy granted me that. As for the Talent . . . something Vaelinar in me lent it." Sevryn sucked in a calming breath. It hissed over his lower teeth and across his tongue and into his throat in a slow, deep, movement. "Stand aside. I've no more time to waste."

"You've an enemy who might have plotted centuries for this moment. Did not Gilgarran warn you of such things?"

Something clicked in Sevryn's mind, like a shopkeeper's lock on a door, as the keyed tumblers fell into place. He made the slightest motion backward, on guard, balancing himself. One unnamed who managed to be everywhere, turning, meddling, directing. "It was you," he answered slowly. "The Vaelinar not named. Gilgarran warned of the meddler, the manipulator, the obstructionist, the schemer. I thought it was Quendius, but it was you."

"It might be both of us, if you live to find out." Daravan moved.

Not a straight-ahead lunge or even to his side, but a somersault that took up his weapon and brought him to his feet at Sevryn's open flank, in under his dagger hand. It did not matter. Cerat had seen him coming, from the corner of Sevryn's heated eyes, and met him, the dagger cutting across his face.

Blood splattered Sevryn's mouth and eyes, burning and salty. Daravan fell aside with a cry, dropping his sword and clasping his hands across his visage. With a growl, Sevryn knocked aside his hands and put his own over the gaping wound, fingers that burned as if they were on fire and Cerat exulted at the feel of the blood, but the Demon made a brand out of Sevryn, and at his touch, the wound sealed. Not entirely cleanly and not without much pain, for Daravan let out a howl of anguish, but without more loss of blood. Daravan fell to his side, curled on the ground as Cerat tasted his life and soul, and Sevryn pulled back in panting effort.

With his Voice, he whispered *Home* to Aymaran and set the horse free. He sheathed his sword and dagger and pitched headlong into the dark mouth of the waiting cave. The Demon light in his eyes gave him sight.

Chapter
Forty-Seven

NUTMEG KNEW TREES and branches intimately. She'd spent most of her life climbing them and leaping from one to another with an abandon that made her father yell in frustration and her brothers nudge one another in admiration at the skill they'd taught her. So when she saw the low-hanging branch coming at her as her horse galloped headlong toward it, she knew it would sweep her from her saddle if she didn't duck. She ducked.

The fool tashya horse swerved in blind panic to the right instead, dumping her unceremoniously, head over rear, onto the ground. Her breath left her with a whoosh, and hurt filled her at the same time as she stared skyward. The branch in question waved languidly over her as if in a mocking salute. Like a fish out of water, she whooped for air and glared at the tree. She didn't think anything on her body could have hurt worse than her legs with which she'd gripped the horse for dear life while he ran, but now her head thumped, her rear must have apple-sized bruises on it from some rock she'd landed on, and she was undoubtedly losing her wits with every breath she could not take! Not to mention that the ground was freezing cold under her. The horse came trotting back and whuffed at her questioningly, his exhalation a misty cloud over her. When she finally got a breath, she rolled to her knees, shaking her fist at the beast.

"For a withered apple core, I'd eat you and walk after Grace."

"Horse chew good, but what carry you then, little one?" rasped a growly voice behind her.

Nutmeg scrambled to her feet, spinning about with another gasp or two for breath out of necessity and surprise, brushing her unruly hair from her face to see a gnarled Bolger hunkered over watching her. She knew the rough visage well although she'd never thought to see him again. "R . . . Rufus? Rufus!"

He grinned, a frightening grimace considering his weathered face and tusks, but she knew that grin! Nutmeg bounced toward him with a fierce cry of her own to hug him. "We thought you were dead! But you're not! You're here!"

"Much hurt," he grunted as he patted her back awkwardly with one great hand. "Gods have thing for me to do. I not journey for a while. Now I travel again."

Nutmeg held onto him for another long moment, enveloped by his strong odor and warmth and muscle-knotted strength. She stepped back. "What do they want you to do?"

He shrugged. "Not know yet."

"Help me find Rivergrace!"

He jerked a thumb over the yellow-green and browning hills toward the jagged peaks. "Gone."

"You know? Which way? Come with me!" Nutmeg tugged on his hand. He rose to his full height.

"I know. Even in nasty caves, she smell like flower. She pass this way." And the Bolger jerked his head this time, toward the rugged stone.

"You can smell her that well?"

"Aye. You smell. Dweller. Apple and spice that bites."
A light twinkled in Rufus' eyes.

"And with every moment the two of you chatter, that
scent has to grow fainter so that soon even you won't be
able to track her."

Nutmeg had to crank her neck to look up at the two
Galdarkans who emerged from the shade of a nearby
evergreen, their leather battle armor and weaponry
muffled by colorful scarves wrapped about them, the familiar haughty expressions on their wide-planed faces.
She had never had much trade with Galdarkans until
their uprooted family had come to the big city of Calcort, but she had never met one who was not arrogant
and thought his worth far more than that of whoever
he met. What was Rufus doing with the enemy Queen
Lariel feared? She chewed on her tongue before spitting
out words she might regret. The speaker tilted his head
to one side rather than lower his chin to speak to her.

"I take it you know this Rivergrace?"

"She's my sister."

His gaze swept her from head to toe in mild disbelief. Nutmeg shifted from one boot sole to the other, her
body aching. A few pine needles drifted from her hair
and blouse as she did. "I am Tiforan, third-in-command
to Lord Diort. This is my scribe, Lyat. You seem to know
our smith and tracker already. If that suffices, I suggest we move and quickly before the queen decides to
strengthen the wards on her borders."

Rufus put his great, rough hands about Nutmeg's waist
and carried her to her horse, tossing her aboard with no
more difficulty than if she were a small sack of grain.
She snatched at the saddle to keep her balance. "Follow," he ordered her as he turned to lead all of them on
the trail he alone seemed to know, his wide-slit nostrils
flared as he moved uphill, his bowed legs carrying him
with greater speed than appeared as the horses moved
out with long strides to catch up.

Rufus took them unerringly to the mountains. Tiforan caught up, his face creased unhappily as he reined to a stop. "Old fool, you've taken us back to the way we came in. We've lost the girl now and whatever advantage Abayan wanted us to take."

The Bolger did not even blink. He made a curt gesture toward the tumble of boulders.

She heard Tiforan's complaint with uncertainty. She did not believe for a moment that Rivergrace had offered a marriage alliance to his warlord, but something was afoot here that she had no idea about . . . yet. She trusted Rufus far more than she could throw either Tiforan or Lyat. Standing in the stirrups, she rubbed one throbbing cheek ruefully. *Big* apple-sized bruises, she thought.

Tiforan spat to the ground, not far from both of them. "Turn back. We need to find the trail."

Rufus stayed unmoving. He jerked a thumb toward the rock, granite and shadows behind him. He pulled a torch from his saddle pack and crouched down, flint and stone in his hand, striking them until it took a few sparks and lit.

"It's a fool who has a guide and ignores him." Nutmeg settled back down and tried not to wince. She slid off her horse, landing with a solid thump as she did and nodded to Rufus. "I'll follow."

The Bolger's eyes flashed in triumph as he turned, leading his horse after him, picking a way through the debris so as not to lame his beast, and Nutmeg came after. She could hear a sound of disdain behind her, then the noise of two more riders on their tail. She was undoubtedly the only one who did not have to duck as a rough stone arch loomed before them, leading into the mountain's depths. Here it seemed narrow and crowding and she felt choked a bit as smoke hung low.

They walked for a good candlemark or two. Dank air hung close about them, smelling of their sweat and rock under mountain that had never seen light, and strange things grew and lived there. They went skittering, chittering about as she kicked loose stone and broken tile for someone, or something, had laid tile down here, as if she walked a very old court's road and for the most part, the tunnels had become very smooth, as if chiseled like some artisan's sculpture. She did not see how Rufus could smell anything down here other than the suffocating smells which cloaked them, but he must, for his head swung about now and then, and he took them down a different branch of the looping tunnels they traveled. Then they reached a dead end blocked by a fall of rock.

Tiforan shouldered his way to them. "Well done," he muttered. "I suppose your keen senses can tell she is on the other side of that."

"Taken that way. Double back, catch up."

Tiforan craned his head. He looked back toward a branch of tunnels, the one they'd just come down, and another Rufus wanted followed. Pathway marks shone in the glow of the torch over the caves they had traversed but none the way the Bolger wanted to lead them. He had no liking for the darkness or the pathways and knew it to be cowardice on his part, but he could not fail Abayan Diort. Not if he wished to stay high in his warlord's estimation. He would not stray from the high and low places marked by the Mageborn. He swallowed with a dry mouth.

"Follow the markings if we're to find her."

"We go." Rufus made a vague motion to the other tunnel.

"There are no tracks that way."

"This cut off. Other way not."

"You can't know that. It's not marked. We're underneath a cursed pile of rock." Tiforan jabbed a forefinger at the signs painted eye-height to his frame. "We go this way unless you think you can track across polished stone."

"Work mines. Know mines. No like."

"These aren't mines. You're on the Pathways of the Guardians," Tiforan snapped irritably.

The gold-and-black eyes of the Bolger fixed on his face for a moment. "Kill all the same," Rufus replied. Flashing his tusks, he turned away.

Tiforan bit down on the corner of his lip. He had no liking for Bolgers of any sort, but this one had been handpicked by Diort to ride with him, therefore he had to deal with it. It had to be a test of his ability to control his men, a test of his ability to command, Tiforan could see no other reason for it. Rufus spat upon the cave floor, and he reached out to the Bolger's shoulder and spun him around.

"This is sacred ground. I will have respect shown, if not to Lord Diort, then to our ancestors!"

Rufus dropped into a crouch, his lips curling back from his massive ivory teeth. He balanced himself with one hand knuckled to the dirt before he straightened. His eyes flashed in the semidarkness. "You think Magesss made these tunnels? These here before you crawled. We know what made these. We hunted it. It hunted us. In our first home and here." He thumped his chest with the hand holding his torch, and sparks flew about him like maddened fireflies. When he spoke again, his breath cut through the smoky cloud with scorn. "A great beasssst. Its mouth drips, and its juice cuts stone. It eats and then sleeps under mountain. We hunt. It eats its way through rock. Great snake but not snake. These tunnels loop back and forth as it wandered. We hunt for many years of fathers. It kill all it hunt but Bolgers. We too ssssmart for it. It kill us but not all. It turned south. Came to great bay of the ghosts. Went into the seas for food and something there ate it. Your Magesss may put magic into the rocks, but never did they make these places at the beginning." Rufus waved his torch, the flame roaring up as he did.

"We own them now." Tiforan's words fell as if dripped in the same acid-venom the Bolger had just described.

Nutmeg's hand curled tighter about her own torch.

"What do you think?" she charged the thin air. "I think he is right. I follow Rufus."

"This is not a vote!"

"You may be right. But you'll look pretty silly walking around in the dark all by yourself. We have the torch." Putting her chin up, Nutmeg led her horse over to stand by Rufus, the Bolger overshadowing her.

Acknowledging her only with a benevolent grunt, Rufus pointed across the cave. Nutmeg obediently trotted toward it, and disappeared into its shadowy maw. Rufus followed.

Tiforan stood for a bare moment longer as darkness descended around him and then, tugging on his horse's reins, he went after the two of them, his jaw tight and his gut hurting. He had already lost the prize Diort had sent him after; what difference did losing his dignity make now? Just inside the stony arch, Nutmeg waited for him. He found himself absurdly happy to see her in a circle of illumination, surrounded by rock that did appear as if it had, indeed, been chewed through. They traded looks. "What," said Tiforan. "No pithy Dweller saying to encourage me with, like 'Many feet make a short trail?'"

"That," Nutmeg told him, "is a given." She presented him with a picture of her back as she led her mount away.

Tressandre deftly wove Jeredon's hair into a war plait, pulling hard with her comb to untangle it before she did, his scalp stinging as she yanked. Jeredon fought to sit still and stay silent, a task not difficult as his thoughts wandered. Her hands quieted suddenly. "You're thinking of the Dweller."

His head jerked even though she had not pulled on him then. "I'm thinking of war," he denied.

She ignored him, returning, "Keep her, then, as a pet."

A bitterness rose in his throat at her words. "She is not a pet."

"You may be right there. Our hounds live longer than she might." Tressandre's fingers began to move again, even harsher than before. Her voice softened a bit. "It is not uncommon to have a bond with those who nurse us. Lariel should recognize that. You're a man of good heart, and she should know better than any of us. Your fondness for Nutmeg is not a flaw. I understand."

He could not see her face to weigh her words, but even if he could, he doubted he would be able to judge Tressandre. The ild Fallyn kept their true thoughts and machinations as veiled as any he had ever met. He knew that even as she now shared his bed it wasn't for him alone. She had her eye, as she'd always had, on the throne of Warrior Queen. She pleased him more in love-making than he pleased her, of that he had no illusions, for she liked it far rougher than he could manage, her taste for pain both in giving and taking something he could not meet. He lay with her only because she knew how to make her touch seduce him, and his thoughts of Nutmeg created an ache that he could not forget in any other way. And today, it seemed, even that no longer worked. He tightened his jaw as Tressandre finished his braid and let it drop along his back.

"It is best she stayed behind," Tressandre murmured, her hand stroking his shoulder. "She won't understand your warrior side as I do. Your returning triumphant to her will mean that much more. She will see you, and understand what all three of us share." Her words lingered meaningfully, stopping his comment in his teeth.

He did not trust her. He wasn't as blind as she thought he was, nor was she, he realized. She lifted him to his feet as he stood, her power bringing strength. His own strength increased every day, but he would not spend it just yet. He used her even as she hoped to use him.

"I will be with Lord Bistel."

Tressandre gave a little half smile, a gracious curve to her beautiful face. "Of course."

He found Bistel easily, his shock of white hair standing out, as the warlord sat upon high ground, watching his troops. Bistel smiled, a genuine smile, that creased his face and warmed his shockingly blue within blue eyes.

"Sit with me a moment."

Jeredon maneuvered as close as he dared, but the old war hound Alfra lifted her head and curled her lip at him in warning as the warlord stretched out one leg and his aryn wood staff. Bistel put his hand on her head. "Steady," he told her. He scratched the flap of her ear gently. "She's an old bitch," he said to Jeredon, "and one of my favorites. She's a brave one. Faced a pack of Ravers with me, took two of them down all by herself. She hates the very scent of them now. I'd hoped to get one last litter from her, but she's gone barren these last few seasons according to the packmaster. They shouldn't have brought her. She deserves to rest at home, but she wouldn't be left behind. And now she snaps at everyone. I can't have that or her pretending she's too deaf to hear orders."

Jeredon put his hand out and let the dog sniff him. She settled against Bistel's leg with a grumble. Jeredon ran his hand along her muscular frame with his hunter's senses, feeling her bone structure and the lines of her body, a hound bred to course battlefields instead of green fields and forests, his palm pausing for a moment on her flank; and then a curious and warm smile came over his face, and a light into his eyes. "Thrash your packmaster for not knowing his bitches," he told Bistel. "She's carrying a litter and a nice-sized one, too, I sense. She's about halfway along."

"What?" Bistel looked at him down his sharp, aquiline nose.

Jeredon took his hand away with a shrug. "It's just one of the things I do. I'm told I knew my mother was carrying Lara days before *she* knew."

"Great news then!" Bistel thumped old Alfra in delight.

"I'd put her with the supply wagons on guard," Jeredon offered. "She'll have shelter there. She's snappish only to protect herself and you."

"That I'll do." Bistel settled back with a pleased look. He let his free hand down and scratched Alfra's head now and again.

"What do we do here, sir?" asked Jeredon. "Besides waiting."

"I'm letting him decide when to make his move. I know Lara wants him broken, and quickly, but I see no advantage to our rushing it. There's a trap here, and I'll draw him into it if he decides to open an attack upon us. If he does not, I'm sure we've enough diplomats tented here to come to terms." He gestured. "Ashenbrook," said Bistel carefully, "is the river that ran red with blood and where Kanako fell. But it wasn't Ashenbrook that killed him. It was the Revela." And he pointed with his aryn wood staff at the other river, a knife of a river, keen and cutting across the landscape, its bones showing because what water remained in it was no more than a trickle.

"How so?"

"It was a wet year that year. A lot of rainfall. Clever brutes, the Bolgers. They knew their land better than we did although, in our arrogance, we didn't think so. But the Revela was high and so was the Ashenbrook. We'd come in through the southern pass and they cut it off. We thought to wade down the Ashenbrook if we had to retreat, but we weren't worried. We should have been. The Bolger clans came sweeping down over the Revela, which ran too swift for any crossing on foot. They had pontoons over it and crossed their infantry at a run and then their horse guards. Most of them made it."

"Wouldn't they have had their backs to the Revela and been cut off if the battle turned?"

"Kanako hoped so, but he was wrong. They swept up

below us, toward the stomach of our troops, because they crossed at night and we had deemed them superstitious devils who wouldn't dare such a maneuver. The sun rose at dawn, and we look out at a floodplain of Bolger troops. They'd never been so organized before—or since. Kanako knew that his sole hope was to so completely annihilate their troops in our defeat that they would scatter and the nation would be broken. That, he accomplished."

Jeredon moved in his cart. It creaked under his impatient weight. "Why are we damming the Revela, then?"

"Because this is a dry year. The queen is counting on Galdarkan arrogance to not know all the stories about Ashenbrook and Kanako's death, that he would not have bothered listening to toback shop tales and there are no Bolger storytellers to listen to. The Revela will once again be uncrossable and even pontoons won't manage it. Now, the Revela is the driest, most dangerous, rock-ridden trench we could have hoped to dig, if we'd the time. Instead, all we had to do was dam her main tributary up in the mountains and she becomes bone dry."

"And the Galdarkans think . . ."

"They think that she will be low, and easily fordable, and their retreat. By the time they see she is gone, it will be too late."

"My sister is brilliant."

"Possibly." Bistel lowered the point of his staff to the ground as he got to his feet, and Alfra scrambled up as well. "She might have had a bit of sage advice, too."

Jeredon had the grace to flush a bit as he tucked his chin in slightly. "I meant that, of course."

"Naturally." Bistel walked a pace and then came back to the side of the cart. "She has plans we formulated together and plans which she has kept to herself. She doesn't intend for us to turn the Ashenbrook red with our blood again. I had hoped she would trust me enough before this day to confide in me what else she has in mind." He stopped, and then added, "You know your sister well."

"We've always been close."

"Then it is likely you know her Talent. I won't ask what it is. Her grandfather made a point of keeping that knowledge under wraps, and I won't press for a betrayal, but we ..." Bistel paused, then shook his head sharply. "There is no 'we' anymore. I am the only one old enough to remember! Once there had been a 'we,' though, and we surmised that one of the secret Anderieon abilities was to prophesy. It followed on the known one, of bridging this plane to the Gods' for treaties such as the one which created Larandaril under the protection of the sacred Andredia. Your grandfather was a very young warlord when Kanako rode out, but records show that he warned Kanako of what he faced. Kanako did not listen. When it fell to Anderieon to take up his banner and scatter what remained of the Bolger clans, he did so, before we all retreated to our Houses and Fortresses and left the citizens of Kerith to fight their own skirmishes for many a century. Luckily, there wasn't much fight left in anyone for quite a long while. I remained a warlord, and he became the Warrior King. There were wars among ourselves, the Secret Wars, about which no one will speak except perhaps in the *Books of All Truth*. That is another matter. What remains is that your sister earned the title she carries now, and it is likely that part of what she does is as knowable to her as it is unknowable to us."

"Prescience."

"Stronger than that, I deem. Let's hope that she has foresight and common sense; otherwise, the same Vaelinar arrogance that doomed us before will doom us again."

"How so, if she knows the rivers?"

Bistel pinned Jeredon with his brilliant blue-on-blue eyes. "A ruler knows what it is to buy an alliance with his or her body, be it in bloodletting or marriage bonding. She's refused to speak of Diort. Arrogance? Or does she know that which I do not? I pray it's the latter. I am too old to risk my life again for the former. I don't wish for history to repeat itself endlessly." Bistel swung aboard his stone-gray charger, his aryn staff tucked up under one arm as if it might be a sword. "Rest while you can. They'll come at us again in the morning, I think. They've licked their wounds and made their repairs and replotted their strategies. There are no trees high enough for them to look over the Revela, and we've managed to keep their scouts either away or dead. They'll be greatly surprised when they put their backs to what they plan as a safe retreat. Greatly surprised."

Jeredon swept his gaze over the river plain as the warlord rode off. He did not know what his sister had planned and from what he could see, they were as trapped as Kanako, only this time by no river instead of a river too high and fierce to cross. But Bistel seemed to think she meant to put Diort's back to it, giving him no place to go. He could only hope it would be that easy. She didn't want to annihilate his forces, only beat them to a standstill. It would take more than that, he feared. And where was she?

Chapter
Forty-Eight

THE ARMY OF QUENDIUS reeked. They held a dry and musky odor about them that filled his nose with strangeness. He tried to outmarch them but was lucky to stay on his feet. Their movement had gone from a walk to a march to a trot, pressured from those at the rear to the front. Those leading dared not slow. Garner still moved easily, but he knew that some of the two hundred or so guards behind him had begun to wheeze and labor yet dared not drop back. He could hear Beezel's loud grunt every time his left boot hit the tunnel floor even though the veteran caravan guard lumbered at the rear of their pack. His shambling discomfort echoed ahead to all of them, warning them what they would be reduced to, all of them. A day, a night, and a day, by Garner's reckoning, they had spent in the tunnels, with little time for a breather and food and none for sleep. The army which followed on their heels would envelop them, run over the top of them, or even devour them. They would not be seen again. The Ravers had taken

their horses and ponies one at a time, bounding forward
to pick one they wished, tearing the reins from its rider's
hands and bringing it down to eat in the middle of their
pack. It could happen to any one of them. That fear prickled the hair on the back of their necks and drove them
more mercilessly than any whip. Bregan paced Garner,
his elven brace moving smoothly, but the rest of his body
had begun to fail him. The Kernan trader's pale skin had
lightened even more except for the slash of color across
his cheekbones. Sweat slicked his forehead. He flicked a
glance over as Garner looked toward him.

"I think we're not here to fight," Garner said quietly,
with a chin point toward Quendius who trotted a handful of body lengths or so in front. "I think we're here to
keep him from *them*."

"I believe you may be right." Oxfort mopped his forehead with his sleeve.

Quendius kept an easy pace with Narskap by his side
although Narskap seemed distracted, winding the stifled
air of the caves and casting forward now and then as
if he searched the dim depths ahead or the occasional
tunnel which shot off from their passage. The pathways
glowed when Quendius reached them, not overly bright
but clear enough they could be traversed. Once or twice,
at the beginning, Quendius had cupped an odd amulet
which hung about his neck on a braided thong, and a
Raver had sprinted forward, touched foreheads with
him and then dropped back as though given an order.
As for the caves themselves, all the ways they had taken
were marked with glazed and painted tiles inset into the
walls and a mere touch from Quendius had brought a
glow up in a faltering, flickering start as if reluctant or
burned out, only to be forced. Garner had wondered if
the glow fed all the way back down their lines or if the
others were driven toward the light and that was why
they kept increasing their paces.

They both watched as Narskap leaned close to Quendius, his wiry frame little more than a skeleton draped in

worn leather armor, his lank hair tied back at the nape
of his neck. Surprisingly, the Hound reached near Quendius in height, something Garner would never have figured, even seeing them side by side. Quendius stood as
a tall man, even among tall men yet Narskap nearly met
him at eye level though Garner had never reckoned
Narskap as a being tall and straight. Something inside
Narskap hunched as if life had dealt him a near lethal
blow and he awaited the second, fatal one. Nonetheless,
Narskap argued with his commander now. What about,
the two could not hear, nor did Garner think that even
those closest could, for they showed no inkling at all
about anything happening. The guards were, quite simply, in a slow run for their lives and knew it, and endeav-
ored only to keep moving.

Quendius snapped an order. Narskap shook his head,
and then, deliberately, swung away from the other, and
took a feeder tunnel on his right. Quendius watched him
go, and then snarled in anger. He made a furious gesture that swung the amulet around his neck to one side,
like a pendulum. It caught the dim light and gave off a
dull glow before disappearing from sight. But Quendius
did not slow nor did he signal any of the guards to follow Narskap. The Hound had not slipped the hold of
the packmaster, but he might have snapped at the hand
which fed him, Garner thought.

Bregan took Garner's arm and pulled him sideways
into the same tunnel as they reached it. The tramp of
boots covered their defection. Bregan reached up and
touched a set of marks painted onto a beautiful though
half-recessed and hidden tile in the wall. It glowed at
his touch.

Garner caught his breath and saw Bregan fighting
to do the same. The trader had spent his frail strength
keeping pace. It was defect or die as the army caught up
and overran him. They both withdrew deeper into the
small cut as the march of other steps drew nearer and
nearer, drowning out even their labored exhalations.

They could not go back now, even if they wished. Or they could only if they had the strength and will to sprint back into place with the caravan guards, but Garner doubted that Oxfort could manage it. He did not know if he himself could, as his sides burned and his breath wheezed slightly. Even as he pondered the choice that Bregan had made for them, the invading army began to trot past.

He saw the Ravers. He knew them by their odd gait. Some hopped and leaped on two legs, others gamboled on four, uneven legs, their black rags in tattered wisps about their shining carapaces. Bregan drew in a hiss and then held it as if afraid they might hear him. Garner worried more about their scent. Heat boiled off him like a kettle even though he shivered and dust coated him, caking over the sweat of his body, dust raised by the troops as they went by. Bregan steepled his hands over his nose in protection as they both watched in horrified fascination.

Things followed after the Ravers. Things like no beings he had ever seen before, and he was not sure he could ever describe to another who had not already seen such a creation. Lean and muscled, they trotted upright like a man, but there all resemblance ended. He would have said nothing that looked as they did could run except that he saw them. Only one scent hung about them, that of blood. Copper, sweet, ripening blood. They hissed as they quick marched, tongues flickering in and out. Panting? Complaining to one another? The noises they made battered at his eardrums, atonal and sharp, pitched lower and higher than he could hear in comfort. They wore armor, or perhaps it was their hide along the back, folded into plates about the shoulders and flanks. Some of them were spined, short and sharp, now and again, heavy and blunt. Armor and weapon were grown out of their own tough hide, in addition to what they carried. Teeth, many, sharp and pointed, glinted in every gaping mouth.

Beezel reeled into his view, his staggering form buffeted uncaring by the tide surrounding him. Sweat poured off his purpling face. He clutched his left arm and cried, "Stop, just let me stop! Help me . . ."

They *sssssisssed* at him as he spun about, helplessly. Their ranks broke around him, as a tide parts around a huge boulder jutting up from an ocean floor, leaving him vulnerable to one huge figure as it bore down on him.

Beezel took a whooping gulp of air as he fell to one knee, cradling his arm to his chest, heavy creases of pain etched into his weathered face. The . . . thing . . . came at him, a hand out.

Long curving claws tipped each finger on that hand. It swiped through the air, catching Beezel by the throat, and ripped it out. Blood spurted out in a wave that flooded the ground. Beezel waved his arms and toppled onto his side. Crimson splashed up and all around him as he did. Garner turned Bregan's face away, hoping only that Beezel was dead before the thing began to feed greedily, tearing flesh from bone in long bloody strips. One or two others joined it, at the end, and they fought over the last scraps and gobbets of meat.

Tears coursed down his face, hot and wet, and dried far too quickly, and were far too few. His body had little moisture it could spare, even in shock and sorrow for a comrade. He took Bregan and shoved him down the feeder tunnel, praying only that they not meet Narskap, less afraid of the dark than he was of what he'd just seen. He did not stop until they'd gone far enough that the sound of the passing marchers was only a mild thrum in their ears.

"If only he could have stayed on his feet," Bregan said, in a low breath. "On his feet."

Even a whisper might be too loud, but he answered anyway. "An army that feeds on itself never stops. No wounded. The enemy losses only fuel it. *No survivors.*" Garner tore his attention away from the main tunnel and put his back to the stone wall. "We can't let it reach its goal. Whatever it is. Whoever they are."

Bregan made a noise in his throat. He wiped his mouth with shaking fingers. "They are the Raymy," he managed. He turned and pressed his face to the stone and then shifted farther down the tunnel into its obsidian depths before finding something and fingering it upon the wall. His touch feathered across an inset tile, and he put his hand forward to it as it lit, as if its coolness, as if its subtle light, could both soothe and guide him. After a moment, he reared back and put his fingertips to it, tracing and strengthening the object. Whatever he worked upon the tile, it answered. "We can outrun them."

Garner felt his lips twist. "I won't go back. I've got to warn Sevryn. I've got to get the warning out."

"Why? What have the Vaelinars ever done for us, but weave a web about us that strangles us, Ways that bind us and tax us . . ."

"Ways that bridged us together after the Mageborn tore us apart."

"It took the Mageborn to turn away the Raymy."

"They went for each other's throats after."

Something glinted deep in Bregan's eyes. "They did not value one another."

"As you don't the Vaelinars? The Galdarkans?"

Bregan spit dryly to one side. "At least defend something of Kernan, if you're going to defend anything."

"They're human! Human enough that many of them have loved us, and we loved them back. They redressed their wrongs. They know the mistakes they've made. They're human," he repeated, adding, "There's nothing human in that army."

"You'll kill us, playing the hero."

"There's no other way. Die this way or go back and try to stay on our feet . . ."

"All right, all right!" Bregan waved a hand, quieting Garner. "We can travel a pathway they cannot, by sheer bulk of their numbers. These side tunnels are narrow. They can chase us if they see us, but not en masse. If I can but know where they were headed ... I saw the tiles ..." Bregan closed his eyes tightly, face screwed in memory. "I read everything in the trader libraries growing up. Everything. It stays with me, even languages long dead."

Garner looked at the brushed-on sigils. He knew a little of the Galdarkan style from his brief stint in Calcort, and he would have staked his life that he looked at it now. "Who made these?"

Bregan gave a shrug. "Perhaps it was the Mageborn you so revile." He leaned over to adjust his brace. "Have you water in your pack?"

"Some."

"As do I. A drink now, and then we go this way." He pointed down the feeder tunnel as he straightened.

"Where to?"

"A place called Ashenbrook." He frowned. "I should know that name."

Garner took his waterskin out and drank a little, slowly, wetting his lips and tongue, and letting it trickle down his throat, before taking a second sip. "Where Kanako fell and the Vaelinars won a blood-soaked victory, according to toback shop tales."

"Then we can only pray history repeats itself." Bregan took his own drink, capped his flask tightly, and waved Garner ahead of him. "Everything is against us. Time, tide, and all manner of flesh."

The wide and treacherous Nylara River stretched sinuously across their view, deeply sapphire, foaming sea green where it etched into the riverbank. Lara looked down at the tradesman they had accosted, he with but a few caravans parked idle at the river's edge.

"There's no Ferryman here. Ay waited better part of a

day, then sent for regular boatman from across t'Nylara. Ropes still in place, and th' barge, but no Ferryman. Took the most of yestiddy and t'day to get my caravan acrosst. This be th' last of it." The trader hitched up the shoulder of his finely embroidered vest as though it scratched him under his heavy winter coat.

"What do you mean, he's not here?"

"Are you daft? Looky around you. No Ferryman! Now, mind you, he takes his time, part'clarly when it comes to trader caravans, ever since th' Oxfort son struck him down. He carries a grudge, that un. Traders sumtimes wait much as 'alf a day t'get him to show up. Now there's sum that says he ferries other rivers, too, but ay can't be sayin' that. You all would know more abut that. Mebbe you'll have more luck gettin' th' ornery beast t' answer." And he leveled his heavy eyebrows to look at them. Despite his heavy northeast Kernan accent, his meaning was clear, his words seeming to hang in the air between them.

Lara's mount stamped restlessly. She looked to Bistane. "Tree's blood." Her mouth worked on words she wanted to spit out, but did not. His eyes reflected both her anger and her worry. The Ferryman was not a being, beast, or man, but a Way, and what if he had spun out of existence just as the Cut had done around Sevryn? Yet there was no sign of anything amiss at the edge of the Nylara River other than the missing phantom. As she glared across the bright blue ribbon of the river, harsh winter sun glancing off it, she saw, she *felt*, no sign of the Ferryman. What she did feel hit her like a blow, the link with her vantane cutting across her vision of the Nylara: a field of war, trampled grass running red-brown with blood, horses down and struggling to get to their feet despite shattered legs, men and women strewn everywhere like broken dolls, and a trap waiting to be sprung that would spare all the rest of the fighters from the same fate—if she and her troops could but get there in time. As planned, by the hand of the Ferryman. She shut her eyes tightly. Bistane's arm went around her waist to steady her in her saddle.

A brilliant trap. If it could be worked.

Bistel and her brother led troops as bait. She and her troops were the jaws.

She opened her eyes.

"What do we do?"

She hauled back on the reins, spinning her mount around sharply as he squealed in protest. "We ride," she answered tightly. "And pray we get there in time to be of some help. Bistel will hold them as long as he can."

"Five days." Bistane sounded grim.

"If anyone can do it, the warlord can."

Bistane signaled the troops to fall in, and they set out at a collected, steady run back the way they had come. They dared not run far or long, but they would press themselves as they could. Lives depended on it. The thought of victory had been swept away. Now the Warrior Queen concentrated only on survival.

Chapter
Forty-Nine

RIVERGRACE DRAGGED HER BOOTS. She walked in gliding, searching strides even though she could see a little in the torchlight cast around her, more in worry that there would be something in shadow she could not see. The weight of the rock pressed down on her. Her throat fought to close against the dust she raised. Last time she had walked a route like this, Cerat had been in her hands, talking to her, taunting her, urging her. Not that she would ever want to hold a presence like that again, but it had distracted her from the reality closing about her. Then, those other forces had driven her, had led her. Propelled by a River Goddess wanting freedom, a souldrinking Demon wanting mayhem, and a trapped elemental Goddess of Kerith seeking cleansing, she had been pulled and pushed to her destination. Now she had no idea where to go except that she could not go back.

How did the Ferryman know to find her, to take her from Larandaril, and for what reasons? Had they been his own or was he nothing more than a thrall to a Way, a Way that even other Vaelinars found a mystery? No one seemed sure what House made it or brought the specter into being or how he tamed his river. Few knew that he could tame other rivers, bridging them with his phantom presence. So did he have a master who lived still, as Vaelinar could and often did? Had that master sent for her, and the Ferryman failed, or did she walk to him now? What could he possibly be, under all this rock, let alone where? Now it seemed she could wander down here, lost, until she no longer had the strength go on.

Grace halted. She put her right hand to her chest to see if her heart still beat as she thought it did. It pulsed strongly under her palm. The gesture echoed the touch she liked to give Sevryn, her palm over his chest to feel the strength of his heart as if she could cradle the life he carried within him. She closed her eyes. She could not feel him, whether he lived or died, whether he had betrayed himself to Lara or whether he kept himself confined and coiled, waiting to strike. He would come after her, she knew, if he could find the means to do it. Even through death, he would find a road. They had done it before. This time, though ... her thoughts faltered and her hand dropped to her side. Lara's attack on her had scattered her trust to the winds. What was she that she had earned that betrayal? What did the queen fear from her? Narskap's daughter. Who was she but lost? And if she were lost, how could she hope that anyone else would be able to find her? She had no way forward unless she found it herself.

Grace stopped thinking, shutting down her doubt, her shadow wavering in the orange-yellow glow of her torch. She stiffened her spine. Betrayed or rescued, punished righteously or persecuted, how could she know what transpired? She could only know herself. And she knew water. Fresh water. Droplets of rain and puddles and the beginnings of the smallest brook to the deepest, white-water current. Water ran through sand and stone, through ash and branch ... it ran wherever it could until it was free. If she found it and followed it, it might take her into depths where only the merest rivulet could run, or it might take her to freedom.

She took a deep breath and let her senses go, senses she had kept tightly wound because of her fears, fear if she touched the rock it would tumble down to crush her. She brushed granite and quartz, jasper and stone, and plain old dirt ... and she found its essence. It ached for sun and water and wind, just as any leaf or flower would. Abandoned in the dark, it lay still and silent and hurting. It was earth, alone and separate, and yet it was not. It was meant to be part of all: earth, wind, fire, and water. Even here in the depths, water would trickle down and run through, touching it, tumbling the stone, bringing out colors with its wet brush, moving it, springing seed to life that could crack recalcitrant stone in two. Lifegiving water, denied. Rivergrace tucked a curling strand of hair behind her ear. A dry winter. As a Farbranch, she understood the cycle of farming and ranching. Wet years, dry years. Trees that harvested well only every handful of years or so and trees that harvested abundantly every year. Vines that grew well only if severely cut back first. Insects that came and went according to the moons and the seasons. All natural.

Save for this.

A dry year which would never end, not until the spiteful River Goddess could be appeased and there was no excuse Grace or anyone else could give Her which would placate Her. Like Sevryn, the Souldrinker had corrupted the Goddess with his merest touch, with his burning presence. Perhaps the only uncorrupted part of the Goddess lay within Rivergrace. She understood now the desperation of the being. Could she heal the Goddess or had Cerat bridged the distance between them, bonding Demon to deity? Could she even survive attempting it?

Had the Ferryman sent Rivergrace under the mountain to make one last sacrifice?

If so, he did not know who he meddled with. She was a Farbranch, and she had family and a love to return to. She curled her fingers tightly about her torch. She would find water, sweet water, and she would find a way out.

Chapter Fifty

"I HEAR WATER."

"What you heard," Bregan rasped, "was me pissing air in the corner." He leaned over, hands on his knees.

Garner took out his waterskin and passed it over, knowing that he carried a bigger store than the trader did, and that Bregan's supply was probably nearly exhausted. Bregan waved it off. Garner shoved it into his hand. "Last thing I need is to carry you. Your legs would drag."

"Aye, the one thought that keeps me going is the image of you attempting to hoist me over your shoulder." Bregan carefully untied and uncorked the skin before sipping gently from it.

"I could carry you, but you'd drag. I cannot help it if you folk grow like weeds." Garner took his waterskin back and tied it off tightly, hefting it a bit before stowing it. Not much left, but it would have to do.

"Weeds, yes, most of the races are weeds compared to the sturdy Dweller. Now as for this water you hear ..."

"No way of knowing if 'tis drinkable or not or if the stone flavors it. Could be full of sulfur or other minerals."

Bregan flexed his shoulders and rolled his neck. "I bow to your expertise. Having been brought up on only the finest wines and liquors, I doubt I will know good water when I see it." He gave a bow before following after Garner who snorted faintly as Bregan fell in behind.

They trudged along for a bit before Garner asked the question that kept simmering at the front of his mind. Bregan would either answer it or ignore it. "So how is it a clever fellow like you came to partner with a man like Quendius?"

"Partner, mmm? A good word. Less than alliance, more than acquaintance. I tell myself it came out of good intentions. I had no doubt whatsoever about those intentions until the Jewel shattered. Istlanthir was not given a good death." Bregan scratched his jaw as he walked. "My hatred of the Vaelinars is well known and I doubt I have to explain that to you. It stems not only from this by virtue of the Ferryman," and he rapped his hand against his brace, "but that they feel they can tax us on our own lands, that they have holdings which they tore from our ancestors, that they enslaved many of us when they first appeared, and that they still feel as if we are beneath them. They strangle us with steel hands hidden by velvet gloves under the pretense that they hold together a nation torn apart. We were mending. We did not and do not need them."

"You can't deny they have given as well as taken. That brace o' yours is Vaelinar."

"Aye, this brace that keeps me on my feet ... I have clerks at the countinghouse who could not see but for the spectacles they make. They gave us better spindles for spinning and looms for weaving. Built bridges that span impossible reaches. Kid yourself not, none of that was done for us out of the goodness of their hearts. They had needs we could not meet, not for centuries, and so they brought their knowledge to us as sparingly as they could, to help themselves. The Vaelinars are infamous for helping themselves to whatever they want."

"They have grafted themselves onto our lives and sometimes the fruit is sweet, sometimes bitter." Garner shrugged.

"What can sweeten that bitter fruit? The petitions they grant us now and again to get our lives back? Never!"

"Seems t' me that if anyone had a stranglehold, it could be the trader guilds."

"The coin purses. Oh, yes, the holder of the purses. Let us never forget that the Vaelinars are uncanny when it comes to the making of fortunes. They can see through stone to the gems that lie within. Refine gold to its purest state. Tan hides so that they are as soft as silk ... and yes, let us not forget the silks as well."

"Yet you have a change of heart."

"The man who said that the enemy of my enemy becomes my friend is a fool. I am trying to be as little foolish as I can. Pray that it's not too late."

"What would you do now?"

"What you would. Stop him. What Quendius truly desires is probably no less than the annihilation of all he sees on Kerith. He is a man full of poison who can't look upon life without despising it. I didn't unleash him, but there is a faint hope you and I can trip him up."

Garner could not argue with him on anything he said. Whatever hope they both held, it was faint indeed. He stopped talking to concentrate on the very faraway sound of water he thought he had heard, a wet lapping against stone, a tip-tapping of a drip now and then. It drew him as a flame drew a moth, and he could only hope it was not a trap.

Demon light played about the caverns with an eerie red-gold glow, giving Sevryn the feeling that he walked into the heart of a forge, melting stone. He would blink or narrow his eyes, and the glow still reflected although it was lessened. He gave it off, and it would not stop unless he stood with eyes closed, and even then he wasn't certain that the light wouldn't seep through his eyelids. He could feel its heat and steam of the forge, its unforgiving fires that melted iron, copper, tin and alloyed them into more than their individual selves. He could feel the toughened ridges on his hands that came, not from handling weapons, but from making them for twenty years under the lash of Quendius and Narskap. Sweat dampened his armpits and ran stingingly into a scratch or two (or perhaps they were deeper, he hadn't taken the time to look) left from his skirmish with Daravan. He had no idea how long he'd been entombed in stone. It could have been a candlemark or two or even the full turn of a sun, although the way his cuts bit at him, he doubted that long. Cerat crawled under his skin, hot and itchy, as if readying to tear his way out. Sevryn scratched at his arms until he drew blood, but nothing stopped the feeling. Nothing would until he laid Cerat down, and that he could not do as long as Demon-sight took him through the underworld beneath the stone. Did he believe Daravan that Rivergrace had been brought this way? He had no choice, but, yes, he did. Not only for himself and his own beliefs, but through the hunger of Cerat who had had a taste of her once and longed for more. Always thirsty, never sated, the Souldrinker quested tirelessly in search of lost but very sweet prey.

So, by the eyes, by the soul, Cerat took him after Rivergrace without hesitation. Rockslide, bottomless abyss, nothing mattered to it, not even the frailties of the flesh which might need to eat or drink or sleep. Sevryn would not deny the demon, not yet. He only prayed that he could deny Cerat once his love was found. Footfalls echoed hollowly within the tunnel as he trotted. If there was a fiery hell for souls who had failed or faltered in their purpose, he knew he glimpsed it now.

If he could do one thing, it would be to deny Cerat a stroll through the battlefield, picking and choosing what souls to harvest among the dying and severely injured, those on the brink of life and death. He had hoped to beat the Demon out of him or extinguish it, but nothing he had done worked. He used it now to find Rivergrace and when he'd found her, and delivered her, he would walk away. He knew the burden she carried. When he found out how to excise that which possessed him, then and only then could he return and help her without adding to that burden. He loved her with all he had, and it was not enough. She had family to lend her strength while she waited for him, and he trusted that would be enough. Love sometimes must mean letting go as well as holding on.

Sevryn stopped in his tracks. He put one arm across his ribs to hug himself as that realization cut through him. What he had decided could apply not only to lovers, but to mothers and sons. . . .

A lump thickened his throat. He swallowed it down with difficulty. He rubbed a thumb across his mouth, found his lips cracked and swollen with dryness, and his eyes stinging without moisture. Never once had it crossed his mind that his abandonment might have been as much out of love and necessity as it might have been self-serving. Then a smile stretched his face. It was a wonder Tolby Farbranch had never knocked that sense into him. He'd taken him to task more than once over the courtship of his beloved foundling daughter. No doubt the imcomparable matriarch Lily Farbranch had talked him out of it and was just waiting for the maturity to sink into Sevryn on its own. He could almost see her now, reigning over her tailoring shop, scissors in one hand and a handful of pins in the other, looking at him as though she could not decide whether to skewer him or slice him or hug him.

Sevryn staggered back into movement. Hot, still heated, everything about him glowing like coals in a banked fire, and he burned from the inside out. Water, he needed water. His blood boiled as if laced with ked-ant, and delirium ruled his thoughts and his words. He talked, he could feel the dry husk of his voice moving through his throat, tearing as it emerged, and yet heard nothing of what he said. Did he spew his thoughts out randomly? He could not hear. He had lost the ability to know thought from voice. But he had to have water, that he knew, and he also knew that where he would find it, he would find his Rivergrace, for she needed water as a fish did. Not that she was a mermaid of legend but that water soothed her and replenished her, and . . .

Sevryn croaked to a halt. He blinked his eyes furi-ously, so dried out he could hardly see through them. He reined in Cerat, strapped down the delirium. He needed water, or neither of them would live. The Demon seemed to agree, or perhaps it sensed as much as Sevryn did that Rivergrace would be found somewhere like that as well.

It led him in a staggering rush through the tunnel. Walls rose from nowhere to slam him in the shoulder. Overhangs snatched at his brow. He had unleashed something terrible in his desperation and if, when, he found Rivergrace, he did not know if she would survive the meeting.

She found a pool. Still and silent and somewhat brackish, normally to be replenished and purified by winter rain, yet the basin held onto its moisture. Rivergrace knelt by it and put one hand into it, singing quietly the song she remembered from her first days in dark, twisted caverns and mines just like this one, a song from her mother that she remembered better than she did the person who'd birthed her. The song flowed with her Talent, twisted through the water, bubbling it up gently, cleansing it. After long moments, the song stopped of its own accord, the last notes falling from her lips into quiet. She swished her hand through the pool. The moisture felt tepid. She put her wet fingertips to her mouth to taste it tentatively. It lingered on her tongue a moment, sweet water, good water, with only a hint of staleness and dirt within it. It would give life. She knew that as soon as she left, whatever lived inside these smooth, carven walls would skitter out to partake of the bounty. She cupped her hands and drank deeply before washing her face.

Rivergrace sat back on her heels, resting. The torch guttered low and she knew it wouldn't burn forever. The water had found a way in, so it might have a slow, trickling, way out. She eyed the widened area of the tunnel. Although cut or chiseled smoothly in the main tunnels, it still had its nooks and crannies, as though the builder had followed the natural geography of the mountain's crevices and caves. She would have to trace it. A weariness settled over her in a cloud of aches and malaise. She secured the torch in a brace of rocks to let it burn. Her eyes dipped once and stayed closed for far too long. Rivergrace forced herself to stand and to move away from the comfort of the water to one of the nooks big enough to hold her body. She sidled into it and then sat down, finding a cradle within the jagged rock, and closed her eyes again. With the dampness of the pool still upon her cheeks, she slipped into sleep.

Click, click. Tap, tap. Click.

Hard nails or talons upon the tile and polished stone of the tunnel. Rivergrace's eyelids fluttered in an effort to open, dried shut in her sleep. How long, she did not know, but she knew what she heard. Something large moved along the tunnels toward her. She wiped her eyes open. Her torch still burned fitfully, throwing its orange glow off the small pond and its environs. Its smoky scent gave its presence away, drawing whatever trotted across the stone toward it.

By the same token, its oily smoke hid her own scent, and threw long shadows to reveal that which approached.

She held her breath as she watched the spiky darkness take form, mutate, and take form again until it became something she could recognize.

Raver.

Her heart leaped once before steadying. Would it scent her? It had come down a different passage, or so she thought, three of them spiking away from the pool. Did it nest nearby or did it come to collect her as part of the Ferryman's offering or did it hunt her? She had nothing, nothing at hand with which to defend herself except that she could stuff gravel down its gullet as it tried to slice her to death. And she had her back to the small crevice, and it would have to work to dig her out. If it found her. She knew little of how the Ravers hunted, whether by sight or smell or some other means, only that she was in mortal danger if it discovered her.

Shadows merged into the being as it approached the poolside, crooking its head on its odd, stilted body, and it clicked. It raised a sticklike, pincered arm that bent at impossible angles with a grace belying its rigid form. It could leap, she knew, but the roof of the cavern wouldn't allow much height, and it could run on all fours at a horse's pace if it had something to chase after. Instead of the rags which usually wrapped a Raver from head to toe, hiding its true aspect, this one wore light armor over its hard-shelled body and weapons, pike and a short sword and a spiked chain, by the looks of them, strapped where it could easily reach them. The pike she feared most because the Raver could strike at her from a distance. She dug her hands quietly into the rock pile surrounding her.

The Raver cocked its head to give off a short, piercing whistle. Her ears throbbed at the noise. They both waited long moments. Did it call for others? She watched it as it turned slowly and then walked about the pool, pausing by her torch. It leaned to sniff at the object. It straightened with a low whistle, head swiveling about, and she swore it searched for her, could see her tucked in the crevice only a few body lengths away from it.

The orange-yellow glow about the pool began to deepen, taking on a crimson hue. It flared wider and stronger as if the torch had found a new source of fuel deep in its wrappings and its heat surged out, like a finger pointing toward her. The Raver turned to look. Had it seen her?

It leaped, pulling its pike free of its harness, and she no longer wondered.

It jabbed at her, but she had each hand full of as large a rock as she could hold and she batted at the pike head with one hand, and lobbed the other at the Raver as hard as she could. Part of its spiny ridge broke off and hung by its skin. The rock bounced off the carapace hide and rolled back at her feet. She grabbed up a handful of dirt and gravel and flung it in what passed for the thing's face, even as it sliced the pike wickedly at her, catching her sleeve and ripping it from collar to cuff. But she had drawn first blood, and she wasn't about to stop there.

A long shard met her search for another piece of stone. Obsidian, curved and naturally sharp, it cut her fingers as she gripped it, and she swapped hands long enough to tear off her ragged sleeve and wrap it about one end, a clumsy bandaging to hold it. She got it back up in time to parry a jab from the pike. Slice and another jab, and she fended them off. Then a downward cut that she barely met in time. The pike head slid off her obsidian blade with a keening noise as her weapon bit into the iron, notching it heavily. The Raver made a loud chitter as it pulled the pike back.

"That's right," Rivergrace told it. "I won't be easy pickings!" She stood, bracing her feet, holding the obsidian shard as she'd been taught to hold a long sword. She only had the front vulnerable and she could hold that offensively and defensively for a bit, perhaps long enough to damage and discourage the Raver.

It withdrew.

"Think I have straw for brains? I'm not coming out to get you." The crevice protected her like a shell did a mud turtle and she had no intention of leaving it.

It drove in again with the pike. They fought furiously till the sweat ran down her, soaking the rag wrapped about her blade, and she thought she might not be able to hold onto it. She parried the pike head and lunged past it, plunging the sharp end of the obsidian deep into the Raver's torso. It sprang back with a hissing chitter as green goo flowed from the crack in its body. It flailed at its body as if putting out a fire, a series of loud spits spilling from it.

Rivergrace held her breath a moment to see if the thing toppled, but she seemed only to have enraged it. It threw the pike clattering upon the stone and then drew forth the spiked chain. Her momentary flush of victory went ice cold.

The creature slung its length at her. With a snap, the chain slid off her blade and the end snapped along her side, tearing cloth and piercing flesh in jagged, hot pain. She cried out and held onto the shard by sheer will as she fell back against the rock wall. The Raver made a noise of what could only be satisfaction as it coiled the chain and prepared to strike it again. Blood slid down her flank, hot and stinging, soaking her blouse and vest.

Even if she could bear to grab the chain, she knew she didn't have the strength or leverage to wrest it from the Raver's hold. All she could do was parry it as long as she could and hope that its wound was worse than hers, and it would fall back. Rivergrace didn't think she had those odds in her favor.

Torchlight danced and grew ever more crimson as it threw darker and darker shadows upon the rock. She wiped her forehead, certain that blood must be veiling her eyes. She pulled her vest off and wrapped it around her left hand and wrist. The chain came slinging at her before she was ready, but she caught it. As the Raver thought she might. As she had to, to keep it from wrapping about her body and slicing her to ribbons.

It did not think she would come charging out of her hole, obsidian blade in her hand, and skewer it between the eyes.

It fell back with a squawl, its momentum and the chain drawing Rivergrace with it. Green ichor spurted from its helmet-thick head with a smell that made her choke. It thrashed at her as she pushed away, the vest tearing loose from her wrist as spikes shredded it to ribbons.

She made it to her knees. She scrambled for her obsidian blade which lay shattered in front of her, under the Raver's flailing body. She pulled back, one hand bracing her as she got to her feet, watching it, spent, having done all she could do.

Then it got to its feet.

A sound of dismay escaped her. Rivergrace hugged her arm to her bleeding side and squeezed as far back into her crevice as she could. Heat flooded the small cavern, heat that made the crimson glow dance and bloom upon the walls. The Raver came after her.

She threw rocks at it. Pea-sized gravel to a boulder she could barely heft. The boulder jolted the creature, nearly knocking it off its stiltlike legs, but it still came. Green slicked its black carapace and what was left of her blade stuck out from the middle of its cranium. It walked with its head tilted grotesquely to one side as though half blind, notched pike in hand. It would jab and peck at her like long-billed birds pecked at snail shells to get the delicacy inside. She found another rock just behind her, a huge one. With a scream of defiance, she lifted it.

The Raver jolted backward.

In a spate of chitters and clacks, it lumbered around, razorlike arms stabbing at the air. She thought it had gone mad, damaged from the splinter in its skull, and then she saw the figure, sword and dagger in hand, cutting the Raver to pieces. Oh, she knew well that tall and graceful figure, muscled and yet lean, face not as slender and chiseled as a true Vaelinar, but a face that smiled only for her. Bathed in crimson light, Sevryn danced on the balls of his feet, his hands in constant motion, the Raver unknowing of what hit it, of what took it down. It toppled, and he stepped aside smoothly, his eyes like lanterns. He sucked in a breath before turning to her.

"Are you all right?"

"I will be."

He bent over, wiping his sword and dagger clean on rags wrapped about the Raver. He took the spiked chain, examined it gravely, and then hooked it to his weapons harness. Finally, he came to her, putting his hand out, fingers under her chin, and drew her to him. The light in his eyes had dimmed by then, and the heat washing over her passed, leaving her chilled, but his flesh warmed her as he held her close. His heart pounded under her cheek and then steadied. She did not wonder how he found her. Demon-touched and Goddess-ridden, it would have surprised her if they had not found each other eventually, though it might not have been with life still in their mortal bodies. He held her tightly and she leaned to him, her curves pressed to his lean, hard body, and neither spoke.

After very long moments, he commented, "I think you could have taken it."

"Only if it choked on the gravel. I hadn't much left for the fight."

He smoothed her hair from her brow. "You had enough. That's all it takes."

She looked up, and the Demon light in his eyes had faded to the merest flicker, like that of a candlewick just taking the flame. His jaw was bruised and scraped, fatigue crinkled his eyelids, and he looked, on the whole, like she felt. Beaten and weary yet glad to be alive. She kissed the cheek under her fingertips as she stroked him.

He found her mouth and kissed her gently, then with

more heat and need as he resettled her in his arms. She broke away long enough to take a breath and ask, "Do you know the way out?"

Sevryn shook his head. "I came in behind you."

"There has to be a way."

A voice spoke dryly from the long, purple shadows across the small pool of water. "There are several and one must be careful choosing them."

Freeing his sword hand, Sevryn broke away from Rivergrace and they both faced the dark as Narskap stepped into the torchlight.

"Do not worry," he said, closing the distance between them in three strides. "I merely came for this." And he plunged his hand into Sevryn's chest.

Chapter Fifty-One

RIVERGRACE SCREAMED. Sevryn uttered a wet gurgle. He raised his hand toward her and sank to his knees. She thrust out at Narskap, her fingers flaring with fire, blue fire that engulfed her arm as she swung at him. He spat a word, and the flames went out, icy cold, and he knocked her blow aside. She picked up a rock, clutching it tightly. This was not her father, not Fyrvae, and yet she hesitated to club him. Before she could strike, Narskap withdrew his hand slowly and painstakingly from the gore of Sevryn's chest. He uncurled his fist and she saw nothing but a small, fiery crescent. No blood, no shreds of flesh or organs. No pulsing, throbbing bit of human life torn free. No mark left on Sevryn as he struggled for breath, his eyes wide in pain. His chest closed.

"Did you not wonder," Narskap remarked, "why the arrow you took for Queen Lariel did not consume you the way it consumed Osten? Did you never think how it was you took only an irritating flesh wound instead of your death from it?" He slapped his open hand to his chest and shuddered as if something forced its way into him. His deathly white skin paled even more, taking on a faint greenish cast, and his eyes looked as if they would be lost inside the depths of his skull. He swallowed tightly. The moment passed, and he dropped his hand to his side. The pallor of his skin and the sunken hollows of his eyes returned to their normal wasted state. "You lived because Cerat never eats his own. He cannot devour himself. Demon calls to Demon . . ." Narskap glanced from Sevryn to Rivergrace and back, "and I am the one who calls Demons and binds them. Just as I am the hunter who tracks other hunters." He gave a desultory wave at the carcass of the Raver.

He grabbed Sevryn by the shoulder and hoisted him to his feet. "You haven't long. An army marches under this mountain. Go this way, and quickly, or you will be devoured by something much less immortal and just as unsavory as the Souldrinker." He stroked Rivergrace's cheek. "Run, Daughter."

He turned away and as he passed, his shadow sucked the last of the light from the torch and all went dark.

Bistel reined in. The drums had stopped again, and there was no veiling by fog this time; the winter wind had sucked every drop of moisture out of the sere land, and even the river could not give them a curtain. He'd had two more days than he thought he would after their initial skirmish, no doubt because Diort had sent climbers around the peaks to avoid the ild Fallyn archers, to stake out the high ground Bistel had been determined not to let him have. That is what Bistel would have done. So now their waiting was done, and the Vaelinars had a warlord but no Warrior Queen. No word or sign of Lariel, no trap to spring, just a war to fight. His mouth stretched in a thin smile. He had prepared for this. This was why he had been raised as a warlord, to make war, to know the contingencies, to plan for victory and defeat and, even more importantly, afterward. Too often the aftermath went unnoticed. The victor had to be as careful with the people he defeated as he had been in defeating them. This was why he had peace in the northern lands he called home, this was why he planted and harvested when he was not making war, because it lay within him to replenish and nurture that which had been cut down. He offered hope, a plan, and a future after conquering.

He held his aryn staff across his legs. It served as a shield as well as a bludgeon in his off-hand. Made following the tradition in his immediate family, the staff was greenwood, cut from the finest aryn tree on his lands. He did not know if it would take root when planted in the ground of his grave by his son when he fell, but he thought it would. He would be truly surprised if it did not. Then again, he wouldn't really know. Bistel's mouth quirked further in an ironic smile.

An aide loped frantically toward him and brought his horse to a pawing stop. "My lord! Diort has men on the upper peak, trying to approach the dam of the Revela."

"Of course he is." Bistel did not doubt that, despite ild Fallyn archers and fog, that the Galdarkans would have discovered the Revela all but bone dry, its source held and cut off by his forces. "Harry them. Let them get close, but keep them contained. The dam will be destroyed when I wish it destroyed, but let the Galdarkan think that he is thwarting our objective. Pick them off sparingly. Is that clear?"

His aide looked baffled but ducked his chin in quick agreement. "Aye, Lord Vantane, understood. Hold them off, bring them down only if necessary, keep them busy."

"That's the idea." Bistel waved him off. The aide put a bootheel to his mount, and the horse sprang away as if spurred within an inch of its life, mane and tail flying.

Traps within traps, and Abayan Diort would have

only the surface of them revealed to him. Bistel settled his boots in stirrups. He watched the shield men fall into position and the archers begin to nock their arrows. Horses neighed in anticipation of a charge as lancers swung into their saddles. The foot soldiers secured their weapon harnesses. Every one of them looked to him at least once before looking away to their own commander for orders. He had already given them his blessing. He would not fight today, it would not do well to have the forces lose their leader if he could help it. But tomorrow ... he glanced at the sky. Tomorrow all might be necessary.

They burst out of the tunnel like a submerged apple bobs to the top of a tub of water. Bregan reeled and fell to the ground, laughing hoarsely until he lapsed into gasping. Garner collapsed into a sitting position, turning his face to the sky, the gray and leaden sky that had been promising rain for days, make that weeks now, without any real release. He did not care. He had thought he would never see the sky or clouds again. He listened as Bregan finally subsided into wheezes that were, comparatively, silent. He freed his waterskin to take a long, satisfying draught that wet his throat and filled his stomach. The trickle of water he'd found and they'd followed led here, to where the trickle became a little more than that, and the grass was winter brown and the shrubs stuck dying leaves into the air.

"This," he observed, "can't be the Ashenbrook. That is a great, wide river, aye?"

"So I've heard. Never crossed it myself." Bregan Oxfort rolled over lazily onto his stomach, propping himself on his elbows, and took the waterskin when it was passed to him. He poured a little over his head and face before drinking deeply.

"I'll see if I can snare something for a bit of supper.

Then we'll need to fill my skin and your flask and anything else we can carry that will hold water."

Bregan looked at him with his fine-boned Kernan face streaked in dirt and water as if he were a Bolger heathen, and he arched an eyebrow. "Might I ask why?"

"We're going back in, to find the passage to Ashenbrook, and warn them, aye?"

Silence met his question. Garner waited a moment or two, then put his hand out and shook Bregan's shoulder roughly. "We're warning them, aren't we?"

Bregan let out a sigh. "That would be the question." He pushed himself into sitting up, his braced leg stretched out in front of him and kneading it as he seemed to gather effort and words. Or perhaps it was courage he gathered, Garner thought. "There seems little profit in life or in coin to go back in and find ourselves a leg behind the Raymy, an encounter we're not likely to survive a second time. On the other hand, time flows differently along those passageways—"

"What do you mean?" Garner interrupted sharply.

Bregan took a timepiece out of the vest under his coat. He tapped it. "Dead it is, and has been ever since we stepped foot into the caves. Its gears aren't broken or jammed nor its winding stem snapped. It's just . . . dead. Well, it did a few things first. First all its pictographs spun in reverse as if its little world had gone mad. Then it worked in fits and spurts but never with the correct time as I reckoned it must have been, and then it spun to a halt altogether." He tapped the timepiece again gently. "Fine workmanship made this. It's never failed before." He slipped it back into his inner vest pocket.

Garner gave a chuff. "Which can mean nothing."

"Or it can mean that we have no chance of cutting them off. They could be days ahead of us in travel."

"As my da would have said, no planting ensures no harvest."

Bregan considered him. "Your father was a fine caravan guard in his day. Disciplined and yet hell on wheels.

Raiders stayed away on the mere chance he might be guarding the caravan that trip."

Tolby spoke little of his youth, yet Garner was not surprised to hear Bregan's evaluation. He gave a nod of comprehension and then toed his boot into the other. "That was then. Tell me how to read the tiles, and I'll be going by myself if necessary." He stood and dusted himself off.

"I would if I could."

"It does you no good to keep me back. You can fend for yourself out here."

"I'm not keeping you back on my account!"

They locked eyes. Bregan sucked in a breath. "Do you accuse me of lying about the tiles?"

Garner lifted and dropped a shoulder diffidently.

"I make deals that could buy and sell most cities at the shake of my hand, the promise of my word."

"When it profits you, I've no doubt of that."

"There is no benefit in this but death."

"Then you're as blind and useless as that timepiece of yours if you can't see that even one life saved is profitable."

Bregan got to his feet. He bent to straighten his trousers under the brace and check the strapping that held it in place, wincing a bit as he did. It might be chafing him a bit, but Garner couldn't find much sympathy. The trader walked and even ran when others less fortunate might be hobbled for life. Oxfort looked up to see Garner considering him and must have read the expression, for he flushed a little. "I'll take you in, show you the first tile we find."

"And then?"

"Whether you can read it or not, first we come out, get water and eat. It doesn't do anyone any good if we drop."

Garner told him, "I'll set a snare first." He patted his pockets down for a bit of twine and a peg, a useful thing Dwellers carried that could be used for snaring or even fishing, if it came to that. He'd rather fish, but the brooklet here was far too reedy and insubstantial to have more than frogs basking in it. He went down to the water anyway and set his snare near a bevy of small paw prints before rejoining Bregan.

The tunnel had grown dark again and they stumbled against each other until Bregan's searching touch found what he was looking for. At the glide of his fingertips over it, the tile lit and its glow illuminated the passage just enough to see by. Bregan drew him to it. "Can you see the brushstrokes over the tile? The sigils and runes?"

Garner all but put his nose to it. The tile had been glazed masterfully and held a pleasing pattern to it, but he could see nothing remarkable about it that could be deciphered and read. Finally, he shook his head in regret. "Maybe a pattern or a decoration, a floret, nothing more."

"I can't see the runes till I touch the tile, although I can sense the tiles wherever they are placed." Bregan put his palm over it. "Magicked, I suppose, like the Elven Ways of the Vaelinar."

"Then I'll go without the tiles."

"You'll never find your way. You'll wander under these mountains until . . ."

"No choice is there? I won't be having much of a life to live if I know that I might have done something to save others, and didn't."

"Dwellers always did have a stubborn streak."

"Aye. That comes from doing things ourselves and not waiting for the Gods to speak to us. The Gods help those who are already doing the deed."

"Do you think? Or perhaps they're just always watching you because you're entertaining?"

Garner punched Bregan in the bicep and the trader laughed. He rubbed his arm and waved. "Out, out, I'm hungry and then we'll brave being the heroes."

As luck and skill would have it, Garner's snare had

caught a small coney. He prepared it gratefully for roasting while Bregan managed to strike a fire and rig a spit. While he cooked and the waterskins were being filled to bursting, he pondered their course of action. As gambling men, he and Oxfort both knew that whatever they planned, it would be against all odds.

Bistane sang. Whether loud enough to be heard by her troops or quietly enough that only his mount, ears flicking back and forth, heard the crooning, he had not been quiet. Lara supposed that he would have a battle chant ready on his lips when, if, they reached the Ashenbrook. Now he paused before starting a new ballad, one that tore at her heart when she recognized it:

> *"Over hills of drifting mist and*
> *valleys cupped low with sun,*
> *we wander yet, our souls in search*
> *of the lost Trevilara.*
> *Her name is forever burned*
> *and yet stays buried,*
> *carried on every wind and treasured breath.*
> *Trevilara is lost and gone before us all,*
> *A final hope, waiting for our death.*
> *Oh, Trevilara, if I could but know you*
> *If I could see and touch you through sorrow's rain,*
> *My spirit would soar beyond the silences*
> *Of all the stars, and my soul come home again."*

She put her hand out to stop his song. Bistane turned wondering blue eyes to her, and then dipped his chin in understanding.

He smoothed the reins in his hand. "I give it five more days before we reach the fighting plains."

"I know."

"My father will hold."

"That, I know, too. Only at what cost." She looked away, over the dry highlands as they rode, past the bountiful lands of Larandaril, out of range of the blessing of the sacred river Andredia. She saw, as she knew Bistane did, land struggling as it was to survive without the bane of armies marching through and blood staining the ground instead of needed rain.

"I am old enough," she murmured, "but I cannot remember a drought like this."

"And I older, nor can I."

"After the battle, we shall have to send engineers throughout the lands. See what conservation we can work. Set to building irrigation canals. We can't depend on chance to break the dry spell."

"It could only be a season or two."

"Or it may be the beginning of a cycle which our farmers cannot survive without our help."

"There are Kernan weather witches . . ."

"I've consulted them," Lara told him. "Dry as a stone, they told me, for years to come. They are frightened."

"Then we shall have to take whatever steps we can."

"Your word on that?"

His blue-within-sharp-blue eyes met hers, eyes of blue with gold and silver, and his face became very solemn. "My word to my queen."

"Good." She put a hand to the nape of her neck and rubbed there, as if easing a tension. "My vantanes show me a pitched battle. The warlord holds his own, but . . . the cost is mounting."

He had no immediate answer. When he found one, his words were cut short by a shout from one of the troops riding point.

"Smoke!"

Lara wheeled her mount around and caught up with the scout. "Yes, I see." She frowned at the very thin snake of blue-gray smoke undulating into the air. "Not much of a campfire."

"Not a lightning strike, or we'd be facing wildfire."

"No." She weighed losing time against finding out who might be camped in the middle of nowhere. She signaled for the scout to proceed. "Let's see who is having an early dinner."

Chapter
Fifty-Two

"I AM FREEZING," Nutmeg grumbled, hugging her arms about herself. She jogged to keep pace with the strides of the others, cursing long-legged humans silently. Even being forced to lead their horses didn't seem to slow them at all. Her hair worked its way loose from its tieback for the twentieth time that day . . . had it been a day? . . . and she *pfuffed* stray curls away from her forehead and eyes in aggravation. The day before she'd worn it braided, so it had been a day and then two . . . she gave up trying to reckon time.

Rufus gave his customary grunt in response. He fumbled for a moment in the pockets of the leathery apron he wore under his armor like some others wore shirts before fishing out a handful of jerky bits and pushing them onto her. "Eat. Chew slowly."

As if she had any choice, jerky being what it was, but she shoved the first one into her mouth with a grateful, "Thank you!" around the tough, dry piece. Salty, sweet goodness swelled in her mouth as she chewed. And chewed. And finally got it softened enough so that she could savor it before swallowing.

"Not good on march," Rufus observed.

"They threw us in the cellar for two days," Nutmeg told him. "Without food! I started off cold and hungry."

The Bolger showed his tusks in a grin. "Little one always hungry."

She had to agree with him. "Lately, anyway." She would have added more, in her defense, but Rufus put up a grizzled hand, stopping her abruptly. He waved back at Tiforan and Lyat, and they all plowed to a halt, the tunnel glimmering faintly about them.

"Hear, smell, something."

When they stopped, she became aware that the muffled noise that she had been hearing for quite a while now, like the drumming of a heartbeat within the mountain, had grown louder. But it was not near, or so she hoped, not knowing what she heard. Was it the pulse of the beast Rufus told them had made the tunnels even though he said it had gone to the sea and died? Could another such great reptile still live within the stone, its venom cutting endless loops of passages around them? Would it have a great heartbeat that echoed and thrummed throughout the mountain?

The Bolger listened for a long while before clucking at the back of his throat. He flashed his tusks. "This way."

Nutmeg balked. "How do you know?"

Rufus patted her back stiffly. "She always smell like flower. Even here." He cast his glance about the tunnel. "Even here."

"Good enough for me, then."

"If not, then I suggest you drop behind and let us finish our mission," Tiforan commented from behind them. "I can have food and water left with you as well as designating a way out."

Nutmeg threw him a look over her shoulder. "And what would that mission be?" He did not know Rivergrace had been charged with treason, nor did he seem to be in pursuit of her. In fact, he seemed to regard Rufus as leading them toward an objective for which Tiforan had no time or patience.

"I think," Tiforan answered dryly, "if you had the confidence of Lord Diort, I would have been informed of it before starting out. Therefore, you do not know because you are not supposed to know, and I intend to leave it at that."

Even in the half-light, he could sound haughty. Nutmeg decided to take a stab at his arrogance. "You won't take her without a fight." Whether it was Lariel or even Tressandre that the Galdarkans pursued, she knew they were not up to the task. Did they not have female soldiers within their nomadic ranks? Barbaric to think they might not and could underestimate capturing either woman with only a man or two. Behind her, she could hear someone stumble and catch himself at her words, and she smiled in satisfaction. She thought she caught a wink from Rufus as they followed a curve in the tunnel and a new tile panel began to glow in response to their presence.

Rufus made a signal for silence and passed it to all three of them. Tiforan made a tsking noise but held his tongue even though the expression on his face looked as if he had been sucking a particularly tart berry. She slowed gratefully when he brought them down to a walk, and then she thought she could hear voices.

"... you're still bleeding."

"I can't be. That must be sweat."

"It's too cold in here to sweat."

"I'm not cold. I am burning up."

Her heart leaped. She knew the voices. Dropping her mount's reins, Nutmeg wheeled her short legs into a run, dimly seen tunnel ahead of her or not. "Rivergrace!" she cried even as Tiforan raced after her to stop her, his hand catching and losing its grasp on her skirt. "Sister!"

"There. Tight?" Rufus asked her, as he knotted a last strapping into place and frowned at Rivergrace. Grace put her hand on his forearm, unable to believe that her old friend had survived and returned to find her, and murmured, "Thank you."

He rubbed a rough finger along her cheek. "Little flower, little one. Rufus never forget."

"We put you on a pyre in honor."

"Like chief. Grateful, but I not dead." He grunted as he wiped his hands on his apron and stood. "Crawled off, healed."

She hugged him.

Tiforan, the envoy of Abayan Diort, looked annoyed at the whole proceeding. Sevryn stood with his back braced to the tunnel as Nutmeg ministered apple vinegar to his cuts in cleaning, the Bolger's packs having yielded a field kit of remedies and bandaging. Tiforan had already handed over an ointment for Rivergrace's wounds. "Is the bleeding stopped?"

"For now, clean and dry."

"Excellent." He unsheathed his sword, swung with the flat of the blade and knocked Rufus flat upon his back. Tiforan addressed the now unmoving Bolger, "I will tell my lord you served us well. My mission could not have been completed without you."

Even as Nutmeg and Sevryn launched themselves at the Galdarkan in one move, the horses panicked and fled down the tunnel. All the Dweller and the half-breed accomplished was to block and tangle each other. Lyat took out Sevryn with a well-placed blow on the back of the head, pinning Nutmeg under his limp form with no chance to fight free before Tiforan had her tied and roped to Rufus. Grace made not a move except to fall back and cling to the tunnel, swaying with the effort just to stay on her feet.

Rivergrace's eyes fluttered. "What . . . ?"

"A little something extra in the Bolger's ointment. Nothing harmful." Tiforan didn't even seem bothered by the loss of the horses, merely flicking a finger at Lyat. "Carry her."

The scribe moved to catch Grace as she wilted help-lessly and he hoisted her over one shoulder.

Nutmeg's mouth curled in contempt. "You wanted her all along!"

Tiforan paused in his binding of Sevryn. "My lord is not the ignorant soldier he's been taken for. He knew the offering of Lady Rivergrace was bait or pawn, in-tended to disservice the lady. Daravan hoped to put off interest in that which he valued most, but at the same time, if taken, would cause the most disruption. There-fore, Diort takes the bait. We will see why this lady is of value to the Warrior Queen and to Daravan." He tugged one last knot tight at Sevryn's ankles.

Tiforan nodded at Lyat, and the two left even as Nut-meg shouted after them until she grew hoarse and they had disappeared from sight.

She quieted only when the ominous drumming grew ever nearer and she could tell then, it was the boot stamps of hundreds.

"I'm disappointed in famed Dweller hospitality. There should be enough roasted—whatever that is—to feed ev-eryone." Lara rested her hands lightly on her mount's with-ers and looked down at Bregan Oxfort who had clearly seen much better days and a Dweller who, by the looks of him, had to be related to Nutmeg Farbranch. That sturdy family clung to her as troublesomely as firestick burrs.

Oxfort, dirty and disheveled, his face barely scrubbed clean, gave her a half bow which was as discourteous as it was body weary. He looked, frankly, as if he had been dragged behind one of his caravans. Her eyebrow arched at him.

"You are late, Highness, for your war."

"Unavoidably delayed."

"Then take my advice and go not at all, for there won't be anything left to save but yourself."

Bistane's horse took a leap forward as if his rider's legs had tightened about his flanks. He reared to a stop just short of Oxfort. Bistane leaned down a little, eyes narrowed at the trader. "Do you suggest Lariel is cowardly?"

"No," Bregan told him wearily. "It's the truth. We saw the Jewel of Tomarq shattered and Istlanthir murdered . . ."

Lara turned her head abruptly to the rear of her troops. "Tranta, can you hear?"

Tranta Istlanthir brought his horse to the forefront, just behind Lariel, and answered quietly, "I do." He squeezed his eyes hard shut a moment, before opening them to stare at Garner. "You would be, if I'm not mistaken, Sevryn's man there?"

"I was. It was not," and Garner's voice shook openly, "not a good death, m'lord. Not a clean one, but a very hard one. His body . . . his body and soul seemed torn apart . . . and little was left but shreds for the kites to fight over. You could not even tell," and Garner swallowed hard, "that a man had died there."

Tranta cleared his throat twice. "He Returned, then, as some Vaelinar do. Gods help him." He cleared his throat a third time. "Who killed him?"

"Quendius, with a most unnatural arrow," Bregan informed him. "The same he used to strike the Jewel. How it shattered it, I couldn't tell you, but it did."

"As Osten died," stated Lariel. Her horse turned in a restive circle, and she brought her mount around so she could face them again. "We know all this, or most of it. It explains none of why you are here and why you would accuse me of dalliance to my advantage."

Bregan put his hand up and came to stand by her knee and stroke her mount's neck quietly. "Lariel, with the Shield gone, a navy came to Smuggler's Coast and landed an army there for Quendius. It marches to Ashenbrook, and there is a small chance we can get there before it, but not much of one. We deserted it and were

gathering strength before trying to find a way to warn
you."

Her face paled. Her hair lay tumbled about her shoulders and she brushed it back in a glinting of gold and
silver. "What army?"

"The Raymy. We ran in front of it, myself and a few
hundred caravan guards, allied to Quendius before we
knew of his foul treachery, and I . . . I bolted at the first
opportunity, and took Garner with me to keep myself
alive." Bregan rubbed the horse's neck as if he could not
bear to meet Lariel's eyes. "Stories of old don't do them
justice. They eat their own dead and wounded, as well as
any they might fight. They're not human but perhaps of
a reptile breed. They will sweep across our lands like an
unstoppable plague."

"Then we must stop them." Lara gathered her reins.
"You mentioned a small chance to get there first. Tell
me what it is."

Garner pointed down the tiny, winding stream to the
foot of the mountain. "Through the caves."

"Mounted or on foot?"

The two men traded a look. "Mounted," ventured
Bregan. "Although led, in some places, where we've
been. The main tunnel is vast, but I can't say about the
other tunnels, and we must see if there's a way to pace
them without being seen."

"Fair enough."

Garner kicked his fire apart, picking up his pack and
Bregan's and tearing the spitted coney in two. He tossed
one section to Bregan. "We'll eat on the run," he said.
Tranta leaned down to give him a hand up.

Bregan stood with one hand full of greasy dinner and
the other still on the horse's neck. Lara's horse sidled
away from him at the smell of the meat as Bistane kneed
his mount over. Bistane smiled ruefully before kicking
a foot out of his stirrup and offering his hand as well.
Bregan swung up, saying, "I need to be in front. There are
tiles, placed tiles, and I need to read them as we move."

"By your leave, Highness," Bistane said, and he gravely moved his horse to the fore of the group.

Just inside the lip of the cave, the group halted. Lara opened herself to the many threads that had created the mountain, winding in and about it, and let the pathways flood her. "Old," she said, "older than the Mageborn, almost older than the mountain itself. The Mageborn took what they found and used it. It is not a Way such as we would weave with the elements, but a backward thing forced on the elements. The tunnels are entwined with magic that is near extinguished, a prideful and spiteful magic, but useful. An evil and ravenous worm ate away the stone, and the Mageborn followed in its path to do their own workings. We need to be careful not to get lost here, either in the flesh or in the soul." Lara twisted about in her saddle. "Any who do not wish to ride with me are excused. The Raymy are a formidable foe." Her gaze swept across the assembled horsemen and women. Not one reined out of line. Her face relaxed into a very slight smile. "Then," she said, "pray our tashya are both swift and courageous. And we half as stubborn as any Dweller."

Chapter Fifty-Three

"MAY ALL YOUR TEETH FALL OUT but one, so it can rot and you still have toothaches!" Nutmeg shouted, her raspy voice echoing down the tunnel. Tiforan and Lyat, long gone, could not possibly have heard her, but she loosed the still potent curse after them anyway.

Sevryn stirred with a moan. She could feel him shifting at her feet. "Damn Galdarkans," he muttered. "They know how to tie a knot. I can't reach any of my blades."

"They took Grace," Meg told him miserably. She shifted and squirmed, but none of her bonds relaxed at all. She would lie bundled up like a stuffed sausage on a drying rack until something interested in untying her—or eating her—found them. She let out a sullen sigh.

Sevryn squirmed about again before sneezing as dust rose and filled his nostrils. At the noise, Rufus growled. "Noisy, both of you. Bring hunters."

"Have you a knife?"

The Bolger snorted. "No need. Have teeth."

Nutmeg felt his heavy form heaving against hers and then a rough tugging and gnawing at her ropes. Strands frayed about her ankles and she gave a little kick, parting them! She rolled. "Get my hands."

"Rope taste bad." Rufus let out a low, rumbling chuckle.

"I'll have them coated with honey next time." Nutmeg bit her lips and fell silent as the rough edge of his tusk tore at the tender inside of her wrist.

His mouth and flat nose snuffled at her fingers. "Honey taste good."

Bolgers had a sweet tooth. Who knew? But she would remember, if they ever won free. "Muffins and honey cakes whenever you ask," she promised him. Her wrists flew apart even as his tusk slipped with a burning rasp, slicing her. She sat up, shedding the rest of her bonds as quickly as she could, parts of her body numb and other parts throbbing in bruised aches. Then she slid her hand over Sevryn and found one of his concealed daggers. She had to put a boot to his ribs for leverage to tug it free. She sawed clumsily with her tingling hands and he shoved off his ropes as soon as he could, grabbing the dagger from her. Rufus had almost chewed himself clear when Sevryn moved to him and knifed away the last of his bonds.

They sat, bruised and bloody, passing around Sevryn's water flask. Nutmeg wiped her mouth with the back of her hand in gusto. "Beaten but not beat," she declared triumphantly.

"Farbranch family motto?"

"Aye! And if it isn't, it should be." She swept her amber hair back and tied it in a knot at her neck, lustrous and abundant for all that dirt caked it and even a stray splinter of quartz and obsidian decorated it. "Now to get Grace."

Sevryn took back his flask and corked it. "That won't be the hard part. We know which way they took her."

Nutmeg's eyes widened in question.

"To Diort, in the middle of Lariel's war. The hard part will be figuring out why Daravan wanted her there and getting her out."

Rufus clambered to his feet. He jabbed a finger at them. "Blood. Draw hunters."

"Last thing we want!" Sevryn sprang up and then handed Nutmeg to her feet. "Can you run a bit more?"

"That's like asking me iffen I can pick apples."

"Good, then. Running in the dark might be a bit harder. Stay close if you can. We'll hear you if you trip or fall, but we'll need quiet." Sevryn cocked his head to one side. The thrumming, drumming of many footfalls had grown closer to them. "Quendius brings an army of his own. Smugglers, bootleggers, and thieves of the worst kind, I wager. We'll do well to stay ahead of them." Sevryn moved to the lead, but Rufus cuffed him aside gently.

"Galdarkan magic caves. Confuse and lose trespassers. But these caves mine first. Not lose me."

Sevryn thumped him on the shoulder. "I have your back, then."

Rufus let out a rumbling laugh and took them down the dark, twisting pathways of long-dead Mageborn and even longer dead worms who could eat stone.

"He is regrouping, m'lord Vantane."

"Good. They need rest, then. Do not let him. Hit him now and hit him hard."

"We . . . we need rest, too, my lord."

Bistel swung about on his commander, Farlen Drebukar, who had the looks of his father Osten Drebukar in his bulk but not the heavily scarred face. "Hit him! The world has not seen the Vaelinar go to war in a century or more, and they have forgotten what we can do. Remind them, Drebukar, and make them pay dearly for that memory! Now go!"

Farlen put his fist to his forehead and wheeled his horse around, shouting hoarsely as he did so. He watched the lancers fall in behind them, raising their spears and shields.

Bistel lifted his chin so he could see over the bloodied plain. He knew what Diort planned now, as clearly as the splashes of crimson on the trodden grass and dirt. He wanted to end the skirmish quickly and decidedly so that the war would be over. No pull back to strike again another day, elsewhere. No posting of troops along the border. No, Abayan Diort wanted a clear and decisive and sound victory so that he could negotiate from a position of absolute strength. Lariel had drawn him into this confrontation, and he would not back down without winning. She had her reasons, he supposed, for being so adamant in putting down the Galdarkan warlord, reasons that had little to do with the altruistic worry that he was forcibly cobbling together a kingdom of his own by conquering town by town with no means to resist his rule. No one had sent for her help. No entreaties had been laid at the feet of the Vaelinars to stop a tyrant. No properties had been wrongly assimilated or borders crossed. Diort warred on Lariel's turf now only because she drawn him there and entrapped him into doing so.

Yet he had come willingly, wanting a resolution that only a battle could bring. Win or lose.

Bistel picked up his helm and settled it over his snow-white hair. Not that either of them intended to lose. His men were tired, uncertain now of why it was they had been brought to fight. It was time for him to join the fray. He signaled his cavalry with a whistle and even the hounds answered, rattling their armored collars, barking sharply as they wove in and about the dancing legs of the tashya horses. He wondered for the last time where Lariel Anderieon might be.

He raised his aryn staff, cried his war cry, "*Scresendan narata*," and charged down the slope of the small hill at the enemy.

"By the Gods," breathed Bistane. He took his hand from the tile even as he'd read it for Lariel when they'd heard the march.

Garner looked into the massive cavern hall. His bowels would have turned to water, if he'd anything in his stomach, but he'd thrown up the half-cooked coney a while back and nothing stirred in him but bile. Still, he stared. Ravers and Raymy marched steadily into the cavern from their tunnel, filling its vast size, and it was like watching ants boil out of an anthill, their single target a drop of honey. Light filtered over them fitfully as if their very presence offended whatever illuminated the hall, swallowing up brightness where it touched. He knew that must be impossible, even as the sparkling quartz lamps that shone overhead were. The amulet inside his shirt burned against his skin as if it, too, held a light within it. He took it out and looked at the odd thing and saw nothing remarkable although it lay warm in his palm. Torn off a Raver, did it sense that its true owners neared him? He stuffed it back out of sight.

"There is no way," Lariel murmured, "that we can pass without being seen. Once we ride into the cavern, we're in full sight."

The feeder tunnel they shared broke through the stone halfway down the cavern. "But we're still ahead of them."

For how long? That question hung in the air, unasked and unknowable. The abominations moved on foot. On two legs and all fours, bounding now and then, their progress ragged. They had been marching for days, and that might be the only advantage Garner and the others held over them. Four or five horses straggled to the front, trotting and loping about with their reins dangling, their saddles askew, riderless. He saw only one being mounted and Bistane pointed the man out as all eyes turned to him.

"Quendius."

"Have they archers?"

"Not that I can see, but they are oddly shaped. I can't stake my life on it."

"Then I won't ask you to," Lara answered softly. "I need two volunteers, if your horses still have bottom to them."

Why did she ask for horses with stamina? Garner's head twisted about as two riders shuffled forward. One woman smiled thinly. "My horse is part mountain pony. He can run all day."

"And mine can run with hers, although she is pure-bred." The two Vaelinars traded looks.

"Naymer. Cayleen. I do not intend for you to be left behind. Succeed if you can, rejoin us at all cost. Clear?"

They nodded at Lariel.

"Drop back. Hamstring the stray horses."

Garner gargled. Her gaze snapped to him. "They will tear the meat to shreds, will they not? From what you've told us?"

"Aye, but . . ."

Her expression softened a little. She returned her attention to her volunteers. "Kill the beasts if you can. But whatever you do, bring them down quickly. That will slow the troops a little. Perhaps enough."

"Quendius?"

"He is an adept archer. Stay clear and out of range. Go in swiftly, do what you must, and get out! Stopping him, I fear, will not stop the Raymy. Now, go!" And she sent them off in a spray of dust and broken tile as they charged from their passage into the main hall.

Lara spurred her horse into the open as well, heading the way Bregan had brokered for them, Bistane's mount shoulder to shoulder with hers. The horses eagerly stretched their legs out after long confinement in the closed tunnels, but she gathered her mount back. He fought her hold with an angry shake of his head that rattled his bridle before settling into the controlled lope she demanded of him. Garner held tightly to Tranta's waist. Over the thunder of hooves, he could hear a hiss rise in sharpness and volume, a thousand throats and more issuing it in gargling, keening measure. It sent chills down his spine and made the gorge rise in his throat. Tranta Istlanthir's body tensed under his hold. Then, without warning, his horse veered out of the pack, arrowing straight down on the only ridered horse leading the dreaded army.

Quendius, the murderer of Kever Istlanthir, Tranta's brother.

Garner bit his lip till the taste of copper blood filled his mouth as he held on dearly. He could hear shouts behind them, of dismay and command, but Tranta never wavered. Garner thought of beating on his back with his fist to turn him even as he knew that nothing on this earth could move Tranta. Would he turn back if he knew Quendius had taken the lives of any of his family? By tree's blood, he would not! He put his mouth by Tranta's shoulder. "I have your back," he said. He pulled his sword.

Tranta's only answer was to draw a dagger, a wickedly sharp blade, with a sea-green jewel of incomparable worth in its hilt as he bore down on Quendius. Foam flew from the bridle of his mount as it pinned its ears back in urging to its rider. They charged across the expanse of the cavern hall which was big enough to have swallowed the city of Hawthorne on its island and all its seven bridges connecting it to the shore. The depth of it took his breath away as they bore down on Quendius and yet never seemed to grow nearer although the horse stretched its long legs out in immense strides, rising and falling, racing headlong into a terrible maw. Hoofbeats sounded on tile and polished stone in a staccato that grew louder and louder. It dimmed as they crossed dirt once again and Garner glanced back at a tile road that transected the hall.

Naymer reached the straggling horses first and took

the leader down with a cut to the jugular. The horse somersaulted and stayed down. The resulting noise from the Ravers and Raymy behind it shivered through Garner as he heard it, a rising and falling exultation over the scenting of fresh blood and hot meat. He swallowed down the bitter tang at the back of his throat and turned his head away. That would slow some but not the bulk of the army. They were disciplined; they had to be, or they would have torn each other apart over the last few days. No, they had their objective in mind. He looked back even though he had sworn to himself he would not and what he saw burned its way into his mind.

Each Raver and Raymy, as they passed the still and in some cases still quivering carcasses of the horses, slowed only long enough to rip off a hunk of bloody flesh to fill their clawed hands as they marched inexorably on. Cayleen and Naymer swung about, whipping reins against their horses.

Garner tore his eyes away from the sight as Tranta moved in the saddle. They charged at the man in the fore, his white-wool longcoat swinging aside from his charcoal-tinged bared chest. Quendius stood in his stirrups as they lunged at one another, and Garner recognized the telltale movement of an archer unslinging his bow from his shoulder.

"Bow!" he cried in warning.

Tranta seemed not to hear him. He twisted slightly on his horse's back, and the horse curved his pathway in answer. They turned, almost broadside now to Quendius.

Quendius filled his hand with an arrow whose arrowhead gleamed ruby red as if carved from a jewel. He knew those arrows. Garner's mouth went dry, and his throat failed him when he tried to yell a second warning.

Two things happened almost at once, so quickly he could scarcely comprehend them. First, Quendius nocked the arrow and fired at them. Second, Tranta's horse slipped on the edge of the old tile road, its legs splaying in every direction. The arrow whizzed by them, so close he could hear its whine, as Tranta fought to bring the horse upright, to keep from losing control entirely, and going down. The horse scrambled and made it up. They whirled about and Garner could see Quendius so close by that his eyes of black jet burned like coals into them.

Tranta cocked his hand and threw his dagger. "*Haviga aliora!*" he spat as it sang out of his hand. It whipped through the air, silent and straight even as Quendius dipped a shoulder and tried to retreat. It dove deeply into flesh with a solid *thunk*. Quendius reeled in his saddle before reaching out and pulling the dagger free as he skinned his lips back in pain.

A deep blow. A hurting blow. But not a killing one.

"Sorry, Brother," Tranta murmured. "Next time." He straightened his horse out and whipped it after Lariel and the others, now so far ahead of them they could barely be seen. Garner held on and fought to breathe.

Behind them, the Raymy loosed their voices in squeals of fury. Tranta hissed back and concentrated on riding. Garner could feel the determination running through his body as he held on tightly. "What was that you said?"

"*Haviga aliora.* Seek the soul. It should have gone to the heart, if Quendius had one." Bitterness dripped from Tranta's answer, and he said no more except to whisper encouragement to his mount who labored under the weight of two riders.

They gained slowly, inexorably, on Lara and the others as the horses scented fresh air and the yawning opening of the cavern's end; a gray light flooded inward. The horses lifted their heads, ears pricked forward, and bugled their triumphant race as the sun silhouetted and then swallowed them up one by one with its presence as they raced into its rays.

Behind, only a length or two, Tranta leaned over his tashya's neck and whistled gently, and stroked his lathered mount. A hiss sounded behind Garner, barely heard over the pounding hooves. He crooked his head to look back under his arm. He saw the thing leap. He braced his short sword, bringing it about as it fell upon the horse's haunches, a thousand sharp teeth and talons sinking into the animal and into Garner even as they, too, gained the sun.

Chapter
Fifty-Four

NUTMEG SQUEALED AS RUFUS GRABBED her and pushed her out of the tunnel like a bottle expelling a cork. They emerged somewhere between the heavens and what must be hell.

Even the sullen sunlight made him squint against the brightness as Sevryn crawled out of the dark. Nutmeg sat tumbled on the ground. Rufus stood with a great popping of joints, his age betraying him. They looked down on the trampled river plain strewn with fallen bodies and writhing horses and a hound here and there, while those still fighting surged around them, following bannered leaders and drummers. They could see the bones of the dry bed of the Revela and the wide blue ribbon of the Ashenbrook, and the struggling troops within their borders. Dead and dying lay everywhere. She scrubbed at her eyes. "Where is he . . . where is he?"

Sevryn put his hand to the back of her neck. "Down there," he said, and pointed, to the line of ild Fallyn archers and bowmen on horseback, following the command of a man in a chariot.

"There," she whispered in soft echo and fisted one hand tightly. "What about Rivergrace?"

"If I could spot Diort, I might know." Sevryn hunkered down on a flat rock. "Where would he be, Rufus?"

The Bolger swung his head in a slow shake. "Not see. White-haired chief leads." He pointed a callused finger toward the white-tailed helm of Bistel Vantane, as distinctive as if the warlord were without a helmet. Bistel headed a wing of infantrymen, cutting a path before him.

"We might be here before them." Sevryn patted himself absently, counting the weapons he still had left about him. "Can you get down to Diort?"

"I can. Not you."

"Will he trust you over Tiforan?"

Rufus snorted as if Sevryn asked a stupid question. Sevryn waved him off. "All right, go. And keep your head down. And . . . may we meet as friends after this." He offered Rufus his hand.

The Bolger cracked a grin and shook his hand mightily. Then he leaped down the face of the crag as if he were a young goat.

"You're . . . you're not going with him?"

"I haven't a chance on that side of the lines. Rufus will find her and get her out of the fray. I trust him for that. He has a love for her like a father for a daughter."

Nutmeg stared down, watching the Bolger's form grow smaller as he picked his way through rock and shrub. "How do you suppose that happened?" Rivergrace never talked about her life before she was pulled from the river. Not the small things, although one could hardly count Rufus as small.

"Before you found her, when she and her parents were slaves in the mines and forge, she shared what little she had with another starving slave. She was a child and recognized his hunger as sharp as her own, his hurts as painful. She gave him what she could, him, a Bolger, a stinker, without regard for what he was or how savage he could be. He never forgot."

"Even then," mused Nutmeg softly, "she was like that."

"Aye, even then." Sevryn set her on her feet. "Now we go down to our side and tell them an army of ruffians is headed their way. Out of this mountain, somewhere, somehow, just like us, the rock will spit them out."

"Will they believe us?"

"Lariel, perhaps not if she were here, but Bistel will."

Nutmeg nodded as she brushed past him, hopping down the rocks much as Rufus had. Sevryn watched her go. "I hope," he added under his breath.

Tiforan found his lord in a small copse of sere, dry trees, drawing lines in the dirt, discussing how to take out a Vaelinar-held position where the Revela seemed to be dammed. The din of the battle could not muffle his warlord's voice nor the chill of the day take the edge off it. Tiforan approached quietly, one hand still holding a great tankard of wine flavored with a bit of water that an aide below had pressed on him before showing him where his lord could be found, and he went to one knee before Diort. Moving through the encampment at the battle's edge had been a trial but nothing compared to what they had already survived. Pride filled his chest. Lyat followed, dumping his captive without ceremony on the ground. She sat up, sputtering, but Diort put his hand up for silence and she, like the others, obeyed. Tiforan could only wonder at that, for the woman had screeched like some demonic wind god since awakening over Lyat's shoulder. Abayan Diort was the master of men (and women) in ways Tiforan could only hope to emulate some day. The air stank of leather and burning and blood and sweat. His eyes threatened to water.

"Tiforan. You were successful, I see, in more ways than one."

"The Pathways of the Guardians are myriad, Warlord, and time flows in them like a river, sometimes in full tide and sometimes even eddying in reverse. I thought we might be lost in them, but with the words you entrusted to me, I accomplished what you asked of me." Tiforan inclined his head and watched the ground, waiting for his praise. "You need only ask it of me, and I will show you the entrance to the pathway that delivered us. If things ... if there is a need ..." he stopped. "If the warlord should require ..."

"If I need a retreat, I know whom to ask," Diort stopped him. "I sent you with two men, you return with one. What happened?"

"We took the prize you requested from the halls of the Warrior Queen herself, but a man followed, the one known as the Queen's Hand. He came after with all intent of either rescuing Lady Rivergrace or destroying her, failing rescue. Rufus gave his life preventing that." The scribe Lyat stayed silent, staring at the ground, as Tiforan spun his story.

The captive sputtered only to stop as Diort gave her a look, and she put her hand over her mouth at the glint in his jade eyes.

"It seems to have gone above and beyond the duty I required of you."

Tiforan lifted his gaze. "Thank you, my lord."

"Oh, don't thank me. Yet. Is what he says true, Rufus?" And Abayan Diort looked behind him, to a pile of threadbare blankets tossed aside on the hillock, as the old Bolger rolled out from under them. Rivergrace let out a joyful, unfettered noise then.

"No," said Rufus flatly, and crossed his arms over his chest, standing bowlegged in anger.

Diort nodded slowly. "I'll have further discussions

with you, Tiforan, and you, Lyat, later. The first thing I will ask is why you neglected to tell me that others move in the Pathways, Ravers and perhaps worse, and then we will move onto outright lies." He made a gesture and the two men were grabbed before they could even stand, and dragged down the hill to where a few supply wagons were tethered and the wounded were being tended.

He looked to Rivergrace. "So now I have you, but I gather you've little use as a hostage."

She cleared her throat and took a shallow breath, for her ribs hurt like fire despite the binding upon them. "At this moment, I have reason to think Lariel hates me as much as she hates you."

"But why does she hate me?" Diort considered her gravely, the sun which burned through clouds that it ought not to have shredded lent a glow to his bronzed skin, glinted off the diadem that held his hair back, and made shadows of the tattoos and carved scars of office and heritage in a face that might otherwise be handsome.

Rivergrace would not tell him of Lariel's vision; she would not give him anything he might use against the Vaelinars. She picked carefully among the truths she did know. "You conquer those she feels ought to have a choice."

"Was she there? How does she know I didn't give them a choice? Does she know they are worse off under my watch and care of them?"

"I don't know more than that. I can't tell you why she thinks what she does." Rivergrace shook her head help-lessly. "I'm not Vaelinar," she told him. "I wasn't raised by them, I've spent nearly my whole life with Dwellers. I know their history through tales and their politics not at all."

"But she hates you."

She nodded. She would not pretend to have a worth she didn't. Either this man would let her remain alive, or he wouldn't. She was done with being a pawn. She could feel the eyes of Rufus upon her. If he lived, Sevryn did and Nutmeg. She was not in the enemy's camp alone.

Diort took a step toward her. He touched her brow and then the bandages about her torso. "Who gave you injury?"

"I fought a Raver in the tunnels."

His eyebrows flew up. "With Rufus and the others?"

"By myself. At first."

"You're a Warrior Queen then, like Lariel. She fears a competitor."

"Oh, no. Not me. I can fight, but I'm not a warrior."

He touched her bandage again. It was wet with her blood, she realized, and it hurt when he touched her. She winced, and he withdrew his hand. "I . . . I had my back in a corner. It could only come at me one way. That— that helped."

He watched her solemnly.

"And then Sevryn came from behind and killed it when I had it down."

"And you say you are not a warrior."

She shook her head emphatically. "I don't kill. It's not what I do, it's not in me. Not like others."

"Mmmmm." Diort's mouth twisted a little. "Perhaps not. She has enough to fear from the bitch of the ild Fallyn." He took a breath. "Then what do you do, Lady of the Grace of Rivers? Why would Daravan think you of value to me?"

She hesitated but a moment, flicking a look to the stoic Rufus and back. If this Galdarkan knew of Tressandre as a thorn in Lara's side and the quest for the river Andredia, then he'd heard of what the tales said she could do. Did he ask for proof? She had no idea.

Tiforan had left his watered wine on the ground. She picked up the tankard. Dipping a finger in it, she hummed a few notes of the song that knitted her soul to her flesh, her memories to her present, her magic to her use. The water cleared as it purified. She handed the tankard to Diort who took it, smelled it, and then drank.

"Wine to water. There are those, milady, who would prefer the transformation in the other direction." He handed the cup back to her and watched as she drank, too, quenching a thirst she'd almost forgotten she had.

"Much of my kingdom is wasteland. I won't pretend that those who can find water aren't precious and those who can tell me if the water is good are even more so. But the Kernan have water witches who can do the same. I don't need to risk a kingdom to hire one of them."

"No, Warlord, you don't."

"The question I need answered, then, is one I should put to Daravan. It is he who stirs the pot, I think." Diort beckoned to Rufus. "Guard her well. There may be a use for her yet, and she becomes my guest until I am no longer fit to protect her."

"Then she my guest."

Diort looked askance at the Bolger before giving a short, dry laugh. "Then she is yours."

He gestured to an aide. "Get down there and spread the word to every commander that we may have an attack from the rear. I want the army ready to turn on my signal if necessary. Make it clear."

Rufus enfolded her hand in his and moved her away from the warlord as he pulled his scouts back into conference, their voices low and quick.

"Where is Nutmeg? Is she all right? Sevryn?"

"Little one talk much. All time. Very noisy. And fierce." Rufus skinned his lips back and made a tiny, kittenish growl.

Grace laughed in spite of her worry. "Yes! Yes, she is."

"Tiforan lucky Diort have him."

She laughed again and it made her side hurt, so she grasped it as she did. Rufus frowned as she winced. He leaned down and picked her up, cradling her in his arms against his broad chest and leather apron. He stank, but she counted it as one of the strong, good smells in her life.

"Sevryn with her. Finding white hair. Much danger to both armies."

"Ravers, then?"

Rufus shrugged. "Many. Not know all. Quendius lead."

The wind skirled around them, chill and with a hint of ice despite its dryness. "What will Diort do?"

Rufus made a noise deep in his throat. "He warrior."

Rivergrace closed her eyes briefly. Wherever Rufus carried her, she could hear the moans and soft cries of the wounded growing louder. The sounds pierced her to the bone.

Chapter
Fifty-Five

THE HORSE SCREAMED in raw agony as it bolted from the cave. It made three great leaps before the Raymy brought it down. Pitching awkwardly, its hindquarters collapsed, throwing Garner free of the attacker and Tranta over its shoulder. At the sound of the stricken beast, all of the Vaelinar circled their mounts around, weapons whipping out. The Raymy tore lose from the horse and bounded to its feet, dancing away from the kicking hooves as the poor animal thrashed. It drew swords in each hand and went after Tranta with a hiss. The blade Garner had sunk into it jutted out from its armpit, only the hilt visible.

Tranta dragged himself away from the flailing horse and fumbled for his blade. He stilled the horse's cries in a single, deep slash with a spurt of crimson, and came up on one knee in time to meet the Raymy's assault. Garner threw himself at the thing's legs, but it saw him coming and leaped straight up, blades whirling at Tranta.

Garner came to rest against the horse's quivering carcass and stayed as the Warrior Queen charged.

It did not have a chance with Lara bearing down on it. It must have known that, but it came down lightly and balanced itself in a fighting stance, meeting Tranta's cuts and then whirling about to face Lara. It staggered back a step when Bistane's feathered bolt struck it in the chest and it let out a defiant whistling hiss like a hot kettle as Lara leaned from her saddle, sword swinging. Its hand and weapon went flying. Tranta dove under its guard then, plunging his sword point deep into its torso before tearing his weapon free. Entrails exploded from the wound, and still it keened at them, its face grimacing in anger.

Lara pivoted her mount and took its head in the second pass even as it tried one last time to cut Tranta in two. The head rolled and bounced, its lips slicked back in soundless fury.

"Gather that . . . up," Lara ordered. One of her lancers threw her cloak down and did as commanded. A stench lay over the corpse as she dismounted where Tranta tried to clean his sword on the bruised and sere grasses. "Are you hurt?"

"Bruised. Garner, though," and Tranta swung his head about, blue-green hair trailing across his shoulders. "You are torn."

"Looks worse than it hurts." Garner sat in a pool of horse blood, fingering himself. "A few rips. The horse took the worst of the attack."

Lara toed the headless form. "It took four of us to bring it down." She pulled Bistane's arrow loose and handed it to him, then pried out Garner's sword. "We've no time to waste." She looked into Tranta's face. "Even to avenge brothers."

Bregan's pale face watched Garner as he retrieved his sword from Lara, and another lancer gave him a leg up while Tranta mounted behind Lariel. Deep lines etched the trader's face, and dark bruises shadowed his eyes. His lips parted as if he would say something to Garner, but it was lost as Lara snapped her reins and they took the downhill run at breakneck speed. The bugler of the company unslung his horn and winded it, heralding them.

Lara never slowed her horse as she took it through the lines. She ripped at her chain mail, tearing loose her soft white chemise underneath. Right hand knotted in the pale silk, she held it up like a banner, over her head. With her left hand laced with her horse's reins and a hank of mane to steady her, she stood in the stirrups and rode through the fighters. She cried, "To me! To me! Truce!" as she rode. Her company flanked her, but they could not protect her from all harm. She rode into the heart of the battle as if the white makeshift flag was the only guardian she needed.

Bistel heard slowly. The scream and clash of fighting surrounded him, filled his ears and mind, muting even the bugle calls. He had not ordered what he heard, and as the sound sank in, he turned his head, chin strap of his helmet chafing his neck, to see what Vaelinar countermanded the attack. Irritation flooded him. He had wedged his way slowly but steadily toward Diort who had come down off his high ground, and the two could just see each other over the surging waves of their infantrymen. While the Galdarkan would undoubtedly kill him if they came to blows, Bistel held a different objective. Now his attention was demanded. Across the bloodbath, across the wounded and fighting and the fallen, their eyes met, his and Diort.

Then he tore his gaze away to see what bore down on him.

Diort entered the fray because he could feel the Vaelinars weaken. Whatever entrapment the queen had planned, it had not materialized nor had the queen herself. Lara's absence made her troops falter, her army second-guess their presence on the field. He could sense the disheartening and feel it grow. He knew the spirit of a fighter, he could feel it like a flame, and that flame had begun to gutter and flicker in the men and women they faced. That was when he took the field. The Lion of the Galdarkans, they cheered the moment he rode from his overlook, took shield and spear from the nearest man who would surrender it to him, and he took his place among them. As the sun arched and rose in the winter sky, he could see the general of the Vaelinar—White-hair, Rufus called him—the legendary Bistel Vantane working his way toward him.

To bring down Bistel would likely turn the battle into a rout. He had no stomach for the senseless killing of soldiers when a decisive blow could stop a war. He turned his horse's head toward Bistel and began to edge his way through. Before the sun set, he would reach his goal and the warlord would die.

A trumpeting winded over his drummers. He thought the winter gusts, always cruel, had come up again although they did not usually rise until dusk. Then he caught the notes, high and strident, as the Vaelinars quieted. The fighting seemed to slow, and the army parted as if a tide rolled through it, and he saw the Warrior Queen come at last to her battlefield, her right arm high in the air with white silk unfurling from it. His first thought was that she had finally come to spring her trap upon him, and his second thought was that if he could take her, he would never have to worry about his kingdom again, and his last thought was the realization that she carried the color of truce. He recognized that last reluctantly before putting up his own hand to signal his drummers. The rhythm stopped, then began a ponderous, different beat.

The fighting stopped. Warriors stepped back, falling back to their own lines, chests heaving, weapons at parry, eyes narrowed in suspicion, but they retreated until Lara rode into an empty circle manned only by Bistel and Diort. She dismounted between them, still holding her silks high. At her gesture, her lancer threw a bloody bundle on the ground and the Raymy head fell free. Death had not softened its fierce expression or settled the lips back over its many sharp and pointed teeth.

"What is this?" Diort stared at the grisly remnant.

"Raymy," Bistel answered him distastefully. "Unless I am greatly wrong."

"Quendius landed an army of thousands. Raymy and Ravers. I was there, I saw it," provided Bregan from behind the lancer's back.

Bistel eyed Oxfort. "I see one."

Diort made a noise at the back of his throat as if in agreement.

Bregan shook his head. He dropped his hands, frustration choking his words. Lara said smoothly, "They travel the trails under the mountains, the old Pathways of the Guardians, and they're on our heels. They *will* overrun us. Our only hope is to call truce and fight together. It took four of us to bring this one down." The admission colored her face, but her eyes flashed in defiance as she finally lowered her hand and the silk of her undergarment flowed softly from her fingers.

"You ask us to meld the armies."

"I do."

Diort's jaw tightened. "The easier, then, to stab us in the back. This is a war you insisted upon. Why should I trust you?"

She stared at him. "We have a quarrel, but I won't see us lose every last fighter to such as this!" She toed the Raymy's head. Its eyes glinted ferociously, death not having leeched that from it yet.

"You thought to bow my head quickly and bring me to my knees at the bargaining table."

Lara answered slowly, "I did."

"You could have sent an envoy."

"Would you have listened to one?"

The corners of his jade eyes crinkled a bit. "Probably not."

"Then I decided a slap would get your attention."

"The dead and wounded were not slapped."

"No." Lara took a deep breath. "I planned other. I was delayed. I have the price of their deaths on me. But I would not accept more, unless there isn't any choice."

What Diort would have countered with was cut off by high-pitched screaming and yelling far behind the lines, and Lara knew they had run out of time.

Sevryn saw the battle part as if a tide had turned. Even on the stony hillside, he recognized Lariel's armor and helm and her upturned hand with the color white billowing from it. Tranta rode pillion a horse or two behind her, distinctive for his bare head of blue-green hair. Bistane held her flank. The sight took him by surprise as did the tenor of the trumpeting and the change of the Galdarkan drummers. They called for a cessation. His pulse quickened.

Too far away for details, he still saw a circle open up about Lara and a bundle drop on the ground. He could not see what it was when opened, but he *knew*. Knew it as if he had been the lancer who had done the deed. He took a step backward at the realization.

Nutmeg clutched at his arm. "What is it?"

It was the end of all he valued. It was the last battle. He could see Bistel and Diort facing one another on either side of Lara, their hands empty for the moment, a transient truce holding. What did she ask of them? Could she bend her pride long enough to hope that Diort would join them?

He had no ears to listen to their words, but he could hear the sounds of battle rejoined again, up on the stony paths, near a gaping hole at the peak. He could hear a hiss boiling out of the depths like hot iron being plunged into salt baths at a forge. He could smell fresh spilled blood on the dirt. He knew why Daravan had taken him to the salt bay to fight that morning not so long ago, so that he would know the true enemy. He had not the eyes of the Vaelinars, but as he looked down into the river valley and over two armies poised on the brink of warfare and annihilation, he saw the threads of all the lives spilled over the lands. Find the *astiri*, the way, Gilgarran used to pound at him. It had never been easy for him to use what pureblooded Vaelinars took for granted. It had been near impossible for him to look at the elements of the world about him and see what composed it and how it might be touched in the most minute manner so that it could be perceived better and perhaps even manipulated. No, he did not have the multicolored eyes of his lineage that gave the sight so easily, but he did have its Talent.

How do you blend two armies together and then turn them as one against the true enemy? What bugling could signal to turn from one army and merge to fight a third? What drumbeat could send the complicated rhythm for all to know what to do know, what was needed? He could hear fresh drumming from the Galdarkan front and saw the soldiers mill uneasily, uncertainly. He could hear the bugles and banners go up for Bistel and Lariel, and the Vaelinars assemble no less unsure. Word would be passed, but would it be clear enough and in time?

Nutmeg pulled at him again. "What's happening?"

"Raymy are attacking. Ravers with them, I think."

"Raymy?" Her voice shook in disbelief. "I thought it was just smugglers. Brigands. Quendius with outlaws."

"No. Quendius brought the most dire enemy he could find."

The two armies drew apart in confusion. They no longer attacked one another but they had no understanding of what poured out of the mountain after them. They would be plowed under. The disciplined ranks that had faced one another began to crumble in chaos.

"They have to fight!"

Slaughter if they did not, he knew that. Nutmeg threw

herself down the hill, running. "I have to tell Jeredon to fight!"

They all had to be told. He did not have their eyes, their sight, but by all the Gods he had their *Voice*.

He pulled the winter wind to him, off the ridges, off the sharp-edged peaks and crags about him. He took a deep breath, felt the ice in that wind, its sharpness deep in his lungs prickling at him. He gathered up all the power of his ability, his soul, the threads of what he knew and what must happen and then, and only then, he Spoke. Fire and power stroked his throat.

The wind roared down off the mountains. Bistel turned as it did, touching him, and it said to him, "The Raymy come. Turn to the western peak and make your stand." It left no doubt in his mind as to the truth and urgency.

Diort raised his chin as the wind shivered past him. "Who is that who speaks?"

"That is the Hand of the Queen."

"Badly named, I think, Lariel." Diort gave her a half bow. He could see the dark forms of fighters already engaged halfway up the great western peak. "I have a way to stop them, I think." He pulled his war hammer from his back. Rakka growled softly in his hands as he tightened his grip about it.

"Close the pass."

"Aye. I can bring the rock down on them, I deem."

"If you can get close enough."

Diort met Bistel's eyes. "True."

"Then you will. Queen Lariel, I think your guidance is needed here. I might suggest you drive a spearhead through that—" and Bistel nodded to the severed head on the ground, "—and use it as your banner. Bistane, with me."

Rivergrace felt her heart warm as she heard Sevryn speak, ignoring the dire message, knowing only that he lived. She came out of the small tent as its canvas rippled in the stiffening breeze and Rufus joined her there.

"He live," Rufus commented with a knowing look in his eye. He smelled of fire and iron and charcoal, and grime covered his hands.

A healer had wrapped her with fresh bandages, but she still carried pain with every movement. "I need to go to him."

The Bolger blocked her body. "He come to you."

"What if he can't?"

"Then too late."

"I can't wait until it's too late."

Rufus stayed immovable. She clenched and unclenched her hands until he patted her on the shoulder and turned her to face the west. "We wait."

Nutmeg saw the sturdy little mountain pony tethered among the fine tashya. She threw her spotted head up with a knowing eye as Nutmeg grabbed her bridle to yank her loose. "I don't know whose mount you be, but you're mine now," she told the shaggy little horse. She threw a leg over the bare back and touched heel to the small mare. She ignored the soldiers scrambling to answer the wind's summons and steered her pony across the lines to where she had seen Jeredon last. She found him in his cart, his chariot, loading quivers with arrows from a supply wagon and shouting orders at his archers. He looked up startled as she called his name.

"Nutmeg!"

"The western slope ..."

"I know, we're called there." He tossed a quiver to a waiting archer before filling his fingers with new shafts.

"You're facing Raymy."

His hand stopped in midair. "Are you certain?"

"Do apples grow on trees?"

His hand unfroze long enough to continue loading the arrows into a new quiver. Jeredon looked about and yelled "Tressandre! I need to be on my feet!" Nutmeg watched him as if she had never seen him before, and in a way, she had not. Not like this. There was blood and grime on his dark green battle leathers and the amber glints of his soft green eyes matched the red gold that streaked his dark brown hair here and there. The teasing curve to his mouth had disappeared into hard lines as he yelled again. "Ild Fallyn! Come bring me my legs!"

Tressandre ild Fallyn did not come to answer. Nutmeg's little pony stamped her feathery leg.

"I can get you up there. I know where to hit them from."

Jeredon looked to the western peak and its jagged base. "I can't drive the cart up there. I need my legs, curse it, Nutmeg, don't you understand?"

She slid off the pony and put the reins in his free hand. "Get on."

"My feet will drag."

"Your feet dragging or your ass, it's your choice."

A pulse along his jawline that she knew well ticked once or twice before he tightened his hand about the reins. He could do that much, and they both knew it. With a grunt of effort, he swung off the cart and with Nutmeg's steadying hand on his hip, he got onto the pony. His feet did not quite touch the ground. She took the headstall as he pulled two quivers over his shoulder and two bows.

"One for me?"

Jeredon snorted at her then, much like a mountain pony. "Lead me in and then I want you on your way to safe shelter."

"There is no shelter in this valley," she told him quietly and tugged the pony after her. The two of them, as agile as any creature climbing the slope, found a path straight into the heart of the new fight.

Baring his teeth at the day, Quendius tied his horse and moved upslope, among the small evergreens that grew twisted and spare among the rock. His army met with pitched effort at the tunnel's exit but they pushed out determinedly, over the bloody and broken bodies of Vaelinar

and Galdarkan alike. He savored the carnage. He knew
the heroes would come to bolster the dam, but it was a
tide they could not stop. It only mattered to him that they
came. He had two arrows left that would answer to him.
Quendius shook his vest out and took a position on a slab
of rock, one that had caught a few slanting rays of the sun
and held a slight measure of warmth. He waited.

And behind him, in jagged long shadows cast by stone,
Narskap moved silently. He knew his master had made
a deal with the Raymy. He knew of only one below who
would be saved from the slaughter, the one a part of
himself wanted to call kin, and that one would be saved
not because Quendius had any mercy in his body but because she carried the touch of the River Demon in her
and his master was greedy. That part of himself would
rather see her dead than in the hands of Quendius.

Barely breathing, he crept along gravel and slate, rock
and sere weed, sigh by sigh closer. Narskap knew his
master's mind as well as he knew his own. Better, perhaps. He had always been able to hear the thoughts running thinly through his own. Quendius was not the ghost
who haunted him, but he was the faithful hound because
he knew his master's every inclination.

Quendius showed no inkling of his stalking. He
watched as his master flexed his longbow and drew an
arrow from a belt quiver, an arrow with the head chiseled from flame-red gemstone, and eyed a target below.

There were three actually. One rode a small pony that
stubbornly hopped and jumped along the rockfall like a
goat, led by a woman hardly taller than the pony, but on
his back, oh, yes, they knew that visage well. The Warrior
Queen's brother, quiet but deadly Jeredon Eladar, son
of the Anderieons, himself a master of earth, of forests
and their creatures, and of death from the air. The small
woman neither watcher counted, not Quendius nor
Narskap, even though it was she who helped the Eladar
from his mount as he moved stiff-legged over the ter-

rain. When Quendius settled, it was on a line with the opening and farther, on a line with the two other targets in sight: Diort and Bistel. The Eladar would block any shot Quendius might have in mind unless he moved, but moving now would likely draw attention to his presence, for the mountain boiled with Raver and Raymy leaping from the tunnel and fighting their way downslope.

Narskap did not think the Eladar's positioning to be accidental. He was poised to give cover to the two warlords whether they knew he was there or not, and he had two full quivers with which to do so.

Quendius put his arrow to string and began to draw it back slowly and carefully. Narskap crouched, weighing his decision in his shattered mind, biting his lip until his mouth ran with blood to keep the howls back, the howls that always plagued him when he tried to reconcile one life within his body with another, always failing. His mouth filled with the coppery taste.

Quendius moved a foot to better brace himself, longbow ready. He stepped on a twig. Here, where little existed but shale and granite and dirt, a scrub pine had gamely pushed its way up and died, leaving a brittle reminder of its fight for life. The twig snapped with a sharp crack that echoed.

Nutmeg's head came about with a cry, and Jeredon threw himself in front of her as he saw the archer standing in position. The arrow flew. Its ruby point sparkled in the graying day. She struggled against his hold to move him, too late, his weight too ponderous for her as the shaft hit home. It struck his broad chest, and Jeredon sank, blood spilling from his mouth as he fell. The arrow dug its way deeper as he gave a yowl of pain. He clawed at the shaft, and she wrapped her hands around his and they pulled it loose together, jerked it free as the thing itself squealed and keened, denied in its attempt to burrow its way through his heart and body. She picked up a rock and smashed it, smashed it as she would a viper, smashed it like a vicious *thing* until its ruby head was nothing but sparkling powder. A cloud leaked from it, dark and oily, a smear upon the day and sunlight until it dissipated.

"Nutmeg."

She gathered him in, hopelessly trying with her embrace to quench the font of blood his chest had become. "Don't talk, don't move. Someone'll find us. Someone will come. Don't talk. Just breathe for me. Just keep breathing!"

"No use. I hear it calling for me. Home. Trevilara." He managed to get one arm about her, curving her body to his. His voice came with agonized effort, gasping, wheezing. "I didn't mean to leave you this way."

"You're not leaving me! I won't have it."

"There's no other way. I'm bleeding inside, I can feel it." His arm tightened around her. He pressed her tightly to him, and inhaled deeply of her scent, her hair, stilled her mouth with a small kiss that he broke away from, and his hands drifted down to her waist. A strange smile of wonder then passed across his face. "Why... Nutmeg," he breathed. The light faded from his eyes, but not the smile, not the expression of joy and contentment overshadowing one of pain. She did not see it for long moments until she realized the blood had slowed, and she could not feel him moving against her. She pushed back to see what was wrong.

It was then she began to cry.

Quendius scrambled back with a muttered curse as both Bistel's and Diort's attention swung their way, but they could not see him or the fallen Eladar either, through the few shrubs that clung to the hillside, nor did they hear the small woman crying as if her heart would break, the clamor of the battle below filling the air. He heard it, and he would have taken her life, too, for destroying his arrow, but there would be time for that. He had at least one more shot he wanted to take before retreating to let his army do their bloody work. Moving downhill stealthily, he found a new pinnacle and knelt in place. Bistel had his hands full as Ravers swarmed. His horse kicked and tossed at least two aside to writhe on the gravel in their shattered carapaces. Diort hefted his hammer.

Narskap moved with him. He filled his hand with his dagger. Quendius straightened and lifted his bow.

Narskap sprang. *"Haviga aliora!"* he cried and plunged the dagger in the back, up under the rib, straight and deep to where his master's heart lay.

QUENDIUS JERKED. The longbow fell from his hand, and the arrow clattered to the stone in front of him. He coughed and a fine red mist sprayed the air. He swept the arrow up and turned in one smooth move to bury it deep into Narskap. Narskap dropped on his back.

They looked into one another's face. Quendius' mouth drew to one side. "If I had a heart where Vaelinars have a heart, you would have succeeded." He screwed his arm around with a grunt and clawed at the dagger hilt. He pulled it free. "Alas for you, my hound, I have a heart where Galdarkans carry it. A little higher and to the center. Thanks to my mother. You, I fear, are not so lucky." He watched as the arrow ate its way into Narskap's emaciated body as his back arched and his heels drummed in agony. "Like all hounds, we knew the time would come when you would snap at me. Your teeth hurt." He coughed and showed pain, but not pain enough. Death did not ride his face. Narskap stared up into flint-black eyes with no heart in them at all.

The arrow churned and ate until it stopped where the rock slab at Narskap's back halted its progress. Quendius grabbed Narskap by the shoulder and pulled the arrow through with a wet, slurping noise accompanied by a Demon squeal of satisfaction. He dropped Narskap's body slumped on the ground. He watched as blood pooled slowly.

Then Quendius nocked the arrow again and took his position. The fighting grew fierce as Bistel opened a wedge for Diort and the tall Galdarkan warlord stood at the tunnel's opening and raised his war hammer Rakka, *earthmover*, to strike.

"Can't have that," Quendius said. He pulled the string taut.

Narskap felt Cerat as the Demon churned hotly inside of him. His mouth drew tautly to either side in a rictus of pain. He drew the strength of the arrow within him. He drew on Rakka, which he could feel nearby. He called on the small but bloodthirsty demon he'd imprisoned decades ago in the sword Quendius carried. He called them all back. All home, to him. To him. He waited to see what kind of death Cerat might bring him.

Nutmeg raised her head from Jeredon's bloody chest. She stared with anger at the rocks above. She knew who had shot the arrow. She gently laid Jeredon's still form down and pulled his short sword from its sheath. By branch and root, leaf and flower, she would take her vengeance or die trying. She climbed over a split boulder and through a handful of stunted pines, their needles gray green with dryness and sharp as sewing needles. She scrambled over a quartz-shot bit of stone that would normally catch her eye with its beauty, and a slide of gravel slipped under her boots, taking her with it in a hail of pebble and dust.

"Now, for the love of the Gods," Bistel said to Diort. With a grunt, he twisted his sword to let a Raymy carcass fall from it, turned, and parried a razor-sharp pincer on his aryn staff. Bistane held the corridor a length away, a sword in each hand, afoot, and busy. Father and son and Galdarkan had carved their way up to this rocky gate and held it free. It would only stay that way for a breath or two, but they had cleared it. Raymy boiled inside, hesitating, their voices in low growls and piercing hisses, bottlenecked at the cavern's exit.

Diort bunched his shoulders and swung his great war hammer upon the rock arch. The hammer hit with a noise like thunder, but he did not hear Rakka's voice sound. Rock split at the impact, but the arch of the tunnel stayed in place. Diort wrapped his hands tightly about the handle to strike again, and he felt the absence. Rakka had gone. Where, he did not know. Died, disappeared, gone. The hammer had emptied of the Demon God. He put his head back and roared in disappointment.

In a curtain of gravel and dirt, Nutmeg slid under the hooves of Bistel's immense warhorse. She let out a tiny squeal as she did, and Bistel stared down in amazement.

"Quendius," she got out. "Arrows!"

Bistel dismounted in a leap and grabbed Diort by the shoulder, swinging him about. As he did, the air whistled and crimson blossomed deep in his left shoulder.

"Father!"

Bistel put a hand to his wound and the arrow. He looked to his son. Blood splattered his stark-white hair and sharply-chiseled face. A knowing expression passed through his blue-within-blue eyes.

"Get the warlord mounted and out of here."

Bistane kicked a body out of the way to get to him. "My lord . . ."

"Do it." He took Nutmeg by the elbow and hoisted her to her feet. In chopped strides, he pulled her over bodies strewn along the trail.

"Father!" Bistane had Diort mounted and stood at the

reins of his own horse as it reared and danced among the blood.

"Son. Go." He paused a moment longer, and then he tossed the aryn staff, its wood bitten and nicked with the blows it had parried.

Bistane caught it from the air. His face hardened. He threw himself on horseback and whipped both the horses with the staff, bolting from the scene.

Bistel turned back. He stumbled. His chest gurgled. He broke the arrow shaft. He looked down at Nutmeg and seemed to really see her for the first time. He touched her wet face. "This is far less safe than a library." He pointed their way.

She could see the copse he led her to, and put her small weight under his shoulder to help him to the shelter. Behind them, the Raymy and Ravers quarreled among themselves over the carcasses of their own as they issued from the cavern, and the two of them were forgotten. He sank gratefully to the ground. He took off his helmet, let it drop, and lay down beside it, his snow-white hair glistening with sweat.

"Did you ... find what you needed ... at the library?"

"Not what I hoped."

"And ..." He paused to take a long, sucking breath. She could only wonder why the arrow had not eaten him inside out, but it mattered little. It had killed him anyway. "And what had you hoped for?"

"I wanted to find out if I could love a Vaelinar, and if he could love me back."

"Ahhhh." He touched her wet cheek again. "That is not ... the sort of thing ... we Vaelinar write in our books. We feel it, but we do not write it." His chest bubbled and she could see his pulse throb in his neck, and his skin pale. "When this is all done," and he turned his head, peering down the slope toward the river savannah where two armies melded to fight a third, "Ask Bistane to tell you about Verdayne." He sucked in a breath. "I have something . . . I want you to take. It is a burden, a trust." He licked his lips. "You can say no."

"There is no one else here."

He smiled thinly. "Bistane will come back for . . . me. But it is not something . . . I wish him to have . . . yet. You are honest. By the very stock of your blood, you are honest." He gathered another breath, in great pain from the creases across his face. "Take the book from inside my mail, tucked in my shirt. Keep it. Give it to your sons to keep . . . until the day you feel it should be given. And to whom you would give it to." His eyes of brilliant blues locked onto hers. She did not quite know what to answer.

"I will," vowed Nutmeg. She unlaced his chain and found the book inside as he told her, wrapped in cloth that had become drenched with blood. She pushed the cloth aside to reveal a hand-sized journal. *Book of Ways*, it read. She tucked the book inside her bodice. "Until the day comes when I think it should be given."

"Thank you." Bistel managed a shallow breath and then shuddered. His body gave a terrible wrench as if it fought to hold on, and failed.

And then his form began to rise from the ground. Nutmeg stepped back, her eyes wide. He floated in the air; a silvery glow came over him, and he turned slowly. Tendrils of gold wavered about him, weaving, and his skin grew as translucent as the finest gossamer. It danced about him, weaving and caging, then wisping away as if a thousand small wings had covered him. Then, as quickly as it had come on him, the glow left and he dropped back to the beaten earth, dead.

She stayed with him until Bistane thundered back, to watch as the son lifted up his father's body in his arms, and looked at her. His horse's nostrils flared at the smell and the mount lifted his head warily.

"Thank you, milady Farbranch, for not leaving him alone."

"He . . . it . . ." Nutmeg stammered and stopped. Then she found a word or two. "He glowed. It was beautiful. Gold and silver, all about him, and peace."

Bistane studied her face. "Truly?"

"Truly." She hugged her arms across her bosom, over the book, which still held the warmth of its previous carrier.

Solemnly, he strapped his father's body to the spare horse, and gave her an arm up to ride in front of him, and took her down to the lines where warriors wept before going back to fight again.

Rivergrace found Sevryn. Or, rather, Sevryn found Rufus, grinding new edges on troubled blades, with Rivergrace perched nearby. He gathered her up and swung her around, murmuring, "Aderro," into her neck, over and over. He finally let her feet touch ground again, but he did not let her go.

"You are mine," he told her, "and no king or queen or kingdom will take me from you again."

" 'Bout time," Rufus grunted. He held a dagger to a grindstone and pumped his legs again, turning it.

She smoothed his tawny hair from his face. "How goes it?"

"The only hope we had was Diort closing the tunnels, but the hammer failed. The Demon held within it is either gone or dead." He kissed her softly again. "We may not leave here alive."

"But we both know what lies beyond death."

"Aye. It's the dying that I don't look forward to. The Raver are not gentle and the Raymy . . ." He stopped.

Grace looked at the sky, the sullen sky, always promising rain but never delivering. But the Ashenbrook held water. It had once fed this grassy plain, although the savannah now was dry as tinder. A thought struck her. "Take me to Lariel."

"Rivergrace . . ."

"Take me to Lariel!"

He blew out a breath and took the newly sharpened dagger Rufus handed to him. The Bolger stood and wiped his hands on his apron. "Go with."

"Good." He cupped Rivergrace's hand within his. "She'll be in the thick of it."

They found her behind the lines, with Bistane as he gave his father's helmet to her, its stiff, white brush of horsehair unforgettable. Lara turned to them, holding it, her lips pale and curving downward. She looked as if she would say one thing to them, and then changed her mind. Instead, she turned the helmet in her palms. "The toll is great. Jeredon is dead. Bistel. Many, many others. I could not get here in time. The Ferryman is gone." Lara looked around, dazed. "The Ferryman is gone. He left the banks of the Nylara and exists no more. He is a Way, and he is undone."

Rivergrace's heart twisted in her chest at the news, but she pressed forward. "Where is Nutmeg?"

"With the body, at the nursing wagons, I believe." But uncertainty flashed across Lariel's face.

She didn't know. She had become unsure about all of what they were doing in that place, at that time. Rivergrace took a step back in realization. She put a hand to the hollow of her throat. With a look at Sevryn, she turned and ran.

Ran to the Ashenbrook where the water called her. She skirted the dead and dying, weaving across the savannah field as though it were a loom and she weaving a crazed pattern upon it. Behind her and to her flank, Grace heard Rufus grunt and the sharp cries of triumph from Sevryn as they kept her path cleared. The sky might rain arrows, but she could not think on it. At the bank of the Ashenbrook, she raised her hands and waded into its chill, turbulent waters, waters swirled with blood and gore. Rivergrace went to her very core, uncaring if she unmade herself by loosing all that she had. Sevryn would live. Nutmeg would live. Tranta. Bistane. Others. If the river took all that she offered it and more, she did not care. She called for it to rise, to rise and sweep away the fools made of flesh who would deny its power.

She could hear Sevryn call to her. Words fell on her ears, but she lost the meaning of them. Water rose to her knees, and she felt the River Goddess in them, full of hatred and fear, and she reached for the deity, and flooded her with her own essence. She gave all that she had and found more.

Fire answered her. Rivergrace blinked at the acrid stinging in her eyes and looked out on the river plains, the fighting fields, and saw flame. It burst in leaps and bounds in the dried grass and shrubs, swirled into the wind in great chimneys of heated sparks and flame. It carried its voice in a dry roar and lay across the parched land, ready to consume all in its path.

Her fire. Cursed fire of her cursed line. She stumbled back in the Ashenbrook. *No.*

Traitor.

Killer.

No.

Cerat leaped and danced inside of her. The Demon capered with an insane joy. Hidden within the tiny spark of the River Goddess she'd carried unknowing this bit of the Demon, welded inextricably together with the Goddess it had not answered Narskap's call. Slowly it had gained strength from Rivergrace. And now, within its element, the fiery Souldrinker took the Goddess first and then struck with all that she had given him.

Rivergrace saw the fire racing toward Rufus and Sevryn. Toward troops locked in combat. Toward Abayan Diort who'd gained a mount and raced along the river, exhorting his troops to turn and fight yet another enemy, on a fire-fury front. *No!*

Her strength gushed out of her body, the dam of her flesh broken, washing her spirit away. Rivergrace took a stumbling step to fight it, to fight herself. She could feel the blasts of heat as the grass fire took hold. Wildfire would sweep the valley and then the hills. As night drew close and the wind picked up, nothing could stop it. Nothing.

Save water.

With her last coherent thought, she called again on the one thing she hoped might save them. Her serenity, her hope. She spun herself out in a singular, brilliantly blue thread. It was not enough. She took a heartening breath, tasted the bitter smoke upon it, and braided that thread with the gold of herself. The gold of abandonment and chaos, of destruction and yet as much life as water was. Water and fire. She threw it out again, seeking. Her soul thinned until it was nearly nonexistent.

She thought of him, the Dark Ferryman, the being who had ferried her across many rivers, and spoken to her, *nevinaya aliora*, remember the soul. The being who broke through the wards of Larandaril to carry her off. The being who left her underground to find herself. She spun out her love of water, her need for it, her hope for it. She called with all she had in her, her life and death and new life . . . and she found him. Time had passed. A tight ring of fighters surrounded them, all with weapons drawn, and she could hear fierce battle nearby. Very nearby. One of them reached her, wading to her, threw his arm about her waist and anchored the shell that was left of her.

Rivergrace felt a tug on her thread, a pull that nearly unraveled what was left of her, and then an answer.

He coalesced in front of her, a towering wraith wrapped in dark and shadow, hooded and caped, and when he raised his head, she saw his face.

Daravan pushed back his hood, storm-gray eyes filled with sadness as he looked down at her, and asked, "What do you need?"

Sevryn bunched to spring at him, but Rivergrace held him tightly by the hand, her fingers laced in his. "Give me the Ferryman. Turn the waters," she said, "Master of Rivers. Wash the battlefield clean. Answer the fire with the only defeat it will accept! Bring me the Ferryman, Daravan."

He shrugged his black cloak from his shoulders and looked at his hands as if they were strangers to him, then looked at her again. "I am the Ferryman. Before I was torn asunder and anchored to the Nylara. But I am still a Way."

Sevryn said, low and urgently, "Forget him. Grace, they're breaching. We have to run now."

Locked in his solemn gaze, she could not move. "It's not you. Stand aside, Daravan, and let the Ferryman through."

Flames had driven the fighters close by to the brink of the Ashenbrook. She could see Lariel from the corner of her eye, and Diort stood with his war hammer defending her, his body in front of hers, hers stained and blossoming with blood, her hair wild about her shoulders, and she wore Bistel's helmet. She could see Rufus wrestling with a Raver and bringing it down. She could hear Nutmeg, muted, crying, "And take that from a Farbranch!"

Daravan looked at her, his eyes creased in sorrow. "Don't ask this of me."

"It's for all whom we love. How can you not ask it of yourself?"

Sevryn set himself between Daravan and Rivergrace. "He'll mislead you. He's unnamed from the beginning, a traitor from the first day he dealt with the Suldarran."

"Suldarran." Daravan shook his head slowly and set his gaze on Lariel. "We were never the lost, my queen. We were always the Suldarrat, the exiled! I was sent with the first, to watch, to guard, to obstruct, to meddle. I had but one love, Trevilara, and I did all that I did in her name, even forsaking the mother of my son. You are the Vaelinars who warred and yet broke from her when she planned a weapon to end all wars. From both sides, you met to carve out a peace, and she unleashed her powers on you, sending you ripping through the planes of existence to another place. You are *Suldarrat*, the exiled, and I am meant to keep you here."

Smoke filled in about them, like a fog off the river. Flames licked toward the lowering sun.

Rivergrace reached for Daravan and pulled at his shadow-cloaked form and drew it out, a single obsidian thread glittering in the air. An icy jolt numbed her, but she felt a familiarity in it, and then the being was there, the Ferryman, as like to Daravan as a twin, but his face was abyss and his form was phantom. Daravan let out a despairing groan.

"Brothers . . ." murmured Sevryn.

"One broken by the journey. The other bound by it. Yes, we're brothers although he is truly only a shade of himself. Together we were a bridge. He wandered until a House reached for a deity of water and air to navigate the Nylara and he could not resist answering. He hadn't the strength, and he was trapped. You freed him, but you cannot heal him. He can't raise your waters, Rivergrace. Not alone."

"None of us are alone." Rivergrace stepped into the arch of both men.

She felt Sevryn move to her back. She had no time to argue with him. She put her hands out, and let her anger rise in her. Anger at the blood and the pain and the desecration of life around her. Let the silvery blue fire fill her and she called to the Ashenbrook and she swung about so that she could fill her vision with the sight of the Ravers and the Raymy as they swept through the flesh of her people. She did not deny the fire. She wanted to, as it grew in strength and speed but instead, she let it herd the enemy toward the tide the Ferryman raised.

And the river answered. It gathered the bloodied, the hissing, the vicious enemy and bore down on the savannah to crush them, curved in a never-ending crest. A tide came from all rivers and even the sea with its sharp salted water in answer to their call, crashing down to drown the wildfire and sweep across the battlefield. The

Revela filled and could not hold them all, the tide of warriors, even in her sharp and narrow bed of flooding water.

"Neither but both," Rivergrace said to herself, and she fell back against Sevryn, spent yet whole.

Raymy boiled down the mountain, a diminished tide but still in numbers they could not meet. The Ashenbrook and Revela crested to sweep over them with no place for the tide to carry them.

Daravan reached for Rivergrace but Sevryn knocked his arm aside and the three of them stood linked, Ferryman, Sevryn, and Daravan. The very air quivered about them in shock as they contacted. Daravan looked at Sevryn in a mixture of disbelief and discovery.

"The bridge is rebuilt. Water, air, earth, and fire."

Daravan raised his right arm as if in benediction, and the air shimmered under it. The seeming of another place came to sight. A world of such beauty that Rivergrace's heart keened to see it. She could see fairness and beauty and flowers that had never bloomed on Kerith and her being longed for it. Lara cried out, "Trevilara!" and would have leaped for it, but Diort's hammer blocked her way as he parried a blow meant to take her head from her shoulders as she stared into wonder. Warriors rose against them, herded by fire and flood.

The Ferryman swept up the Raymy as if they were nothing but a scattering of toys, swept them and flooded them into the window of the world they beheld. "We can hold them," Daravan said. "For a time. A season. Maybe ten years of seasons but then the Way, this bridge, will weaken and they'll be back." With that warning, he, the Ferryman, and his charges disappeared.

Driven by fire, Quendius crawled to the outcropping where he had left Narskap's body. He would loot his hound of all the weaponry he could find, crafted by a man who could coax and cage both God and Demon into his steel. They would serve him well even as their maker had. His army lost, he would take the Pathways in retreat but not defeat. Yet he crouched over a rock stained with blood and nothing remained. Not flesh or bone or ash. Quendius ran his palm over the killing ground. He felt an essence he did not know, neither dead or alive, but undead.

And no sign of Narskap.

Chapter
Fifty-Seven

RIVERGRACE LIFTED HER EYES to the sky, dappled gray and lowering over her, the sky that remained sterile despite all their hopes, and then looked down to the trampled ground, to the ashes of the fire pits and the pools of blood that the earth might never be able to soak up, there was so much of it. They had been burning the bodies for days now and finally finished. Sevryn walked beside her quietly, his presence bolstering her, his love warming her. She lifted her hands, palms up, and a shudder ran through her at the inescapable gravity of so much death. No matter what she had done, it hadn't been enough. The incredible loss weighed on her so that she could hardly breathe, hardly even feel. He put his arm about her waist in comfort, but there was not comfort enough for what she saw and felt.

She'd left Nutmeg behind, in mourning, with Lariel, and she'd taken Sevryn because only he could understand and feel as she did about death. And because she loved and needed him.

A veil lay over her sight, a translucent curtain of men and women still locked in combat upon the river plain, still fighting, still falling, still dying, a vision of which she might never be rid. So many dead. So many maimed for the rest of their lives. So many. She would name the ones she could, but it seemed a gross injustice for the many lost that she could not name. Sorrow shivered through her body, dancing upon her skin when it emerged like tears. It sighed through her. It fell from her as a tree sheds its leaves in the fall, without thought or hesitation because that was the way of things, naturally, to let go. It took the veil from her eyes as it fell.

Drops began to fall from above. Large, cold, hugely wet drops. They fell in hesitation, and then steadied into a pattering rhythm upon the parched and trampled earth. Blood washed away in rivulets, and puddles began to form in beaten hoofprints. Ash dissolved. The world seemed to let out a sigh born of relief and need. They stood unmoving for the longest time before she looked at Sevryn as it soaked them. She could feel the dampness upon her face, at the corner of her eyes, and skittering down her cheeks; she saw it upon his lined face and glistening in his hair and spotting the shoulders of his cloak. Wonder lightened her face.

"I can make it rain," she said.

Tales from the Toback Shop
Told with a hope to illuminate the mortal condition

THE MILLER, HIS FINE VEST strained to its buttons over his chest which was ample even for a Dweller, took a deep breath and began to regale them.

"This," the tale-spinner said, after filling and tamping his pipe to perfection, lighting it, and sitting back, "I heard from a Bolger chieftain himself, and since we've had hardly any stories from these folk, I remembered it well. Knowing that they are a people but not as we reckon people, I cannot say whether it is the truth or not, but only as they view it. This is how they say they came to be.

"The world began as a steaming ball of mud, floating through the sky and clouds. The Gods looked down it, a-thinking to themselves what they might do with it. They called up the one known as Digger, who appeared with his rounded talons and rounded ears and his sharp-pointed stick. He was not a God, but a great, strong creature, and listened to them. 'Go down,' they told him. 'Dig about and make us lakes and rivers and great seas as you wander, and grub about and tell us what you see.'

"So Digger went to the newborn world and did as he'd been told. With his clawed and padded feet, he dug out the massive oceans. He paddled in the waters that flowed over the mire, and he tickled the fish with his claws and tail. When he tired of that, he trudged over the steaming lands and searched for other life that made him curious. With his point-sharp stick, he etched out the thin and swift rivers. The mud he flung aside stacked into towering mountains and vast, wide plains. He did many things heedlessly, interested only in what he might dig up from under the steaming mud. Almost, the Bolger chieftain told me," reminisced the miller, who may or may not have actually had the tale from a chieftain but was far more likely to have heard it in another toback shop, "the Digger did not notice the people he brought up. Colored as the muds, brown and gray and greenish, the people were, and grubbers like the Digger and with sharp sticks of their own, they set off across the new lands fashioned from the Digger's cast-aside sludge.

"Finished with the new world, the Digger returned to the Gods and let them see what he had found, and done. Now it drew their interest and closer attention, so they fashioned new people with their own hands, and reshaped the lands themselves with fire, ice, and flood, until the world was nearly what we know today.

"The mud people, the Bolgers, stayed to themselves for many a century until one day, they found a bridge between their land and another, and traveled it, astonished to find they were not the only people in the world. How they dealt with that discovery is another tale." And here, the miller closed his story, and the ponderings of his words began—including whether he had ever met a Bolger chieftain, for he was well known to have rarely strayed from the fine millworks his family built and owned—and many other things were discussed in the shop, until the talkers were too weary of it and

begged for another tale rather than decide upon returning home.

Someone, whose cheeks sounded stuffed with toback
leaf being chewed, shouted out for a telling of, "Why the
Kernan Grew Tall," and so that tale was launched by a
quiet, straw-colored man in the corner who recited:
"Why the Kernan Grew Taller—

"In the early days, it is told the Gods came down to
the top man of the Dwellers as he sat taking his leisure
with his pipe, and said to him, 'Bad times are coming for
our peoples, for your kind and the Kernans.'

"The Dweller, who was a little surprised but not dis-
concerted to see a God emerging from a cloud of toback
smoke, put his pipe down to answer, 'I am sorry to hear
that, my Lord. Is there something I need to do?'

"To which the God replied, 'It is We who will do the
doing. I have come to make you taller, so that you will
be closer for hearing and talking with Us, so that We
may help.'

" 'Me? Taller?'

" 'All Dwellers,' the God told him, not unkindly.

" 'If there are bad times coming, You will need all of
Your strengths, then! No need to make us taller—there
isn't a tree we can't climb to get closer to you and to get
a leg up on trouble.'

"The God frowned a bit. 'This is a great honor We
offer you.'

"Our Dweller responded in his sturdy way, 'Of that
I have no doubt! But we like ourselves quite as we are,
and I thank You, knowing that You wish to be close by
when trouble comes.' And the Dweller bowed in great
respect and when he looked up, not only the fragrant
cloud of good toback smoke had faded away, but so had
the God.

"He might have wondered if he had seen what he
thought, but other events occurred to prove the truth of
it. Determined in the way of Gods to do something with

Its omnipotent powers, the apparition then made Its way to the leader of the Kernans. To the God's declaration, the Kernan smiled shrewdly and only asked, 'May we listen to You from our cities?'

" 'Of course.'

" 'Done, then,' the Kernan told the God. 'There will be paperwork and new buildings to build, and new jobs to assign to those who will be speaking with You, and You will find no more capable hands than ours for this work.'

"So the deal was struck, and the Kernans, one by one, were made taller to the dismay of those who found it quite painful to be stretched by bone and sinew and flesh to a height the Gods deemed necessary. Their children after were born taller but the remaking of those already living was not a thing to be borne lightly. Some to this day are still quite disagreeable over their lot in life. They did as they said they would, and built tall buildings in their cities for listening and talking to the Gods and created the priests and the Mageborn, and talked and talked until they began to fight over the Gods and their newly gained magics and things turned out quite disastrous, in the way lofty plans can go wrong. It is said, after the Mageborn Wars when the Gods stopped talking to anyone, that it was as much out of embarrassment as anger and punishment, but who can say for sure? Only a God would know Their minds.

"As for the trouble said to be coming, there have been many difficult days but no one knows if the times the Gods feared have passed or are yet to be. So it is a good thing the Dwellers have remained nimble and strong and the trees are still growing tall enough that one might shinny skyward up them, just in case the Gods might decide to speak and listen once again." The straw man grew quiet, as did the entire room, for that warning of dire times seemed to echo the words Tolby Farbranch had spoken earlier in the evening though every Dweller and Kernan in the room had held some hope of forgetting them.

A Recollection of Some Curious Events

300—Magi create Galdarkan guards.

223—The Raymy are defeated and retreat across the ocean, leaving Ravers stranded behind.

90—Magi wars. Most magic users die and magic fades from Kerith.

0—Collapse of the Empire.

90 AE (After Empire)—Creation of City States through trader guilds.

112—Galdarkan Rebellion, the collapse of which sends the survivors into the barrens as nomads.

312—Vaelinars invade Kerith, starting a hundred years of slavery, strife, impressments.

423—Accords signed, principally between the Houses and Strongholds of the Vaelinars for their own civil wars, but are extended to the City States.

501—Bolger clans unite, begin warfare.

511—Vaelinars step in to help defeat Bolger clans, but then retire to a deep seclusion, as their numbers are hard hit. Kanako defeats the Bolger tribes, but his lineage dies with him.

700—Vahlinora is born.

703—Gilgarran dies.

721—Bolgers emboldened, and Raver raids begin anew.

723—Nutmeg Farbranch pulls a waif from the Silverwing River waters.

723—A major assassination attempt in Calcort signals new animoisites toward the Vaelinars.

733—Ravers and Bolgers join together in raiding groups with new aggressions.

737—Accords Conference in Calcort brings riots, and the Accords are contested.

737—Abayan Diort begins forcible unification of the Galdarkans.

Glossary

aderro: (Vaelinar corruption of the Dweller greeting Derro) an endearment meaning little one

alna: (Dweller) a fishing bird

astiri: (Vaelinar) true path

avandara: (Vaelinar) verifier, truth-finder

Aymar: (Vaelinar) elemental God of the wind and air

Banh: (Vaelinar) elemental God of earth

Calcort: a major trading city

Cerat: (Vaelinar) souldrinker

Daran: (Vaelinar) the God of Dark, God of the Three

defer: (Kernan) a hot drink with spices and milk

Dhuriel: (Vaelinar) elemental God of fire

emeraldbark: (Dweller) a long-lived, tall, insect- and fire-resistant evergreen

forkhorn: (Kernan) a beast of burden with wide, heavy horns

Hawthorne: capital of the free provinces

kedant: (Kernan) a potent poison from the kedant viper

Lina: (Vaelinar) elemental Goddess of water

Nar: (Vaelinar) God of the Three, the God of War

Nevinaya aliora: (Vaelinar) You must remember the soul

Nylara: (Kernan) a treacherous, vital river

quinberry: a tart yet sweet berry fruit

Rakka: (Kernan) elemental Demon, he who follows in the wake of the earth mover doing damage

skraw: (Kernan) a carrion eating bird

staghorns: elklike creatures

stinkdog: a beslimed unpleasant porcine critter

Stonesend: a Dweller trading village

tashya: (Vaelinar) a warm-blooded breed of horse

teah: (Kernan) a hot drink brewed from leaves

ukalla: (Bolgish) a large hunting dog

Vae: (Vaelinar) Goddess of Light, God of the Three

vantane: (Vaelinar) war falcon

velvethorns: a lithe deerlike creature

winterberry: a cherrylike fruit